The Westbrook Affair

A R DANCE

ARUNDEL
BOOKS

First published in Great Britain in 2013 by
Arundel Books, 2, Audon Avenue, Chilwell,
Nottingham, NG9 4AW
www.arundelbooks.co.uk

ISBN 978-0-9558133-5-1

Typeset in Adobe Garamond 11pt

Printed and bound in Great Britain by
CPI Group (UK) Ltd, Croydon, CR0 4YY

In memory of my father Geoffrey Dance
1912–1988

whose reminiscences of stories related to him by his
mother about certain events in the lives of some of her
ancestors, inspired the plot for this book.

FOREWORD

This book is set in Yorkshire and Nottinghamshire between the years 1828 and 1867. It chronicles the lives of two families from opposite ends of the social divide; of the discovery of a lost family fortune; and how a man-made disaster eventually leads to a search for justice and the truth.

And yet, whilst it is a work of fiction, accounts of real events that occurred in both Nottingham and Sheffield will be found in the pages that follow.

Nottinghamians might be reminded of one of the most brutal and notorious murders ever to have been committed in the town, which resulted, at the subsequent public execution, in an even greater loss of life than that perpetrated by the murderer.

And many residents of Sheffield will undoubtedly be aware of one of the greatest man-made disasters ever to have occurred in the country, resulting in a massive loss of life and damage and destruction of unimaginable proportions in their home town.

Parts of the plot, and some of the characters, are based on actual events and real people, although their story has remained untold. Until now.

Every effort has been made to ensure historical accuracy as far as can be established. Any errors that remain are entirely of my making.

CHAPTER ONE

Black sheep of the family

'Damn you! Damn your cards! A curse on you all!' The man rose from the table, pushing his chair furiously to one side. He took a full glass of port from the table and downed the contents in one swift gulp. Wiping his mouth on his sleeve, he hurled the glass into the fireplace and turned towards the door.

'Aren't you forgetting something, Miles?' asked one of the four men seated at the table, a touch of sarcasm in his voice.

'Yes,' added another, 'we all have a run of bad fortune from time to time. Can't be helped. You know how fickle lady luck can be.'

Miles turned to face his tormentors. He stood almost six feet tall, a handsome man of nineteen years, broad shouldered with straight auburn hair reaching down to his collar, and eyes of piercing green. When he had a mind, he could use those eyes to charm the very birds from the trees, and many a young girl could testify to his beguiling and persuasive ways. But when he was in a temper those same eyes could signal danger, and anyone who had ever crossed him once would keep their distance when he was in such a foul mood.

'The devil can take lady luck for all I care. She's been no friend to me this last week. If I didn't know you all better I'd say you'd made a pact with Old Nick, either that or you've been cheating. I've never known the cards run so badly for so long. Oh, don't worry, you'll get your money, you always do.'

'Ah, that's true Miles, but then you've never been in debt before for anything like a thousand pounds, have you? Will we be seeing you tomorrow night?' A chuckle went round the table but for one man in the room there was little to smile about. Miles Lambert threw open the door, and with a snarl on his lips repeated his promise.

'Don't worry, you'll all get paid soon enough,' he shouted as he descended the stairs noisily and entered the back parlour of the inn. 'Bates, Bates, where the devil are you, man?' he yelled. The landlord came running through from the bar.

'I'm sorry sir, what's the matter?'

'Nothing's the matter you fool; nothing that a few decent cards won't cure! Now get me my horse, I'm away home.'

'Very well, sir,' said Bates, as he poked his head into the bar and shouted to his potman to go and fetch Miles's horse. Miles loitered impatiently, conscious of those present, silently watching him. Most of them were employees and tenants of his father, and they knew that a word out of place could lose them both work and home. Miles stepped outside into the cold and snowy November night as the potman brought his horse from the stable where it had been put some five hours earlier. Angrily, he climbed into the saddle, dug his heels deep into the animal's side, and with a crack from his whip urged it forward.

It was but a short distance from the Black Boar, the only inn in the village of Westbrook, to Westbrook Manor, where he lived with his father, Henry Lambert, the local squire and owner of several thousand acres in this remote area of the West Riding of Yorkshire. The estate, although relatively small, had been in the family for over three hundred years. The manor house itself was a replacement for an earlier structure, and was built of limestone hewn from quarries on the nearby moors, and bore the date 1626, carved deeply into the stone lintel above the solid oak front door. The family's wealth, originally acquired from a marriage between one of Miles's sixteenth-century ancestors and the daughter and only heir of a much wealthier neighbour, now depended mainly on agriculture, although Squire Henry had recently been investigating the potential of coal deposits, which he was assured lay beneath his land on some parts of the moor.

Five minutes after leaving the inn, Miles turned off the lane and into the drive leading up to the house. A near full moon lit his way along the avenue, now carpeted white by the snow that had been falling steadily since dusk. Even without the light of the moon his horse would have brought him safely home, so often had Miles taken this route, frequently in a state of inebriation. The horse came to a stop outside the front porch, and almost before Miles could shout for assistance the door opened and a man stepped out. Alfred Hough, who acted as both butler and footman, and one of only six servants now employed at the manor, was all too familiar with the demands of the young master, having watched him grow from a child to a man. He was a respected and trusted servant, having given loyal service to the family for nearly forty years, the second generation of his family to do so. Alfred believed his position to be safe, for he and his wife Jessie, who acted as both cook and housekeeper, were regarded by the squire almost as part of the family. But he was always careful not to cross Miles, especially when he was in such a dark humour.

Miles dismounted and, ignoring Alfred, stormed purposefully up the steps, through the doorway into the great hall, and straight to the library. Not bothering to locate the groom at such a late hour, Alfred took the horse by the reins and led it round the side of the house to the stable. By the time he got back, Miles had already poured himself a large brandy and was stretched out in an armchair in front of the dying embers of the fire, his feet resting on the iron fender.

'Where's father?' Miles demanded of Alfred.

'Your father's been retired an hour or more, sir,' Alfred replied.

'Damn; I need to speak to him. Still, I suppose it can wait until the morning.'

'Will there be anything else you require tonight, sir?'

Miles yawned loudly as he settled deeper into the chair. 'No. I've got everything I need tonight in this bottle; off you go.'

'Very good sir,' said Alfred, as he left the room. But barely had he closed the door behind him when he heard a loud snoring, followed by the sound of breaking glass as the brandy slid from the limp hand of the now sleeping Miles.

◆

He was still there, sleeping soundly, when Alfred opened the door to the library the following morning at seven o'clock, to check on him. Henry, as was his custom, rose at seven thirty precisely and went straight to the dining room. He was a creature of habit and would do nothing until he had taken his breakfast, which Jessie brought in as soon as she heard him coming down the stairs. But sometimes, when alone at the dining table, he would sit brooding, playing with his food, and Jessie noticed that he seemed to be far away, as if daydreaming. In truth, he often awoke in a melancholy state, frequently following a disturbed night, during which his dreams took him back to happier times, now gone forever.

Henry Lambert was forty-eight years old, and despite his advancing middle age he already had the look of a much older man. His receding hair had begun to turn grey, and the bags under his eyes, and heavily lined forehead, bore all the outward signs of an inner torment. He had begun to age prematurely, so those who knew him well had declared, following the untimely and tragic death of his wife some thirteen years earlier.

He had been born in 1780 and had been forced to grow up quickly, for his father had died when he was only sixteen years old, placing upon him the responsibility of squiredom at an early age. With the support of his mother, an uncle and the estate factor, he had been determined to fulfil his role as the new head of the household, and had set about this task with a zest and energy which astounded those around him and belied his youth. He worked hard, and over the next ten years or so had brought to the estate a prosperity that had not been enjoyed for many years. He soon became a popular and genial host to his neighbours, and a fair employer to the many estate workers who relied on him for their livelihood. Those with whom he did business had not a bad word to say about him, and he was universally acknowledged to be dependable, honest and trustworthy.

There was, therefore, a great rejoicing when he became engaged to Miss Amelia Bussey, a renowned beauty with flaming-red hair, the daughter of a farmer who had a substantial landholding near Wakefield, about twenty miles from Westbrook. Everyone agreed that they were a well-matched and much devoted couple, and when they married in May 1807 their future seemed to promise nothing but joy. But how easily can the hopes of mankind be dashed. For their time together was to be short.

On their wedding day, which now seemed just a dim and distant memory to Henry, he and Amelia had both looked forward to a long and happy marriage, with many children to brighten their days and look after them in their old age. But ill luck had struck, not once but four times. Miles, their first son, was born a year after their marriage, but the next three children, all daughters, had each died within a year of their birth. And then came the worst blow of all. They had been married for only eight years when, in September 1815, Amelia died giving birth to their second son, Joseph.

Amelia was only thirty at the time, and Henry's one consolation was that the child survived. And so he suddenly found himself a widower at thirty-five, with two young sons to bring up. His friends and relations rallied round and offered their help, and many believed that after a decent period of mourning it would only be a matter of time until Henry remarried. For he was a man of considerable wealth, and there were, amongst the families of his friends and neighbours, many eligible young ladies, any of whom would have been flattered to become the second Mrs Lambert.

But it was not to be, and Henry seemed to descend into a slough of depression. Gone was his lively disposition, his ready wit and natural charm, and he devoted his days entirely to the running of the estate. There were to be no more parties at the manor, no more jolly evenings with friends, and despite receiving numerous invitations from neighbours to attend their social gatherings, he would always politely decline. In spite of his wealth he reduced the number of servants at the manor to an absolute minimum, and managed the estate almost single-handedly. After his wife's death he seemed to have little enthusiasm for bringing up his new son, and within weeks of his birth, Joseph's wellbeing was left in the hands of Emily, Amelia's elder sister. A spinster, she still lived with her elderly parents, but she readily agreed to move to the manor and help her brother-in-law to raise his two sons.

But within a few years another black cloud had appeared on the horizon to darken Henry's life. Miles, who had always been such a friendly and likeable lad, gradually changed following the death of his mother, whom he had loved dearly. He resembled her in so many ways – his striking features and the colour of his hair and eyes – and everyone said that he was his mother's double. He had always been educated at home by a private tutor, and was a model pupil, ever eager to learn, attentive and enthusiastic. But after Amelia's death the tutor began to find it increasingly difficult to control him. Miles became headstrong, argumentative and lazy, and possessed a rudeness and arrogance which he readily demonstrated to those with whom he had the slightest disagreement. And following one particularly nasty outburst by Miles, the tutor simply upped sticks and left. But it was towards his younger brother that he exhibited a degree of spitefulness that disturbed Henry greatly.

More than once, Emily had gone to the nursery and found young Joseph in tears, with marks on his arms or legs that could only have been made with a stick. It soon became apparent that Miles was the culprit, and despite Henry's frequent reprimands, it seemed that nothing could prevent him from developing a profound hatred of his younger brother.

Emily, too, became the target of his attention, and although she made valiant and patient attempts to befriend the boy, he showed no respect for her whatsoever. Daily, she would bear the brunt of his surly and aggressive ways, and when this failed to upset her, Miles found other ways to hurt her. She had recently acquired a pet kitten, and one day it went missing. A search soon discovered the poor thing hanging from a tree in the grounds of the manor. Henry and Emily were both quite certain who the guilty party was, but when questioned Miles not only denied responsibility, but also displayed a complete indifference to the cruelty shown to the animal. And then, his father had watched horrified one day as Miles unmercifully taunted a lame old dog which had been a family pet for many years. Henry reprimanded him severely but this seemed only to make things worse, and it was towards Emily that all his attentions now turned. The taunting, the tricks and the vindictiveness continued for several more years without respite, until eventually Emily declared that she could stand the situation no longer. With great regret, but also with much relief, she returned once more to her family home, leaving Henry to cope as best as he could with a nine-year-old child and his increasingly unruly seventeen-year-old brother.

Henry did his best, but what with spending most days running the estate he could find little time to devote to his sons. He therefore came to rely more and more on Jessie to keep a watch on them, but she began to find it impossible to carry out her own duties and at the same time keep the peace. On many occasions, Henry had returned to the manor to find uproar, and eventually Jessie told him that unless something was done she would have no alternative but to seek another position.

And so, after much thought, Henry concluded that there was only one thing to be done. Joseph was now approaching ten years of age and so far had received no formal education, other than the little that Henry had been able to instil in him. Miles's tutor had never been replaced, and so his mind was made up. Henry decided that the best course of action would be to send Joseph away to school.

Henry had, amongst his acquaintances, an old friend from his youth, Jacob Parsons, who was now the proprietor of a boys' boarding school near York. He knew that he was a man he could trust, and at least Joseph would be safe there from the harmful influence and unwanted attentions of his elder brother. In no time at all the arrangements had been made for Joseph to attend, and a week after his tenth birthday, Joseph was all packed and ready to leave.

It was a tearful farewell for the boy, but Henry assured him that he would be in good hands, that he would come and visit him as often as he could, and that he would, of course, be returning home during the holidays. But as Joseph left the manor in the company of his father, Miles was conspicuous by his absence. There were no goodbyes or words of encouragement from him. He sat in his bedroom and gazed out of the window as the coach made its way down the drive, and silently congratulated himself that he had at last rid the home of the one he blamed for the death of his mother. It was in giving birth to him, Joseph, that his dear mother had forfeited her life; it was Joseph who was to blame for taking away from him the one person whom he had loved more dearly than anyone. And he secretly hoped that Joseph would never return.

Joseph quickly discovered just how tough life could be at the school, with none of the comforts he enjoyed at home. It took him some time to accustom himself to this new regime, and for the first year there he felt dreadfully homesick. But gradually he began to settle in. He worked hard; he was a keen student and he made many new friends. He was now looking forward to spending many more years at the school, but little could he have known how soon and how dramatically his world was about to change yet again.

CHAPTER TWO

Not thy will but mine be done

Henry finished his breakfast and got up from the table, although he had eaten little of what Jessie had cooked for him. He walked through the great hall and into the library, where he found Miles lying asleep in an armchair, exactly where Alfred had left him the previous night. He approached his son, kicked his legs from the fender and shook him by the shoulder. With a start Miles awoke, and looked up, bleary-eyed at his father. Henry looked down at him in disgust, for he knew exactly why he was here instead of in his room, and where he had been the night before. And the state he was in! This was not the first time he had found him here of a morning.

'Drunk again, I expect,' he said, disapprovingly. 'How many times have I warned you against the evils of excess?'

'Father, don't preach,' implored Miles, holding his head in his hands to try and ease the throbbing pain.

'I suppose you're now going to complain about your hangover. I'd have thought you would have learnt your lesson by now.'

Slowly Miles rose from the chair, yawned loudly and stretched himself in an attempt to wake up.

'I need a drink and some food. Where's Jessie?'

'You know what time breakfast is served. But if you go into the kitchen and ask her politely, I've no doubt she'll find you something.'

Miles made his away across the room, then stopped, and turning round said hesitantly, 'Father, there's something I need to talk to you about urgently. Are you going out this morning?'

'I'm going over to Langdale Farm in about an hour. Why, what do you want to talk about?'

'Let me get something to eat first,' said Miles.

Henry sat down in the chair his son had just vacated, and stared morosely into the smouldering ashes in the grate, for he knew instinctively what his son was going to ask him. Miles was soon back, a large tankard of ale in his hand, and sat down opposite his father. 'Hair of the dog?' asked Henry sarcastically.

'That's right; best cure I know,' and he took a long and satisfying drink. He emptied the mug and put it down in the hearth. He looked across at Henry, and then without any hesitation declared, 'Father, I need some money, and quickly.'

'Whatever for? You've only just had your allowance this quarter. Surely you've not spent it already?' Henry had guessed precisely why Miles needed the money, for he was only too aware of his gambling habits, but he pretended otherwise, determined to make him sweat for a while. But Henry was unprepared for the shock he was about to receive.

'Oh, I need much more than that. I need a thousand pounds,' replied Miles, nonchalantly. 'The honour of the family's name is at stake. I'm sure that's worth a thousand, isn't it, father?' For a few seconds Henry sat in silence, undecided whether it was the amount his son had demanded or the way he had so casually asked for it, that was the bigger shock.

'A thousand pounds! Good God! Are you serious? I assume you've been gambling again. Are you never going to learn? I've bailed you out enough times before, but a thousand pounds! Have you no sense of values? Don't you realise that many of our tenant farmers manage to support themselves and their families on less than a tenth of that for a whole year?'

'Oh, stop mythering, father. You don't expect me to live like those peasants, do you? How can I be expected to move in the right circles and not indulge in their pastimes? The occasional hand of cards is no crime; I've had a run of bad luck, that's all. This time next week I'll probably have won it all back and more besides. I made them a promise I'd repay it and I intend to do so. You wouldn't want me to go back on my word now, would you, father?'

'You're out of your depth with those so-called friends of yours. *They* might be able to afford it, or rather their *fathers* might. But from what I know of them they're all lazy good-for-nothings; gambling, boozing, womanising. To tell the truth, I don't feel inclined to let you off the hook again. And to think, I sent your brother away to school. Maybe I should have sent you away instead, to learn a trade or do something useful, instead of letting you stay here and fritter away *your* time and *my* money. I'm sorry, Miles, but the time has finally come to put a stop to your dissolute ways.'

This was not the first occasion that Miles had had to ask his father to help out with his gambling debts, and in the past he had always, eventually, given in. But the amounts had always been much smaller, never more than fifty or sixty guineas, and Miles was beginning to realise that this time his father was not going to concede so easily. He would need all his powers of persuasion to get his hands on the money. He pleaded, he begged, he stressed how shameful it would be to the family if news got round that he was unable or unwilling to settle his debts.

Henry sat for a while, thinking. 'Very well,' he said at last, 'this is what I'm prepared to do. I'll pay your debt, but on the following conditions. Firstly, you cease gambling and mixing with those rakes. Secondly, your allowance will be halved, until the thousand pounds has been repaid, and thirdly, you knuckle down to some hard work. There's plenty to be done on the estate. I'll put you under the charge of Sykes, he'll soon lick you into shape.'

Abraham Sykes was Henry's estate factor, a man of immense knowledge and industry. He had only three men to assist him, and there were times when they were hard-pressed to manage all the jobs that needed doing. Miles had little time for Sykes, and the thought of having to get his hands dirty and work for his keep horrified him. But he had no choice. If he wanted the money, he would have to agree to the terms – for now, at least. But he was confident that he could soon wriggle out of them, one way or another.

Miles nodded his head. 'Thank you, father, I agree. But I did promise that I'd settle up without too much delay, so if you could arrange ...'

Henry interrupted him. 'I've told you what I'm prepared to do and you know I'm a man of my word. You'll have the money in a week or two, when it suits me, and not before. I'm sure your avaricious friends can wait till then. Now, I must get off to Langdale Farm. I'll speak to Sykes on my way out and tell him that you'll be starting work tomorrow morning at seven o'clock sharp. Meanwhile, I suggest you go and find some old clothes to wear; you won't want to spoil that fancy dandy outfit, will you?'

Henry got up and without further ado set off on his business. Miles was left to ponder his immediate future. It was only minutes since he had agreed to his father's terms, but already his devious mind was working on ways to avoid carrying out his part of the bargain.

For the next few days neither Henry nor Miles had much to say to each other and the atmosphere in the house remained chilly, almost as icy as the hoarfrost that had formed overnight and clung to the trees and bushes in the garden.

Henry was away for most of the daylight hours visiting his tenants, but not too busy to ensure that his son was buckling down to his new occupation. Henry had spoken at length with Sykes and told him that he wanted Miles to find out exactly what real hard work was like. And Sykes was not a man to disappoint his employer. But how Miles hated it. He hated having to rise so early, especially on these dark winter mornings; he despised the filthy work he was given to do, the monotony and repetitiveness of manual labour, and of perpetually smelling like the very farmyard animals he was forced to spend every day attending to – feeding, herding, milking and mucking out.

But worst of all he resented the fact that for this enforced labour he was receiving no wages. At least those he was working alongside received some pay. And to make matters worse, it was now mid-December and the weather had turned bitterly cold. Much of the estate was high up, near the edge of the moors, and the north winds that came howling down bit with a vengeance. As he toiled in barn or field, he determined that this little episode in his life would be as short-lived as he could possibly make it.

About two weeks after their discussion, since when there had been little discourse between father and son on the subject of the money, Henry suddenly announced at dinner one evening that he had something for Miles. Rising from the table he went over to a bureau, and opening a drawer took out a small leather bag. He returned and dropped it in front of Miles. The bag rattled as it hit the table, and Miles eagerly untied the string round the top. He opened it and tipped out the contents; gold coins and bank notes spread out before him.

'There's no need to count it; it's all there,' said Henry, forcefully, 'but I think you'd better get your debts paid as soon as possible. I don't like keeping large amounts of money in the house, and I have no doubt that your friends will be anxious to get their grubby little hands on it.'

Miles's face lit up. 'Thank you, father,' he said, gleefully. 'You're right. I'll go and see them tonight. They're probably wondering what's happened to me.'

'But don't think you can forget your side of the bargain,' added Henry, pointing his finger meaningfully in Miles's direction. 'If you've got any common sense in that head of yours you'll take heed of what I told you and give up gambling for good. There's many a man been ruined by that vice. And remember; I'll not bail you out again. If you run up any more debts, you'll have to sort them out yourself. I'll not come to your help any more, whatever people might think.'

Then, changing the subject, Henry continued. 'By the way, did I mention I've invited your Aunt Emily to come and stay with us over Christmas? Joseph will be home from school early next week and you know how fond he and Emily are of each other. I do hope you'll remain civil while she's here.' Miles mumbled something in response, but was more interested in finishing his dinner and setting off to meet his friends.

It was just after eight o'clock when he rode into the yard of the Black Boar, dismounted and shouted for someone to come and attend to his horse. A boy soon appeared, and handing him the reins, Miles made straight for the door of the inn. As he stepped inside he removed his hat, and used it to brush the light powdery snow from his coat. He went over to the fireplace, where he stood for a minute, drying himself in front of the welcoming blaze.

'Your friends are all upstairs, sir,' said Bates, the landlord; 'I expect it's them you've come to see.'

'Yes, I'll join them shortly after I've thawed out,' he replied, as he removed his coat and slung it with his hat over a chair. 'And while I'm doing that I'll have a large rum to warm me up. And a pint of ale to follow.' Bates obliged and Miles downed the rum in one gulp. He belched loudly. 'You can't beat a tot of rum on a night like this,' he exclaimed, then picking up the ale, he left the bar and climbed the stairs to the room where he had spent so many evenings in recent months. He entered the room, a small but inviting place, brightly lit with oil lamps and candles, and warmed by a fire crackling merrily in the hearth. In the centre stood a large circular table, covered in green baize cloth, on which stood an assortment of glasses, tankards and plates of food, whilst on a sideboard were bottles of wine, brandy and whisky, and a large jug of ale. Around the table sat five men, the air thick with the smoke from their cigars and pipes. Miles's entrance was met with a mixture of greetings and ribald comments from those present. They looked up from the table around which they were seated, as one of them shuffled the cards before dealing.

'Well, look who's here! It's the elusive Miles Lambert. Shall I deal you in?' asked the man with the cards.

'I think before he plays again there's the small matter of some debts to be settled,' said another.

'Looks like St. Nicholas might have arrived a week early,' added a third. 'Let's hope he's brought presents for us all!'

The men laughed loudly. They were all young and wealthy; two were brothers, the sons of a distinguished Knight of the Realm who owned estates not only in Yorkshire but also in many other parts of England, Scotland and Ireland. His Yorkshire estate bordered Henry's land and his ancestral home made Henry's seem positively humble in comparison. A third was a cousin of the two brothers, visiting his relatives from his home in Shropshire, whilst the other two owed their wealth to the fortunes made by their fathers through sugar and cotton plantations in the Americas, and in the slave trade. The money having been made, and the slave trade now having been abolished, their families had settled down to a life of rural domesticity in the neighbourhood, and with no need to work for a living the two men devoted most of their time to the usual pleasures and pastimes of country life.

Compared to them, Miles was barely of the same social standing, particularly in terms of wealth. But he was welcomed amongst them for his ready wit and sense of adventure, and his willingness to join in those escapades which young men with too much time and money are prone to enjoy. This upper room in the Black Boar had, for a while, been a convenient meeting place for this group of like-minded friends, a place where they could indulge their passions for drinking and gambling. Not only drinking and gambling, for there were other diversions which could also be enjoyed here, away from the prying eyes of their families. There were several young ladies in the village who could easily be persuaded to tender their favours in return for a few shillings, and no questions asked, especially from the landlord who welcomed the custom these young men brought to the inn.

Miles approached the table, and taking the bag from a pocket he emptied its contents in front of them. 'There you are,' he declared, vehemently, 'I told you you'd get your money!'

'We were beginning to wonder,' said one of them, 'we've seen neither hide nor hair of you for weeks. We thought you might have emigrated! But then a little bird told us that you'd got a job as a farm labourer, presumably trying to earn what you owe us. I said you'd be a hundred before you made enough to pay us back.' Miles smiled sardonically but refused to rise to the bait. He knew that it was all being said in jest, but was annoyed that news of his current situation had leaked out; that was one indignity he could do without.

'Anyway, are you playing?' enquired the dealer. Miles hesitated for a moment before replying. Nothing would have given him greater pleasure than to join in, and his natural instinct was to say yes. But he could not ignore the dire warning his father had given him. What if he were to lose heavily again? But he might not lose; why should he? He'd had a run of bad luck before, so perhaps it was now time for his luck to change. He was about to say yes when he looked down at the money he'd just emptied onto the table, and saw the others dividing it out between them, according to their dues. The stakes were bound to be higher tonight now that they had all been repaid. And he only had a small amount with him. Reluctantly, and much against his will, he allowed common sense to rule, something that rarely happened.

'No, not tonight,' he replied. 'I only came to repay you. I'll stop for a while and have a drink, but I told father I wouldn't be late back.'

'And since when did you want to hurry back home of an evening?' asked one of the others. 'I reckon it's all these early mornings; up with the lark and out into the fields. The man clearly needs his sleep, now that he's one of the labouring classes!' he added to a roar of laughter. Miles could take a joke anytime, but he really was beginning to tire of this.

'Look, I'll be here for a game soon enough, you can be sure of that. But it won't be until after Christmas. My brother comes home from school next week and we've an aunt coming to stay as well, so it's going to be a bit awkward.'

'Well,' said another, 'if it's that same aunt you've spoken about before, I'd have thought you'd have wanted to spend as much time away from her as possible.'

'Maybe,' agreed Miles with a sigh of resignation, 'but you know how it is. Sometimes you have to put up with these tiresome domestic arrangements for the sake of peace and quiet.'

'But I hope you're not going to vanish totally over Christmas, are you? I take it you and your father will be joining us for the hunt on Boxing Day.'

'Oh yes, you can rely on that,' replied Miles, emphatically. Hunting was the one pastime that Henry had not ceased to enjoy, and about the only one when father and son could be seen together socially.

The cards were now dealt and Miles looked on as the others continued their game. He was right; the stakes were higher than usual and he was glad, in a way, that he had not joined in. But he was determined that, by hook or by crook, he would soon be back in that card school. He had a cool head and a quick brain and he considered himself as skilful a player as any of them. Yes, he decided; he might have to miss out for a while, but not for too long, and then it would be his turn to win.

He finished his ale and bade his companions goodbye, and as he turned to go he said to them, 'I want you all to remember that that thousand pounds was just a loan. I'll be here again to recoup it shortly, and with interest!' and he chuckled to himself as he descended the stairs to the bar. He called for his hat and coat, and Bates sent the lad to fetch his horse. Bates was astonished to see Miles leaving so early and wondered why, but reckoned his own interests would be best served by not asking.

Miles arrived home to find Henry sitting at his desk in the library. It was covered with papers and documents, and by the light cast from an oil lamp he was busily sorting through them and making notes. As Miles entered, he looked up from his work. 'Ah, there you are, Miles. You've paid your debts then?'

'Yes, father, all settled up.'

'Good. Let's hope you've learned your lesson this time!'

'Don't worry, father. I'll not be asking for any more money, I can promise you that. What are you doing?'

'Something I should have done years ago. I bumped into old Cartwright today, you know Nathaniel Cartwright, the solicitor. I called in at the vicarage on a small matter and he was there talking to the parson about his will. And I realised that I've still not made one myself; very remiss of me, I know. It's something I keep putting off, but as Cartwright reminded me, one never knows when one's time is up and if it comes suddenly, well, it would be too late then. So I've made an appointment to see him early in the new year to get it sorted out once and for all. I've been going through some estate papers, checking the extent of my assets, and once that's done I shall draft out exactly how I intend to dispose of everything, and he can have it properly drawn up.'

Henry looked at his son and could tell that he was thinking deeply about what he had just been told. 'Oh, don't worry, Miles. You'll be well provided for, have no fear of that. And of course, as the eldest son, you would, quite rightly, expect to inherit the estate. But I do want to make sure that Joseph is also catered for. I have heard of cases where younger sons have been left almost penniless after their father died. And I'm going to make some other bequests, too. To start with, I shall leave something for Emily. She was very good to us after your mother died. And then there are the Houghs. They've given us years of sterling service, and we owe it to them to see that they are financially secure in their old age. In fact, I intend to ensure that all our employees are left with at least a token of my esteem. You see, Miles, we're very fortunate in our position and I believe we have a duty to help those less well off than ourselves. And finally, there are a number of charities I have decided to patronise. I've already promised the parson that there'll be something for the upkeep of the almshouses.'

'Well, that's very noble, father,' replied Miles. But it took all his efforts to make himself sound convincing and hide his true feelings, for he felt nothing but contempt for Henry's philanthropic intentions. As far as he was concerned, the matter should be a simple one – the eldest son inherits everything. That's the way it had always been and that's the way it should continue, he thought to himself. 'Anyway, I'm tired. It's been a long day and I'm off to my bed, so I'll leave you to carry on. Goodnight, father.'

Miles left his father at his desk and made his way to his room. As he lay in his bed he pondered over the next week or two; his brother returning home from school, the visit of his Aunt Emily, and his father's continuing warnings about his behaviour. None of these gave him any particular cause for joy, in truth, just the opposite. But worse still was what his father had been telling him, and he realised exactly how much he stood to lose. So long as his father failed to make a will, he would inherit everything. But now that was all about to change, and he knew he had to act swiftly. If he was ready to take his chance, if he was daring enough to strike whilst the iron was hot, then he could still have everything that he had ever desired – the estate, money, power and position; all there for the taking. But he had to be bold. And once he had made up his mind to be so, there could be no turning back.

CHAPTER THREE

From a view to a kill in the morning

The days leading up to Christmas were tedious in the extreme for Miles, particularly when he contemplated having to spend time with his brother and aunt. His tedium was only made bearable by the prospect of the Boxing Day hunt, and the anticipated departure soon afterwards of Aunt Emily back to her home and Joseph's return to school. But for the time being he had to play the part of the dutiful elder son.

Joseph arrived home from school on the twentieth of the month, a cold, grey day, with heavy snow clouds gathering. As the coach bringing him back made its way down the long drive, Henry went out to welcome his son. It was three months since he had last seen him, but even in that short time he seemed to have grown somewhat. Joseph was now eleven years old, a bright and cheerful boy with blond curly hair and deep blue eyes, and it was clear for all to see that he took after his father in appearance. He jumped down from the coach and ran excitedly towards his father, throwing his arms around him, glad to be home once more, for whilst he now enjoyed his school days he was pleased to be back in familiar surroundings. And when Henry told him that Aunt Emily would be joining them for Christmas he was even more thrilled.

Miles, on the other hand, made no fuss of his younger brother and showed no interest in his welfare or how his schooling was progressing. Indeed, it was over an hour after Joseph's return before he even made an appearance, and when he did so he displayed a pronounced indifference towards him, and they might as well have been strangers rather than brothers.

Miles decided he would try and keep himself to himself as much as he could, and that he would simply let Christmas pass with as little participation in its rituals and ceremonies as possible, for he had no desire to be in the company of either Joseph or Emily any more than necessary.

The weather remained much the same for the next few days, and as he sat by the fire, whiling away the hours, Miles longed to be with his sporting friends at the Black Boar. Emily and Joseph, however, were determined to enter fully into the festivities of the season, and even Henry's spirits seemed to lift a little. The church choir came carol singing on Christmas Eve, a long-standing tradition in the village, and as part of that same tradition, Henry invited them all in to partake freely of the food and drink that Jessie had laid on specially for them.

On Christmas morning Henry, Joseph and Emily attended the church service. Miles, however, did not join them. In fact, he slept the whole morning, and only appeared shortly before Jessie entered the dining room carrying a magnificent roast goose. But the effects of his previous night's imbibing were still apparent for all to see as he slowly and silently made his way to his seat at one end of the table. Christmas lunch at Westbrook Manor had always been a time when feelings of goodwill would abound, and despite the underlying rift between Miles and the others present, they were content to put this to one side. Even Miles, briefly, seemed to reciprocate, to the extent of wishing his aunt the compliments of the season. But within an hour or so, during which time he consumed a full bottle of claret and a considerable quantity of his father's best brandy, his demeanour began to change once more.

Sitting by the fire, the talk had inevitably turned to times past and to nostalgic reminiscences of former Christmases at the manor. It was Emily who first made reference to her dear departed sister, and Henry, nodding his head in agreement with Emily's tributes to the memory of his fondly remembered wife, suddenly raised his glass and proposed a toast. 'To Amelia, the kindest and most loving wife and mother a man could ever wish for,' he proclaimed, and Emily could not help noticing a hint of sadness in his voice. The other three raised their glasses, and although Joseph had never known his mother he seemed to share a memory of her, if only through the stories told him by Emily and his father.

'To mother,' he responded.

'Aye, to mother,' said Miles, 'and God forgive the one who sent her to her grave,' he added, bitterly, glowering fiercely in the direction of his brother. Joseph stared back, a look of bemusement on his face. Henry turned to Miles and looked him straight in the eye.

'And just what do you mean by that?' he demanded, although he was sure he knew exactly what Miles was implying.

'You know very well what my view is on that subject, father. She'd have still been here but for him. She died so he could live.'

'That's a terrible thing to say. Now, just you apologise!'

'I don't have anything to apologise for. It's the truth and we all know it. She died so *he* could live.' And Miles spat out the word 'he' with venom. 'I was only nine at the time but I remember it as if it were yesterday. I overheard what the midwife told you. She said she could save the mother or the child, but not both. You had a choice, and you chose him over her.'

Henry glared furiously at his eldest son, the anger on his face clearly visible for all to see. 'That's unfair and you have no right to say it. Her labour was difficult, that's true enough, and the doctor was sent for. But there was nothing he could do to save her, nothing at all. God knows, we all miss her, none more than I, but I'll not have you blaming Joseph, do you hear me?'

'I hear you, father,' replied Miles, grudgingly, but no apology was forthcoming as he rose from his chair and clumsily staggered out of the room.

For a while there was silence, then Henry spoke again. 'Don't worry Joseph, I'm sure Miles didn't mean what he said. I'll talk to him later. And it's not true what he said. Nothing could have been done to save your poor mother, that's a fact, whatever he might think.'

Miles spent the rest of the day in his room, leaving the other three to amuse themselves. But his outburst had cast a cloud over what, until then, had been a happy and peaceful Christmas Day.

It was not until the next morning that he appeared, dressed and ready for the hunt. It was a tradition going back over fifty years that the Westbrook Hunt would meet at the manor on Boxing Day morning before setting out for a day's sport. Jessie had been up early to prepare the pre-hunt refreshments, along with the food that the huntsmen would take with them, for it was likely to be a long day. She was assisted by some girls from the village, and for a couple of hours all was hustle and bustle. Emily did not hunt, but Henry and Miles were keen followers and this year, for only the second time in his young life, Joseph was to join them. The day dawned crisp and clear, the early-morning frost casting a white dusting over the trees and hedges; ideal weather for an exhilarating chase across the countryside.

The hunt was to commence, as was customary, at eleven o'clock, and by ten thirty small groups of hunt followers were beginning to gather at the manor, most on foot, some on horseback, followed shortly afterwards by the Master of Fox Hounds and the Whippers-in with the hounds. Henry had generously provided some bottles of his finest port for the occasion, and the huntsmen made a fine sight in their brightly coloured jackets, as they drank from the stirrup cups being handed round by the serving girls.

As the time approached to set off, the horses, sensing the sport to come and eager to be on their way, were getting restless, their hooves noisily scraping the ground, whilst the hounds milled around excitedly, yelping impatiently in anticipation of the sound that would signal the start of the chase. Eventually, the time-honoured formalities having been completed and the port having been drunk, all was ready. The Master of Fox Hounds put the hunting horn to his lips and with three short blasts he urged his horse forward and led the pack down the drive and out into the lane in search of old Reynard, followed enthusiastically by twenty or more huntsmen and almost twice as many followers on foot.

They had been gone about two hours, and all was calm once more at the manor. Jessie, Emily and the village girls were busily preparing the feast which, as tradition dictated, the squire would provide for the returning huntsmen, when suddenly there came a frantic knocking at the front door. Alfred, answering the call, opened it to find the towering figure of Ben Hall standing there, panting heavily. Ben was the local blacksmith, and a lifelong follower of the hunt.

'Whatever's the matter, Ben?' asked Alfred, for he could see well enough that something was amiss.

'It's the squire; there's been an accident,' exclaimed Ben, breathlessly, 'he's had a fall and seems in a bad way. Get some blankets and a hurdle, or something we can use as a stretcher. We need to get him back here as fast as we can. I've already sent a lad to fetch the doctor.'

Emily, overhearing the voices, had come out from the kitchen to see what all the fuss was about. Alfred quickly explained to her what had happened, and while he went to the stable to find something to use as a stretcher, Emily, as efficient as ever, fetched some blankets. Within a few minutes, Alfred and Ben were on their way, leaving Jessie and Emily anxiously awaiting their return.

It was just over an hour later that the two women, watching patiently from a window, saw a small group of riders and followers turn from the lane and into the drive. Together they rushed to the door, and stood there silently as the party gradually made its way towards the house. Ben, Alfred and two of the huntsmen were carrying the improvised stretcher, whilst Joseph and Miles walked alongside, and as they got closer, Emily and Jessie could see Henry lying motionless on the stretcher. The men carried him into the house and the doctor, who was with them, immediately requested that a bed be made ready.

'How is he?' asked Emily uneasily.

It was the doctor who replied. 'It appears that the squire fell from his horse. He's suffered a nasty blow to his head and he's not regained consciousness yet. It was Miles who found him.' Miles was standing at the back of the small group, and so far had kept quiet.

'Miles, whatever happened?' Emily enquired fretfully.

'We'd not been gone an hour when I had to stop to tighten the saddle girth on my horse, and got left behind. I was catching up with the rest of the field, and was halfway through Hangman's Wood when I noticed father's horse. Then I saw him lying on the ground.

He must have ridden straight into a low branch and been thrown off. I rode as fast as I could, and once I'd caught up with the others we all went back to where he was lying, and then Ben set off to get help.'

'I don't understand it,' said Ben, shaking his head, 'the squire's one of the most experienced horsemen hereabouts. He knows that wood like the back of his hand; I can't see how he would ride into the branch of a tree, not in broad daylight. In any case, we'd all ridden round the *edge* of the wood, not *through* it, so what was he doing in there anyway?'

By now, Henry had been taken to his room and was being attended to by the doctor. For several hours he stayed with him, bathing his wounds and bandaging his broken bones as best he could. Across the front of his forehead was a long deep gash, and his right arm and wrist were fractured. He also had some cracked ribs and was breathing with great difficulty.

'There's not much more I can do at this stage,' said the doctor to Emily and Jessie. 'Have someone keep an eye on him and send for me if his condition deteriorates. I'll call again tomorrow, but if he does regain consciousness, you can give him some brandy and a little hot broth.'

Emily and Jessie took turns in watching over him, and Joseph also stayed at his father's side until, exhausted by the day's activities he could barely stay awake, and at Emily's insistence he went to his room to get some sleep. But Miles insisted on staying, suggesting to Emily and Jessie that *they* should both retire and leave him to sit with Henry. Emily thought this strange. Miles had never been that close to his father and had never exhibited as much concern for him as he did now, but despite his suggestion Emily remained with Henry, just as the doctor had ordered. Once or twice, they thought that he was about to wake up, for he moved slightly and seemed to be trying to open his eyes. On each occasion that this happened, Miles showed some apprehension, almost as if he dreaded his father regaining consciousness.

Then, just as it looked as if he was about to awaken, his breathing became heavier, louder and more irregular, until suddenly, with one final breath he sank back, as lifeless as the bed on which he lay. Emily looked down, sorrowfully, at her brother-in-law as tears began to run down her cheeks. She turned towards Miles and although the tears blurred her vision, he appeared to have lost the anxiety that until then he had been unable to hide. It was almost as if his father's passing had lifted a great weight from his shoulders.

It was a sombre party which, three days later, made its sad and slow journey from Westbrook Manor to the village church, where over ten generations of the Lambert family had been laid to rest.

Memorial tablets on the wall of the south aisle commemorated the more notable members of the family who had served the district in various positions of power and responsibility. Some of them had been interred inside the church, but Henry would lie next to his wife in a corner of the churchyard where many of his forebears were also buried.

The hearse was drawn by two black stallions, bedecked in black feathers and crêpe. The funeral cortège was led by Miles and Joseph, walking slowly and with dignity with their Aunt Emily by their side, and behind followed many friends and neighbours, tenants and estate workers. Emily had sent a messenger to advise her parents of the unexpected death of their son-in-law, and of the funeral arrangements. But they were both now getting on in years and, regrettably, felt unable to make such a long journey, particularly in the depths of winter. And of other relatives there were none, for Henry had no brothers and his only two sisters had both died as spinsters.

The church was packed, and the vicar, in his eulogy, paid tribute to a man whom, he avowed to general agreement, was both universally liked and admired. A man who treated his tenants fairly, and who could always be relied on to deal justly and compassionately with those less fortunate than himself. He commented on the death of Henry's young wife, all those years ago, and how equally untimely and tragic had been Henry's own sudden passing, at such a relatively young age. The vicar added that it was not only his wish, but surely that of everyone present, that his heir, Miles, would carry on the administration of the estate in the same benevolent manner which his father had during his lifetime. But Miles's reputation was already well known in the area and some of those in the congregation, particularly Emily, could not help thinking that the vicar's pleading was, in reality, a subtle warning to him. For those who knew Miles best also feared that things would never be quite the same again on the Westbrook estate.

Following the funeral, the party returned to the manor, where Jessie had laid on food and drink for the mourners. It was during this gathering that Miles was approached by Nathaniel Cartwright, the family solicitor. The firm of Cartwright and Dickens had been solicitors to the Lambert family for three generations, and Nathaniel felt it his duty to suggest a meeting to discuss those matters affecting estate policy that he knew would require attention. Nathaniel was himself nearer seventy than sixty, and whilst he had known the Lambert family all his working life he was still somewhat naïve, especially with regard to Miles's reputation. He explained that it was only shortly before Christmas that he had met Henry, who had told him that he intended to come and see him early in the new year to make a will.

'I was very surprised he had left it so long before doing something about it. I knew he hadn't made his will, and I did mention it once or twice, but I didn't feel it my place to pressurise him. I suppose he was always too busy and just never got round to it.'

'Yes, I expect you're right,' said Miles.

'Still, unless he had anything unusual in mind, I don't suppose it will make a great deal of difference. You and Joseph are his next of kin, and as the eldest son you'll now inherit the estate. But I've no doubt you'll be making provision for your brother's continuing education and to secure his future; that's what usually happens in these circumstances.'

'Oh, rest assured, Mr Cartwright, you can rely on me to make the very best use of all the estate's assets.'

'Well, Miles, I'm delighted to hear that. Young Joseph has been telling me how much he enjoys his time at school, and after what's happened I'm sure that's the best place for him. I know he's taken his father's death very badly but I really do believe that school will help to take his mind off it. When does he return?'

'Later this week, I think. And I'm sure you're right; the sooner he gets back there the better. Now, if you'll excuse me I need to speak to Jessie, but I must call and see you so we can finalise everything for handing over the estate. Shall we say Friday next at two o'clock? I assume you can have the relevant documents ready for signing by then.' And without waiting for a reply he turned away, leaving Nathaniel standing alone and looking somewhat bemused.

After the last of the mourners had gone and Joseph had retired for the night, Miles sat in front of the fire, a large glass of brandy in his hand, and contemplated his new circumstances. He was now the squire, the owner of the estate and all its wealth. In a few days time Joseph would be back at school and Emily would be returning home, and he could then indulge himself as he wished. Naturally, there'd have to be a decent period of mourning on his part. There'd be nothing to be gained by upsetting the neighbours, and the next morning he'd talk to Sykes. It was important that the estate continued to prosper but he certainly had no intention of getting *his* hands dirty any longer. No, he'd leave that to Sykes, for he had other plans about how he intended to pass his time. And getting involved with the messy and smelly business of farming certainly didn't number amongst them. What he'd really like to do, right then, he thought, was go to the Black Boar and meet up with his friends for drinks and a game of cards. After all, there'd be no worries now about paying his debts, should he incur any. But he'd have to be patient for a little while, and he could be patient if he had to be. He now had years ahead of him as master of all he surveyed. Yes, he decided, he could wait. Not for too long, but just long enough for his father's death to be replaced as the main topic of conversation in polite society by some other event.

Three days later, on New Year's Day, Joseph returned to school. Emily, who had delayed her return home until Joseph had left, was there to see him off, and even Miles bid him goodbye as he climbed into the coach. Joseph had been very upset by his father's death. He was now an orphan, as was his brother, but he felt the loss far more than Miles. And yet he was looking forward to returning to school. The proprietor, Jacob Parsons, was an old friend of his father, and unlike so many boarding schools Joseph had heard about, this was one establishment where he felt happy and knew he was safe. Mr Parsons, of course, didn't yet know of Henry's death, but Joseph was sure that when he heard the news he would be saddened to learn of it.

Joseph said his farewells to Emily and Miles and wished them both good health until he would see them again, some three months later at Easter. But as the coach set off down the driveway, he was blissfully unaware of just how quickly and to what extent his life was about to change. Neither did Emily, as she waved him *bon voyage*. But Miles, standing by Emily's side had already made plans for his brother's future. Tomorrow, he would visit Cartwright to sort out the estate's transfer into his name and a smile came over his face. Yes, one by one his plans were slowly but surely falling into place.

CHAPTER FOUR

Debts and threats

It was a couple of months later that Miles's life gradually started to return to normal. He began once again to frequent the Black Boar, and occasionally he would invite his friends back to the manor, where their drinking and gambling would often go on all through the night. Sometimes, when they became tired of their all-male pursuits, they would arrange for some of the local girls to join them, and there was never a shortage of willing participants to be tempted by the promise of good food and wine, and a generous tip in return for offering female entertainment of a more intimate nature.

Jessie soon became upset at the activities of her employer, and whilst her livelihood, and that of her husband, depended on him, she increasingly found it difficult to stop herself from voicing her disapproval of his behaviour. For a while she kept her opinions to herself, hoping that as time went by Miles would realise that, as the new squire, he now had a position to maintain. But despite her hopes, things only went from bad to worse. It was after one particular night of unrivalled drunken debauchery when she was left to clear up the mess, that she could no longer hold her tongue.

'I'm sorry, sir, but this can't continue. It was never like this in your father's day, God rest his soul. You might be the new squire, but I've known you since you were a child and I can't stand by and see you ruin yourself without saying something. It's a disgrace, the way you're behaving. Your father would turn in his grave if he could see what you're getting up to; and as for your poor mother, well, I can't even begin to think what she would say.'

Miles, who was clearly suffering from a severe hangover, at first ignored her, but when she continued with her diatribe he turned on her with a degree of malice she had rarely witnessed before.

'Don't you ever dare speak to me like that again! You might have been with the family for more years than I care to remember, but don't forget who the master is now. If you hadn't been here for so long I'd dismiss you instantly, but I'll give you one last chance. I'll do exactly as I please, and you'll do exactly what you're paid to do. And the same goes for your husband, too, and you'd be well advised to remind him of that. Right, I'm off out now but I'll be back at about six o'clock. And when I do get back I expect this room to be tidied up and my dinner ready. Is that clear?' And without waiting for an answer he swept out, leaving Jessie speechless.

Once Miles had left she went in search of her husband. She found him in the butler's pantry, cleaning boots, and as soon as he saw her he knew from the expression on her face that something was wrong. 'Jessie dear, whatever's the matter?' Soon she had related, in detail, the whole distressing episode.

Alfred pondered for a little while before replying. 'You know, Jessie, I fear we're going to have nothing but trouble with young Miles. He's returned to his old ways with a vengeance, and now there's nobody to stop him. When Henry was alive, at least he was able to rein him in a bit, but now he's gone Miles can do whatever he likes. It's almost as if Henry's death was just what Miles wanted. I know it might sound fanciful, but I'm beginning to wonder whether his death really was an accident. I was talking to Abraham and Ben about it the other day, and the more we talked the more we convinced ourselves that there was something not quite right. The way he was supposed to have hit his head on a tree. He'd never have done that, would Henry; he was far too good a horseman. If you ask me, Miles had a hand in his father's death. We were all agreed on that, and I don't think we're the only ones round here who believe it was an accident.'

'Maybe, but what can we do about it?'

'Nothing, absolutely nothing, except keep our mouths shut if we want to keep our jobs. Henry's dead and buried and Miles is the new squire, and that's the long and short of it. We've got to accept it and get on with our lives; either that or leave. And where would we find other positions at our time of life? No, Jessie, I'm afraid we'll have to grin and bear it and stay out of his way as much as possible.'

'Yes Alfred, I'm sure you're right. But as you've heard me say often enough, a man's dark deeds will eventually come back to haunt him. And if he really was behind Henry's death, he'll get his just deserts one day.'

Over the coming weeks the situation did not improve; indeed if anything it deteriorated. Miles was now spending more and more of his time drinking, gambling and womanising, and he had begun to lose all interest in the running of the estate, which he now left entirely in the hands of Sykes. Even when there were important decisions to be made, Miles was reluctant to get involved.

Sykes was particularly concerned by the large number of unpaid bills. These were piling up, and try as he might he could not get Miles to authorise payment. Many of the local merchants and tradesmen were now owed substantial sums. One of the biggest creditors was a local wine and spirit merchant, who was owed over £200, and he declared that unless he was paid soon he feared he would be put out of business. It was becoming increasingly embarrassing for Sykes, who was friendly with all the local tradesmen, that his employer was so tardy when it came to settling his accounts. Of course, they were used to having to wait some time for payment, especially from the gentry, and at first they were reluctant to press the matter further lest Miles took his business elsewhere. However, the situation was becoming so serious that one night a group of them met to discuss what could be done, and they agreed there and then on a plan. It was one that was not without risk, but they had reached the point where something had to be done. They would all demand immediate settlement of outstanding debts, with the threat that if they were not paid they would refuse to supply anything further, and if that didn't work they would take Miles to court. They would also ensure that all other potential suppliers were made aware of the circumstances.

Letters to this effect were written and handed to Sykes to present to Miles. This was one task that Sykes was not looking forward to, for he knew that Miles was always ready to shoot the messenger if the message did not suit him. He waited until Miles was reasonably sober before broaching the subject and presenting him with the various demands, which he knew totalled over £500.

At first, Miles had no wish to listen to what Sykes had to say, and it was only with the greatest difficulty, and with much persuasion, that he was able to convince him that the matter he had to discuss was of the utmost importance. Eventually, Miles opened the letters and read them one by one, and as he did so Sykes could see that he was becoming angrier and angrier with each letter. His face was getting redder and redder until the veins stood out on his forehead, as if he were about to burst a blood vessel.

'How dare they! How dare they threaten me like this! I'll not have common tradesmen dictating terms to me. If they don't want my business I'll take it elsewhere, and hang the lot of them!'

'I think, sir, you might find it difficult to find others willing to do business with you. News spreads quickly amongst tradesmen and if it got round that you are, how shall we say, a little tardy in paying, you might find there is nobody else willing to supply us.'

'So what do *you* suggest then, Sykes?' demanded Miles in an accusing tone.

'I think, sir, the only option is to pay, and in future to make sure we don't hang on to bills for too long. I also think that in the long term it would be to everyone's advantage to maintain good relations with all the local merchants and tradesmen.'

'Damn them all, I say!' Then, after a long pause, during which Miles's demeanour changed from one of resentment to one of resigned acceptance of the facts, he said to Sykes, 'All right then, you'd better arrange for them to be paid. I'll give you a note to take to the bank to withdraw the money. I'll see to it first thing tomorrow, then perhaps we can silence these tiresome busybodies once and for all.'

For once, Miles was as good as his word, and the following morning Sykes set off for the bank with the authority to withdraw the money. Within a few days he had visited all the creditors and settled all outstanding bills, much to their relief and satisfaction. But at the same time that Sykes was going about his business, Miles was also involving himself in a little financial manoeuvring. For the week before, he had received another bill of which Sykes was unaware, not from a local tradesman but from Joseph's school, for the fees due for his continuing education and accommodation. The previous bill had still not been paid, it having arrived shortly before Henry's death, and the next amount was now due. Miles looked down at the two bills, added them up, and realising just how much brandy could be bought for the total, decided that it was now time to do what he had promised himself when he had waved his brother off to school some three months earlier.

'What a waste of money!' he said, out loud. 'Why should I continue paying out so much for such little return? What good will Joseph's education ever do for me?' And taking up pen and paper, he wrote a short note, addressed to Jacob Parsons Esquire, proprietor of the North Riding Academy for Boys, near York.

CHAPTER FIVE

Creeping like a snail unwillingly from school

Jacob Parsons was a sallow-faced, middle-aged man of above average height, his thick grey side whiskers contrasting with the rapidly thinning hair on the top of his head. As a schoolmaster of many years standing, he knew exactly how to manage the boys in his care. He maintained a firm and strict regime, and where necessary could instil a sense of fear in any pupil who stepped out of line. Most of them soon learned this, and consequently, the occasions when he needed to come down with a heavy hand were few and far between. But he was, by nature, a kind and caring man, and earnestly protective of his pupils' welfare. He also possessed the driest sense of humour and – so it seemed to the boys in his charge – an unparalleled knowledge of every branch of learning to which the keenest of them might apply their enquiring minds.

Whilst Jacob, ably assisted by one aspiring young schoolmaster, concentrated on providing the scholastic needs of the forty or so resident pupils at his academy, Emma, his wife of over twenty years, acted not only as matron and housekeeper but also *in loco parentis* for those boys whose parents had entrusted them to the school's care. Jacob was usually slow to anger, and it was therefore somewhat of a surprise to his wife when she entered his office one morning to find him sitting at his desk, a letter in his hand and a look of utter exasperation on his face. He shook his head in disbelief, as he waved the letter in the air. 'Just look at this, my dear,' he exclaimed tetchily, peering at the letter over the top of his silver-framed spectacles. 'I don't know how the fellow could be so insensitive; it's beyond my comprehension that someone could be so unfeeling, and to his own brother!'

'Whatever's the matter? Who's the letter from, Jacob?' she asked.

'I'll read it to you. It's from Miles Lambert, young Joseph Lambert's elder brother. You know their father died at Christmas and Miles inherited the estate. Well, it would appear that his inheritance has gone to his head; just listen to this,' and repositioning his spectacles on the bridge of his broad nose he continued:

Sir

I write in regard to your invoice recently received in respect of my brother Joseph. I have to inform you that I have decided that your services are no longer required, and I therefore have no intention of settling these bills. You are, of course, perfectly at liberty to maintain and educate him at your own expense should you so desire, but under the assumption that this will not be the case, I expect that you will send him back home immediately.

I remain, sir,

Miles Lambert

'Oh, the poor boy,' declared Emma, 'what are we to do?'

'I'm not sure, my dear. He's such an attentive scholar, and since his father died he seems to have come to regard the school as his home. I had known his father, Henry, since we were both young men, although we hadn't met for a number of years, so Joseph does seem rather more like an old family friend than a pupil. But we can't really afford to keep him here at our expense forever; you know what our finances are like at the moment. We might be able to let him stay until the Easter holiday, but unless he can persuade his brother to change his mind, I'm afraid he'll have to leave then. I'll talk to Joseph and see if he can shed any light on why his brother should have decided on such a course of action.'

Later that evening, after the boys had finished their supper,

Jacob summoned Joseph to his office. 'Ah, there you are Joseph,' said Jacob as the boy entered, a look of some bewilderment on his face. 'Come and sit down, I have something to discuss with you,' and he opened a drawer in his desk and took out the letter. 'I received this today from your brother. There's no point in hiding its contents from you, and sooner or later you'll have to know what it says, so I think it best if you read it for yourself,' and he handed the letter to him. Joseph sat in silence as he read it, and then buried his face in his hands. Jacob could see that its message had cut Joseph to the quick and he knew that he had been severely hurt by what he had just read.

'Please, Joseph, don't upset yourself. If we try, we might persuade your brother to see reason and change his mind. In any case, you'll not have to leave immediately. Mrs Parsons and I have discussed the matter and we're agreed that you may stay here until the Easter holiday; that should give us some time to see if we can talk him round.'

Joseph quickly composed himself. 'I don't think he'll change his mind, sir. I've dreaded something like this happening ever since father died. I know my brother better than you do and I don't think that anything you or I could say will make any difference.' Joseph then proceeded to open his heart to Jacob and tell him all about his brother; that Miles had never liked him, that he blamed him for their mother's death, and that one of the reasons his father had sent him to the school was to get him away from Miles. 'And now my father has died and Miles has inherited the estate, there's nobody to prevent him from treating me exactly as he wishes.'

After Joseph had finished talking, Jacob sat calmly for a minute, carefully mulling over in his mind what he had been told. 'Now look, Joseph, I don't want you to worry. As I said, you can stay here until Easter, and that will give us time to try and reason with your brother.'

'But you don't know him, sir. He won't change his mind. And if you try and contact him it could only make matters worse. I'm not sure what I will do, but it's now up to me to fend for myself. I'm very grateful for your help, sir, but I'd like to go to bed now. I have a lot to think about.'

In the dead of night, when all was still, a boy crept quietly from his bed in the dormitory. He gathered together the few possessions he had, some spare clothes, a couple of books, a little money, and most important of all, the only thing he had to remind him of happier times – his father's gold watch and chain, the one item he had managed to keep after his father's death. He bundled them carefully inside the blanket from his bed, and tiptoed carefully down the stairs to the back door of the school. He stopped only to write a brief note to Mr Parsons, then unlocking the door slipped silently out into the darkness. In the morning, Joseph's absence was soon discovered, and it was not long before the ensuing search uncovered the note he had left. It was short and to the point, and read:

> *Dear Mr & Mrs Parsons*
>
> *Don't worry about me and please don't contact Miles. I know where I'm going and I know I'll be safe. Thank you for everything.*
>
> *Yours truly,*
>
> *Joseph Lambert*
>
> *p.s. I promise to return the blanket one day.*

It was a clear, starlit March night with a near full moon, when Joseph set off from the school where he had been so happy and content for over three years. As he headed south he looked up at the moon and stars and said a silent prayer in thanks for the light that they provided. But the cloudless sky meant it was also a chilly night. Frost pinched at his ears and fingertips, and he wrapped his coat closer around him to try and keep the cold at bay. At one point, as he passed a barn full of hay, he was tempted to stop and rest, but knew that keeping on the move was the best way of staying warm. He had gone about ten miles when the dawn slowly began to break, an orange glow over distant hills heralding a bright day to follow.

He had decided that he would head for his Aunt Emily's house, as he wanted to let her know what had happened, and was quite certain that Miles would not bother to tell her. He also knew he would be welcome there, and he looked forward to seeing his grandparents again, for it was some time since he had last seen them.

And then what? He was not sure. He had thought long and hard about where he could go and what he could do. There was no sense in returning home; Miles would not help him. He could appeal to Abraham Sykes or the Houghs for help and he had no doubt they would be only too willing to assist, but they were employees of Miles and if he found out they had helped him, their own jobs might be at risk. No, he thought, he must fight his own battles now. He knew Emily would let him stay with her, but he had already made up his mind that it would only be for a short time, for she had her elderly parents to care for. He was determined that, painful as it might be, he must put his past life behind him, strike out and seek his fortune elsewhere. Where that would be, or what he would do he had no idea, but he knew that, somehow, he would survive.

It was some thirty miles to his aunt's home, a rambling old farmhouse a few miles south of Wakefield, an enormous distance for young Joseph to travel on foot. And although he was fit and healthy he had never had to walk so far in one day. Several times he stopped to rest, and with the little money he had he was able to buy some food. It was late afternoon when he eventually found himself, cold, tired and hungry, knocking on the farmhouse door. He heard steps approaching on the stone-flagged floor inside, then a bolt being drawn back and finally the large oak door slowly opened. His aunt stood on the doorstep, a look of astonishment on her face.

'Joseph, whatever are you doing here? Why aren't you at school?'

'Can I come in please, Aunt Emily?' An hour later Joseph had warmed himself by the fire, eaten a hearty meal and had finished telling his aunt and grandparents the whole sorry story.

'I never had much time for your brother,' said Emily, 'I think you know that; but I would never have thought he'd do something like this! It's shameful. If your father had made a will, I know you would have been well provided for and I think Miles knows that, too.'

For a while, Joseph stayed with his aunt and grandparents, Edwin and Lidia Bussey. Joseph had never had much contact with his grandparents, certainly not as much as he might have had, if his mother had lived. He had accompanied his father on occasional visits to their home when he was much younger, and they in turn had made the odd return trip. But that was in the past, and in more recent years it was only Emily's time spent living at Westbrook that had really kept him in touch with his mother's side of the family. Both Edwin and Lidia were now getting old, and they relied on Emily to look after them and undertake most of the housework. They no longer farmed the land, which they leased to another, neighbouring farmer.

Emily explained that she had had no contact with Miles since Henry's funeral, but news of his increasingly debauched lifestyle had reached her. She had met Sykes one day when he was over at Wakefield on business, and he had confided in her that he was deeply worried about the effect that Miles's behaviour was having on the finances of the estate. Evidently, he could be found in the Black Boar most nights, drinking and gambling, and there were also rumours of wild orgies taking place at the manor. But those who relied on him for their employment were reluctant to say too much, for fear that their livelihoods might be put in jeopardy.

Joseph had already decided that he would make no attempt to contact his brother and let him know where he was, but he was anxious that Mr Parsons should know what had happened to him. So he parcelled up the blanket he had borrowed and arranged to have it returned to the school, along with a note, explaining where he was and that he was safe.

One evening, after supper, Joseph was helping Emily clean and put away the utensils, when Edwin, who was sitting by the fire, noticed that he was busily admiring the cutlery.

'Sheffield silver-plated steel that is, my lad – best quality in the world – you'll not find better anywhere,' said his grandfather. Joseph was examining the hallmark and maker's insignia, inscribed in fine detail on the blade of a bone-handled knife. 'It's made by Yates and

Sons, one of the most respected firms in the town,' continued Edwin. 'Solomon Yates was an old friend of mine, and he founded the business. But he's been dead for some years, and his eldest son, Titus, is now in charge. It's certainly well made is that knife; the man who made it knew his craft all right.'

'I can see that,' replied Joseph, admiring the workmanship, then after a moment's thought he added, 'how does a man become skilled enough to make such a piece?'

'Years of training, lad. A seven-year apprenticeship, and if at the end of it you can prove you're good enough you'll be accepted as a true cutler.'

Joseph continued to admire the knives, forks and spoons. He had always had a love of beautiful, man-made objects, and had often thought how rewarding it must be for those with the skill to create such beauty. He had always been adept at drawing and painting, and often, as a child, he had whittled away at pieces of wood, carving figures or animals. And then, suddenly, an idea struck him. 'Grandfather, do you think I could be taken on as an apprentice at Yates's?' he asked. Emily, who was busy putting away the crockery and had overheard Joseph's conversation with her father, stopped and looked across at him.

'I don't think that's exactly what your father would have had in mind for you,' she said, somewhat curtly.

'Well,' replied Joseph, 'I don't suppose father would have expected Miles to do what he's done, either. But he has, so it's now up to me to do the best I can for myself. You know I can't stay here forever, Aunt Emily. I have to find work and I don't want to be anywhere near Miles. I should like to learn a trade, and what better than making fine objects like these.'

'Good for you, lad,' said Edwin. 'If you really are serious about this, I could write to young Titus and put in a good word for you. And if he does need another apprentice, well, he might agree to take you on; how would you like that?'

'Oh yes, grandfather, I'd like that very much! Please write to him.'

It was over two weeks before a reply was received to Edwin's letter, two weeks that seemed like two months to Joseph. Happy as he was staying at his grandparent's house, he felt that time was slipping away. He longed to do something and make something of himself, but when the letter eventually came he suddenly realised that the answer might be no; that they might not be taking on any more apprentices. What then? He had convinced himself that his life was about to take a new and exciting turn, and it never occurred to him that he might be disappointed. He waited apprehensively as Edwin opened the letter and read aloud its contents to the assembled audience:

Sheffield
30th April 1829

My Dear Mr Bussey,

I was most gratified to receive your communication of the 16th inst. You will, I am sure, be pleased to hear that our business is currently thriving, and with that in mind I am willing to offer your grandson a position. I understand that the young man has no immediate family, and under the circumstances I assume you will oblige by acting in loco parentis and signing the enclosed apprenticeship indenture. I suggest that the boy comes to Sheffield on Monday week. I know of a widow woman who has a room to let and she has kindly agreed to take the boy in. In the meantime, perhaps you will acknowledge your acceptance of the aforesaid. Trusting this finds you well,

I remain, sir,
Your obedient servant,

Titus Yates

'Well, lad, there you are, he'll have you. How does that suit you?' asked Edwin, as he removed his spectacles and placed them on the table alongside the letter. Joseph eagerly grabbed the letter and read it to himself, the broad grin on his face showing just how delighted he was. But Emily and Lidia were both a little concerned that Joseph, who was still only thirteen and who had never had to fend for himself, would soon be setting off, alone, to a strange town he had never been to, away from family and friends. But Joseph himself had no fears, and Edwin sought to reassure his wife and daughter. 'He's my grandson, and if he's anything like I was at his age he'll be fine, won't you, lad? Don't let these silly women worry you, Joseph. We men know how to look after ourselves. Why, when I was twelve I ran away to go to sea.'

'Yes, and your father soon caught up with you and brought you back home before you'd got anywhere near the coast,' Lidia reminded him. 'Heaven knows what might have happened if he hadn't. You'd probably have been drowned at sea and then we wouldn't all be sat here now talking about it.'

'Oh, never mind that, my dear. I'm sure Joseph will do all right. He'll be working for a reliable man who is known to me. If he works hard and applies himself, who knows, twenty years from now he might be taking on apprentices of his own.'

And so it was arranged that, ten days later, Joseph would start out on his journey. He had made up his mind to walk the twenty odd miles to Sheffield, but Emily and his grandparents would hear none of it and insisted on paying his fare to travel by coach.

'There's a stagecoach that runs every morning from York to Sheffield and calls at Wakefield,' said Edwin. 'You'll have to go into the town to join it, but it's not far, and I'll get one of the farm lads to take you in on the cart. It leaves the King's Head at eleven o'clock and you don't want to miss it. Titus will be expecting you and you mustn't be late on your first day.'

At ten o'clock the following Monday, Joseph said goodbye to his grandparents. They were both sad to see him go, but Edwin shook his hand firmly and told him to work hard and always do right by those he worked with. Emily went with him into the town, where the coach called to change horses and give the passengers time to partake of food and drink. The coach was already at the inn when they arrived; the horses had been changed and those who had travelled from further north were beginning to rejoin it after taking refreshments.

Soon they were ready to leave. Joseph said his goodbyes to Emily and thanked her for looking after him since he left the school. She wished him the very best of luck and made him promise to write and let them know how he was getting on, and to come back and visit them if ever he had the opportunity.

Joseph had very little luggage with him – just one bag with some clothes, a handful of books, and two pounds which his grandfather had given him. He found a seat on the top, and Emily was thankful that the weather was fine, for there was no protection for outside passengers should it rain. As the coach pulled out of the inn yard, Joseph continued to wave to Emily, until they turned a corner and she was out of sight.

And so, his great adventure began.

CHAPTER SIX

Nerves of steel

The journey to Sheffield took almost four hours, with one short stop at Barnsley, and Joseph was fascinated by the ever-changing landscape. He was, of course, familiar with the open moors and farmlands in which he had grown up, and whilst most of the countryside through which they passed was devoted to agriculture, there were areas where industry had begun to encroach into an otherwise rural setting. Coal mines, quarries and ironworks were at once evident from the scars they made on the landscape, and often the sound or smell of these industries could be sensed before they actually came into view.

Soon they were approaching Sheffield. His grandfather had told him something of the place, and he knew that he would have to get used to a new way of life here. Sheffield was an industrial town and its wealth depended heavily on coal, iron and steel, but principally on the manufacture of knives, scissors, scythes, swords, chisels and every conceivable item of cutlery for which it had long been renowned. But no matter how much Joseph had been told, nothing could have prepared him for the shock as the coach passed rapidly through the outskirts of the town and into the heart of its thriving centre.

The buildings seemed to get taller and more tightly packed the further they went; narrow lanes, alleyways and courtyards led off in every direction, and the noise and clatter told him loud and clear that this was indeed a hive of activity. All around there were factories, mills and workshops, smoke billowing from their chimneys, and the nearer they got to the centre of the town the slower they were forced to go, as the narrow, cobbled streets became ever more congested with horse-drawn vehicles jostling for space. And people! Everywhere there were people. He had never seen so many in one place, even on his occasional visits from the school into the ancient City of York. Wherever he looked, there they were, scurrying hither and thither, shouting and shoving, laughing and joking, swearing and cursing; carrying hampers, bales and boxes; pulling carts and pushing barrows as they went hurriedly about their business like a colony of ants on the march. Intrigued and excited as he was by these new sights and sounds, there was a certain foreboding about them and he was unsure whether or not he could be happy living in such an unfamiliar and hostile environment.

Joseph was still in a daze when the coach pulled into an inn yard opposite the old church of St. Peters, and he climbed down from the roof, clutching his solitary bag. Throughout the journey, he had shared the top of the coach with three other travellers, and had felt perfectly at home and in good company. But now, here, despite all this frenzied activity, he suddenly felt utterly alone, silently gazing around and trying to acclimatise himself to his new surroundings. He took from his pocket a piece of paper on which he had written the address of Yates's premises. Eyre Street was all it said, but it might as well have been at the other end of the country, for all it meant to him. The coachman had just finished helping the last of the passengers from the top of the coach, and peering down at Joseph, he noticed him puzzling over the piece of paper.

'Can I help thee, lad?' he asked, 'tha seems to be lost.'

'Thank you,' replied Joseph with a sigh of relief. 'I need to get to this address,' he said, handing the piece of paper to the man. The coachman took it reluctantly, scrutinised it closely and then handed it back.

'Well, lad, my eyes ain't too good today,' he said, unconvincingly, 'but if tha reads me what it says, I'll see if I can tell thee how to get there.' It had never occurred to Joseph that the man might not be able to read. Everyone he knew could both read and write, and he had just learned the first of many lessons he would learn in the coming years – that a big town was a very different place from the safe and privileged world he had been used to. Joseph read the address out loud. The coachman stroked his chin pensively for a moment. 'Eyre Street, is it? That's easy, lad, it's not far. Go along the High Street here a little way,' he said, pointing down the street past the church, 'then cut through George Street, past the Baptist chapel and turn right into Norfolk Street. Then it's left into Surrey Street and tha'll soon come to Eyre Street, straight opposite the concert hall. It's quite a long street, mind. Who's tha trying to find?'

'Mr Yate's cutlery factory,' Joseph replied, 'do you know it?'

'Aye, I know where it is, lad. Tha can't miss it. Just carry on down Eyre Street and tha'll find it on the left.'

Joseph thanked the man and set off, repeating to himself as he went the directions he had been given and in no time at all he found himself in Surrey Street. Soon he reached a large imposing stone building, erected in the classical style, which he took to be the concert hall, and immediately opposite he saw the cast-iron sign he was looking for – Eyre Street. Crossing over, he stepped out with a confident stride, his anticipation increasing with each step as he looked up at the buildings on his left, searching for the signboard that would indicate his new employer.

The street was quite wide, but other, narrower streets led off on either side, and he soon realised that this part of the town was laid out in a grid formation. The whole area appeared to be devoted entirely to the cutlery trade in all its various guises. There were numerous workshops both large and small, each with its signboard outside declaring the name of the owner and his particular trade – *scissor maker; scythe and sickle manufacturer; knife and sword maker; supplier of agricultural implements;* and of course, *manufacturers of the finest cutlery.*

None of the properties, particularly the smaller ones, gave any hint from the exterior of the valuable and high-quality items made therein. Indeed, many of them seemed to him not only run down, but almost about to fall down. Rickety wooden stairs led up the outside of some of the buildings to upper rooms, and some of these housed a different business to that conducted on the floors below; here and there, roof tiles were broken or missing and the small dirty windows sported many a broken pane of glass. How strange, thought Joseph, that this ramshackle area of a Yorkshire town could produce items as exquisite as those he had admired at his grandfather's home. But as he soon came to appreciate, the owners of these numerous businesses were practical men, especially when it came to parting with money. The quality of their finished articles was of paramount importance, and for the most part they clearly believed that money should never be wasted on such unnecessary luxuries as the outward appearance of their premises.

It didn't take long for Joseph to find the address he was seeking. It stood on a corner, a two-storey brick building with an identical row of six windows on both sides and on both lower and upper floors. The door was on the corner, above which was affixed a wooden board with faded white letters proclaiming this to be the premises of *Solomon Yates & Sons. Cutler.*

Joseph remembered what his grandfather had told him about Solomon, who had been dead for some time, and the weather-beaten lettering on the sign bore witness to the fact that it must have been there for years. He walked up to the door, which stood slightly ajar, and taking the large brass knocker in his hand, knocked loudly. There was no immediate reply and he knocked again several times until, his curiosity getting the better of him, he slowly pushed the door open. It creaked noisily, and when it was sufficiently wide open, he quietly crept inside. Just as he did so, a door at the far side of the room opened and a man entered.

'All right, all right, I'm coming. I heard you the first time. Now then, what can I do for you, young man?' The speaker was elderly with greying hair and stooping shoulders.

'I've come to see Mr Titus Yates,' replied Joseph hesitantly.

'Ah, so it's the mester you want, is it? And who shall I say wants to see him?' he asked.

'Joseph Lambert. He is expecting me.'

The old man stared intently at Joseph, eyeing him up and down. Eventually, he spoke. 'Right you are. Stay there and I'll go and find him.' He turned round and disappeared through the door he had come through, and Joseph could hear his footsteps as he slowly climbed a wooden staircase.

Joseph gazed around him at this somewhat dingy room. It was small, about eight feet high and twelve feet square. The walls were covered from floor to ceiling in dark wood panelling, giving the room a sombre appearance. On each of the exterior walls were two tiny windows, and between them were rows of shelves stacked high with an assortment of boxes. To the left of the door was a narrow wooden counter, cluttered with papers, books and ledgers, and a solitary, unlit, oil lamp. Behind the counter, up against the wall, stood a high stool and sloping desk, on top of which were an inkwell and more documents. In front of the counter was a single wooden chair, presumably, thought Joseph, for the benefit of visitors to use whilst conducting their business.

The only light came through the windows, and he wondered how effective the single oil lamp would be when dusk fell. He was just comparing the dim and gloomy atmosphere here with the bright and cheerful library at Westbrook Manor, when once more he heard footsteps descending the stairs, this time much firmer and quicker than the old man's. The door opened and in stepped a much younger man. Joseph judged him to be about forty years of age. He was of medium height, chubby, with a round, friendly face, clean-shaven, with a shock of ginger hair and short bushy side whiskers. The man smiled broadly as he approached. 'You must be young Joseph, Edwin's grandson, I'll be bound,' and he grasped Joseph's right hand in his own and shook it vigorously.

'Yes sir, I'm Joseph and I'm very pleased to meet you.'

Titus stepped back, as if to get a better view of his new apprentice. 'Follow me,' he said. Joseph picked up his bag and followed Titus through the door and up the wooden stairs. These led to a large oblong workshop in which a score or so of men sat at benches, surrounded by a variety of tools, each man working meticulously at his appointed task. Joseph followed Titus into his office, a small, partitioned room in one corner, with a large window that allowed him to keep an eye on his workmen.

'Sit yourself down there,' said Titus, pointing to a simple wooden chair, as he himself sat down in a large high-winged leather seat behind his desk. 'Now then young man, let's hear all about you!'

For the next half-hour, Joseph told Titus a little more about his background and why he was looking for work. Titus already knew something of Joseph's history from what Edwin had told him in his letter, but he always thought it best to get the story direct from the horse's mouth. When Joseph had finished, and had answered a few questions, Titus got up from his chair. 'Come along with me and I'll introduce you to your workmates. You can have a look round and see what you make of us all. I've no doubt everything will be strange to you at first, but tomorrow you start work in earnest and I'm sure you'll soon get the hang of things. I'm going to put you with Dan. He's been here longer than anyone and knows the business inside out. Anything you want to know, you just ask him. The men finish at six and I'll get Dan to take you to your lodgings. It's not far from here and it's on his way home. Mrs Whitworth is expecting you. Now, I have an important client to visit, so I'll leave you in Dan's capable hands and we'll expect you here tomorrow morning at six o'clock on the dot.'

Dan Ellin was small, thin and wiry, clean-shaven but with long straggly white hair. He seemed to Joseph to be very old, and on his own admission had worked at the factory for upwards of fifty years. He was a native of the town and spoke in the distinctive local accent. He sported a mischievous grin and as Joseph would soon discover, possessed the most perfect ability at mimicry. No one was spared his impersonations, and many were the times he would reduce the workforce to fits of laughter, especially when a particularly pompous or difficult customer became the victim of his wicked sense of humour. Joseph was to get to know Dan well over the coming years, for he was assigned to teach Joseph the trade.

At six o'clock work stopped and the men set aside their tools, put on their coats and left the factory. Joseph accompanied Dan to the home of Agnes Whitworth, a widow and old friend of Titus and his wife. She lived in a house in Norfolk Street, less than five minutes walk from the factory. Dan knew Agnes well, but then it seemed to Joseph that Dan knew everybody in Sheffield, judging by the greetings and banter he exchanged with most of the people they passed in the street. He knocked on the door, and when it opened it was a girl of about eleven who stood there. 'Hello there, young Hannah, and how are you, little un?' asked Dan.

'I'm very well, Mr Ellin,' she replied, timidly, eyeing Joseph rather suspiciously. 'Is it ma you want? She's in the kitchen doing some baking.' But before he could answer, a lady appeared in the hallway.

'Hello Dan,' she said, wiping her floury hands on her apron as she walked towards the door. 'I guess this must be the young man Titus told me to expect.'

'This is him all right, Agnes. Let me introduce you to Master Joseph Lambert; Joseph, meet Mrs Agnes Whitworth, widow of this parish, and one o' finest pastry cooks in t' town o' Sheffield, probably in t' whole West Riding o' Yorkshire. By heck, lass, if I didn't still have my owd lady waiting for me at home, I'd offer to make thee an honest woman again!' exclaimed Dan with a huge grin on his face.

'Get away with you, you old rogue,' she laughed, 'you're old enough to be my father. Even my grandfather! You wait till I see your Nellie, I'll tell her all about you.'

'Too late, lass, she already knows,' chuckled Dan. 'Well, young Joseph, I must get off. Tea'll be on table soon, and if I'm not there missus'll be on doorstep wi' frying pan in her hand! So I'll leave thee to settle in, and we'll se'thee tomorrow at six o'clock. And don't be late mind, he's a stickler for timekeeping is the mester,' and with that Dan set off along Norfolk Street towards his home.

'He's a right character is that Dan,' said Agnes, shaking her head in amusement as she shut the door. 'Anyway, come on in lad. Titus has already told me a bit about you, and from what he said, I do think you're very brave, leaving home all by yourself and coming to a strange town. You must have nerves of steel for one so young, and steel's the one thing you're certainly going to see a lot of, working here in Sheffield.'

Whilst all this had been going on, Hannah had remained

standing shyly behind her mother, almost frightened at this stranger who, it seemed to her, was about to invade the happy and cosy world she had known for as long as she could remember. And she stayed close to Agnes, clinging to her skirts, as Joseph followed them into the house which was now to become his new home.

CHAPTER SEVEN

Matches hatches and dispatches

On a Saturday evening in May 1829, in a back room of the Hanging Gate, a hostelry nestling snugly beneath the steep sandstone rock upon which stands Nottingham Castle, the party was in full swing. Ale flowed, food was plentiful, music played and the revelry went on late into the night. It was not often that those present enjoyed such a feast, for they were ordinary working folk – framework knitters, factory hands, labourers and warehousemen. Many were employed in the lace trade, as were the groom, David Brown, and his bride Margaret Hubbard. Most of the revellers did not have much money to spare, but a couple don't get married every day, and Christopher Hubbard was determined that his daughter's wedding would not be forgotten for a long time.

Christopher was a widower and farm labourer from over Bingham way, where he had worked diligently for many years for one of the largest landowners in the area. He had managed to save a little money for a rainy day, and had now decided that this was the time to put some of it to good use.

David had completed his apprenticeship with a master lace maker the previous year, and as a fully fledged journeyman twist hand was now free to marry. His father, George, a framework knitter, had also insisted on contributing a little something to help make sure the happy couple's wedding would be a day that everyone would remember.

It was three years previously, at the age of sixteen, when Margaret had arrived in Nottingham looking for work. Jobs were difficult to come by in the country at that time. Unless a girl could find a position in service at one of the big houses there was little option but to spend long days toiling in the fields for a pittance, and the farmers gave no allowance for the fact that they were women. And she had seen at first hand what this work could do to a woman. Her own mother had died, worn out after years of such hard labour and raising a family, and now Margaret's eldest sister, still only thirty-two, was rapidly going down the same road. Margaret had no desire to follow her. She had heard that there was employment to be found in the expanding lace industry in Nottingham, and whilst the hours could be long and the work hard, the pay was better and the conditions much more agreeable than the drudgery of labouring on a farm. And it was here that she had met David shortly after arriving in the town.

Most of her friends were now in Nottingham and so she had decided to marry there, rather than return to her native village for the ceremony. Naturally, her father, her sisters and brothers and their children, along with some of her childhood friends had come over to Nottingham for the wedding. They had persuaded the local carrier to bring them on his largest wagon, and with the promise of free food and drink he was happy to oblige. It was a heavy but perfectly sober group that the two horses strained to haul the ten miles to Nottingham that morning, but it was to be a somewhat heavier and considerably less sober gathering that returned much later that night. It was fortunate that the horses were familiar with the way home, for not a man and barely a woman was in a fit state to guide them, and most of the children were fast asleep.

The party came to an end shortly after one o'clock on the Sunday morning. Nottingham folk knew how to celebrate, and not for nothing was the town famous for its ale. And so, the Nottingham guests made their way slowly and unsteadily back to their homes. Most of them lived nearby in the warren of narrow streets and alleys that were rapidly occupying the former open space between the town centre and the canal to the south, and they had little distance to go. Only the Bingham guests had a long journey home and glad they were that it was a fine dry night. But at least the night air might help to alleviate the effects of the day's overindulgence.

When the last guests had departed, the happy couple made their way to an upstairs room of the pub. The landlord had been a good friend of the groom's father for many years and had offered them the room for the night as his wedding gift. The following day would be their one free day before a return to work on the Monday morning. But work was the last thing on their minds as they shut the bedroom door behind them, and started their married life together.

At first, David and Margaret lived with David's parents, George and Nancy. They rented a property on Eland Street, but it was small, and there were two other children still living at home. So when Margaret fell pregnant almost immediately, they decided it was time for them to move. They had a bit of money saved, and now that David was a skilled lace maker, his wages had risen. They soon found accommodation round the corner in Mortimer Street, in a row of three-storey, terraced houses. It consisted of four rooms on the first two floors; a living room and small rear scullery downstairs, and two bedrooms upstairs. The top storey was one large room with wide windows at both front and back, and this was rented out by the landlord to framework knitters for use as a workshop.

Margaret spent all her spare time making their new home as comfortable and inviting as she could. A neighbour, who worked in one of the canal warehouses, appeared one day with two big pots of paint and no questions asked, and she and David were soon busy brightening up the dull plaster walls. Friends gave them bits of old furniture and some rugs, and an aunt who had died recently left them some pictures, which David hung on the wall.

Margaret carried on working in the lace factory until just after Christmas, but the work was hard and tedious and the hours long, and by then the baby was almost due and she found it too tiring to continue. They were fortunate that the lace trade was quite buoyant and that David was bringing home a reasonable wage. Many other women in less happy circumstances would have had no option but to carry on working right up to their confinement. Or starve.

By the end of January, Margaret was finding it difficult to climb the stairs to the bedroom, so David brought the bed downstairs and placed it in the living room. A lot of the women in the neighbourhood, most of whom already had children, thought she might be having twins, so big had Margaret become. But when her time came it was just the one child, a boy who weighed in at over nine pounds. They named him Matthew, after David's grandfather, and two weeks after the birth the christening took place at St. Nicholas's Church. Margaret did not return to work. Many mothers did, leaving their offspring with relatives or neighbours, and there were plenty willing to help. But she wanted to stay at home with her baby, and David was now bringing home enough money to feed them all and pay the rent, with a little left over.

By early 1832 Margaret was pregnant again and by the summer of that year was looking forward to the birth of their second child. But then one day in July a frightful rumour began to spread round the town. A child over in Narrow Marsh had died the previous night. Nothing unusual in that, but the word was that the cause of death was the dreaded cholera. There had been occasional outbreaks before and it was always the poorest and most densely populated parts of the town that suffered the worst. And Mortimer Street, whilst not as crowded and poverty-stricken as some other areas, could certainly not be regarded as a safe place to be.

Margaret stayed in the house for the rest of that day, not daring to venture out lest she came into contact with someone who might be infected. By the time David arrived home from work he had already heard the rumours, and suggested that Margaret should go and stay with her father in his cottage near Bingham until such time as the danger was over, and take Matthew with her; but he would have to stay in Nottingham and carry on working. Margaret readily agreed and they decided to leave immediately. Within the hour she had packed a bag with some spare clothes and they set off to walk the ten miles. David carried young Matthew on his shoulders with ease, but Margaret, who was nearly seven months pregnant, was beginning to find the going hard. They had gone about four miles and dusk was falling when a farmer, returning home from the market in Nottingham, noticed her condition as he passed by on his horse and cart. He was going through Bingham and kindly offered to take them the rest of the way.

By the time they reached Margaret's childhood home it had turned dark. They were lucky that Christopher had not already retired for the night, and he was both surprised and delighted to see them. He hadn't yet heard about the suspected cholera outbreak, but was pleased to have his daughter back home, as he rarely saw her, or his new grandson. They all agreed that Margaret should stay there for a while, at least until the new baby was born and the cholera scare had subsided. David managed only a couple of hours sleep that night, then set off early the next morning to be back in time for work, promising that he would come and visit them the next Saturday afternoon when he had finished work for the week.

And so it continued for a month or two, with David coming to visit each Saturday evening, and returning to Nottingham in the early hours of Monday morning. Every week he brought news of the epidemic, for that is what it had now become, and every week the death toll rose. As the weeks wore on, David became ever more anxious about Margaret, but he knew that she would be well looked after by her sisters and other friends in the village, who would be there to help when her time came. And it was much to David's relief when, one Saturday evening in September, he arrived at the cottage to find that he now had a daughter. She had been born the previous morning but there had been no way of getting a message to David to let him know the good news. They named her Sarah, after Margaret's mother.

By October the epidemic seemed to be over. More than three hundred had perished, but when two weeks went by without a death the authorities declared that the danger had passed. The following week David took his wife, son and new daughter back to Nottingham, this time in the luxury of the local carrier's cart.

For the next few years life went on with little excitement or incident. David continued to prosper at his trade and so there was no need for Margaret to return to work. They had only two young children to care for, whilst some of the families in the street had a dozen or more, living in just two or three rooms. Margaret always felt sorry for the mothers, many of them exhausted by the sheer drudgery of trying to make ends meet on the meagre pay their husbands brought home. Some of the men spent most of their wages on drink before they even got home, and often Margaret would see their children in the street, barefoot and ragged and sometimes crying with hunger. When she could afford to, she would take food to the more needy families, but always waiting until the husbands had gone out, as most would have been angry and embarrassed if they knew their wives were accepting charity.

It was to be four more years until their next child arrived, another boy who came into the world in May of 1836, just as the blossoms were appearing on the trees. Thomas they named him. Thomas Brown.

CHAPTER EIGHT

A cutler by trade

At about the same time that young Thomas was raucously making his presence felt in the Brown household in Mortimer Street, Nottingham, forty miles to the north Joseph Lambert was about to finish his apprenticeship. For almost seven years he had worked long and hard at Yates & Sons in Eyre Street, Sheffield, where he had now become a skilled cutler, and in a few weeks' time he would be a Freeman. He would then be able to set up in business and work on his own account, should he so wish, but he had already been offered, and accepted, a position with his employer at a much increased wage, so highly were his skills regarded. No longer would he be required to abide by the petty rules and regulations that had governed his life as an apprentice, and consequently he would now be at liberty to marry his beloved Hannah.

Often he would tease her by reminding her of the first time they had met, when, despite being eleven years old, she had clung to her mother's skirts and hid, shyly, from the young boy who had turned up at their house as the new lodger. But if truth be known, Joseph had been equally as shy that day when he had first arrived in the town, as Hannah seemed to be towards the stranger who had come to share their lives. But their shyness soon faded, and as time went by what had begun as a simple boy-girl friendship gradually developed into a much closer relationship.

Hannah was two years younger than Joseph and was an only child. Her father had died when she was barely a year old and her mother had never remarried. Most women, finding themselves in such circumstances would have had no choice but to find another husband to support them. But Agnes was fortunate, for shortly before his untimely death her husband had received an inheritance from a maiden aunt. On his death this had passed to Agnes, and although not a large amount it provided her with a small annuity, sufficient to enable her and Hannah to live comfortably, albeit frugally. Agnes supplemented this income by taking in the occasional lodger, and also by supplying some local shops and hostelries with her home-made bread and cakes, pies and pastries.

Apart from Hannah, Agnes's cooking was another reason why Joseph had never even considered looking for anywhere else to live whilst he worked through his apprenticeship. And forever after, he could never smell the aroma of freshly baked bread or pastries without recalling the happy time he had spent lodging with Agnes Whitworth. She had become almost like a mother to him, for he had never known his own. And before long, she was to become his mother-in-law.

During those seven years in Sheffield, Joseph had never once returned to his childhood home at Westbrook, and had never tried to contact his brother. Indeed, he had ventured north only twice, for the funerals of his grandparents. Edwin had died a couple of years after Joseph had come to Sheffield, and Lidia had followed only three months later. The couple, who first met as children, had been devoted to each other and since marrying had never been apart. Emily was convinced that her mother had died of a broken heart, for she had been in reasonable health, but after Edwin's death she seemed to have lost the will to live.

Emily was now left alone in the family home, and for a while after Lidia's funeral she and Joseph would write to each other fairly often. But gradually the letters became less frequent, until no correspondence had passed between them for over two years. Joseph felt guilty about this, for if it had not been for his Aunt Emily and his grandparents he would have been left totally alone in the world when he had been forced to leave his school. But his working days were so long and tiring that he rarely found the time or motivation to put pen to paper. And of Miles, he had heard nothing for years. He had not attended their grandparents' funerals and Joseph had never mentioned him in his letters to Emily, nor had she in hers. It was as if both of them wanted to erase him from their memories.

In fact, Joseph always did his best not to reveal any details of his past to Agnes or Hannah, and whenever they asked him about his family he would say very little, and always sought to change the subject. The only relatives he had ever mentioned were his Aunt Emily and his grandparents. When questioned about his own parents, he would merely say he could not remember them, not even attempting to explain what had happened to them, and that he had been brought up by his grandparents. But Hannah was sure that there were things from his past that he wished to hide, and although she was inquisitive to know what they were, she never pressed him to reveal his secrets.

But now that his apprenticeship was coming to an end, Joseph decided he must make amends and get in touch once more with his aunt. And so it was much to Emily's surprise and joy when she received a letter from Joseph, inviting her to come and stay with them in Sheffield, to celebrate not only the end of Joseph's apprenticeship, but more importantly his marriage to Hannah.

He and Hannah had known for a number of years that they were made for each other, and they would have married earlier, had the terms of Joseph's apprenticeship not strictly forbidden it. But now there was no impediment to prevent their happy union and they had decided to wait no longer. And so the wedding was arranged for the last Saturday in June. The house was far too small to accommodate all the friends who they wanted to invite, so Agnes hired the Cutler's Arms for the day, one of the establishments she supplied with her home-made baking, and where Annie, the landlady, was an old family friend.

A week before the big day Joseph heard from Emily, and was delighted when she confirmed that she would travel to Sheffield the day before the wedding and stay for the weekend. She said she would be on the coach which arrived at about one o'clock, and asked him to meet her. There was no time for him to reply, so the following Friday he set off to the inn near St. Peter's where the coaches from Wakefield arrived. He had not been waiting long when he heard the familiar sound of a posthorn, and rounding a corner, the coach came into view. The sight vividly brought back to him the memory of when he himself had arrived in Sheffield for the first time.

The coach turned into the inn yard and came to an abrupt halt. Immediately, the passengers began to alight. He could not see Emily on top, but he would not have expected her to travel outside. And then, just when he was beginning to wonder whether she had changed her mind, there she was. Stepping from the coach, she gazed around her, looking for her nephew, and as soon as she spotted him a big smile spread across her face. It was five years since they had last met, and whilst Emily had changed very little – or so it seemed to Joseph – the same could not be said of him. Emily stared in amazement, for the skinny youth whom she had last seen at her mother's funeral had now grown into a strapping young man.

'Joseph, my boy, it's so good to see you; and look how you've grown! I hardly recognised you,' she exclaimed as she threw her arms around him.

'It's good to see you too, Aunt Emily, but you've not changed a bit; just the same as ever,' he said as he picked up the well-worn carpetbag she had brought with her. 'Now, you must be hungry after your journey, so I suggest we go into the inn for something to eat. We'll be having supper later, but I expect you could do with some lunch now. I know I could. Agnes and Hannah are busy baking and getting all the food ready for tomorrow, so we'd better not disturb them. I told them we'd probably have a bite to eat before we returned, and anyway I'm sure we have a lot to catch up on.'

Soon they were seated comfortably in the dining room, tucking into a delicious mutton pie. Joseph was eagerly relating to his aunt the events of the past two years, and telling her all about Hannah. Emily could still hardly believe that this was the same person who, as a young lad of thirteen, had turned up at her door one day, all alone in the world and with no one to turn to. Now here he was, a skilled craftsman and about to be married. For over an hour they talked, bringing each other up-to-date with all the latest news. And then, suddenly changing the subject, Joseph pointedly asked Emily the one question she really didn't want to hear.

'Have you seen anything of Miles?'

Emily paused briefly, and then, breathing in deeply, she replied. 'Seen, no. Heard of, yes. I recently met an old friend who lives over at Westbrook, and she told me that he is often the main topic of conversation whenever a crowd of them get together. It seems he's still up to his old tricks; drinking, gambling and womanising. His antics up at the manor are the talk of the village and servants never stay for long, not the way he lords it over them. And they reckon the place is in a poor state. It needs money spending on it but he's too mean to part with it, although he always appears to have plenty for his own pursuits.'

'Has he ever married?' enquired Joseph.

'Miles? Married?' said Emily derisively. 'I don't think any woman in her right mind would have him. Oh, there are plenty of young women happy enough to be in his company, so long as he wines and dines them, but none of them sticks around for long, not once they find out what he's really like. He treats them well to begin with, but he soon gets fed up with them and kicks them out. That is, if they haven't left already. No, I doubt if your brother is ever likely to settle down. It'd be a brave woman who took him on, that's for sure! Anyway, Joseph, enough of Miles. Isn't it time we went? I want to meet the young lady who's brave enough to take you on!'

'Right, Aunt Emily, follow me then. But just one thing before we go. I've never mentioned the truth about my past to Hannah or Agnes, not about mother or father and certainly not about Miles; and I really want to keep it that way. All I've ever said is that I can't remember my parents and that I was brought up by my grandparents. The past's behind me and that's where I'd like it to remain. The future's what matters now.'

'Very well, Joseph. I understand; you can reply on me not to say a word.'

Before long they arrived at the house, and Joseph introduced his aunt to Hannah and Agnes.

'Now, Aunt Emily, I'll show you up to my room. I'll be staying with a workmate of mine tonight, Bob. He's my best man tomorrow. And after the wedding Hannah and I are going to spend a week at a cottage in Hathersage, so the room's yours for as long as you're here.'

'A honeymoon as well!' declared Emily. 'How wonderful for you both. There's not many as can afford that, on top of the cost of a wedding.'

'Yes. It came as a surprise to us, too. The cottage belongs to Mr Yates, and he's kindly offered it to us for our honeymoon. Said it's his wedding present. He says Derbyshire is a beautiful county, and Hathersage is not too far away. We've never been there, so we're really looking forward to our visit.'

Agnes and Hannah had at last finished baking, and the bread, the cakes, the pies and the pastries were being packed into boxes for Joseph to take along to the pub. Two of his workmates came to help him, and in no time at all the job was done.

'Right,' said Joseph as he returned from delivering the last of the food. 'All I need to do now is get myself cleaned up, Sunday best clothes on, then it's back down to the Cutler's to meet the lads from work. Can't miss my last night of freedom as a single man now, can I?' he added with a grin.

He said his goodbyes to Emily and Agnes, then taking Hannah in his arms he gave her a kiss, and said with a twinkle in his eye, 'Now, young lady, we have a date tomorrow morning. Ten o'clock at St. Peter's church. I'll be waiting. And don't you be late!'

'Joseph Lambert,' Hannah replied mischievously, 'I'll have you know it's the bride's prerogative to keep the groom waiting; did nobody ever tell you that?' and placing her lips close to his ear, so only he could hear, she whispered, 'Don't worry, my love, I won't be late.' Then, in a somewhat louder voice said, 'Off you go now. Enjoy yourself. And don't let the lads touch any of that food – or else!'

Whilst Joseph spent the night with his work colleagues in the bar of the Cutler's Arms, where he was, as is customary on these occasions, the object of much ribaldry regarding his soon-to-be-lost freedom and imminent initiation into the ranks of married men, Hannah spent a quiet, and fairly sober, evening at home with her mother and Emily.

The following morning Joseph began to wish that he, too, had been a little more abstemious, for he awoke early with a thumping head, and feeling as delicate as the fine lace curtains through which the sun was already brightening up the room. But after Bob had frog-marched him up and down the street a time or two, and with the help of a large mug of strong sweet tea and a plate of fatty bacon and fried eggs which Bob's wife helpfully served up, he rapidly began to recover from the effects of the previous night's overindulgence.

'Hurry up, Joseph,' said Bob, 'you'd better get yourself ready; you don't want to keep Hannah waiting, do you? An hour from now, and you'll be a married man!'

This was a day both Joseph and Hannah had been looking forward to for a long time. Most of their friends and some of Hannah's relatives joined them for the church ceremony and the wedding breakfast that followed, and a fine time was had by all. Ale flowed freely and the mountain of food was rapidly reduced to little more than a molehill. The usual speeches were delivered by the best man and the groom; songs were sung and tall tales were told; jokes were cracked and reminiscences recalled. Old Dan, still sprightly despite his advancing years, amused everyone with hilarious anecdotes from his youth and his mimicry of some well-known local characters. An old uncle of Hannah's began to play the fiddle, accompanied by a cousin who was adept on the accordion, and before long everyone was up on their feet and dancing.

The celebrations went on for most of the day, but by early evening were drawing to a close, and the exhaustion of a day's non-stop merrymaking was beginning to take its toll on many of those present. Mr Yates, who had loaned the happy couple the cottage, had also arranged for his coachman to take them in his horse and trap to their honeymoon retreat, and soon they were settled cosily inside, ready to leave. As they set off from the pub and rattled on down the street, they turned and waved goodbye to their guests, who cheered them until they were out of sight.

'What are you thinking?' asked Hannah as they left the town

behind and headed out into the countryside.

'Just how much life has changed for me since I first arrived in Sheffield. I came here with almost nothing – no friends and no money; only the clothes I stood up in and little else, other than the prospect of seven years hard graft. And now look at me. I'm a fully fledged cutler with the promise of a well-paid job and I've a host of good friends. But most of all, I've got you, my darling. What more could a man ask for?'

The journey took about two hours, a pleasant drive through countryside which was new to both of them, but it was high summer and still light when they arrived. The coachman, of course, knew exactly where to head for, having been here many times, bringing his employer and his family whenever they were able to escape from the dirt and grime of the town. The cottage was situated a short distance down a lane off the main road through the village. It was of modest size and built of traditional Derbyshire stone, as were most other buildings thereabouts, and stood at the end of a well-tended front garden. The coachman showed them in, where they were surprised to find a fire already laid in the hearth, and a basket of food and a bottle of wine on a table in the parlour.

'Mrs Bagshaw will have left that for you. Mr Yates must have let her know you were coming. She and her husband live at the top of the lane and they look after the cottage for Mr Yates, see to the garden, and keep the place neat and tidy. She's a good old soul is Mrs Bagshaw. If you need anything while you're here, just ask her. There's a couple of decent inns in the village where you can get a meal, so you'll not go hungry. Well, I must bid you goodbye and get back home. Have a nice time, and I'll be back to collect you next Friday evening; that's the arrangement.'

'What a pretty little cottage,' said Hannah, once they were left alone, as she inquisitively inspected each and every room. 'So tastefully decorated and furnished, and so cosy. And just for a rural retreat! I expect Mrs Yates chose all the furnishings.'

'Yes, I expect she did, Hannah. And this shows what money can buy. I went to Mr Yates's house once. It's ten times the size of this, and equally well appointed.'

'Do you think we'll ever be able to afford anything like this, Joseph?'

'You never know. Mr Yates inherited his wealth from his father, Solomon, but I believe he started out in life with very little and built up his business through sheer hard work. So if he can do it, why not me? But let's not talk about work; there'll be enough of that when we get back to Sheffield. Let's enjoy the time we have here. Now, Hannah, how do you fancy some of that food and a glass of wine? It's not very often we have wine. And then, Mrs Lambert, I have something else in mind!'

'Oh, really?' replied Hannah demurely, 'and I wonder what that could be?'

'Ah, well, you'll have to wait and see, won't you!'

CHAPTER NINE

Ambitions and suspicions

Hannah and Joseph quickly settled down to married life, and before long their honeymoon seemed but a distant memory. Not that they ever forgot that week, a week which they both agreed was the best and happiest time of their lives.

They began their married life living with Agnes, which at first suited them all. Hannah continued to help her mother with the baking, whilst Joseph started his new job at Yates & Sons. He was soon revelling in his position as a journeyman cutler with the freedom to work unsupervised, producing high-quality cutlery, as fine as those pieces which belonged to his grandfather and which had inspired him to take up the craft.

But as summer turned to autumn and autumn to winter, Hannah had a hankering for a home of their own, and when, the following May, she told Joseph that he was to become a father, they decided that they should look for somewhere else to live. Joseph was now earning a decent wage and they could afford to rent their own house. Hannah wanted to live near to her mother so that she could carry on helping her, for her little enterprise was now thriving, and she also wanted her to be close by when the baby was born. They looked around and before long found a neat little terraced house in Charles Street, only three or four minutes walk away from Agnes, and for Joseph, very handy for the factory. Hannah fell in love with it the moment they walked in, for it was just what she had in mind, and she would always remember the day they moved in, the very same day that King William died and Britain had a new monarch on the throne, the young Queen Victoria.

Hannah immediately set to, redecorating some of the rooms and purchasing ornaments, pictures and items of furniture, mostly second-hand from stalls on the market. Agnes would come and help her daughter whenever she had the time, and seemed to derive as much pleasure from doing so as Hannah did. Hannah spent most of that summer getting the house just as she wanted it. She worked almost non-stop for weeks and Joseph was amazed at her energy, but he knew it was the approaching happy event that was spurring her on. Sometimes he would return home from work to find her still beavering away at some little task or other until finally she had the house exactly to her liking.

By the autumn all was finished, and before long the nights began to draw in as winter loomed. A cold north wind would often come whistling down the street, but inside, with the curtains drawn and the coal piled high in the grate, they felt as cosy and safe as could be.

Christmas Day that year was spent with Agnes. It was a Monday, and Mr Yates closed the factory for two days, a welcome break for all the workers, but with no pay, of course. Hannah was not far off her confinement, and she was thankful that, for once, someone else was doing the cooking. They spent a quiet day together, just the three of them, but on Boxing Day evening Joseph took Hannah to a concert at the new Cutlers' Hall, a magnificent building recently constructed in Church Street, opposite the parish church, and home to the ancient *Company of Cutlers in Hallamshire* of which Joseph was proud to count himself a member. Only freemen, who had completed their apprenticeships, were entitled to attend, and whilst Joseph had visited on a number of occasions this was the first time Hannah had been inside.

She climbed the steps to the huge entrance doors and was astonished at what lay behind. The sight that met her eyes as she entered the great hall almost took her breath away; the sheer size and splendour of the room, the opulence of the furnishings and decor, and the grand staircase, wide enough for those ladies wearing the largest and most fashionable crinolines to pass each other with ease. Hannah enjoyed that evening, but when the concert was over and they had returned home, she was glad to be back by her own fireside.

Three weeks later, just as Joseph was about to leave for work one morning, there was a sudden panic when Hannah cried out that she thought the baby was on its way. Joseph immediately ran to a neighbour's house, where there lived a woman who had become a good friend. She had had eight children of her own, and had kindly offered to come and help Hannah with the birth. It was then along to Agnes's to alert her, and finally round to the midwife's house. By the time Joseph got back home, the neighbour and Agnes were already there and saucepans of water were simmering gently over the fire. The midwife arrived shortly afterwards and soon had everything organised and ready, at which point she promptly dismissed Joseph from the bedroom and told to wait downstairs, or better still, go off to work. So he did as he was told, and off he went to work. But finding it almost impossible to concentrate fully on his latest commission – a particularly expensive banqueting set of silver-plated, bone-handled cutlery for a minor European royal household – he was excused and told to go home, but to return to work as soon as the baby was born.

He didn't have long to wait. He had barely been back in the house for a quarter of an hour, when, following on from much screaming and yelling and the raising of female voices from above, he heard the much more soothing sounds of a baby crying. After a short interval, Agnes appeared and invited him to come upstairs and meet his daughter.

Hannah had already decided on a name – Eliza. Not Elizabeth, as Joseph had preferred, but Eliza; after Hannah's own grandmother. And so, a month later, a small gathering of family and friends made their way to St. Peter's Church one Sunday morning for the christening. Afterwards, everyone was invited back to their house for the traditional celebration, Agnes, as usual, providing the refreshments.

When all the guests had left, and whilst Hannah and Agnes were clearing away the pots, Joseph sat by the fireside, thinking about his past life. He began to compare his present situation with the time when he was a young boy, living with his father at Westbrook Manor.

There was no similarity between the two; between his lifestyle then, when money was no object and he could have anything he wanted, with servants to do all the work, and now, when he had to work hard for a living. And instead of a two-hundred-year-old manor house with all its grandeur, his new home was a terraced house in the centre of a busy manufacturing town. But he knew that he would not swap his life now for the life he had once had.

For the next couple of years Joseph continued working for Mr Yates, where he was highly regarded. Titus Yates was undoubtedly a very fine cutler, but Joseph sometimes thought him a little too old-fashioned and rather set in his ways. He was somewhat reluctant to try anything different, whilst Joseph had his own opinion about the variety and styles of cutlery he would like to make. Increasingly, he had a yearning to be independent and to set up on his own account. He carefully weighed up all the pros and cons. So long as he worked for Mr Yates, he knew he would never become rich but would always have a steady income, with none of the risks of running a business of his own. But he also realised that he would never be able to achieve his potential and do those things he really wanted to. Being self-employed, however, would give him the freedom to work just as he wished and to make his own decisions. He had a number of business ideas that he believed would be successful, if only he were allowed to try them.

Whenever Joseph read the newspapers, he couldn't help noticing the numerous advertisements offering opportunities to invest in newly formed railway companies. New lines were rapidly spreading their tentacles to all major towns and cities throughout the land. Locally, the Sheffield and Rotherham Railway had opened in October 1838, nearly two years previously. This had recently been connected at Masborough to the North Midland Railway, which ran from Derby, and an extension of this line northwards to Leeds was due to open shortly.

He judged that as more people travelled around the country there was bound to be an increasing demand for hotel accommodation and dining facilities. Hotels needed dining rooms, and dining rooms needed cutlery. He knew that many of the railway companies had already started building their own hotels close to their stations, and if he could establish himself as a supplier to these companies, offering them their own individual and unique sets of cutlery, perhaps engraved with their coat of arms, or company name, he believed that he could become a wealthy man.

Naturally, he would have to find his own premises and equip it with the necessary machinery, and take on some workmen of his own. But the prospect enthused him. He had already mentioned these ideas to Hannah, and whilst she seemed a little averse to his taking any risks, he knew that she would not stand in his way if he was determined to branch out by himself.

One Saturday evening in June, after they had eaten their supper and Eliza had been put to bed, Joseph sat quietly reading the weekly newspaper, whilst Hannah busied herself making a dress for Eliza. He spent some time perusing the advertisements on the front page, where he spotted an announcement about the imminent opening of the North Midland Railway's extension from Masborough to Leeds. He then began to turn the pages, and had reached page five when suddenly a name leapt out at him from an article towards the bottom of the page – *Miles Lambert*. Had it been any other name, he would probably not even have noticed it.

He read the article with a mounting feeling of dismay and disbelief, for it immediately became clear that this was not any Miles Lambert – this was indeed his own brother.

ALLEGED MURDER OF HOUSEKEEPER

The trial of Mr Miles Lambert, of Westbrook Manor, who has been charged with the murder of his housekeeper, Mrs Jessie Hough, has now been set for Saturday the 11th July at the York Assizes. A detailed account of this sordid affair was reported in some detail in our issue of Friday last, but we repeat here the brief events which have lately caused so much discussion in the area. Mrs Hough, a well-respected widow, and lifelong servant to the prisoner's family, was found dead in the dining room of the manor house early on the morning of 6th June by the scullery maid, who had arisen early to commence her duties. On entering the dining room she found the deceased lying dead in the hearth, with serious injuries to her head. It being early, about six o'clock, and not wishing to arouse her employer's wrath by waking him, she immediately ran, in fright, to her mother's house in the nearby village, where the alarm was raised. The constable was summoned and the maid told him that she had retired to her bed just before midnight, and shortly afterwards had heard her employer and the housekeeper engaged in a furious argument. She reported hearing Mr Lambert shouting violently at Mrs Hough, followed by the sound of a scream, after which no further noises were heard. She was reluctant to go and investigate the cause of the disturbance herself, knowing that Mr Lambert often returned home late at night, the worse for drink, and because of this she had been too afraid to venture downstairs. The constable then went to the manor house, where he arrested the accused and conveyed him to the gaol at Wakefield. An inquest on the body of Mrs Hough was held at Westbrook the following day, and the jury returned a verdict of 'wilful murder'. The accused, who has denied any responsibility for this crime and stated that he will defend himself vigorously, was subsequently taken to York gaol where he now awaits trial.

Joseph read the article again and putting it to one side, sat back in his chair, deeply troubled. This was the first he had heard of the incident, but then he remembered that he had been so very busy the previous week that he hadn't found the time to read the newspaper in any detail, as he usually did. He said nothing to Hannah, as he had always refrained from telling her anything about his past. And there was little danger of Hannah reading the report herself as she had never been to school, nor learned to read and write properly, although she could now read and write a few simple words since Joseph had started to teach her. But even if she were able to read the newspaper article, he doubted that she would associate the name Miles Lambert with her own husband.

Joseph made a decision – he would attend the trial. Mrs Hough had been so good to him when he was a child, and now she was dead, seemingly murdered by his own brother. Furthermore, the newspaper stated that she was a widow. He didn't know that Alfred had died, and so felt it his duty, more than ever, to be there. It was to take place on a Saturday in a fortnight's time. He normally worked on Saturdays until midday, but he was sure that he could persuade Mr Yates to allow him the morning off if he offered to work extra hours during the week. Yes, he decided, first thing on Monday morning he would broach the subject with him. Suddenly, he was aroused from his daydream by Hannah.

'A penny for them, Joseph,' she said. 'You look miles away. Where were you?' Joseph was almost tempted to explain how appropriate was her use of the word 'miles' but thought better of it, and had to come up quickly with a suitable explanation.

'Oh, yes, sorry Hannah, I was miles away. I've just been reading about the number of railways being promoted. Do you remember me talking to you the other week about possibly going into business myself, and supplying the new railway hotels with cutlery? Well, there's an item here about a proposal to construct a hotel near to the railway station in York. I think I'll take a trip up there and see what I can find out. There's a new line north from Masborough to Leeds opening next week, and according to the announcement in the paper it will be possible to change at Normanton and get a train to York. I've always fancied seeing what it's like travelling by train, so if I can persuade Mr Yates to let me have a Saturday morning off, I'll go up there for the day.'

'Oh, what a lovely idea! Maybe I could come with you. I know mother would have Eliza for the day.'

Joseph hated what he was doing, not telling Hannah the truth, but he couldn't allow her to come with him to the trial. 'Well, love, I think it might be better if I went by myself. I expect I'll be busy, assuming I can find someone connected with the hotel who I can talk to. And if I don't get my business finished in time I'll have to stop over and return on Sunday. But I could take you another time, when we'd be able to spend all day looking round York; I'm told it's an interesting old city.'

'Yes, you're probably right, Joseph. And in a year or two, when she's a bit older, we could take Eliza with us, and mother might like to come, too. We could make it a real family outing.'

On the Monday morning Joseph spoke to Mr Yates and asked if he could take the time off. As Joseph had hoped, he was agreeable, provided he put in the extra hours beforehand. After work that evening, Joseph walked down to the railway station in The Wicker to confirm the train times and to book a ticket. The railway timetables and fares were regularly advertised in the newspapers, but this mode of transport was completely new to him and he wanted to make sure that he had the correct information. The clerk at the station confirmed that there would be a North Midland Railway train at 7.30 am to Leeds, and by changing at Normanton he could reach York by 10.15 am. The last train back from York was at 4.00 pm, but Joseph couldn't be sure that the trial would be over by then and he did not want to miss any of it. He knew that if he missed that train he would have to stay overnight in York and come back the next day, but the clerk warned him that there was only one train on Sundays, at 7.45 am. He could travel first class for twelve shillings and sixpence, each way, but knowing he might have to pay for overnight accommodation, he booked a second-class ticket for nine shillings, instead.

As the day of the trial drew near, Joseph became restless and agitated, unsure as to how he would react to seeing his brother on trial for his life. Would Miles be able to see him in the public gallery? And if he did, would he recognise him after all this time? It was eleven years since they had last met, and Joseph had changed a great deal since then. Hannah noticed Joseph's agitation, and on asking what was troubling him, he simply told her he was a little apprehensive about what would be his first ever business meeting.

On the morning of the 11th July he rose early, put on his best clothes, and just in case he did have to stay the night in York, he packed the few things he would need into a small brown carpetbag. Hannah also got up as she wanted to go with him to the station to wave him off. After breakfast, the three of them set out, Eliza toddling along beside them. She was only two and a half, but could manage short walks. It wasn't far, just up Charles Street and along Norfolk Street, passing Agnes's house en route towards the town centre, down the Haymarket past the fruit market – a scene of feverish activity at this time of the morning – across Lady's Bridge over the River Don and into The Wicker. The station was a little way along, between Spital Hill and Saville Street; an impressive stone structure constructed on classical lines.

As they approached it, they could see steam and smoke rising over the top of the building, indicating that a train was ready and waiting. It was ten minutes past seven as they entered the station through a tall archway, into a bright and airy entrance hall lined with seats, with doors leading to various offices, and a small window where passengers were queuing to purchase tickets. Joseph already had his, so they all headed straight for the platform. A gate guarded the entrance to the platform, and by it stood a man in the uniform of the railway company, inspecting the ticket of each passenger before they were allowed through.

'I don't think you can come any further, Hannah, unless you're travelling. I'd better go now and find a seat. All being well, I should be back by about seven o'clock. But if I'm not, don't worry. I'll find somewhere to stay and I'll be back home tomorrow morning.'

'All right, Joseph, and good luck. But I hope you do get back today; I don't like being left on my own.'

'Oh, I'm sure you'll be fine. Anyway, you said you're going to spend the day at your mother's, so you'll have her to keep you company. And there's always this little rascal to keep out of mischief,' added Joseph. He placed his bag on the floor, then bent down and picked up his daughter. 'Now then, you be a good girl for mummy. Daddy's going for a ride on that train, but I'll soon be back. And when you're a bit older, we'll take you for a ride on one. You'd like that, wouldn't you, Eliza?' He gave his daughter a hug and a kiss, then handing her back to Hannah, leant over and hugged and kissed her, too. 'Take care, the pair of you. Give my love to Agnes, and I'll see you all later. If I get back tonight I'll go straight to her house first. If I'm not there by eight o'clock, it means either the train is late or I'm staying the night at York. But if I do get back tonight, we can go along to the pub for a drink; I'm sure Agnes would look after Eliza for an hour or so.'

'Yes, I'd like that. It seems ages since we had a night out.'

Joseph picked up his bag, joined the queue at the gate and showed the man his ticket, then turned and blew one last kiss to Hannah and Eliza. Beyond the gate and the platform stood the train, but before boarding it, Joseph went to take a closer look at the engine and carriages, such was his curiosity for anything new. The locomotive was almost entirely finished in black, except for the boiler, which was clad in varnished strips of wood. Behind the engine were two first-class and three second-class carriages, each painted in a deep shade of brown, lined out in black. The first-class carriages reminded Joseph very much of the stagecoaches which he had travelled on occasionally. Indeed, their construction was very similar except, of course, that these were designed to run on rails rather than the highway. But they were longer and wider and were divided into three separate compartments, and just like stagecoaches, each door contained a window, lowered and raised by a leather strap. The inside of each compartment was luxuriously fitted out. Two long bench seats faced each other, deeply upholstered and divided by padded armrests into three separate seats, with velvet curtains and a deep-piled carpet, all in matching shades of crimson.

The second-class carriages, however, were spartan in comparison. They had five compartments, each with two wooden benches capable of seating up to six passengers, a bare wooden floor and neither blinds nor curtains. In fact, there were no windows at all, only low doors through which the passengers gained access, the upper half of the carriage being entirely open to the elements on each side with only the roof for protection. Had Joseph realised the difference between travelling first and second class, he might have spent an extra three shillings and sixpence for the added comfort. Fortunately, it was

summertime and the weather was fine; but he shuddered to think
what it would be like travelling second class on a cold, wet and
blustery winter's day.

Joseph was fascinated by everything he saw and would have
liked to have spent longer examining the train. But the departure
time was imminent and so, selecting one of the coaches, he climbed
into a compartment where just one man was seated. The man was
deeply engrossed in studying a catalogue, which Joseph observed
consisted of diagrams and drawings of machinery components, and
Joseph took him to be a commercial traveller, perhaps employed by
one of the engineering firms in the area. Five minutes later, after
much commotion and the ringing of a bell, there was a sudden jolt,
and the train lurched forward. By this time they had been joined by
three other passengers, a man, a woman and a child, who, Joseph
soon learned from their conversation, were travelling to Leeds to
visit an elderly uncle they had not seen for many years, and who, it
became clear as the journey progressed, had no other living relatives;
was wealthy and, so the woman continued to assure her husband, was
not long for this world. Judging by their demeanour and the nature
of their discussion, Joseph had no doubt that these three facts about
their unnamed relative was the principal reason for their making the
journey.

The train gathered speed, and after a journey of almost twenty
minutes along the valley of the River Don, it slowed down on the
approach to Masborough Station, close to Rotherham. Joseph was
impressed both by the speed and the smoothness of the journey,
compared with the usual slow, bumpy and bone-shaking journeys
he had undertaken by stagecoach, especially on those roads where
little, if any, maintenance was ever carried out. At Masborough,
the train joined the recently opened North Midland Railway from
Derby. Shortly after arriving there, Joseph heard the sound of another
approaching train, which presently drew alongside on an adjoining
track. This, he was told in a matter-of-fact way by the man with the
catalogue – who, Joseph judged, must be a regular train traveller,
well versed in the mysteries of railway operation – had arrived from

Derby, and that the two trains would now be 'put together'. There then followed a noisy sequence of uncoupling and coupling of engines and coaches, and a shunting to-and-fro, until the coaches of the train from Sheffield had been attached to the rear of the one from Derby and made into one long train, bound for Leeds. A few minutes later, after much clamour, the bell rang and they were once more on their way.

As they bowled along, Joseph soon overcame his initial trepidation at this, his first experience of train travel, and was now beginning to enjoy himself. The constantly changing scenery seemed to fly effortlessly by, like some panorama painted on a moving canvas and rolled out continuously before him for his personal entertainment, interrupted only briefly at the various stations where the train called. After almost an hour they arrived at Normanton, the junction for the line to York. Joseph got off here, as he had to change trains, and was joined by the man with the catalogue. As soon as everybody not travelling to Leeds had alighted, and others had joined, the train continued on its way, leaving Joseph and a score of other passengers awaiting the train for York.

Joseph looked around him, and expressed his opinion that this station was nowhere near as grand as the one at Sheffield, and seemed to him to be very rudimentary. His travelling companion, who was clearly a fount of knowledge on all things railway, then proceeded to explain that a new station was to be built in due course, with an accompanying hotel. When completed, Normanton was to become a principal station, where long distance trains would call for a short time to enable passengers to take refreshments and avail themselves of other conveniences. And Joseph made a mental note of this.

After a short interval, the distant sound of escaping steam and the rumble of iron wheels heralded the approach of the train from York, which was to terminate here, and then return whence it had come. As soon as the engine had been uncoupled, its tanks replenished with water, and then attached to the other end of the train, they were ready to set off. Shortly after departing there was a lurch as the train swung to the right across a set of points, and onto the line for York. After about an hour they slowed down as they rounded a long curve and came to a stop at their destination. Joseph, who by now was beginning to consider himself something of an expert on the architectural merits of railway stations, felt that this one, a crude, wooden affair, somehow didn't do justice to such a large and important city. But his new-found companion explained that this too, like the one at Normanton, was only a temporary building and that a much larger and grander station was soon to be erected within the old city walls.

But Joseph's thoughts now returned to the purpose of his visit. For almost three hours he had been totally captivated by the journey and all the novel experiences it had presented. He dearly wished Hannah and Eliza could have been with him to enjoy them too, and he promised himself that, one day, he would bring them here, just as he had said he would. But for now, he had to concentrate his mind on what was to follow – witnessing the trial of his own brother on a charge of murder, with the possibility that he might be found guilty and condemned to death. He had reason enough to hate Miles for everything that had happened between them when he was a boy. And his alleged murder of Jessie Hough, who had always been so kind to them both in the past, was something that horrified him.

And yet, Miles was still his flesh and blood, and a man is innocent until proven guilty. Joseph genuinely believed that he *was* guilty, but hoped that somehow Miles would be able to prove his innocence beyond any doubt.

Such trials rarely lasted more than a day, and he realised that by that evening his brother would either be a free man, or be locked up in the condemned cell, awaiting his rendezvous with the hangman. And so, with feelings of nervousness and unease, Joseph set off for the court, and whatever the day might bring.

CHAPTER TEN

Trials and tribulations

Leaving the station, Joseph stepped out into Queen Street and walked towards Micklegate. He had a fair knowledge of York from the time when he had been at school, when the boys would occasionally be allowed to visit the city. He knew that the prison and courthouse were situated next to the castle, only a short walk away. He turned left into Micklegate, immediately passing under the old city walls and through Micklegate Bar, one of the ancient gatehouses that guarded all roads into the city. Passing St. Martin's Church, he crossed the Ouse Bridge, then turned right down Nessgate and along Castlegate. As he passed St. Mary's Church he could see ahead of him the medieval Clifford's Tower on top of its huge mound. Close by the tower were a number of large grey stone buildings, made up of a felons' prison, male and female debtors' prisons, the governor's house and the courthouse; and it was to the latter that he made his way.

He paused outside for a minute and looked up at the imposing and awe-inspiring structure before him, designed, he assumed, to evoke a feeling of inferiority in even the most self-assured or influential citizen. But this was not the view that prisoners would see as they were taken there for their fate to be determined. For those awaiting trial were housed in cells below the court, and were brought along an underground passageway and up a flight of stairs, straight into the dock of the courtroom.

Joseph's entry, however, was far less intimidating, as he mounted the steps and walked between the tall stone pillars, through the double doors and into the entrance hall. A quick enquiry to a court official soon established that the preliminary procedures had begun, and that the grand jury had been sworn in and had already vetted the various indictments and statements for that day's cases to decide which were to proceed to trial and which were to be rejected. But since the charge against Miles was one of murder, as formulated by the coroner's jury, no approval was needed from the grand jury and Joseph was advised that his trial was to be the fourth of the day in court number one.

He quickly made his way to the public gallery, situated directly behind the dock, and facing the judge's bench. Most of the seats were already taken, but he found a vacant one on the back row at one end. From here he had an excellent view of the whole court, but reckoned it unlikely that he would be spotted by the prisoner in the dock. He particularly did not want to be seen by Miles, although he suspected that his brother would not recognise him after so many years. The courtroom was a little smaller in area than Joseph imagined it would be, but this was more than compensated for by its lofty height, with twelve pillars supporting a magnificent domed roof, in the centre of which was a large circular glass window to admit natural light. The lower half of the room was panelled, whilst the upper part had plastered and painted walls with panels decorated with intricate friezes. The height of the building allowed for the provision of a large balcony, which extended for three sides of the courtroom – above where Joseph was now seated, and along each side. This upper balcony afforded additional accommodation for the public, such that those seated there had a grandstand view of the proceedings below, and looking up, it appeared to Joseph that every seat there was now occupied.

The judge, resplendent in his full-bottomed wig, red flowing robes, a lilac and white shawl covering his upper body and a fancy lace jabot running from his neck to mid-chest, was already seated in his majestic, high-backed, throne-like chair, comfortably upholstered in brown leather and with deep, wide arms. On the bench before him lay his gavel, and next to it a piece of black cloth. He was positioned at a level slightly higher than the dock, and immediately below him, in the well of the court, was the large bar table, where the Bailiff, the Judge's Associate and the court recorder and other clerks sat, and from where the attorneys would conduct their business. A bewigged gentleman, whom Joseph took to be the attorney for the Crown, was already seated there. On the right-hand side of the court were two rows of seats where the jury sat, and on the opposite side stood the witness box.

As Joseph settled in his seat, the petty jury, which would hear the cases and decide on the verdicts, was being sworn in. Once this procedure was completed and the twelve men were seated, footsteps could be heard from below, whereupon three men emerged from the stairway leading directly up into the dock from the holding cells. Two were dressed in the uniform of prison guards; the third, quite obviously the prisoner, was a miserable-looking individual, a man of about twenty-five years of age, clad almost in rags, unshaven, thin, and with a look of fear on his face. As soon as he appeared, a gasp and cry could be heard from the end of the row where Joseph was sitting, and turning his head he saw a young woman leaning forward as if to get a closer look at the prisoner, her hands clasped together before her in a gesture of despair. 'Oh, John, John,' she wept, loud enough to be heard by everyone in the court.

'Silence in court,' rang out a voice in stentorian tones. The judge, who until now had remained silent, had made his presence felt in no uncertain terms. On hearing the woman's cries, the prisoner had turned round as if looking for the one who, Joseph assumed, was his wife, or sweetheart, or maybe a sister. But he was soon put in his place as the judge, once more, demonstrated his authority in this, his court.

'Prisoner in the dock, you will face the bench!' he bellowed, but before he did so Joseph noticed the deathly white pallor on the man's face, and the dread which he must have been feeling. And well he might, for the Judge's Associate now rose to his feet and read out the indictment. On hearing this, Joseph knew that if found guilty, there was likely to be only one outcome.

The trial that followed seemed to Joseph to be a total travesty of justice. The prisoner, a farm labourer, had been accused by his former employer of stealing valuable items from his house, allegedly in revenge for having been sacked. Yet there was no clear evidence against him, no witnesses to the offence, and Joseph thought that those who gave evidence were either dim-witted, short-sighted, or bore personal grudges against the accused.

During the previous week, Joseph had taken the trouble to find out something about court procedures. He had learned that only the wealthiest of defendants were able to afford an attorney to conduct their defence, but that defendants were allowed, should they wish, to cross-examine any witnesses themselves, and to call witnesses in their own defence. They were not allowed to enter the witness box and give evidence under oath, but were allowed to give an unsworn statement from the dock. Whether anyone had advised the prisoner fully of all this Joseph did not know, but the prisoner appeared to be unaware of the facts.

All the evidence having been heard, the judge then gave a brief summing-up and directed the jury that they should now consider the evidence and return their verdict. The twelve men huddled together, talking amongst themselves, and whilst they were doing so Joseph himself contemplated what he had seen and heard. It occurred to him that the accused had been allowed little chance of defending himself. If he had had an attorney to speak for him, someone skilled in the law and the art of questioning witnesses, he was sure that a fairer trial would have ensued.

In less than ten minutes the jury had completed its deliberations. The Judge's Associate rose to his feet, and asked the foreman if they had reached their verdict.

'We have,' replied the foreman.

'And how do you find the prisoner? Guilty or not guilty?'

'Guilty.'

There was an immediate and audible outcry from the public gallery, and it was obvious to Joseph that he was not the only one there who thought as he did. The young woman at the end of the row began to weep uncontrollably and had to be comforted by those near to her. The prisoner was visibly shaking, and a look of utter disbelief and terror had spread across his face, now drained of all colour. The judge, anxious to get on with the day's proceedings, brought his gavel down heavily on the wooden sounding board and peace was instantly restored to the courtroom.

He quickly pronounced the prisoner guilty but explained that, since all the stolen property had subsequently been recovered, he was prepared to show leniency, and instead of the death penalty usual for such an offence, he sentenced him to be transported beyond the seas for a period of seven years. As the guards roughly dragged him back down the steps towards the cells, Joseph looked round, and saw the poor young woman being helped out of the court by a man and a woman. So this was how English justice worked; short and swift. So swift, in fact, that almost at once the next prisoner was brought into the dock. According to the long list of his past offences read out to the court, he was a hardened criminal. His offence this time was assault and theft on the highway, leaving the victim, an elderly gentleman, badly injured and twenty guineas the poorer. After a trial lasting no more than fifteen minutes, the verdict was guilty, and the judge immediately picked up the black cloth and draped it over his wig before passing the sentence of death. There were no gasps of dissent from the public galleries this time, and the prisoner himself seemed barely interested in the outcome, as he was taken back 'from whence he came, and from thence to a place of execution, and there to be hanged by the neck until dead'.

Next came two young women, domestic servants in a large house, jointly charged with stealing some items of clothing from their employer, a lady of some standing in the county. To Joseph they looked no more than girls, perhaps thirteen or fourteen, seemingly very nervous and completely bewildered by their predicament. They each received a term of six months hard labour in the House of Correction. Better than death or transportation by far, considered Joseph. But when they were released – what then? Without a reference they would certainly find it hard to secure another similar position, and poverty, destitution and the streets seemed the most likely outcome for these unfortunate wretches.

After they too had been taken down, the judge announced that there would be a lunch recess, and that the proceedings would recommence at half past two. The court soon emptied, and Joseph quickly found a nearby public house where he was able to get something to eat. Over his lunch, he thought about what he had witnessed that morning. None of the defendants had had anyone to speak for them, and seemed reluctant to challenge or question the prosecution witnesses. He asked himself whether Miles would. Knowing him as he did, he couldn't see him being left alone in the dock, not when his life depended on the outcome. Miles was too worldly-wise not to do everything in his power to leave the court a free man, even if he was guilty of the charge he faced. But Joseph would soon know the answer to that question, and by a quarter past two he was back in the same seat in the public gallery. He was relieved he had returned in good time, for this case had attracted much interest and the public galleries were once more rapidly filling up.

At a minute before the half-hour, the Bailiff rose to his feet and ordered everyone to follow suit, then opened a door immediately behind the bench and escorted the judge back to his seat. No doubt, Joseph surmised, His Lordship had dined on something rather more sumptuous than the cold pork pie and pint of ale that he had partaken of. Once the judge was seated, everyone else was allowed to do likewise, and the perceptible air of expectation became an audible buzz as the next prisoner was heard being brought up the steps into the dock.

As Miles came into view, Joseph's memories of him came flooding back; of the years of torment and distress he had suffered at his hands, and then of being abandoned and left to fend for himself. And now, here he stood, about to face a trial that could end his life, but looking just as arrogant and cocksure as he always had. He was dressed as if he was on his way to a reception or a ball, but then, Miles always did like to play the part of the dandy. He wore a white, high-collared silk shirt and scarlet cravat tied fashionably in a large knot; a double-breasted waistcoat of a matching shade; a tightly cut marine-blue frock coat and a pair of grey, checked trousers. If he had chosen his apparel with a view to impressing the gentlemen of the jury, he may well have succeeded, for Joseph noticed some of them casting envious and admiring glances towards the accused. As he entered the dock, he turned and smiled knowingly to a small group sitting at the far end from where Joseph was seated. Leaning forward, Joseph was able to see about half a dozen men who had not been there during the morning session. He did not recognise any of them, but he knew their type. They were not dressed quite as stylishly as Miles, but these were, without doubt, his friends and supporters. The judge used his gavel once more to call for silence, and the Judge's Associate read out the indictment.

'Miles Lambert, you are charged that on the sixth of June you did wilfully murder Mrs Jessie Hough, widow, of Westbrook Manor in the West Riding. How say you, Miles Lambert, are you guilty or not guilty?'

Miles inched forward, threw back his shoulders and, sentry like, stood to attention and declared in a loud and clear voice, 'not guilty.'

Charles Downing, for the Crown, then rose from his seat at the bar table. 'I now call Martha King to the witness box,' he said, and a young slip of a girl was quickly ushered into the witness box by the Bailiff. She seemed almost as nervous as the two young girls who had been convicted that very morning, whilst Miles stood dispassionately, a look of quiet confidence on his face. Joseph observed that there were now two attorneys at the bar table, the one who had been there throughout the morning's proceedings and was now about to prosecute the case, and another whom he had not seen before. The Bailiff instructed the girl to take the oath, and taking the Bible in her right hand, she repeated, in a frail and faltering voice, the words that the Bailiff read out to her:

'I swear by Almighty God that the evidence I shall give will be the truth, the whole truth and nothing but the truth. So help me God.'

Having confirmed that her name was Martha King, Downing began his questioning.

'Now, Martha, please tell the court where you live.'

'I live in Westbrook, sir, with my mother.'

'And where do you work?'

'I don't work anywhere just now sir, not after what happened to

Mrs Hough.'

'But you used to live and work at Westbrook Manor, did you not? What did you do there, and why do you no longer work there?'

'Well, sir, I was a scullery maid, but after what happened, the master dismissed me.'

'Do you see the master in court today?'

'Yes, sir.'

'Would you please point to him?' Martha looked towards the dock and raised a shaky hand in the direction of Miles. 'For the record, the witness has pointed to the prisoner,' added Downing. 'Now then, Martha,' he continued, 'I want you to tell the court exactly what happened on the sixth of June, when you found Mrs Hough.'

'I got up at six o'clock to start work and went into the dining room. I saw Mrs Hough lying by the fireplace with her head on the hearth. There was a lot of blood and when I went closer I could see she was dead. I was scared so I ran to my mother's house in the village.'

'Now tell the court about what you heard earlier, when Mr Lambert had come home, late the previous night, wasn't it?'

'Yes, sir. I had gone to bed, just before midnight, and shortly after I heard voices from downstairs. Mr Lambert was shouting, and so too was Mrs Hough. Then the master started cursing and swearing and threatening to kill her if she didn't do as she was told. Then I heard a scream. After that, I didn't hear anything more. I was too frightened to go and see what had happened so I stayed in my room.'

'And why were you frightened to go downstairs?' For a moment or two Martha wavered and looked nervously towards the prisoner. 'There's no need to be afraid. Just tell the court the truth. Nobody here can harm you.'

'Well, the master often comes home late at night, sometimes drunk, and sometimes he brings other people back with him and they carry on drinking and gambling. Once or twice when I was still up, he shouted at me and threatened to throw me out.'

'But you say you don't work at the manor any longer.'

'No, sir. Not now. After the constable went up to the manor and took the master away, he sent a message saying I was dismissed and not to go there again.'

'Thank you, Martha. Now, please remain where you are. My learned friend Mr Garrett may wish to ask you some questions.' Downing sat down, and immediately the other attorney rose to his feet. Just as Joseph suspected, this was Miles's advocate. Alexander Garrett stepped away from the bar table and stared intensely at Martha for a few seconds, which clearly appeared to upset her.

'Now then Martha, are you an honest girl? Do you always tell the truth?'

'Yes, sir. I always try to.'

'Good, I'm sure the court is pleased to hear that. And I expect when you worked at the manor you were a hard-working girl, too. I suppose you worked long hours each day.'

'Yes, sir. I started work at six o'clock and sometimes I didn't finish till about midnight.'

'That's a very long time. No doubt you were very tired when you went to bed.'

'I was, sir.'

'So, when you heard voices, how can you be certain it was Mr Lambert?'

'I heard him arguing with Mrs Hough.'

'But how do you know it was Mr *Lambert* you heard? You were upstairs, in your bed. It could have been anybody. You have already told my learned friend here that Mr Lambert sometimes brought other people back home with him. How do you know there weren't other people with him that night, and it was one of them you heard?'

'Well, it sounded like Mr Lambert.'

'Oh, I see. So it *sounded* like Mr Lambert. But that doesn't mean it *was* Mr Lambert, now, does it? You didn't actually *see* Mr Lambert arguing with Mrs Hough, did you? And another person might sound the same, especially when they are in one room, downstairs, and you are in another, upstairs. You were in your bed. You've told us that you had been working all day and that you were tired, so how can you be *sure* it was Mr Lambert you heard? It could have been somebody else and you just *assumed* it was Mr Lambert. You've said you're an honest girl who always tells the truth, so I suggest you tell it now. Can you put your hand on that Bible and swear that the person you heard arguing with Mrs Hough was Mr Lambert, and nobody else?'

By now, after this intense cross-examination, poor Martha was a bundle of nerves. 'Well, come along, tell the court. Can you be positive? It's a simple answer, yes or no. Which is it to be? And remember, you are under oath.' There was a slight hesitation before she answered.

'No,' came the reply, in a barely audible whisper.

'I'm sorry,' said Garrett, 'I didn't quite catch what you said. Please repeat it, a little louder, so that everyone in the court can hear.'

'No,' Martha repeated, this time much louder than before.

'Thank you, Miss King. You've been most helpful. I have no further questions for you.'

The Counsel for the Crown also had no further questions for her, and the judge accordingly excused Martha, who gratefully stepped down from the witness box.

Joseph looked down at Miles, and although he could not see his face, he could almost imagine a smile of smug satisfaction spreading across it.

Two more witnesses were now called by Downing, firstly the constable and secondly the doctor who had attended the scene. In giving his evidence the constable stated that he had been sent for by Mrs King, Martha's mother, and after hearing the girl's account he had summoned the doctor and then gone to the manor, where he found Mrs Hough exactly as Martha had described, with a severe wound to her head. The accused was found in a drunken stupor in an armchair in the study. After a brief altercation, he had arrested Mr Lambert and conveyed him to the gaol at Wakefield.

Garrett then stepped forward to cross-examine the constable, but had only one question for him. 'Did you find any weapon, or heavy object, anywhere near the body which you suspected might have been used to cause the head wound?'

'No, sir.'

'Thank you, constable. No further questions.'

The doctor then went into the witness box, and stated that having been requested by the constable to go to the manor, he had examined the body and confirmed that Mrs Hough had died from loss of blood following a severe blow to the head.

Garrett rose once more from his seat at the table.

'What, in your opinion, caused the wound on the deceased's head?'

'I am certain it was caused by a heavy blow to the forehead.'

'Such as might be caused by, for example, a poker?'

'Yes.'

'Or, possibly by the victim falling heavily and banging her forehead on the stone flags of the hearth? We have already heard the constable state that he found no weapon at the scene.'

'Well … yes, I suppose that could account for it.'

'Precisely. But you cannot be certain which?'

'No. Not absolutely certain.'

'So, doctor, you cannot say, beyond any reasonable doubt, that the wound *was* caused by a blow deliberately inflicted on the victim by another person?'

'Not if you put it that way, no, I can't.'

'Thank you, doctor. That is precisely how I am putting it! No more questions, your honour.'

From the far end of the public gallery, Joseph could hear muted laughter. Miles's friends were enjoying the way the trial was going.

There being no more witnesses, it now remained for Miles to speak in his defence. From his position in the dock, he merely stated that he had no knowledge of how Mrs Hough came to meet her death, and that he was completely innocent of the charge of murder. Charles Downing, for the Crown, then rose to begin his cross-examination.

'Mr Lambert; I put it to you, that on the night in question you returned home in a state of inebriation and in a foul mood, you had an argument with Mrs Hough, as you have been known to do on previous occasions, and that you then struck her with an object which you subsequently disposed of. That's what happened, isn't it?'

'Not at all. I had nothing to do with her death.'

'But you were overheard by your maid arguing violently with Mrs Hough and threatening to kill her.'

'The maid's already admitted that she can't be certain it was me.'

'So, are you saying it was someone else?'

'The truth of the matter is, I can't be certain either. It might have been me, but then it might have been one of the others who had come back home with me that night. I really can't remember.'

'So, there were others with you, were there? Be so good as to tell the court what did happen.'

'Gladly. I had been to the Black Boar to meet with some friends for a game of cards, and I have to admit I had had a substantial amount to drink; maybe a little too much, as I've no doubt the landlord could confirm. It was gone eleven thirty when we left and I suggested that we all return to the manor and carry on our card game there. There were about half a dozen of us. I do remember that when we got back I asked Mrs Hough to prepare us some food and bring it through to the study, but she refused, saying she'd been up all day and was going off to her bed. I told her she was employed as my housekeeper and she should do as I instructed her. Then she began to give me one of her usual lectures about the evils of drinking and gambling, which I regarded as rather impertinent, as I could tell that she herself had been drinking. I could smell it on her breath. Her husband died recently and since then she's taken to the gin. Anyway, we did have a bit of a heated discussion and I suspect that's what the maid heard. The others told me to forget about it and let her go to bed, so I did.'

'And what about the scream that the maid heard?'

'Oh, that would be Connie, I expect. She does possess the most strident voice. And she always gets a bit giggly and loud, especially when she's had a few drinks and Guy starts to tease her,' replied Miles, to a ripple of amusement from the public gallery, and smiles on the faces of some of the jurymen, and it seemed that he was now beginning to revel in his performance, like a leading actor on the stage. He continued. 'I'm sorry, I should have explained, Guy and Connie, they're two of the crowd who came back with me from the inn. I know they'll be able to confirm all this, if you ask them.'

I bet they will, thought Joseph to himself, as Downing resumed his questioning.

'You state that Mrs Hough went off to bed. So how do you account for her being found dead the following morning in the dining room?'

'I can't. A terrible accident I expect, poor woman. We only had a few more hands of cards, and shortly afterwards, the others left. I poured myself another drink and must have fallen asleep in an armchair there. The next thing I knew, that constable chap woke me up and arrested me!'

'And you expect the court to believe this fairy story of yours?'

'Well, I can only tell you what I know. I've told you that Mrs Hough had taken to drinking gin since her husband died. Perhaps she went into the dining room for some reason or other, passed out, fell onto the hearth and cracked her head on the flags. I wouldn't know. I was fast asleep.'

There was to be no more questioning of Miles. Alexander Garrett announced he had nothing to ask his client, insisting that he had satisfactorily rebutted all the accusations levelled against him by the prosecution.

The time now came for the final addresses to the jury. Downing spoke first, insisting that the case against Miles was unshakeable, that the cause of death could have been nothing other than murder, and that Miles was the only person who could have been responsible.

It was then Garrett's turn to try and persuade the jury otherwise. He stated that his client had adequately explained the events of that night, and that there was no evidence whatsoever that he had been in any way involved in Mrs Hough's death. The maid, the principal witness, who on her own admission had been very tired, had simply misunderstood what she had heard. The constable had found no weapon, and the doctor had admitted that the wound could have been caused by a fall, occasioned, Garrett suggested, by inebriation. In short, he stressed, the evidence clearly pointed to Mrs Hough's death being nothing more than a tragic accident, but one in which his client had taken no part. And he told the jury that there was only one possible verdict they could reach; and that was to find his client not guilty.

Garrett took his seat for the last time and after a somewhat lengthy summing-up, the judge directed the jury to consider the evidence they had heard and return their verdict.

But Joseph was sure that he already knew what it would be. He was as convinced that it would be *not guilty* as he was that Miles really *was guilty*. But then, he knew Miles better than anyone on that jury; better than anyone in the courtroom. Miles had always been able to turn on the charm when it suited. He could tell a lie and make it sound like the truth; he could manipulate and twist others to his will and with the help of his advocate, whom, Joseph knew, would be handsomely rewarded, he would ensure that justice was not done.

In almost as little time as they had taken with any of the day's other three trials, the twelve men of the jury had concluded their deliberations. Once more, the Judge's Associate rose to his feet and asked the foreman if they had reached a verdict.

'We have,' replied the foreman.

'And how do you find the prisoner? Guilty or not guilty?'

'Not guilty.'

A resounding cheer rang out from Miles's friends, and from his position in the dock Miles turned, looked up and waved to them, then clasped his hands together above his head in triumph, like a prize-fighter after a famous victory. Joseph looked down in disgust. He was as certain as he could be that Miles had killed Mrs Hough, just as he had always harboured a suspicion about his involvement in their father's death. And then, for a brief second, as Miles continued to celebrate his acquittal, Joseph got the impression that he might, after all, have been spotted, for a frown appeared on Miles's forehead, and he seemed to be staring at him, as if trying to identify a half-familiar face. Joseph hastily turned his head to one side. Why he should have done this, he wasn't sure. Miles might have been able to intimidate him all those years ago, but he was now a grown man; stronger and taller than his brother. Not as rich, not as powerful, but he had no need to fear him.

Once more, the judge used his gavel to demand silence in his court. 'Prisoner at the bar, you have been found not guilty and are free to go,' he announced.

There were to be no more trials that day, and the public galleries swiftly began to empty. As he left the court and walked down the steps, Joseph took out his pocket watch, a beautiful timepiece in a solid gold case attached to a rose gold chain. It was the one memory he had of his father, the one memento that he had been able to keep for himself, and inside the case were engraved the words – *For HL with fondest love from AB 8th May 1807.* It had been a gift from his mother to his father on their wedding day, thirty-three years earlier. He opened the cover and looked at the hands; three thirty-six they indicated. His train was due to leave at four o'clock. If he hurried, he would be able to catch it, and by seven o'clock he could be back home with Hannah and Eliza. He stepped out briskly along Castlegate and had just passed St. Mary's Church when he noticed, up ahead, a small group of men, one of whom he recognised as Miles. Suddenly, they turned right into Coppergate, so he quickened his pace even more, and followed them round the corner, just in time to see them disappearing into a public house on the right-hand side of the road.

He had a sudden urge to confront Miles. But if he did so he would, as likely as not, miss his train and then he would have to wait until the following morning before he could go home. What should he do? He was in a dilemma. He dearly wanted to tell Miles what he thought of him, and yet catching the train home to be back with Hannah and Eliza was equally as important. He was about to continue on to the station when he changed his mind. He felt, within him, a burning rage at the injustice he had witnessed that afternoon. He knew Miles was guilty and he wanted to tell him so, to his face. Not that the verdict could be overturned, but at least he would have the satisfaction of confronting his brother and telling him that he hadn't fooled everyone. So he walked down Coppergate to the pub, the Three Tuns, a narrow, ancient-looking gabled building with a door in the centre, and went in. It seemed a respectable enough place. Not a dive like some of the pubs found in the back streets of towns, but the haunt, he suspected, of decent working men. Definitely not the sort of place one would normally find men of property, like Miles and his friends, but then Miles and his friends were not typical of most of the landed gentry. Anywhere with alcohol was good enough for them, if need be, and no doubt they had a need right now, the need to celebrate.

A short passageway led past two small side rooms into a slightly larger room with a bar at the far end. Two old men, sitting together at a table, were the only customers, and Joseph was about to ask the barman if a group of men had just come in, when he heard the sound of raucous banter, and looking across the bar he could see through a small hatchway into another room at the back. So he ordered a pint of ale, took the mug, and upon entering the room found them seated round a large table. As soon as he walked in, it all went quiet.

'Sorry,' said one of the men in a supercilious tone, 'we're having a bit of a private celebration here. Be so good as to remove yourself, there's a good chap.' Joseph stood his ground. The man looked up. 'You still here? I told you to move. Are you deaf or just plain stupid?' Joseph continued to ignore him. Miles was sitting with his back to Joseph, and so far had not turned round. 'I'll only tell you once more. Get out, or I'll have to throw you out.' Joseph had met his type before – brash, arrogant, rich, and usually all mouth and trousers. Miles had always had plenty of friends like that. But this one didn't scare him. Joseph was normally tolerant and even-tempered, and slow to anger, but when he was riled he was a match for anyone. Ten years toil in the factory had toughened him up from the skinny boy he had been when he had first arrived in Sheffield, and now, at six foot two and with muscles to spare, he wasn't in the least bit concerned by threats from this foppish pipsqueak.

'I came here to speak to the organ-grinder,' said Joseph nonchalantly, as he nodded towards his brother, 'not to his monkey.'

'I do believe he means you, Miles,' bleated the fop, tetchily. 'I hope you're not going to let him talk to me like that, calling me a monkey! Tell him to apologise, or I'll be obliged to give him a thrashing.'

'The only apology needed here would be to the monkey for being compared to the likes of you,' retorted Joseph, 'but if you really want to have a go at giving me a thrashing, I'll be delighted to step outside with you right now. Otherwise, keep your lips sealed,' and placing both his carpetbag and his pint on a table, Joseph took a pace forward towards the group. The fop had suddenly lost his voice. 'This is the one I've come to see. Miles Lambert; the man who murders old ladies.'

Miles had now turned round and was staring up at him from his seat at the table, and Joseph could tell from the look on his face that he had been recognised.

'Well, well, well. My young brother. This is a surprise,' declared Miles, sarcastically. 'So it was you I saw in the courtroom. But you really ought to be careful, making accusations like that. I have a lot of witnesses here.'

'Who? This bunch of dimwits? They don't frighten me, and neither do you. I saw your performance in court today. You might have fooled the jury, but you didn't fool me. I know you too well, Miles. I can always tell when you're lying. You might have got away with murder, and probably not for the first time, but you'll pay, one day; mark my words.' Joseph had hit a raw nerve. Miles didn't like being spoken to like that, especially not in front of his friends.

'What do you mean, not for the first time?'

'You know exactly what I mean. How strange that father should die while out hunting, something he'd done a thousand times before, and you the only one within spitting distance of him. And how convenient for you that it happened just as he was about to make his will. So he died intestate and you inherited everything.'

'Not quite everything,' replied Miles. 'Isn't that father's watch you have there?' he asked, pointing to the rose gold fob looped across Joseph's waistcoat to his watch pocket.

'It is, and it's the one thing you will never get your hands on. You kept everything else, and you're welcome to it. But I have something far more valuable than you could ever have. The knowledge that I haven't had to commit crimes to get where I am today. I know the truth about you, Miles. But you can keep it all; the house, the land and the money. And much good may they do you.' Joseph made to walk towards the door.

'Oh dear, not stopping for another drink then?' sneered the fop, who had suddenly regained his bravado, now that Joseph appeared to be leaving. 'You haven't even finished your first one yet!' he added, to much ribaldry. Joseph stopped in his tracks. Turning round, he picked up his half-empty mug, walked over to where the fop sat and picked up a full tankard of brown ale from the table.

'No, I shan't be stopping for another drink, thank you all the same. I don't particularly like the company here. But you're quite right, I haven't finished my drink yet. Pity to waste it though. Here, you can have it, along with this other one,' and slowly he poured the contents of both over the fop's head. Then, without saying another word, he turned round, picked up his bag and walked away.

'Just look at my coat; it's absolutely ruined,' whimpered the fop. 'Miles, what are you going to do? He's your brother; surely you can't let him get away with it!'

'Don't worry, Sebastian. I'll wipe the smile off his face. And if you stop your whining, I might even give you the money for a new coat.' Miles then leant over to another of his friends and whispered something in his ear. The man nodded, got up and left the room.

Joseph walked back up to Castlegate and glanced at his watch. Five past four. He'd only been in the pub for about fifteen minutes, but it meant he'd missed the train and would have to spend the night in York. He headed towards the city centre and soon found a small inn in Stonegate, the White Hart, which looked clean and respectable, so he stepped inside to enquire about booking a room for the night. But as he stood talking to the proprietor, someone else was standing, unnoticed, just inside the doorway, observing and listening carefully to what was being discussed. And having heard everything he needed to hear, he quietly left and retraced his steps back to the Three Tuns in Coppergate.

Having made his reservation for the night, Joseph went up to his room, and was soon followed by a maid bringing him a jug of hot water and a towel. He quickly refreshed himself, and satisfied, if not entirely pleased, with the day's events, he decided to set off and spend a little time looking round the ancient city. It was over ten years since he had last spent any time here, when he had been at his boarding school, and there were one or two places he wanted to see again. He had also decided that he would buy presents for Hannah and Eliza to take back with him, then he would have some supper and a drink or two, and then off to bed. He would have to be up early the next morning, for his train left at 7.45 am, the only one of the day, and he knew he must not miss it. So, with a bright and breezy step, Joseph left the inn and headed up Stonegate in the direction of the medieval minster, the place he wanted to visit first.

CHAPTER ELEVEN

Where is my wandering boy tonight?

When Joseph did not return home on the Saturday Hannah was a little disappointed, as she was looking forward to their night out, but then he had told her he might have to stay overnight in York. However, the next morning, when eleven o'clock came and Joseph had still not returned, she began to get a little bit worried. By twelve o'clock, she was getting rather anxious. The train was due to arrive in Sheffield at 10.15 am. She had heard terrible stories of collisions and derailments leading to injury and death and by one o'clock she was most concerned. So, leaving Eliza with her mother, she set off to walk to the station and enquire about the train from York. When she arrived there, all was quiet with scarcely a soul in sight. A train of carriages sat, silently, at the platform, but with no engine at the front, and none of the clamour and commotion of the day before when she had come along to see Joseph off on his journey.

She went to the booking office, where she found a clerk sitting at a high desk making entries in a large leather-bound ledger. Her enquiry soon elicited the information that the train from York had arrived a few minutes late, and that there would be no more trains that day. But, he explained, the following day, Monday, there would be four trains, due at 10.00 am, 11.15 am, 2.45 pm and 6.45 pm. Hannah made a mental note of these times, and tried to console herself with the thought that his business meeting might have been so encouraging that he needed to extend his stay for a further day. So she went back to her mother's and explained what she had learned.

'There you are, dear, I'm sure there's nothing to worry about. He'll be back tomorrow, just you see. And if I know Joseph, he'll have made his visit worthwhile.'

'Well, I hope you're right, mother.' But deep inside, Hannah sensed that something was amiss. Joseph had only been given permission to take the Saturday off work – not the Monday as well. He was always most conscientious to stick to any arrangements he made, and she knew that something extraordinary must have happened to make him act in such a way and so out of character. She hardly slept that night, tossing and turning with worry, not knowing where Joseph was and wondering if he was safe. Only Eliza, completely unaware of the trauma her mother was going through, slept soundly.

By a quarter to ten the next morning Hannah had already been to the factory to tell Mr Yates of Joseph's absence, and was once more at the station, waiting for the first train to arrive from York, praying that her beloved husband would alight, smiling and laughing, possibly with presents for her and Eliza and an explanation for his delay. But he was not on it. Nor was he on the next one. After the arrival of the third train, again without any sign of Joseph, she returned to her mother's house, feeling utterly disconsolate and fearing the worst.

As soon as she opened the door she heard voices coming from the parlour, her mother's and that of a man. But it wasn't Joseph's voice. Neither of them heard her come in, but the second she walked into the room their conversation abruptly ceased. A gentleman, whom she had never seen before, was seated in an armchair whilst her mother sat on the settee. And the look on her mother's face made Hannah's heart miss a beat, for her usual happy and cheery countenance had drained away, and in its place was a look of sorrow and desolation.

'Hannah love, come and sit down here beside me,' she whispered in a soft, almost apologetic tone, as she moved along the settee to make room for her daughter. Hannah did as she was told. 'This is Mr Archibald from the Parish Constables' Office in York. He came on the train this morning. Oh, Hannah, he's brought us some dreadful news. I don't know how to tell you.'

Hannah sat by her mother, staring straight ahead, then without showing any emotion, she said, 'Joseph's dead, isn't he? I know he is. When he wasn't on the train, I knew something must have happened.

He wouldn't have stayed away for so long, not when he had his work to go to.' Hannah turned to face Mr Archibald. 'What's happened to him?'

Mr Archibald was a middle-aged man, short and portly and round of face with a good head of hair. In other, less harrowing, circumstances he would have undoubtedly manifested himself as being of a naturally jovial disposition, with a ready smile that he was now doing his best to hide. Hannah could tell that he was feeling awkward and wasn't sure how to begin. 'Please don't concern yourself about upsetting me, Mr Archibald. I need to know the truth, however terrible it might be.'

'Very well, Mrs Lambert. I'm afraid your assumption is correct. I'm awfully sorry to have to tell you that your husband's body was found yesterday, next to the Old Star Inn in Stonegate. A new shop is currently being erected at the front of the inn where the old coaching yard was, but that's no longer needed, not now the railway's arrived. As it was a Sunday, when the builders don't work, the landlord went out early in the morning to check that everything was all right, as some building materials had recently been stolen. He had his dog with him, and as soon as they went inside the shop, the dog started barking and made straight for a tarpaulin, lying up against one of the partly built walls. The landlord lifted it up and found the body of a man underneath. He immediately sent one of his potboys for a constable, and I went back with him. I examined the body and then arranged to have it taken to the mortuary.

'The landlord said that he recognised the man as he'd been to the inn on Saturday night. He said he particularly remembered him as he'd never seen him before and he was by himself. He had a couple of drinks then left at about nine o'clock.'

'Are you sure it's Joseph?' asked Hannah.

'I'm afraid there's no doubt about it. His pockets were searched for any means of identification, but all we could find was a receipt from the White Hart, further along Stonegate. We showed it to the landlord there, a Mr Todd, and he confirmed it belonged to a man who had booked a room on Saturday evening. Mr Todd also said that he had gone out about half an hour after booking his room, then briefly returned a couple of hours later. He was quite certain about this, as he had some parcels with him that he said he wanted to leave in his room before going out again. That was the last time he had seen him and he didn't remember him coming back in; but then he had been very busy and might not have noticed him. Mr Todd took us to his room and it was obvious that the bed had not been slept in. We found a bag with a few possessions, including a notebook which contained the name Joseph Lambert and an address here in Sheffield, along with a railway ticket.

'First thing this morning I advised the coroner, who told me that he would arrange the inquest for tomorrow, but I think it's pretty clear what the verdict will be. It seems your husband was stabbed several times in the back. No weapon has been found, and I don't suppose it will be.

'I then caught the 8.45 train and went to the address we'd found, in Charles Street, but there was nobody there. I made some enquiries with the neighbours, and one said Mr Lambert gone to York and that you were staying with your mother, so I came straight here. I've brought his bag with me,' he added, pointing towards a corner of the room. Hannah hadn't spotted it before, but there, in the corner, was the same brown carpetbag that Joseph had taken with him.

Throughout Mr Archibald's explanation of this horrific affair, Hannah had remained silent. Both Agnes and Mr Archiblad were astonished at her composure, but this was not the first time that he had been required to break similar sad news to near relatives, and he knew that sometimes this was the way they dealt with such agonising revelations. All too often, the anguish and the grieving would come later.

Hannah went over and picked up Joseph's bag, and sitting down again, she undid the leather strap and looked inside. Slowly she removed the items it contained; a clean shirt, a small bar of soap, a toothbrush, a razor and a shaving brush, the notebook and the railway ticket Mr Archibald had mentioned, and a copy of *Life and Adventures of Nicholas Nickleby* by Charles Dickens. This had been her

Christmas present to Joseph nearly seven months earlier, but he had only recently started to read it. In addition to these items, all of which were familiar to her, there were three other packages wrapped in fancy paper and tied with ribbons. Curious to know what these were, she untied the ribbons and carefully unfolded the paper. The first was a child's doll, the second a box containing a silver charm bracelet, and the third a silk handkerchief. She could only guess that these were presents Joseph had bought for her, Eliza and Agnes, and as she held them tenderly, knowing that they would have been amongst the last things touched by her darling husband, tears came into her eyes.

'Is this all there was? Did you find anything else in his pockets?' asked Hannah.

'I'm afraid not. The only thing we found on him was the receipt from the White Hart. No money was found, so robbery might have been the motive.'

'What about his watch? He was wearing it when he left home. It was a gold pocket watch on a rose gold chain. Has that gone, too?'

'Well, there was no sign of a watch on him. Of course, we weren't to know of its existence, so perhaps that makes it even more likely that robbery was behind the attack. I'll advise the coroner of what you've told me.'

Before he left to return to York, Mr Archibald gave details of the time and place for the inquest, should Hannah and her mother wish to attend, but they decided there and then that neither of them could face the ordeal. He therefore kindly agreed to let them know the verdict, and said that once the inquest was concluded, Joseph's body would be sent back to Sheffield for burial. He also said that they would be kept informed of any developments regarding the hunt for the perpetrators of the crime. Should anyone eventually be apprehended and charged, Hannah was told that she might be called as a witness at the subsequent trial. He asked Hannah the purpose of her husband's visit to York, and whether she knew the names of anyone there whom Joseph intended to call on, as they might have further information. She explained his intention of seeking out those concerned with the opening of a new hotel at the station, but beyond that was unable to provide anything further.

Soon, Mr Archibald departed, leaving Agnes and Hannah alone with young Eliza. The house seemed empty, despite the three of them being together. The knowledge that they would never see Joseph again was beginning to sink in. Eliza was too young to understand properly what had happened, and yet she somehow seemed to sense that something was the matter, and that her mother and grandmother were not their usual happy selves. And Hannah was already beginning to wonder how she was going to explain to Eliza that her father would not be coming home.

The next two weeks were the worst that Hannah could remember. Four years previously she had been married to Joseph, the love of her life. Two years later their daughter had been born, and now, just when she believed she and Joseph had every reason to look forward to an even happier and more prosperous future, she found herself a widow at the age of only twenty-two.

Four days after Mr Archibald's visit, they received the result of the inquest. The coroner's verdict was that Joseph had been murdered by a person or persons unknown. On the same day, his body was returned and arrangements quickly made for his funeral. There was a huge turnout. All their friends, along with Joseph's work colleagues were there, and after the church service at St. Peter's they slowly followed the coffin along to the General Cemetery. But an unwelcome scene awaited them there – a large crowd of sensation seekers, none of whom had ever met Joseph, and who, a week before, had not even known of his existence. But the news of Joseph's murder had been reported in the Sheffield newspapers, which were always eager to publish details of any gruesome or shocking incident, such is the morbid curiosity displayed by many of their readers.

After the funeral was over a small group of family and close friends was invited back to Agnes's house, and one of them casually asked where Joseph's aunt was, the one who had come to the wedding. And Hannah suddenly realised that Emily, Joseph's only known relative, had not been informed of his death. So preoccupied had she and Agnes been that it had entirely slipped their minds. They had met her only once, when she had come to Sheffield for the wedding, and she had said nothing about either herself or Joseph and his family. All they knew about Emily was that she had come from somewhere in the West Riding. They understood she was a sister of Joseph's mother, but beyond that they knew nothing more. And whenever Hannah had asked Joseph about his past and his relatives he had always been reluctant to tell her anything. They believed that Emily was a spinster, but her surname was unknown to them, and they did not have her address. So, on reflection, trying to contact her would have been almost impossible.

Hannah did not return to live in the house in Charles Street which she had so lovingly decorated and made just to her liking. It held too many memories for her. In any case, she could not afford the rent, not now that she was a widow with only a small income. She had received a generous, but small, donation from Joseph's work colleagues, and Mr Yates had doubled the amount they had collected. But half of this she had already spent on a headstone for Joseph's grave. And so she sold all the furniture she and Joseph had bought, and moved back to live with Agnes. Hannah made one final visit to Charles Street, to collect all her personal possessions. The worst task she had to face was disposing of Joseph's effects. There were a dozen or more books, which she kept, hoping that one day she would learn to read properly; his tools she was easily able to sell, and his clothes she gave to a charity. A month after Joseph's funeral, she heard from the authorities in York that no progress had been made into the investigation of his murder, and that they now considered it unlikely that they would ever recover any of the stolen items, or apprehend the guilty party.

The months passed quickly, but only slowly did the pain of Joseph's death begin to heal. Hannah busied herself by helping her mother with the baking, and together they were beginning to expand their little enterprise. And then, towards Christmas, Hannah began to notice that Agnes often seemed tired. She had never been one to relax; she was always on the go and if she wasn't baking and preparing another batch of cakes, pies or pastries for her growing number of customers, she would either be busy around the house, out shopping for more provisions, or assisting some elderly neighbour who needed a helping hand. But one by one, these tasks became too much for her. She had far less energy than before, and Hannah was sure that Agnes had lost weight. As time went by, these symptoms became more pronounced and she slowly began to lose her appetite. The business began to suffer, too, as Agnes was finding it difficult to fulfil all her orders, even with Hannah's help. And then the coughing started. Mild at first, but gradually getting worse. And by mid-summer, there was no denying the truth; Agnes was suffering from consumption.

It was a month after the anniversary of Joseph's death, Friday 13th August to be precise, when Agnes breathed her last. And once more, Hannah followed a coffin from the church to the cemetery. Agnes's husband had died many years before, in 1819, tragically killed in an accident at work, and so they laid her to rest in the same grave.

When the mourners had finally left, Hannah sat with Eliza on her knee, thinking about recent events. She had never known her father, who had died when she was just a year old. And now her own daughter would grow up barely remembering hers. Fate had dealt her two cruel blows in little over a year, but had not yet finished dealing. With the passing of her mother, the once-thriving bakery enterprise was all but over. Now that she was left by herself with a young daughter to look after, she was finding it hard to cope. What little money Hannah had saved was almost gone, but the rent still had to be paid. There was only one thing for it, and that was to try and find other employment. And just when everything seemed stacked against her, suddenly, there appeared a glimmer of hope.

Late one Saturday afternoon in the autumn, Hannah took Eliza down to the market, hoping to pick up some meat and vegetables on the cheap, for sometimes, when they had perishable stock left but were keen to pack up for the weekend, the stallholders would reduce their prices significantly. She had managed to buy some onions, potatoes and other root vegetables, not the best quality, but they would make a good stew with some oxtails she had bought cheaply from a butcher's stall. They were on their way back home, when they bumped into one of Hannah's old friends, Annie, the landlady at the Cutler's Arms, where she and Joseph had held their wedding feast. It was a while since they had last seen each other and Hannah was delighted to spot a familiar, friendly face. She and Joseph often used to call in at the Cutler's for a drink, leaving Agnes to look after Eliza, but those happy times were now little more than a fond memory.

'Oh, hello Annie, it's so good to see you, how are you? We're just on our way home from the market.'

'As well as can be expected,' replied Annie, with a smile, 'what with old age and poverty creeping on!'

'Well, I don't know about old age, but poverty's something I know all too much about.'

'I guess things must be pretty hard for you now, Hannah. How are you coping? I don't think I've seen you since your mother's funeral. And young Eliza here seems to have grown since I last saw her,' she added, looking down at the little girl, tightly holding on to her mother's hand.

'Yes, she's the one that keeps me going. I don't know how I'd get by if I didn't have her; she's all I've got left, now that Joseph's gone and …' but before she could say another word, she burst into a flood of tears, sobbing uncontrollably. Little Eliza looked up at her mother.

'Don't cry, mummy,' she whispered.

Hannah bent down and picked up her daughter, cradling her in her arms, as if frightened to let go lest anything should happen to her, too.

'There, there, Hannah, I'm sure everything will turn out all right,' said Annie, as she placed a comforting arm round Hannah's shoulders. 'Now, never mind going back home; you two are going to come along with me to the pub. I've got a big juicy chicken in the oven; it's far too much for Harry and me to eat by ourselves, so you can help us out, and we'll have a good old chinwag at the same time. And it's Saturday, so there'll be the usual knees-up and singsong later on; that'll help cheer you up, I know it will.'

Hannah had hardly socialised at all since Joseph's death, having had neither the time, the money nor the inclination, and Annie detected that she seemed to have lost her enthusiasm for life.

'Come along now; I'll not take no for an answer! I'm sure you've not got anything planned for tonight, so I insist,' and before Hannah could reply, Annie had taken her arm and was steering her down the street towards the pub, Eliza trotting along beside her mother.

'Harry!' Annie shouted as they entered the back door of the pub, 'come and see who I've brought back with me.' Harry, Annie's husband, came through from the bar. 'Look, Harry, Hannah's here, and young Eliza. I met them in the town and invited them back for supper. We've plenty to go round.' Annie took Hannah and Eliza into the kitchen at the back of the pub. A large oblong table stood in the middle, big enough to seat a dozen. 'Just you sit down there, and I'll get you both a drink first, then I'll see to the supper. I hope you're both hungry.'

Annie left Hannah and Eliza with their drinks, then went and had a word with her husband, who was busy tidying up in the public bar. She told him about how upset Hannah had been and that she seemed to be in a bad way. It was early evening and there were only a few customers in the pub, but later on it would be different; Saturday nights were always busy. 'Don't be long, Harry. I'll be serving up in about twenty minutes.'

Soon they were seated round the kitchen table, tucking into their meal. This was normal fare for Annie and Harry, but for Hannah it was a real treat. She rarely cooked a roast dinner; she couldn't see the point, not just for herself and Eliza, and in any case, a whole chicken was a luxury she simply couldn't afford. As they ate, they talked, and from what Hannah was saying, Annie and Harry soon realised what a terrible predicament she was in.

'I don't know what I'm going to do,' she admitted, 'I've hardly any savings left and the rent's due next week. The landlord's a stickler for being paid on time. If I get behind, as likely as not he'll send the bailiffs round. And if we got evicted, there's only one place we could go, and that's the workhouse. But I'll move heaven and earth before we end up in there.'

'Kelham Street's the last place you want to go to,' said Harry, referring to the Union Workhouse. 'There's an old couple who sometimes pop in for a drink who spent a couple of months there when they were down on their luck and out of work, and it made me shudder hearing them talk of the conditions inside. Men and women are kept strictly apart, including married couples, and even young children are taken away from their mothers.' Eliza, who had obviously understood some of what was being said, looked up pitifully at her mother.

'They won't take me away from you, will they, mummy?'

'Of course not, darling. We're not going anywhere near that horrible place, and I'd never let anyone take you away from me.'

'Well, we'd not see you homeless, would we Harry? We can lend you the rent money, if you need it, just to tide you over until you find a job. And if you do get thrown out of your house, you can come and stay with us. We can always find you a room. There's only the two of us living here, now all our brood have flown the nest.'

'That's very kind of you, Annie, but I'm desperate to find work. And it's not easy when you have a youngster to look after. I really can't think of a way round the problem.'

'I might be able to,' said Harry, all of a sudden, and much to their surprise. 'I can't promise anything, but I've just remembered something I was told last week. You know Albert, the drayman from the brewery. Well, he was here last Monday and we were having a quiet pint after he'd dropped off the barrels, and he was telling me about his missus who does a bit of cleaning twice a week up at a big house on the Glossop Road. It's owned by a solicitor, Brentnall, I think they call him. Anyway, Albert was saying how they'd asked her to work some extra days as a stand-in for their cook and housekeeper who'd suddenly upped sticks and left. They haven't found the right person to replace her yet, but she hopes they do soon, 'cause she's not much of a cook, and she's finding it difficult doing the extra days as she has other houses to clean as well. And it's a fair old trek up there, right out on the edge of town. The woman who left used to live in, and Albert thinks the Brentnalls are looking for someone who can do the same. And *you* know how to cook and keep house, don't you, Hannah? You could do far worse than try your hand there; you never know, you might be lucky.'

Hannah was encouraged by what she had just heard. A job with accommodation included would solve all her problems; but would they want someone with a young child? Best not to get too optimistic, she thought.

'Do you know how I could apply for the job, Harry? Has it been advertised yet?'

'I'm not sure, but Albert will be in again on Monday. I'll try and find out a bit more and let you know, if you like.'

'Oh, yes, please do. And thank you for telling me about it.'

Hannah enjoyed the rest of that evening at the Cutler's more than any other evening since she was last there, and that had been with Joseph. After they had finished eating, they all went into the bar, where a jolly party was getting underway. There were quite a few people there whom Hannah knew, including some of Joseph's old work colleagues, and she was pleased to renew acquaintances. Harry had recently installed a piano, one of the first pubs in the town to have one. A neighbour of theirs was an accomplished pianist, and he would come in on a Saturday night and entertain the customers. As the evening wore on, and more beer was consumed, a general sing-along began, with the most popular songs being sung with gusto. Some individuals, who fancied themselves as singers, insisted on performing their solo renditions for the entertainment of all and sundry. But as Hannah soon found out, most of them had grandiose ideas about their musical talents which far exceeded their actual abilities. Still, it was all good fun, and by ten o'clock Hannah was worn out, and young Eliza had managed, despite all the noise, to fall asleep. So Hannah said her goodbyes to everyone and thanked Annie and Harry for their hospitality.

'You will let me know about that job, won't you?' Hannah reminded them.

'Of course we will. We'll be in touch as soon as we hear anything,' Annie assured her.

Eliza was still fast asleep, so Hannah had to carry her back home. Fortunately, they hadn't far to go, and before long they were both fast asleep in their beds.

The following Thursday morning, there came a knock on the door. Hannah's first thought was that it was the landlord, but peeking carefully between the curtains, she was relieved and delighted to see Annie on the doorstep.

'Oh, thank goodness it's you, Annie, I thought it was the landlord after the rent. Come on in. I've enough put by for another two or three weeks, then I might be coming to see you about that loan, unless something turns up.' Annie came in and sat talking to Eliza while Hannah went and made them both a cup of tea.

'I've got some news for you about the job with the Brentnalls. Albert's wife has put a good word in for you, and Mrs Brentnall says if you're interested, you can call at their house either today or tomorrow between four and five o'clock. But she did say they've placed advertisements in the *Mercury* and the *Independent* this weekend, so if I were you I'd get up there as soon as you can.'

'You're right. I'll go this afternoon. I don't want to let such a good opportunity pass me by. But what am I going to do about Eliza? I can't really take her with me.'

'Don't worry about that. I'll look after her. Just drop her off on the way and you can pick her up when you get back.'

At three o'clock Hannah, dressed in her Sunday best, went round to the Cutler's Arms. 'Now Eliza, you be a good girl for Annie this afternoon. I have to go and see a lady, but I won't be too long.' She kissed Eliza goodbye, then set off for the address that Annie had given her. She walked into the town centre, past the cathedral and along West Street towards Glossop Road. Annie had described the house, which was called *Aysgarth Villa*, explaining that it was at the top end on the right-hand side, shortly before open countryside was reached. Several large villas were dotted along the road, and it was evident to her that anyone living here was well heeled and would never have to worry about where the next meal was coming from. It was a steady, uphill walk all the way, and after about half an hour Hannah arrived at what she thought was the correct house. There was a name board on the gate pillar, but Hannah could only read the simplest of words. As she stood there, wondering whether it was the right one, she noticed a man pottering about in the garden of a house on the opposite side of the road. She crossed over and was soon able to establish that it was, indeed, the home of Robert Brentnall.

The house was a large, square, Regency villa standing in its own grounds, built of Yorkshire sandstone and fronted by a low wall topped with wrought-iron railings, whilst neat hedges separated it from the adjacent properties. A pair of solid wooden gates guarded the entrance to a driveway, which led through the front garden and along the side of the house towards a group of outbuildings including a coach house and stable. A footpath led directly to the wide front door which stood inside a generously sized porch. The house had three storeys, a twin-gabled roof of Welsh slate, and sash windows, and all its architectural features indicated that no expense had been spared in its construction.

Hannah decided that, bearing in mind the purpose of her visit, it would not be the done thing to go to the front door, so she followed the drive round to the back of the house and found the tradesmen's entrance. She knocked loudly, and the door was soon opened by a short, middle-aged, rosy-cheeked lady with an apron tied around her ample waist. Hannah introduced herself, and as soon as she mentioned her name the lady smiled, knowingly.

'You must be the girl that's come about the job, the one my Albert mentioned.'

'Yes, and I'm very grateful he told Harry all about it.'

'Well, come along in. Sit yourself down at the kitchen table, and I'll go and tell Mrs Brentnall you're here. Mr Brentnall is at his office in town, but it's Mrs Brentnall who looks after the domestic arrangements. She'll be the one to decide who gets the job. I'm Ellen, by the way.'

Hannah did as she was told, sat down and looked around her.

She had never seen such a large kitchen, provided with all the latest devices and fittings, and so designed as to make a cook's work as easy as it could be. This is where she would be spending much of her time, she thought, should she be lucky enough to be taken on. As she continued to look around, her attention was suddenly drawn to some items which seemed familiar. At the end of the table was a tray containing silver-plated cutlery, which she recognised as coming from the factory of Yates and Sons. But before she had time to inspect them in more detail, Ellen returned and told Hannah to follow her. She led her out of the kitchen into a short corridor, then through another door and into a grand and spacious hallway. The most striking feature here was the floor, laid out in a stunning geometric pattern of brown, yellow and blue tiles.

Ahead was the front door, inset with brightly coloured panels of stained glass, through which the late afternoon autumn sun shone. To the left, a wide, curving, mahogany staircase led up to the first floor, whilst to both left and right were doors leading to other reception rooms. Ellen opened the first door on the right and showed Hannah into the drawing room, which was exquisitely decorated with dark-red flocked wallpaper above a dado, and intricate plasterwork friezes and cornices above the picture rails. The room was tastefully furnished with cabinets, sideboards, bureaus and an arrangement of comfortable sofas and chairs. A large sparkling glass chandelier hung from an elaborate moulded ceiling rose, whilst the polished wooden floor was liberally scattered with rugs and carpets of the highest quality. To the right, a large window draped with embossed velvet curtains looked out over the back garden, and on the far wall was an ornate marble fireplace and mantelpiece with a fire burning cheerfully in the grate.

As they entered, a lady rose from her chair by the fire, placing a book and pair of spectacles on a low table by her side. Hannah guessed she was in her early fifties, about the same age as her mother would have been. She was tall, slim and elegantly dressed, her silvery-grey hair fashioned in a coiled chignon at the back of her head.

'Good afternoon,' said the lady, stepping forward and reaching out to shake Hannah's hand. 'Mrs Lambert, I understand. I'm Mrs

Brentnall. Please come and sit down,' she added, pointing to a chair facing the window. 'Ellen has already told me a little about you and that you are interested in the position of cook and housekeeper. I had better begin by explaining our domestic situation. My husband is a solicitor with an office in the town and spends every weekday there, other than when business calls him away. Much of my time is spent on charity work, so I too am frequently out of the house during the day. There are only the two of us living here, and whilst we tend to be creatures of habit we do sometimes entertain in the evenings, and occasionally our son or daughter, who are both married and live elsewhere, will come and stay for a while.

'Your duties would entail doing all the cooking and serving of meals, and the ordering of food and provisions, but we do have our regular suppliers who will deliver as required. We always take breakfast at eight o'clock and dinner at seven, except on Sundays when breakfast is at nine and dinner at six. I will take a light lunch at midday if I am at home. We invariably dine out on Saturday evenings, so you may have Saturday as your day off, once you have finished serving breakfast. You will also be free on Sundays during the day, as we take lunch in town after church. In addition to your culinary duties, you would be expected to keep the kitchen clean and tidy, make the beds, light the fires in winter and do some general light cleaning around the house. We do have our cleaner of course, whom you have met. She comes in twice a week, and is responsible for all heavy cleaning and washing. We also have a gardener-cum-handyman who lives nearby and who also acts as our coachman. I think you know that the position does require you to live in, and you would be provided with your own room on the second floor, and of course all your meals. There is also an annuity of twenty pounds. Now, I think that adequately describes the nature of the position. Perhaps you would care to tell me a little something about yourself and your past experience. I take it you have references from previous employers.'

Up to that point, Hannah had been feeling quite relaxed. Although Mrs Brentnall was very precise and formal in her manner, she was in no way intimidating, and Hannah could even detect a kind disposition behind her austere exterior. But the request for references came as a shock. She had never worked for anyone other than her mother. Nothing for it, she thought; she must simply tell Mrs Brentnall the truth and explain her present circumstances.

'Thank you for telling me all about the position. I suppose I'd better start straight away by saying that I do not have any references, as I've never worked for anyone other than my own mother. My husband died in July last year so I returned to live with my mother, but then she died in August this year, and I now find myself in need of a job. I am used to doing all the housekeeping tasks you mentioned, and I do know a lot about cooking. After my father died, when I was only a child, my mother started to make ends meet by supplying some local shops and inns with her home-made bread, cakes, pies and so on, and this eventually grew into quite a thriving little business. And from a very early age I used to help her, so I consider myself to be a fairly good cook.'

'I see. But might I ask why you haven't continued with your mother's business?'

'Unfortunately, the business had started to suffer a few months before she died. She was becoming ill and unable to work much herself, but however hard I tried we began to lose some of our customers. Then mother got worse and I had to devote more time to nursing her, and I also have a young daughter to look after. So, you see, it became impossible to carry on as before.'

'So, you have a daughter too?' asked Mrs Brentnall, somewhat taken aback.

It then occurred to Hannah that her having a child had not been made clear, and she began to think that this might ruin her chance of being appointed to the position. But Mrs Brentnall then surprised her with her next comment.

'Do tell me about her. How old is she? We have no grandchildren of our own, but we adore children and I am on the committee of a children's charity in Sheffield.'

Suddenly, things looked brighter, and Hannah began to relate to Mrs Brentnall the events of the last few years. How she had originally met Joseph when he first came to live with them as a lodger; his apprenticeship and work as a cutler; the dreadful circumstances surrounding his visit to York and then her mother's death. Mrs Brentnall appeared a little troubled as Hannah explained all the sad things that had happened to her.

'Oh, you poor girl. I am so sorry for everything you've had to endure. But if I did offer you the position, I expect you would want to bring your daughter with you, wouldn't you?'

'Well, yes, I would. She's only three, and there's nobody I know who could take her in and look after her. I'm sorry; I should have thought about that before coming here.'

'That's all right, Mrs Lambert. I'm sure it wouldn't cause any problems that couldn't easily be resolved. Of course, you would have to share the same room, but it's quite big and nicely furnished, and we could easily provide another small bed for your daughter. What's her name?'

'Eliza.'

'That's a lovely name. But do tell me more about your husband. You say he was a cutler.'

'Yes, and a very good one too, although I say it myself. I think, had he lived, he would have done well for himself. He had lots of ideas and wanted to start his own business one day and I'm certain he would have done. I noticed that you have some cutlery in your kitchen made by Yates and Sons; that's where he worked.'

'Well, I never! We purchased that set only recently. It's one of the finest we could find. Perhaps your husband might have made some of the pieces himself. And I believe my husband has met Mr Yates on a number of occasions through his dealings with The Cutlers' Company. But heavens, just look at the time! Mr Brentnall will be home shortly, so I must go and make sure Ellen has started preparing supper. She's a very good cleaner and washerwoman but cooking's not her forte – and I know she'd be the first to admit it! That's why we want to find a new cook as quickly as possible.'

Mrs Brentnall went to the side of the fireplace and tugged on a silk rope hanging from the ceiling. Hannah heard a distant bell ring, and soon Ellen appeared.

'Ellen, would you please show Mrs Lambert out – we've finished our little chat for now. There's no need to go round the back, you may use the front door. And thank you for coming, Mrs Lambert. I shall talk to my husband tonight, and I'll contact you to let you know whether you've been successful or not. However, we've already placed advertisements in the newspapers this weekend, and it's only right and proper to wait and see if we receive any other applications. But I promise that I won't keep you waiting too long.'

Hannah thanked Mrs Brentnall and said her goodbyes, and Ellen showed her to the front door. She had just left the property and started to walk back down the hill towards the town, when she saw a pony and trap trotting briskly up the hill. As it passed by, she spotted a gentleman in the back, apparently studying some papers. She looked round and saw it turn in through the gates that she had just come out of. Mr Brentnall, she assumed. And she wondered whether she would see him again. And she hoped and prayed that she would. For the only thing she wanted now was to become the cook and housekeeper at *Aysgarth Villa* on Glossop Road.

Almost two weeks had gone by, and Hannah had heard nothing. She had no idea how Mrs Brentnall would contact her. Would she write a letter, send Ellen with a message, or call herself? Hannah was beginning to think that she had not been successful and that she would have to start looking for work elsewhere, when a knock came at the door. Hurriedly, she ran to open it, and there stood Annie.

'Hello, Annie, come on in. I've just put the kettle on; would you like a cup?'

The two of them were soon busy having a natter, and Annie was keen to know whether Hannah had heard anything about the job.

'No, not yet. Maybe they've found someone with more experience, a bit older and with no children in tow.'

'Well, I don't want to raise any false hopes and you know I'm not one to gossip. But Albert dropped by this morning with a couple of barrels and he told Harry that Ellen had overheard the Brentnalls talking over breakfast yesterday, and from what she heard, she thinks they want you as their new cook. Now, how does that suit you?'

It suited Hannah very well. And it suited her even more so when, a few days later, she received a letter. The envelope was of the highest quality, as was the notepaper inside. Hannah didn't receive many letters, and the problem was that she could only read the odd word or two. She recognised her name, printed in capitals on the envelope, but the letter itself was written in a very fancy script. So, without delay, she put on her coat, dressed Eliza in hers, and hurried round to the Cutler's Arms, hoping that Harry would be in.

'I've just received this,' Hannah said, handing over the letter. 'I think it might be from Mrs Brentnall. Could you read it to me please, Harry?

'Of course,' he replied, as he put on a pair of wire-rimmed spectacles and began to read:

> *Aysgarth Villa*
> *Glossop Road*
> *Sheffield*
> *14th October 1841*
>
> *Dear Mrs Lambert*
>
> *I am very pleased to offer you the position of cook and housekeeper, as per the terms and conditions we discussed. Perhaps you would be good enough to confirm your acceptance, and advise when you will be able to take up the position, which we trust will be by the end of the month. In anticipation of a prompt and positive reply, I remain,*
>
> *Yours sincerely*
>
> *Frances Brentnall*

'I expect you'll be accepting the offer,' added Harry, as he handed the letter back to Hannah.

'Oh, yes! Will you help me to write a reply, Harry?'

'Of course I will. Now, Annie, I think it's time for a celebration. I'll go and fetch that bottle of sherry you've been keeping back for a special occasion!'

A fortnight later, having sold every bit of furniture and the other items she would no longer need, Hannah paid the landlord the rent still owing, packed into boxes those few treasured mementos she wished to keep, along with her and Eliza's clothes, and with the help of Albert and his brewery dray prepared to set off for her new home. And as she locked the door for the last time and climbed up onto the dray, she turned round and looked back, sadly, at the house she had lived in for most of her life, and she shed a tear as she remembered all the happy times she had spent there, and some not so happy ones, too.

She felt somewhat embarrassed, she and Eliza riding up front with Albert, with all their worldly goods stashed between the barrels of beer behind them. But she could easily cope with that. She didn't turn round again. She had made her decision; a new start and a new life. That was all that mattered now.

In next to no time, Hannah and Eliza had settled in at *Aysgarth Villa* and quickly got used to their new surroundings. They had a good-sized room on the top floor with views towards the town. Two beds, a washstand, a dressing table and wardrobe, a cupboard and chest of drawers, two armchairs, and a small table and chairs where they could sit and eat, or play games.

The work was not too hard, although the hours could sometimes be quite long, especially when the Brentnalls had guests for dinner. But Hannah didn't mind that, and whenever she had to work those extra hours Mr Brentnall would always bring a little gift back home the next day for Eliza, as a thank you. And on Saturday or Sunday Hannah would take Eliza and head off down to the town and visit some of her friends.

Mr Brentnall was in many ways a male version of his wife.

About the same age, equally tall and slim, with thin facial features and swept-back grey hair; neat in his appearance and very precise; and always courteous in his dealings with Hannah. He appeared to be very learned, and was always busy. Even in the evenings he could often be found in his study, reading through piles of documents which he had brought back from the office. But what pleased Hannah most was that both Mr and Mrs Brentnall seemed genuinely happy to have Eliza there, too, and she herself soon became friendly with them and was not in the least bit intimidated in their presence.

Hannah had decided to try and improve her reading and writing, and Mrs Brentnall was kind enough to spend some time helping her. And as Hannah's skills improved, she in turn was able to start teaching Eliza.

And so the months went by and Hannah got into the routine of her new life. But she never forgot Joseph or her mother, and every year on the anniversary of their deaths she would go to the cemetery and place fresh flowers on their graves. But her one regret was that she had never been able to find out anything about Joseph's background, and she knew that as Eliza grew up there was so very little she would be able to tell her daughter about the father she had only known for such a short time.

CHAPTER TWELVE

Farm hand to frame hand

On Monday 15th May 1843, the day after his fourteenth birthday, John Glover left his home in the tiny village of Barton-in-Fabis and set off on the six-mile walk to Nottingham. He was small for his age, a slender youth with jet-black hair and blue eyes which he had inherited from his maternal grandmother. But despite his size he was agile and strong, and had no difficulty carrying on his back the large bag into which his mother, Joan, had packed all his spare clothes, a purse with a little money, a copy of the Bible, and some bread and cheese and a bottle of cold tea for his dinner. For tomorrow, he was due to begin his apprenticeship as a framework knitter. John's father, Zachariah, was a farm labourer, and from a very young age John had assisted him with many of the jobs on the farm. And whilst this helped to toughen up the young lad, it also served to convince him that this was not the life he wanted for himself. Fortunately for him, both his mother and father agreed that his future prospects would be much enhanced were he to move to the town and learn a proper trade.

Zachariah had an old family friend, George Brown, who lived in Nottingham and was a master framework knitter, working at home. George's own family hailed from Barton-in-Fabis, and he still had relatives living there, so it was easy for Zachariah to make contact with him and ask whether he would be willing to take on his son as an apprentice. Although now approaching his sixtieth year, George readily agreed. Indeed, the arrangement suited him well, for a former apprentice of his had just left and he was now looking to replace him. So the indenture was drawn up and the date set for John to go and live with George and his wife, Nancy, at their house in Eland Street, not far from the canal wharves and a stone's throw from the castle.

George and Nancy now lived alone, their three daughters having long since married and moved away, while two sons had joined the army and were currently with their regiments overseas. But their other son, David, lived just around the corner in Mortimer Street, with his wife Margaret and their three children Matthew, Sarah and Thomas. George had always hoped that Matthew or Thomas might join him as an apprentice, but David was a skilled lace maker and wanted his sons to follow him in the lace trade, which he believed had a brighter future than the older trade of framework knitting. Matthew, the eldest, now thirteen, had recently started work in the same small factory where his father worked. Sarah, although only eleven, helped her mother around the house and was already accomplished in many of the skills that make a good housewife, whilst the youngest, Thomas, a lively and boisterous seven-year-old, did very little but annoy his sister, if she was to be believed.

And so, with the prospect of a new life beckoning, John Glover kissed his mother, bade her and his father goodbye and walked down the garden path to the lane. As he reached the gate he turned round to wave a last farewell, only to see his mother wiping a tear from her eye. He knew that she was sad to see him leave, for he was the youngest of five children, and all the others had already left home.

'Don't fret, ma. I'm only going to Nottingham, not to the ends of the earth. You can come and see me next time you go to the market, and I'm sure I'll be back at Christmas for a day or two.'

And so he set out through the village. Ignoring the lane to Clifton, he took a short cut through the fields until he reached Clifton Grove, where he had often come with his parents and brothers and sisters for a picnic on a summer's day. This long, wide avenue of oak, elm and beech trees was a local beauty spot, a regular haunt for the inhabitants of Nottingham, especially on Sundays. Then, for a few precious hours, they could forget work and escape the cramped, dirty and smelly streets and enjoy the purer, healthier and pleasanter surroundings it afforded. The path through the grove stretched for over a mile, skirting the village of Clifton, whilst below and to the left flowed the River Trent, running a little faster than usual that day following late spring rain. In some places there was an almost sheer drop to the water below and John was careful not to venture too close, for he knew that others sometimes did that with fatal results, occasionally self-inflicted. As he walked on, the noonday sun shone through the tall branches, casting thin shadows across the path, and on either side wild flowers were beginning to blanket the ground in a patchwork of colour.

Leaving the grove behind, he soon reached the village of Wilford, where he strolled on down the main street, past its rows of thatched cottages and old riverside inn, until he reached the ferry which would take him across the Trent to Nottingham. He had used this ferry on a number of occasions when travelling to the market with his mother or father, but he was always wary of it. For although the river was comparatively shallow at this point, the currents could be treacherous, especially if it was running high after heavy rain. And then, what would normally be a simple journey over some forty yards of familiar water could turn into a breathtaking half-hour's battle for survival against the forces of nature.

And to make matters worse, John had always had a fear of water and of drowning. He had a recurring nightmare of being locked in a room, unable to escape, as floodwaters rushed in and rose up all around him. Then, just as the waters were about to engulf him, he would suddenly wake up and sit bolt upright in his bed, shaking from head to foot. And then, just as quickly, he would lie back down again, thankful in the knowledge that it was but a dream. Where this fear came from, and what prompted this nightmare, he did not know. Maybe it was hearing about those unfortunate wretches who had lost their lives whilst using this ferry, for some had. Only six years earlier, on a stormy January night, the boat had been swept against the chain that was used to haul it across the river, and which lay just below the surface. All five occupants had been thrown overboard; one man had drowned, the other four managing somehow to struggle through the icy water and reach the shore. They were lucky, thought John. For he remembered his own grandfather telling him of another such catastrophe many years before, when six men and women had lost their lives under similar circumstances.

And so it was with a degree of trepidation that he stepped off the landing stage and into the small, open boat along with five other travellers. The ferryman skilfully steered the boat, using a long pole, while his assistant laboriously turned the handle of a winch connected to the chain, and slowly the craft inched its way across. Fortunately, the wind was blowing no more than a gentle breeze, although the river was running a little fast, but John was mightily thankful when the opposite side was reached in safety. It had cost him a halfpenny, but had saved him a walk of almost four miles to Trent Bridge and down the Flood Road into the town. But had the wind been stronger, or the river running even faster, he would gladly have walked those four miles and saved his halfpenny fare.

As he stepped out once more onto dry land he looked ahead of him. Nearly a mile away, beyond the railway and the canal, was the town of Nottingham, his home-to-be for the next seven years. This dense mass of buildings, clustered tightly together within the town's ancient boundaries, rose upwards on a sandstone escarpment, a stark contrast with the lush, green, open meadows before him where cattle and sheep grazed. Adjacent to the landing stage were some benches where passengers could sit whilst waiting for the ferry, so he sat down, and opening his bag he took out the bread and cheese that his mother had packed for his dinner and hungrily consumed every last morsel, washing it down with the cold tea. His hunger and thirst assuaged, he set off along the path towards the town. Smoke drifted lazily from the many chimneys, and as he drew closer he began to both hear and smell those telltale signs, confirming what he already knew – that this was indeed a growing industrial town.

To the left, high on its bare sandstone rock, stood the empty shell of Nottingham Castle, now just a blackened ruin since being torched by rioters some twelve years before, their anger triggered by the refusal of the House of Lords to pass the Reform Bill and their pent-up fury vented against the castle's owner, that arch opponent of parliamentary reform, the Duke of Newcastle. The bill did become law the following year, but in a deliberate fit of pique the duke simply abandoned his castle, leaving it as a stark reminder to the citizens of their handiwork that fateful October night in 1831.

And to the right, another prominent building pointing towards the heavens, but this one a far more reassuring sight; the square tower of St. Mary's Church rising high above every other building in the town, as it had done for over three hundred years.

John followed the well-worn path, admiring the profusion of white, yellow and purple crocuses which carpeted much of the meadow through which he walked. Just like Clifton Grove, this was another popular spot regularly frequented by the townsfolk, especially those who weren't inclined to risk the ferry or who couldn't afford the fare.

The town had now almost been reached, and the path was rapidly losing its rural appearance, becoming wider as it came to the point where it crossed the railway line. As John approached, a man emerged from a wooden hut alongside the tracks to close the gates across the lane. No sooner had he completed his task, when John heard the unmistakable sound of a train approaching in the distance. He was familiar with this sound, for his childhood home was about a mile as the crow flies from the railway line on the far side of the river, and whenever the wind blew from the north, trains passing on their way to or from Derby or Leicester could clearly be heard, if not seen.

A rhythmical clattering of iron wheels on iron rails, the steady *whoosh, whoosh* of escaping steam and a thin rising trail of smoke indicated the train's approach. And then it appeared, gliding forwards as it slowed down and entered the station, a little way to the right of the crossing.

Behind the engine stretched a train of a dozen coaches, four of them being first class and of a most luxurious and superior quality, larger but not dissimilar in design to the stagecoaches which only a few years before had been such a common sight on the roads. Five were for second-class passengers, and whilst fitted with roofs had no windows, just low wooden sides about three feet high, and wooden seats. The final three were third class, without even the benefit of roofs, thus being totally open to the elements, and more like goods wagons with wooden benches.

John stood gazing at the train as it passed by. The engine had four large driving wheels and was finished in shiny black with gleaming brass and copper fittings, and carried the name *Bloodhound* in red letters on a brass plate fixed to the side of the wooden-lagged boiler. Both the first-class and second-class coaches had their upper halves painted black and the lower halves green, lined out in red, whilst the third-class carriages were red with black lining. He had only been close to a passing train a couple of times before, but the experience both fascinated and excited him, and he wondered whether he would ever have the opportunity to take a ride on one himself.

As soon as the train had gone by, the crossing keeper emerged once more from his hut and opened the gates. John walked across the tracks and within a dozen yards or so, a rickety wooden bridge took the lane over the tiny Tinker's Leen, a poor excuse for a river compared with the mighty Trent, thought John, but this was followed almost immediately by a larger, stone bridge which carried the lane across the canal. In less than five minutes John had left the quiet tranquillity of the meadows and was now entering this noisy, bustling town. He stopped on the canal bridge and peered over the left-hand side into the inky black water below, where two boats, breasted together and fully loaded with coal, were slowly descending in a lock as the water level dropped. The towrope lay limp and loose, one end fastened to one of the boats, the other to the harness of a horse which stood silent and motionless by the lock side, its head buried deep in bag of oats as it waited for a signal from the boatman to move on.

In both directions, as far as the eye could see, the town-side bank of the canal was lined with wharves and warehouses. A number of side cuts led off from the canal, where boats were tied up whilst they were loaded or unloaded. Labourers scurried back and forth, pushing barrows and carrying bales and boxes to and from waiting carts or to be stored in the warehouses; others were busy shovelling coal from boats into great heaps alongside – coal mined in the local pits a few miles to the north, and now waiting to be taken away to feed the ever-hungry factory engines, or keep the townsfolk warm on a cold night.

As he was taking in the scene, the boatman and a young lad began to heave open the massive wooden lock gates, and at a shouted signal, to which it was clearly well accustomed, the horse dutifully ceased its repast and gently walked on, until the towrope became taut. Then, digging in its heels and powerfully straining every muscle, it slowly began to ease the two boats, with their forty tons of coal, out of the lock and towards a nearby coal wharf. John crossed to the other side of the bridge, and noticed another horse a little way along the cinder-covered towpath, waiting patiently to haul a pair of empty boats into the lock, destined no doubt for the Erewash Valley mines and another load of coal.

But duty called, so tearing himself away, John walked on a short distance and turned left into Navigation Row, right into Castle Road then right again into Isabella Street. Eland Street lay at the far end of Isabella Street, and John knew exactly which house it was, as he'd been there twice before with his father when they came to make the arrangements for his apprenticeship. George and Nancy Brown lived near the top on the right, close to the junction with Mortimer Street.

All the houses hereabouts were built of brick, three or four storeys high, and most of them constructed back-to-back with another matching terrace of houses, so that each house had only one door, fronting either onto the street or into a central courtyard. These courtyards contained communal water pumps and privies, since none of the properties was provided with such conveniences, and access to the courts for those whose houses had doors to the street was by narrow alleys, more like tunnels, linking the street to the court. This could be an irksome journey should water be required, or an urgent call of nature need attending to, especially on a freezing winter night, along an unlit street and through an even darker alleyway. Because of this, and in order to avoid such unwelcome night-time forays, it was usual for householders to maintain a good supply of water in buckets, whilst the sellers of chamber pots, or guzzunders as they were commonly called, never seemed to suffer from a downturn in trade.

John climbed the two steps to the front door and knocked loudly.

After a short wait he heard footsteps approaching and the door was opened by a petite but bonny woman with a kind round face, short, brown hair and brown eyes. 'Ah, John, you're here at last. Come on in; we've been expecting you.' He followed her into the tiny hallway with the stairs directly ahead, and a door on the left. Nancy opened this door and took him into the living room. 'Sit yourself down and I'll go and fetch George; he's up in the workshop.' Nancy left the room, and John heard her as she climbed the wooden stairs, calling to her husband as she went.

The room in which he was now seated, indeed the only downstairs room, was oblong and occupied the whole depth of the house. The floor was of wood, with rag rugs scattered around, and some framed pictures and a sampler hanging on the walls. To the front was the one and only window, looking out into the street. A pine table, scrubbed almost white, and four chairs occupied the middle of the room, whilst two armchairs, which seemed to have seen better days, stood one on either side of the fireplace. This was the most striking feature in the room. It consisted of a large cast-iron cooking range with an open fire to the right and two small ovens to the left, heated directly by the fire. Above the top oven was a space for standing pots and pans and keeping food warm, whilst above the fire was a horizontal bar to which were attached hooks of differing lengths from which pots could be suspended whilst cooking. A soot-blackened iron kettle hung from one of these hooks, sizzling and whistling softly to itself, whilst on each side of the range were various cooking utensils – ladles, spoons and a toasting fork; and in the hearth below, a variety of fire irons. Above the range was a deep mantelpiece, in the centre of which stood a clock in a plain but highly polished oak case, quietly ticking away the minutes.

The range was the engine room of the house, where water was heated and all the cooking done. Although it was a warm spring day, a welcoming fire burned, and John was soon to learn that whatever the month, whatever the weather, his first job of the day was to clear out the ashes from the grate, and lay and light the fire.

On the wall opposite the fireplace stood an old oak dresser, with open shelves above and drawers and cupboards below, and facing the window, a curtain suspended from a pole near the ceiling served to separate the living area from a tiny kitchen-cum-scullery. The curtain could be pulled back to provide some natural light to this part of the room, which contained a cupboard in one corner, some shelves holding pots, pans and crockery, and a stone sink with four buckets underneath, each full of water.

It was a sunny afternoon with barely a cloud in the sky, yet the living room seemed somewhat gloomy, for the narrow streets and surrounding tall buildings shielded the sun, casting long shadows and preventing much light from penetrating the room. John wondered what it must be like once the sun went down. A gas company had been established in the town in 1817, but the poorer areas, such as this, were not yet connected. Once it turned dark, other than the glow from the fire, oil lamps and candles provided the only light, and John noticed some of these standing on the mantelpiece and the dresser. Although John's boyhood home at Barton-in-Fabis was only a humble cottage, it did at least have two separate rooms downstairs, each with windows which not only admitted light but could be opened on warm days to let in the fresh air. Things were different here, thought John, not that there was much fresh air to let in.

He looked around him at this simply furnished but homely room, where he would be spending much of the next seven years. The Browns were clearly not rich, in fact just the opposite, as was proved by the sparse and modest furnishings, but the room was clean and tidy. He went up to the sampler on the wall and examined it closely. There was a similar one hanging on a wall back home, completed by his own mother when she was a girl, and she had used it to teach him his letters and numbers. There was no school in his village, but using the sampler and a copy of the Bible, he had learned to read and write. Around the borders ran a decorative and elaborate pattern containing little figures and motifs, whilst the centre contained rows consisting of the letters of the alphabet, both large and small, and the numbers from one to ten. Below these were the words *Worked by Nancy Simpkins in the ninth year of her age, 1795.*

Nancy must be very skilled in the art of needlework to have achieved that standard by the age of nine, he considered. He was still examining it, when the door opened and in she walked, followed by George. 'Hello John,' he exclaimed, smiling broadly and offering his hand, 'glad you've arrived safely. I see you're examining Nancy's handiwork. Her mother taught her well, didn't she? Now, Nancy's going to make a pot of tea, and then we'll go upstairs and you can see where you'll be working and sleeping.'

George was almost sixty years old, of medium height but stocky in build. He still had a good head of hair, most of it now turning white, and his bright hazel eyes and almost permanent smile radiated a sense of bonhomie to all who met him.

After a cup of tea, and some scones that Nancy had baked earlier, John was taken on a tour of the rest of the house. On the first and second floors was a bedroom. In most of the houses, each bedroom would have been shared by a large number of people. Many families had a lot of children, who had to share not only the same room, but also the same bed, assuming the family could afford a bed; otherwise it would have been a straw-filled mattress on the floor. George and Nancy had had six children, and John tried to imagine how they would all have fitted into such a small space. But now they had all left, so George and Nancy had a bedroom to themselves, and John, too, the luxury of a room all to himself. It was certainly large enough for one, although part of it had been turned into a storage area for some of the materials and equipment used in the workshop above. There was a single bed, a wooden chair, a chest of drawers on top of which stood a salt-glazed pottery bowl in which to wash, and two shelves with hooks underneath on which to hang a coat or other clothes.

From the second floor another short flight of stairs led to the top storey of the house, where the room had one large window so as to admit as much light as possible. John had noticed that most of the houses in the neighbouring streets were similarly constructed, being designed to house stocking frames. This was a job which needed plenty of light, so that the knitters could see clearly when setting up the machines with the delicate cotton or silk threads, and whilst undertaking this most intricate and demanding work. There were two stocking frames, one of which had not been used for several months since George's previous assistant had left.

To begin with, George described to John the way the trade was organised. He explained that he did not own the frames, but rented them from a hosier, who also supplied the raw material and paid for the completed items, most of which were hose, but also shawls and other knitted garments. At first, John merely helped around the house and in the workshop; bringing in water from the courtyard; clearing out the grate and lighting the fire each morning; sweeping up in the workshop and keeping the frames clean; collecting the cotton from the hosier and delivering the finished products; running errands and generally getting to know the others in the trade with whom George dealt. And then George began to teach John how to use the frame, how to set it up and make plain pieces of material.

As the months went by, John slowly began to learn all the little things he needed to know, and gradually he became more skilful and adept at using the frame. But it was not easy and there was much to learn, especially when it came to producing the most complex patterns.

John quickly made new friends, and within a week or two he had almost as many here in Nottingham as he had back in his home village. The first were George's three grandchildren, who lived just round the corner in Mortimer Street. They often called to see their grandparents, and on the very day John arrived they came scampering round, curious to meet their grandfather's new apprentice.

Matthew was the eldest, nearly a year younger than John, and the two lads quickly became good friends. Matthew's younger brother was Thomas, only seven, and a bundle of energy, although at times intensely irritating to Matthew and John. He wanted to tag along in whatever they did and wherever they went, but they regarded him as too young to join them on their explorations of the town's hidden places – the numerous sandstone caves for which Nottingham was famed and to which they could sometimes find access; and the rabbit warren of courts and alleys for which many of the less desirable areas were notorious, and which became a never-ending source of fascination, and sometimes of dread, for the lads. On these expeditions they were invariably joined by another of Matthew's pals, James Marshall, the son of a blacksmith who lived in nearby Isabella Street and who soon became a close friend to John. He was about the same age, a ginger-haired youth of forceful personality who had no fear of anyone or anything, and was always the ringleader whenever it came to doing something different or ferreting out a new place to explore.

The third of George and Nancy's grandchildren, and secretly their favourite, was the youngest – Sarah. Although she was only ten when John first arrived in Nottingham, he was immediately struck by her pretty, smiling face, her dark-brown eyes and waist-length, chestnut-brown hair, and her kind and loving nature with never a bad word for anyone. And she, too, took a shine to the new arrival, this blue-eyed country boy with his fine looks and tousled jet-black hair.

John gradually settled into the routine of work, and within a few months began to feel that he was at last beginning to achieve his aim of becoming a framework knitter, although he knew he had many years hard work ahead of him before he became truly skilled.

When he had first arrived he had felt a little homesick, but both his working hours and his free time were so full that these longings soon faded. But he did miss his parents, so he was delighted when, towards the end of September, he received a letter from his mother telling him that she and Zachariah would be coming to Nottingham on the 7th October, the final Saturday of the annual Goose Fair, and that they would come straight to the house as soon as they arrived. Saturday was usually a normal working day, at least until noon, but when John announced that his parents were coming over, and as it was the last day of the fair, George agreed that there would be no work that day. As the day approached, John looked forward eagerly to their visit, and they must have left home quite early for it was just gone nine when there came a knock at the door. He peered through the window, and seeing his mother and father on the doorstep he rushed to let them in, and before long they were all enjoying a cup of tea and some of Nancy's scones.

'Well, John, you do seem to have grown since you left home,' observed his mother. 'Nancy's obviously feeding you well – it must be all these delicious scones!'

'That and all the hard work he's been putting in,' replied Nancy, 'running up and down the stairs and working at the frame. And he helps me round the house with any heavy work. He's a good lad.'

After a long chat and another cup of tea, they decided it was time to head down to the Market Place and see what delights the fair had to offer. John had already made a couple of visits that week, in the evenings after work, but it was several years since Joan and Zachariah had been to the fair. John had already told Matthew that his parents were coming over for the day, so as Joan and Nancy cleared away the teacups, and George and Zachariah sat reminiscing and enjoying a smoke, John ran round to Mortimer Street to let him know what was happening. The Goose Fair was such an important event in the calendar that some factories closed on the final Saturday to allow their workers to attend. The lace factory where Matthew and his father worked was one of these, so that the whole family was able to go along, and five minutes later they were all on their way round to Eland Street, and were soon trooping off down Castle Gate towards the town centre.

There was a larger than usual gathering in the Market Place, for the fair was always a big attraction and drew in crowds from all the nearby villages. For hundreds of years there had been an autumn fair, the biggest of the year, when country folk and farmers would come to the town to sell their supplies of seasonal fruit and vegetables, cheeses and cured hams. And whilst there, they would stock up for the winter with all those items not always available at other times of the year.

Many stalls encircled the Market Place and lined most of the adjacent streets. There were cutlers from Sheffield with knives and scissors, scythes and sickles; potters from Staffordshire; shoemakers from Northampton and hatters from Luton; cloth merchants from Leeds and Halifax and linen weavers from Barnsley; and ladies from Grantham with their gingerbread and sweetmeats. And, of course, geese, fattened up and ready for the oven, driven from as far away as Norfolk.

But for many, it was the sideshows and other attractions that were the main draw. And for others the opportunity to get even drunker than usual, for the numerous inns and taverns were open continuously and always did a roaring trade. The variety of entertainers and showmen was a wonder to behold. There were Punch and Judy men, freak shows and merry-go-rounds, actors and comedians, strollers and singers, dancers, jugglers and magicians; and Wombwells were always there, with their Wild Beast Show. All these, and more, vying with each other for the townsfolk's attention and money.

It was later that afternoon, after several happy but exhausting hours, that they made their way slowly back to Eland Street, well fed and watered and a few shillings lighter. Joan and Zachariah didn't stay much longer, as they wanted to make sure they reached home before darkness set in. John walked with them as far as the ferry to see them aboard and on their way, and waited until it had reached the far shore and they had disembarked safely. His mother had said they would try and visit him again before the year was out, if they could, but in any case looked forward to him coming home for a day or two at Christmas.

John didn't really expect to see his mother and father again until Christmas, and was surprised when he heard from them in November that they would be visiting Nottingham again on Monday 4th December. For it had been announced that Her Majesty, Queen Victoria, accompanied by Prince Albert, would be travelling to Nottingham by train on their way from Chatsworth House in Derbyshire to Belvoir Castle. Joan had persuaded Zachariah to take her to Nottingham to witness this momentous event. The Queen had never visited the town before and Joan could not remember any previous time in her life when a ruling monarch had done so. She had heard that the old King's widow, the Dowager Queen Adelaide, had twice, in recent years, passed through but this, she had told Zachariah, was different, and she fully intended to be there to witness it. She asked John to meet them at the ferry at Wilford, if he could be excused work that morning. Nancy persuaded George to agree to this, because she too wished to see the Queen and wanted George to accompany her.

In the weeks leading up to the royal visit there was intense activity in the town, especially close to the railway station, where a number of temporary wooden stands were erected, so that those prepared to pay the appropriate sum could avail themselves of a better view of Their Majesties as they arrived and made their way through the town. But the biggest single undertaking required the drafting in of scores of workmen to construct a new road from near the station entrance in Carrington Street, through the West Croft to the Flood Road. This was to be used by the royal party on its journey to Belvoir, thus avoiding the usual route along Canal Street and Leen Side, through an area constituting some of the worst slums of any town in the land. And in honour of the visit, the corporation announced that this new road would henceforth be known as Queen's Road.

The appointed day turned out to be dry and sunny, and straight after breakfast John walked down through the meadows to the ferry. As he approached the railway he observed last minute preparations for the event being made. In the station yard, on each side of the line, and on nearby roads, the large wooden stands were hurriedly being adorned with bunting and flags, and already crowds had started to gather. John hurried on, anxious to arrive at the ferry by nine o'clock as his mother had requested. The ferry had just arrived, full to bursting, and the passengers were beginning to disembark. His parents were not amongst them, but he could see another large crowd on the far shore, waiting for the next crossing. Obviously, Joan and Zachariah were not the only ones wishing to come and view this royal spectacle.

Once everyone had disembarked the ferry set off across the river, this time carrying only a couple of passengers, but before long it was full again and heading back towards him. He watched, feeling a little anxious as it cast off, for there were clearly more than normal aboard, but it was a calm morning with only a light breeze. As it neared the landing stage he spotted his mother and father, waving to him from the boat. They were soon ashore, and without delay the three of them set off along the path towards the town.

It didn't take them long to reach the railway, and whilst there was over an hour until the royal train was due to arrive, Joan was keen to find a place with a good view. Zachariah made enquiries and established that there were some seats left in one of the stands for the princely sum of two shillings each. He considered this a large sum to pay, but Joan was insistent that they should take the seats whilst they were still available. She told him that such an occasion might never occur again in their lifetimes, and that she had saved some money for this day and was not going to miss any of it. And so Zachariah, who over many years of married life had learned that it was unwise to argue with his wife when she was in such a determined mood, reluctantly untied the cord on a leather money bag and handed over the six shillings, and they quickly made their way to three empty seats towards the rear of the stand. Six shillings, he thought to himself. That would have been a month's wages for him when he was a boy!

Joan looked around in wonder at the scene that surrounded them. Never in her life had she witnessed such a display of patriotic fervour. The stand was now almost full, and nearer to the station platform was another, much grander stand with more comfortable seats and a better view of the proceedings to come. This was reserved for special guests, the Lord Lieutenant of the County, the mayor and magistrates, the directors of the railway company and other dignitaries. Who, Zachariah remarked dryly to his wife, and with a degree of cynicism, presumably did not have pay two shillings each for their seats, and who, no doubt, would also be provided later on with a sumptuous feast at no cost to themselves.

Everywhere were flags, bunting and decorations, and the crowds continued to grow, filling every seat and every possible vantage point. Suddenly, at twenty past eleven, a royal salute from guns placed high upon the castle rock indicated that the train had been spotted in the distance. And then, as the Inniskillen Dragoons began to play the national anthem and a detachment of the 64th Foot presented arms, the train slowly passed by and entered the station to the accompaniment of enthusiastic cheers, the engine and royal carriages resplendent and glistening in the midday sun. John had never seen such a splendid carriage as that in which Queen Victoria and Prince Albert were travelling. The train came to a halt, and from their seats they watched as Their Majesties stepped out onto the crimson-carpeted platform, to be greeted by the Earl of Scarborough, the Lord Lieutenant, who then conducted them along the platform towards the station entrance. Soon they were out of sight, and there was an immediate rush as the throng left the stand to hurry round to Carrington Street to try and see the royal couple as they continued their journey by road. Here, directly outside the station entrance, a temporary porte-cochere had been erected, underneath which stood the carriage that would convey them to Belvoir Castle.

John and his parents got round to the front of the station just in time to see the carriage setting off towards the new road. The route was lined not only with cheering crowds, but also soldiers from the Inniskillen Dragoons, the South Nottinghamshire Yeomanry and the Sherwood Rangers, who guarded the road for some distance. Nine triumphal arches had been provided specially for the occasion, three on the new Queen's Road, three on the Flood Road and three at Trent Bridge. Here, next to the Town Arms, the wherry *Nautilus* had been suspended over the road, its crew inside in full naval costume, to salute the Queen as she passed underneath and crossed the river on her way to Belvoir.

An hour later and the crowds having dispersed, the three of them made their way back to Eland Street. Joan had only managed to get a brief glimpse of Her Majesty, but was not disappointed. She had come to see the Queen and her ambition had been realised. Nancy explained that she and George had found a spot close to the station entrance, from where they had seen the royal couple emerge and climb aboard the carriage. Nancy put the kettle on the fire to make a brew and she and Joan began to swap stories and talk excitedly about what they had witnessed. Meanwhile, George, Zachariah and John, much as they had enjoyed the morning's spectacle, but being somewhat less keen than their womenfolk to relive it all again over a cup of tea, decided to toast the Queen's health in something a little stronger and announced that they were going to walk round the corner to the Hanging Gate.

'Don't be long, Zach,' said Joan to her husband as the men got up to leave, 'we must try and get back home before it gets too dark. You know how quickly the nights draw in at this time of the year.'

'No dear, we won't be long. We'll be back by three.'

'Well, make sure you are. And don't you go letting John have too much to drink, he's only fourteen.'

'Don't fuss, ma, I'll be fine,' John assured his mother.

'I certainly hope you will be. But you know that apprentices aren't supposed to frequent pubs and taverns.'

'Oh, I think we can make an exception,' added George, winking at John, 'seeing as it's a special occasion and I'll be there to keep an eye on him.'

By four o'clock, just as it was getting dark, John had walked with his mother and father down to the river, seen them safely onto the ferry, and had arrived back in Eland Street.

'They got the ferry all right did they, John?' enquired Nancy, as she hung a pot of stew over the fire to warm up.

'Yes, but it was busy; there were a lot of other people from Clifton and Barton who'd come over to see the Queen. And it'll be dark before they get back home, but they've got company and they know the way well enough, so they'll come to no harm.'

Nearly three weeks later, having finished work at midday on a Saturday, John set off on the very same journey and arrived at his home in Barton as dusk was beginning to fall. The following Monday was Christmas Day, and George had given John two days holiday. He would have to be back in Nottingham on Wednesday, but for now he had three whole days to spend with his parents and meet up with some of his friends in the village whom he hadn't seen since he left there in May that year. On Christmas Day two older brothers, who lived not far away, came over with their wives and children. For the rest of that day, life in the Glover household was much as it used to be years before – a house full of boisterous children with boundless energy, laughing and playing noisily together.

Once they had left to return home, Joan and Zachariah sat by the fire. 'What are you thinking about?' asked Zachariah, looking across at Joan, who was staring thoughtfully into the flickering flames.

'I was wondering which I prefer; having our kids and grandkids here, with all the noise and mayhem that causes, or the peace and quiet now that they've left. And when John goes back to Nottingham on Wednesday morning, it'll be just you and me again, Zach.'

'That's easy, my dear. They can come visiting whenever they want; they all know that. But give me the peace and quiet anytime,' he replied as he settled back in his chair, folded his arms across his chest, and closing his eyes, gently began to snore.

CHAPTER THIRTEEN

A razor a rope and a rumpus

The short Christmas holiday was soon over and John returned to Nottingham to continue his apprenticeship. It didn't take him long to get back into the swing of things and as time went by he became more adept at working at his frame. Most weeks he would have to work six full days, with just Sunday off, but sometimes, when they weren't so busy, or if George was feeling particularly generous, he would close the workroom at midday on Saturday and they would both have an extra half-day off. On these occasions, George and Nancy would invariably head off into the town, Nancy to do a bit of shopping while George would meet up with some friends for a pint or two, and they would return a few hours later, George acting as porter, laden down with the items Nancy had purchased. But for John, a free afternoon meant meeting up with Matthew and James, who had every Saturday afternoon off, and the three of them would often set out, seeking amusement or adventure. The castle, still an empty, burned-out shell, was one of their favourite haunts whenever they were able to sneak past the caretaker and gain entrance to the grounds, and fishing down by Trent Bridge was another of their regular pastimes, when they would first call at Walter Wells's fishing tackle shop in Sussex Street to pick up a bag of bait before heading off down to the river.

One warm sunny Saturday in May, straight after breakfast, George declared they would be finishing at midday, and as soon as they had shut the workshop door John ran round to Mortimer Street, where he found Matthew and James sitting lazily on the doorstep, whittling sticks.

'Ey up, John. Got the afternoon off?' asked Matthew.

'Yes. What are you two up to?'

'Nothing much. We're a bit bored. What do you fancy doing? Got any ideas?'

'I know,' said James all of a sudden, as if John's unexpected arrival had stirred him into action. 'Let's go and catch some rabbits. I've got some wire snares; they're in dad's workshop. We'll go up to Colwick Woods, I've heard it's full of the little buggers. We can do a spot of bird-nesting as well while we're there. Come on, it's only a couple of miles; we'll soon be there and with a bit of luck we'll be having rabbit stew tonight.'

Without further ado the three lads set off, and having picked up the snares from the workshop, which was down an alley at the end of Isabella Street, at the back of the waterworks, they carried on along Canal Street and Leen Side. They soon reached Bridge Street, then into Plumptre Square and along Fisher Gate, Willoughby Row and Pennyfoot Stile, crossing over the little Beck Burn by a rickety wooden causeway. They were nearly out of the town now and on the road towards Sneinton, but all around there were signs of building work, with new roads being laid out and houses already being erected to accommodate the growing population. They took the lane leading to Colwick and almost immediately the 'Hermitage' came into view, a peculiar row of cottages built within a large outcrop of sandstone rock, with doors and windows cut out of the front of what was, in effect, an enormous man-made cave. Passing this local curiosity, they were soon in the countryside, and before long the woods appeared on their left and they took the path leading up to them from the lane.

As it was a Saturday the lads fully expected plenty of other people to be about, for this was a pleasant spot, often frequented by folk relaxing in their spare time. But they were not prepared for what they were about to see. They had no sooner entered the woods and were strolling along the path, looking for likely places to set their snares, when they suddenly noticed ahead a large group of people, seemingly congregated in one particular area. Some were collecting handfuls of grass from the ground, others cutting bits of bark or small branches from trees and hedges.

'I wonder what's going on here?' exclaimed Matthew.

'I'll soon find out,' said James, as he strode off at a pace in their direction. 'What's all this about, then? What are you all doing?' he asked, of anyone who might answer.

'We're getting souvenirs,' replied a small thin woman accompanied by three or four ragged-looking children.

'Souvenirs? Why? What for?'

'You mean you don't know?' she continued. 'This is where he did it, the very place!'

'Where who did what? What are you talking about?'

By now, John and Matthew had joined James, and all three listened in awe as the woman, clearly not one to keep a good story to herself, gave them a blow-by-blow account of the horrific event.

'Saville; this is where he done 'em in, all of 'em, 'is wife and kids, cut their throats he did. Last Tuesday they reckon, but they didn't find the bodies till Thursday. Poor little mites. All three of 'em lying 'ere on the ground, a boy and two girls, 'uddled together and the mother over there, just behind that bush,' she added, pointing to a spot a few yards away. 'Old John Swinscoe from Carlton found 'em when he were out walking wi' his lad, and he went and fetched the constable from Colwick. My Fred knows 'im and got all the gory details. The razor was still in 'er hand, but the constable ses he thinks it were put there by Saville to make out it were 'er what dun it. Anyroad, they've got 'im locked up now and everyone reckons he's the guilty one. Be all accounts, he's a bad lot and bin in trouble no end o' times. But he'll swing fer this one, you mark my words, young un. But, 'ow come you ain't 'eard owt before now? Where you bin fer the last day or two? Everyone round 'ere knows about it and they're all wanting souvenirs.'

And it was true; none of the lads had heard anything about the murders. That sort of news always travels fast, but this had obviously passed them by. Now, though, it was the only subject on their lips, and all thoughts of bird-nesting or rabbit-snaring had simply been forgotten. They hung around for a bit longer, joining the crowd of morbid bystanders and listening to ever more exaggerated accounts of what was supposed to have happened, much of it, of course, pure speculation. But the lads were itching to get home and tell everyone the lurid tale of the bodies in Colwick Woods, so they hurried back as quickly as they could. James dropped his snares back in his father's workshop, then it was round to Eland Street, and just as they turned the corner they saw George and Nancy coming the other way. They followed them into the house, bursting to give them the news, but it soon became apparent that by now the story was all over the town. George and Nancy had been there for most of the afternoon, and in every pub and at every stall in the Market Place, there was only one topic of conversation.

Over the next few weeks the details of what had happened became clearer, and every Saturday Nancy would buy a copy of the one of the weekly newspapers, each of which carried lengthy reports of the incident. And after their supper, whilst George and John sat in stunned silence, she would read aloud the latest news about one of the most sensational crimes ever to have taken place locally.

The accused, who was now languishing in the town gaol awaiting trial, was William Saville, a thirty-two-year-old man who hailed originally from Arnold, some three miles north of Nottingham, but who had drifted from place to place, never settling for very long in any particular location. According to the reports, he had himself suffered greatly as a child. His mother had died when he was only about two years old, and his father, a framework knitter and habitual drunk, would often abandon William and his two brothers for days on end while he went to Nottingham to spend all his wages on alcohol and debauchery. It was only the kindness of neighbours who had kept the three boys from an early grave, and William had therefore grown up in ignorance of any knowledge or understanding of the finer virtues of mankind, nor of the intellectual culture which even the most humble person can aspire to.

Some years before, Saville had met a young woman named Ann Ward, a native of Lincolnshire, who already had a child by a man she had met soon after moving to Nottingham, but who had abandoned her as soon as he learned of her condition. William and Ann had subsequently married, and despite two more children being born,

William, just like his father before him, cared little for his family, often disappearing for weeks at a time. In January of that year, 1844, he deserted them yet again, and they were forced to go into the workhouse. Meanwhile, William found work and lodgings in another part of the town, passing himself off as a single man, and whilst there he met a virtuous young woman to whom he made numerous offers of marriage, all of which she sensibly rebuffed.

Towards the end of May, Ann Saville and her three children left the workhouse and went to stay with friends, a Mr and Mrs Wardle in Wood Street. Mr Wardle had found out where William was living and went with Ann to confront him. He eventually agreed to come to Wood Street the next day, saying he would take Ann and the children to a relative's house at Carlton, a village a few miles away, but Ann confided to Mrs Wardle that as long as she had known William, he had never spoken of any relatives living there. He duly arrived the next morning, and took his family with him. But in the early afternoon he returned alone to the Wardle's house, asking if they had seen Ann and the children, claiming that they had only gone a short distance when he and his wife had had an argument and she had stormed off. He returned to the house again later that evening, telling Mrs Wardle he thought his wife had done away with herself and the children. But Mrs Wardle told William she did not believe him, and becoming very suspicious as to his behaviour she sent for a policeman who took him into custody.

The next day he was questioned at length by the police, and told them the same story he had told Mrs Wardle. In his possession were found some items that Ann's sister had given to her when she came out of the workhouse. Some spots of blood were also found on his trousers, and whilst he was being questioned, news arrived that the bodies of a woman and three children had been found in Colwick Woods, all with their throats cut.

An inquest was immediately arranged, at which a number of witnesses swore to having seen William, Ann and the three children on the road between Nottingham and Colwick, close to where the bodies were later discovered in the woods. They had been found by a man named John Swinscoe, who was out walking with his son. The woman's body was a few yards away from those of the children, and there were clear signs that she had been dragged along the ground to where her lifeless body lay, her left hand holding a bloodstained razor. But this fact did not sway the jury, and after three days they returned a verdict of murder against William Saville, and he was committed for trial at the next assizes.

These were not due to be held until the end of July, and throughout the ensuing two months speculation in the town was rife about the outcome. In most people's minds, the accused man was guilty and there was little in the way of sympathy for him.

At last the day of the trial arrived, Saturday 27th, and at the Shire Hall, Lord Chief Justice Denman presided. There was plenty of circumstantial evidence, such as the razor found in Ann Saville's hand, which was identified as belonging to William, but the nature of her injuries meant she could not have cut her own throat. There was no actual witness to prove that it was he who had committed the murders, yet one damning piece of evidence was enough to seal his fate – a confession he was alleged to have made whilst being held at the police station, and overheard by two witnesses, that he *had* committed the crime. The jury soon found him guilty and the inevitable sentence followed, to be carried out eleven days later, on Wednesday 7th August.

A few days after the trial, John, Matthew and James were down at Trent Bridge one evening, doing a spot of fishing.

'Are you two going along to see Saville swing next Wednesday?' asked James.

'Not me,' replied Matthew. 'Me ma's always said she's against public hangings, so she wouldn't let me go, anyway. And me and dad have to be at the factory bang on seven or we don't get paid.'

'What about you, John?'

'I doubt it. I don't think Nancy and George would want me to go, either.'

'You could always sneak out the house,' suggested James.

'But they'd know I'd gone, and there'd be hell to pay when I got

back. It's all right for you, James, you work for your dad, and he's a
bit more easy going.'

'Yes, and we'll both be there. Eight o'clock sharp. Dad reckons
the whole of Nottingham's going to turn out, and *I* ain't going to
miss it.'

Many executions had been carried out on the steps of the
Shire Hall over the years, and they always attracted a large crowd,
for a public hanging was regarded by those with a penchant for
the morbid as pure entertainment, whilst even the more squeamish
were sometimes attracted by a sense of curiosity. And this particular
execution had really caught the townsfolk's imagination. For weeks
it had been the principal topic of conversation, and James's dad had
been right when he said that the whole of Nottingham was likely
to turn out to watch it. And not just the Nottingham folk. For the
case had gained such notoriety that it had been widely reported in
newspapers throughout the land, and many people from further
afield, who had the inclination and the time, were also expected to
come to Nottingham to witness Saville's gruesome end.

The morning of the execution dawned bright and warm, and
long before the appointed hour of eight o'clock the crowds had been
converging on High Pavement. Those from surrounding villages had
been setting off since daybreak, and never had so many people been
seen walking from all directions along the roads leading to the town.

The gallows had been erected in front of the steps of the Shire
Hall, and only a flimsy wooden barrier separated it from the road,
a narrow thoroughfare made even narrower by the presence of the
instrument of death. Fine houses lined both sides of High Pavement,
as far as St. Mary's Gate in one direction and Weekday Cross in the
other, so that along this short length of road a vast assemblage of
people was packed in tightly. Every window looking down on the
scene was filled by the wealthy owners and their friends, who had a
grandstand view, free from the surging mass below. By seven thirty,
the immediate area of the place of execution, where the best views
were to be had, was heaving, but still they poured in – up Garners
Hill from Leen Side and Narrow Marsh; along Low Pavement from

the town centre; down St. Mary's Gate and up Hollow Stone; from every direction they came. There must have been many who chose not to go to work that morning, for rarely had such an immense crowd been seen in one place and at one time, not even on the last Saturday of the annual Goose Fair.

James had continued to badger John and Matthew to join him and his father, but Matthew had stood firm by his decision. Although he wouldn't admit it to his friends, he was quite apprehensive at the thought of witnessing such an event, but in any case his mother would not let him go. John, on the other hand, wanted to go, but knew that George and Nancy were not in favour of the idea. So long as he was George's apprentice and lived in their house, he remained under their jurisdiction. But temptation got the better of him. As usual, he was up early to do his chores, but that morning he arose slightly earlier and before seven o'clock, when George and Nancy came downstairs, he had quietly sneaked out of the house. He went down Isabella Street, calling at James's house on the way, but Maria Marshall, James's mother, told him that he and her husband had left about five minutes before. So hoping to catch them up, he hurried along Canal Street and Leen Side, into Sussex Street and then up the steep steps of Garners Hill. But by the time he got to the top and into High Pavement, the crowd was so huge that he gave up any chance of finding them. And then he began to feel a little nervous. He was not used to crowds, but somehow he managed to force his way to the edge, towards Weekday Cross, and although his view of the gallows was somewhat poor, he felt safer here.

There was still almost an hour to go until Saville would be brought up from the condemned cell and out onto the gallows, but already the area directly in front of the Shire Hall was full. Once or twice John heard cries from that direction, and then a child appeared, being passed along over the heads of the crowd. More children followed and it was obvious that a tremendous crush must have been building up there. By a quarter to eight, John himself could barely move, being hemmed in on all sides. For what had been the edge of the crowd thirty minutes before had now become part of it. Already, some of those in the upper windows of adjacent houses were shouting and gesticulating to those below, urging them to move back, as yet another of the crowd fainted or collapsed from the pressure of the multitude surrounding them.

Then, suddenly, as the clock on St. Mary's Church began to toll the first of its eight peals, there came a shout from those at the front, followed by a rising wave of sound, and out from the Shire Hall came a small party of men. In the middle was Saville, his hands already manacled in irons in front of him and everything seemed to follow so swiftly, as if those in authority wished to put an end to this spectacle in the shortest possible time. Without ceremony he was quickly led up the steps onto the wooden platform and positioned on the trapdoor, whereupon the hangman, with the deftness that comes with practice and experience, reached for the rope hanging from the beam above, and placing the noose around the condemned man's neck, tightened the slip knot under his left ear then pulled a white cotton bag over his head. A parson, prayer book in hand, stood by his side, and appeared to be reading from it, not that anyone could hear a word of what he was saying, such was the noise of the crowd. And then, with no further warning, the hangman performed his morning's work and Saville was thrust into eternity. As his body dropped the short distance and the rope tightened, there came forth a deafening roar, followed at once by an eerie silence, during which all that could be heard was the rhythmic creaking of the rope as it slowly swung to and fro, like a giant pendulum, counting down the last remaining seconds of life ebbing away from the human form it supported.

The spectators, at first so keen not to miss the execution, now all wanted to be as far away as possible from this ghastly scene. But so many had congregated in such a small area, and so tightly packed were they, that as each individual struggled to move one way or the other, an uncontrollable burst of energy began to spread out from immediately in front of the gallows, forcing its way through the crowd like a gigantic wave rolling relentlessly towards the shore. This sudden movement caused those at the edge to fall down, but before they could stand up again, more bodies had toppled over them. In his position near Weekday Cross, John suddenly felt this powerful surge and within an instant found himself lying face up on the ground, but before he could move, a body fell on top of him, and then another on top of that. An enormous and growing weight was now pressing down on his chest and in desperation he tried to call out, struggling to force the weight from off him. He could feel the air being gradually expelled from his lungs, and as he fought frantically for breath he could sense himself slipping into unconsciousness.

Then, just in time, the burden began to ease, as first one, then another of those on top of him managed to extricate themselves, or were dragged away by others coming to their aid. There was a piercing pain in his chest; he felt bruised and battered and somewhat disorientated, but at least he was now able to breathe a little easier, and slowly he began to regain his composure. The one, enormous wave of pressure had passed; the pile of bodies on top of him had gone, enabling him to sit upright, so that he could now see, laid out before him like a Boschesque painting of Hell, the terrible consequences of the morning's event. Everywhere there was panic. Men were crying out and women were screaming, but John soon realised that it was not only for themselves they cried, but for others. Husbands bewailed the loss of wives, and wives of husbands and children who had vanished in the crowd. All around, the injured were lying or sitting dazed on the ground, their clothing reduced to torn and tattered rags. Some had blood streaming from their wounds; others had broken or hideously twisted limbs. Some lay still, and would never again move by their own efforts. Compared to them, John thought, he was lucky; very lucky.

The occupants of the houses on High Pavement were now able to open their doors and get out into the street, and several began to help and comfort the injured and dying. Saville's body was still there, dangling motionless on the end of the rope, his fate seemingly forgotten as that of innocent people now became the only concern of the survivors.

As the wounded were being attended to where they had fallen, John remained where he sat, continuing to recover from his ordeal.

At last, feeling a little stronger, he stood up and decided he must get back home, for George and Nancy would know by now that he was missing, and had probably guessed where he had gone.

He brushed himself down as best he could and ran his hands through his dishevelled hair. His shirt and trousers were badly torn and there were cuts and grazes on his arms and legs, but at least he had survived. Slowly he walked towards the top of Garners Hill, and once there the realisation of what had happened was plain to see. Those standing close to the top of the hill had been forced down the steps without warning by the avalanche of bodies cascading from above. There was no escape, and this narrow, steep, stepped hill, lined with houses on each side, formed the only outlet for this writhing mass of humanity. Like an army of tin soldiers they had toppled over and plummeted headlong down the steps, their screams and cries echoing until, for many, a brief interval brought insensibility or the silence of death.

John, having narrowly escaped death himself, felt the need to see the worst of this disaster, and so he returned the way he had come and made his way back down Garners Hill, treading carefully between the bodies lying on the steps. Most had someone by their side, trying to help them or tend to their wounds, but for others it was too late. Never in his life had he set eyes upon such a scene of carnage, and the most distressing fact was that nearly all the dead seemed to be of a similar age to himself, or younger.

Once he had reached the bottom of the hill and walked through Middle Marsh into Sussex Street, he had left these awful scenes behind him, but small groups of people were milling about, discussing the catastrophe. As he walked along, those he passed seemed to be in a state of shock. So close-knit was the community here, it was likely that everyone would know someone who had been affected in one way or another by the tragedy.

John decided he would call and see James first to make sure he and his father were safe. That would also delay his return home, for he was dreading the reception he might get when he finally showed his face. But as soon as he turned the corner from Castle Gate into

Isabella Street, he could see ahead a large crowd congregated outside the Marshall's house. His heart skipped a beat, wondering what the fuss was about, and he noticed both George and Nancy amongst the neighbours. As he approached, he observed that many of them were distraught, and some of the women were weeping openly. Then Nancy spotted him and rushed towards him, throwing her arms around him.

'Oh, John, thank God, you're safe,' she sobbed, 'but look at the state of you!' John was taken aback. He had fully expected to be scalded, for he knew he had done wrong in sneaking away to go to the hanging and was prepared to accept whatever punishment might be forthcoming.

'I'm all right, Nancy, just a few cuts and bruises. But did you think I'd come to some harm?'

'Yes, John, I did. And you must know what's happened. We've heard there's hundreds been injured and some killed. You went to the hanging, didn't you? When we found you'd left the house we suspected that's where you'd gone so we started to ask around. We knew James had been badgering you to go along with him and his dad, so we came round here and Maria told us you'd called just after they'd left, and you were going to try and catch up with them.' There was a pause, and Nancy looked over towards the group standing outside the Marshall's house. 'You didn't, though, did you?'

John didn't answer immediately. He was still wondering why there was such a crowd gathered here, in this particular street. 'No, I couldn't find them,' he replied, at last. 'There were such a lot of people it was impossible. Have they got back yet?'

George had now come over and joined them. John had never seen him look so sad. 'Come on, the pair of you. We'd better get back home. There's nothing more we can do here at the moment.'

'But what's happened?' cried John. 'Something's the matter. What is it?' George looked down at John, still wearing the same expression of sadness on his face.

'He's dead, John. Your friend James is dead. He was killed in the crush. His father's just brought him home. Poor Maria's in a terrible state.'

Once they were back home, George told John as much as he knew, but that wasn't much. He said that by eight thirty that morning, only half an hour after the execution, news was spreading like wildfire about the tragedy that had followed. Soon, everyone was out in the streets, talking to neighbours, as rumours continued to abound. Then, at about nine o'clock, the dreadful news came that young James Marshall, the blacksmith's son, was amongst the dead, and that his father had been seen carrying his body back home. James's death had probably saved John from an immediate dressing down for his own wrongdoing, but he would gladly have faced any reprimand to have James back.

Within a few days, the full horror of that morning became clear. Twelve had been killed in the crush, most on the steep steps of Garners Hill, and the majority of them were children or young men and women. The eldest to die was twenty-three, the youngest only nine. Over a hundred more were seriously injured and five of them subsequently died from their injuries.

The following Sunday morning, John Marshall placed a simple wooden coffin containing the broken body of his son onto a cart, and with the help of his brother pushed it slowly up the Derby Road to the General Cemetery. The coffin was followed by his heartbroken wife and other relatives and a long line of neighbours and friends. This was not the first, nor would it be the last of the funerals of those who had set out on that fateful Wednesday morning to High Pavement to see a man hanged for the heinous crime of murder, oblivious to the fact that before his body had even been cut down from the gallows they themselves would also have gone to meet their maker.

James's tragic death affected Matthew deeply at first for they had been friends for many years, but his sunny outlook on life helped him to cope with his grief much easier than John. He, being of a more sensitive nature, and despite having known James for only a year, took his death very hard and it had a profound and lasting effect on him. His happy-go-lucky, dare-devil pal who was always ready for a new and exciting adventure had gone for ever. Without him, life quickly became duller, and much of John's time was now spent in quieter pursuits.

But as his apprenticeship progressed and he slowly grew from a boy to a man, John's grief at the loss of his friend gradually faded, and whilst he would never forget him, the major part that he had once played in his life was replaced by another; a gentler and quieter soul – Matthew's sister, Sarah. He had always had a soft spot for her and he could recall vividly when they had first met, on the very day he arrived in Nottingham. She was only ten years old then, he just fourteen, and although he never knew it at the time she too had taken an immediate liking to her granddad's new apprentice.

As time went by they grew ever closer, and John's frequent visits to the Brown's household in Mortimer Street were increasingly not to call on Matthew, but Sarah. Soon, they became inseparable, and shortly after Sarah's sixteenth birthday in September 1848, she and John announced, to nobody's surprise, that once he had finished his apprenticeship they would be married. But that would not be for another two years. In the meantime Sarah continued working in the same lace factory where Matthew and her father were employed and where she had started work when she had turned thirteen.

Meanwhile, the youngest of the Brown children, Thomas, was now twelve and his father decided it was high time for him to start earning, too. But unlike the rest of his family he had no inclination to work in the hosiery trade. He simply wasn't interested and no amount of persuasion could get him to change his mind. What Thomas did have was a leaning towards anything connected with heavy industry, and in all things mechanical. He would often wander off, singing to himself as he went, and go down to the railway crossing on Wilford Lane to watch the trains go by, and wagons being shunted in and out of the station; or sneak into the nearby waterworks, where he had become friendly with one of the foremen. Sometimes, he would allow Thomas into the engine house to watch the giant steam-powered pumping engine at work, and would even let him help to oil some of the moving parts and polish the brass fittings.

His father, knowing of this interest, had enquired at the factory where he worked about an apprenticeship so that he could train as a framesmith and eventually become a mechanic on the lace machines, but even this didn't tempt him. For Thomas, it had to be big, heavy and noisy. Then one night, after he had been missing all day, he came home and announced that he had found a job at a small iron foundry in Radford, a couple of miles away, and would be starting there the following Monday. By now, he was nearly thirteen, and every morning he would leave at six to walk the two miles to work, often not getting back until twelve hours or more later.

Over the course of the next year or two there were to be some significant changes for the Brown family.

At the end of June 1850, a month after John had completed his apprenticeship, he and Sarah were married and moved into rented rooms in a house just down the road from Sarah's parents. The following year, Matthew also got married and went to live on the other side of the town. This was something of a whirlwind romance, for Matthew hadn't known his wife-to-be, Betsy, for very long. He met her when she came to work at the lace factory, and in less than six months they were wed. Four months later, a daughter was born, who was christened Isabella, and Matthew said he had chosen this name in memory of his friend James, who had lived in Isabella Street. This was David and Margaret's first grandchild, for John and Sarah had had no luck yet in starting a family.

John carried on working for George, but his health was beginning to suffer, and after a few more years he decided it was time to give up work. So John took over the rent of the stocking frame and paid George a small retainer for the use of his attic workshop. George and Nancy were happy with this arrangement, as John was company for them, a familiar face to have around the house during the day.

Thomas had continued to work at the iron foundry where he was rapidly becoming a skilled moulder. But then, one evening, in April 1855, he arrived home from work with a worried expression on his face. He came in and sat down at the table just as his mother was about to serve tea. As soon as she walked in from the scullery she could tell something was wrong.

'What's the matter, Thomas? You look as if you've got the weight of the world on your shoulders.'

'I'm afraid I've some bad news, ma. We've all been laid off; every last one of us. No warning. The boss called us all together this afternoon and told us. Paid us what he owed us, and that was that. Seems the works has been losing money for months. He said he's tried to find new orders but has had no luck and that we can't compete with the big modern foundries in Sheffield. That's where most of the orders are going. The trouble is, we're a bit old fashioned compared with them. There's a lot of money being invested in new machinery up there and the boss can't afford to do the same.'

By now, David had joined them. 'Well, son, that's a blow. But there must be other foundries where you could get a job, and with your skills you shouldn't be out of work for long.'

'There aren't many round here. Only a few, and I guess they'll be in as bad a way as us.'

'So what will you do?' asked Margaret.

'Well, if Sheffield's where the work's going, I think that's where I'll have to go, too.'

And that's precisely what Thomas did. His former employer had provided him with a reference, extolling his virtues as a skilled iron moulder, and two days later he took a train to Sheffield and started to look for work. Three days later he returned to Nottingham, having found a position with a large iron and steel producer in the Neepsend district of the town. He had also secured some lodgings in the area, and the following Saturday, he packed a large bag with all his worldly possessions and set off once more for his new home and job. But not before his family and friends arranged a farewell gathering on the Friday night at the Hanging Gate, to say goodbye to Thomas and to wish him well.

On the Saturday afternoon, his parents, along with Sarah and John, went with Thomas to the station to see him off.

'Look after yourself, Thomas,' said Margaret, a little tearfully, as she gave him a hug.

'I will, ma. And don't fret, I'll be fine. I'm only going to Sheffield,

not the other side of the world. I'll come back and see you all as soon
as I can, and you can always come up and visit me if you want to;
you've got my address.'

'That'd be nice,' said Sarah. 'I've never been to Sheffield.'

'Me neither,' added John.

'Well, I'll hold you to that,' replied Thomas, as he opened the
carriage door and climbed into the train.

'Work hard, son,' said David, shaking Thomas by the hand, 'and
don't go getting into any trouble!'

'I won't, dad; you know me.'

They stood on the platform, watching until the train was out of
sight, then slowly walked back home.

'Just us two now, David,' said Margaret, trying to hold back
the tears. 'Matthew and Sarah both married and left home, and now
Thomas has gone.'

'I know, love, but there's no need to be sad. We'll be all right,
you and me; and we'll not be lonely. Sarah and John are just down the
road, and Matthew's only a ten-minute walk away. And as Thomas
said, he's not gone far. We'll be fine, Margaret, you'll see.'

But sooner than they could have imagined, they once again had
family around them. Shortly before Christmas, John and Sarah came
round one evening to ask whether they could move in with them.
John, working by himself, was finding it hard to compete with some
of the small hosiery factories that were springing up, and with the
growing lace trade. He still had to pay rent for the stocking frame and
give George something for the use of his workshop. And all that on
top of the rent for their own rooms. So they went to live with David
and Margaret, and had the frame moved from George's house into
the attic room which had been used as a workshop many years before,
by previous tenants.

David didn't say anything to his son-in-law, not wanting to
upset him, but what had happened didn't altogether surprise him.
He himself was a skilled lace maker and had long believed that the
lace trade had a brighter future than the older trade of framework
knitting, which he saw as being in decline.

At Christmas, Thomas came home for a couple of days, and Matthew and Betsy, along with Isabella, who was nearly four, called in to see the family on Christmas Day. And when George and Nancy joined them, there were barely enough chairs for everyone.

That evening, as they all sat talking, John quietly confided to Thomas that he was very unsure about the future, and didn't know how long he could continue to work by himself as a framework knitter and support his wife, let alone any children that might come along.

'I sometimes wish I hadn't spent seven years learning the trade,' he said to his brother-in-law. 'I wish I'd chosen something else. But don't say anything to Sarah; I don't want to alarm her.'

Quick as lightning, Thomas replied. 'You could always come to work in Sheffield. It's a thriving town and there always seems to be plenty of jobs going.'

'But I don't think I'm cut out to work in the steel industry.'

'Well, it doesn't have to be in steel. There's other work to be had. There's a big tannery not far from where I live, and they're always advertising for hands.'

'I'll remember that. I think I'll give it another year and see how things turn out. But if it doesn't get any better, I might just take a trip up to Sheffield and see how the land lies. But remember, Thomas, not a word to Sarah, not a word.'

CHAPTER FOURTEEN

A lady comes a calling

Late one Friday morning in early April of 1856, just as the trees were beginning to blossom and the daffodils were starting to flower, a two-seater gig pulled up outside *Aysgarth Villa* on Glossop Road in Sheffield. The coachman quickly jumped off the box and helped an elderly lady to climb down from the comfortable leather seat behind. She was slender and stooped slightly and was neatly dressed in clothes of a fine quality, although clearly not of the latest fashion.

'Thank you so much. If you could please wait here for me as we agreed, I'd be much obliged. I'm not sure how long I'll be, but if the lady I'm looking for is here, it could be some time.'

'That's all right, my dear,' replied the coachman, 'I've got all day. Now you take your time; there's no rush.'

The large wooden gates guarding the entrance to the property were open, and with the aid of a black silver-topped cane, the old lady slowly walked up the drive towards the house. Upon reaching the front door she pulled on the bell handle, and a few moments later came the sound of footsteps approaching along the tiled hall floor. The door was opened by a young woman whom she judged to be perhaps eighteen or nineteen. She was of medium height, slim, with blond hair and blue eyes, exceedingly pretty and with a captivating smile.

'Good morning. May I help you?' enquired the young woman. The visitor did not reply immediately, but simply stared at the girl, as if lost for words. 'Is something the matter? How can I help you?' she repeated.

'Oh, I'm terribly sorry, I do apologise. I really didn't mean to be rude. I'd like to speak to Mrs Hannah Lambert, if she's available.'

'That's my mother, she's the cook and housekeeper but I'm afraid she's out at the moment. Can I help you? I'm her daughter, Eliza.'

'Yes, of course you are. I knew that as soon as I saw you.'

Eliza looked puzzled. She had never seen this old lady before and had no idea who she was, but was intrigued to know more.

'Would you like to come in? The master and mistress are also out, and mother won't be back until this afternoon.'

'Yes, I would, thank you. And I think I should explain who I am and why I'm here.'

The old lady followed Eliza into the large hallway. At the side of the staircase stood two small armchairs. 'Please take a seat,' said Eliza, pointing to the chairs. The old lady sat down and Eliza did likewise.

'My name is Emily Bussey. I met your mother once, but it was a long time ago, before you were born. In fact, it was at her wedding and I am related to the man she married, Joseph Lambert, your father. Poor Joseph. I don't suppose you remember him; I know you were very young when he died.'

And as she spoke his name, she took a dainty lace handkerchief from her purse and wiped away a tear from her eye. 'I've made a special journey from my home near Wakefield as I have something important to tell your mother. When would it be convenient to call again? I'm staying at the Commercial Hotel.'

'Well, as I said, mother's not here. She's had to go into town to fetch some supplies. Mr and Mrs Brentnall are having guests for dinner tonight, and there were some last-minute items the mistress particularly wanted included on the menu. I think it might be a while before she gets back, and then we'll be very busy preparing the meal. But she'll be free most of tomorrow. Saturday is our day off and as likely as not we'll be going into town. Maybe she could call and see you at your hotel. That would save you having to come out here again.'

'What a splendid idea; and how thoughtful of you. Yes, that would suit me very well. And you must come along too, Eliza; what I have to say also concerns you. Why don't you join me for lunch? Shall we say about one o'clock? I expect you know the Commercial Hotel, in the Haymarket.'

'Oh yes, we know where that is, and I'm sure we'll be there as you suggest.'

'Well, that's agreed then. I'd better go; I've kept the cabman waiting outside. I'm very pleased to have met you, Eliza.'

Eliza walked with Emily down the path to the cab, and helped her in.

'Thank you again, and I look forward to seeing you both tomorrow. There's so much I have to tell you.'

It was another hour before Hannah arrived back, and Eliza was bursting to tell her the news.

'You'll never guess what, mother, but we had a visitor this morning, an old lady who said she has something important to tell you. She said her name is Emily Bussey and that she is a relative of father.' Hannah seemed somewhat baffled.

'Bussey? No, I don't think I know anyone of that name.'

'She said she'd come specially from her home near Wakefield and that she'd met you once before, at your wedding.'

Suddenly, the penny dropped. 'Of course! She must be Joseph's Aunt Emily. She came from somewhere in the West Riding, but I never did know her surname and I only met her the once. I can't think who else it could be.'

'And she was very insistent that she sees you, so I told her we'd be in town tomorrow, and she said to go to the Commercial Hotel at one o'clock for lunch. That's where she's staying.'

'How very mysterious. Can you describe her?'

Eliza described Emily as best she could.

'Well, that does sound as if it might be her, but it's almost twenty years since I married your father, and if I remember rightly she only stayed for a few nights. I do remember, though, that she was the only relative of Joseph who was at our wedding, but she never said much about herself. And Joseph never told me anything about his family, and whenever I tried to ask him he always changed the subject. I wonder if we'll find something out tomorrow.'

'And another thing,' said Eliza, 'when I opened the front door, she just stood there, staring at me. It was strange. Then, when I told her who I was she said, "Yes, of course you are. I knew that as soon as I saw you". But how could she know that? We'd never even met before.'

Hannah looked at her daughter. 'Oh, I think I know the answer to that. But perhaps we should leave it until tomorrow. Come on now, we've a lot to do. There's eight guests coming for dinner tonight, and you know what a stickler Mrs Brentnall is for timekeeping!'

The next morning after breakfast, once Hannah and Eliza had cleared away all the breakfast pots and finished washing the mountain of crockery and cutlery left over from the previous evening's dinner party, the rest of the day was their own. They soon changed from their working clothes into their Sunday best and in no time at all were closing the back door behind them and heading out onto the road. It was fine and sunny, a lovely spring day, and as they headed down towards the town Hannah wondered just what lay ahead. It must be something important, she thought, for Emily to have come all the way specially to see her. And she reckoned that Emily must, by now, be well into her seventies. It was almost midday by the time they reached the town centre and they had about an hour to kill before meeting her. So they wandered round the market, whiling away the time and looking at what the various stalls had to offer. But neither of them was taking much notice of what they saw, for their thoughts were elsewhere.

'Come on, Eliza, it must be nearly one o'clock. Let's get along to the Commercial; we can sit and wait in the lobby for Emily.' It wasn't far to the hotel, and on entering they went directly to the reception desk, behind which stood a smart young man in the hotel's uniform.

'Good afternoon, ladies, how may I help you?'

'I believe you have a lady named Emily Bussey staying here. We have a meeting arranged with her for one o'clock.'

'Yes, I believe we do have a Miss Bussey staying with us. Now let me see if she's left a message for you,' and turning round, he soon located the appropriate pigeonhole, from which he took a piece of paper. 'Here we are,' he added as he looked down at the note. 'You must be Mrs Hannah Lambert and her daughter Eliza.'

'That's right.'

'Miss Bussey has asked you to take a seat in the lounge, where she will join you. I'll send a porter to her room to let her know you're here.'

'That won't be necessary,' they heard in a softly spoken voice from behind them, and they immediately turned round to see an elderly lady standing there, leaning on her stick. 'Hannah, it's so good to see you again after all these years and such a pleasure to have met Eliza yesterday morning. I have so much I wish to tell you both, so shall we go along to the dining room? I'm ready for some lunch. I may be getting old and frail, but I haven't quite lost my appetite yet.'

They were quickly shown to a table by a window. Both Hannah and Eliza were looking forward to dining at one of the biggest hotels in the town. They could not afford such extravagance and rarely ate out, certainly not at such an expensive establishment as the Commercial. It was usually they who served others at table, so this would be quite a treat for them. And secretly, Hannah was interested to see how the food here matched that which she regularly served for dinner parties at *Aysgarth Villa*. Orders were taken, and the three of them were soon enjoying a glass of sherry whilst waiting for their first course to arrive.

For several minutes they engaged in small talk, renewing their acquaintanceship. Hannah felt a little unsure as to how to continue the conversation, not wishing to interrogate Emily about her visit, or rush her into explaining the reason for it. But she needn't have worried, for Emily soon took charge of the situation.

'Now,' she said, 'I know you must both be wondering why I am here and what it is that is so important, so if you're happy for me to proceed, I'll begin.

'I think you know, Hannah, that I am your late husband's aunt. I know he would have explained that to you when I came to your wedding, the only time we ever met. But beyond that, I doubt that he told you anything about his family or his background. In fact, I distinctly remember that he asked me not to say anything to you on that subject.'

'Yes, that's right; and whenever I tried to ask him anything he always changed the subject, or gave some vague reply. I always wondered whether there was something terrible he wished to keep from me. In the end, I just stopped asking.'

'Well, in a way you're right, he did have something terrible to hide, but not in the way you might think. There was nothing in his past for which he could ever have felt ashamed; rather the opposite. And I would never have betrayed his trust, but there is a very good reason why I must now tell you the truth. You see, I might appear to be well for someone my age, but I have an illness that can't be cured and I'm afraid I don't have very much longer left to live. I'm the only one who can tell you what you need to know and I'm quite sure that Joseph wouldn't blame me for what I'm about to tell you.

'I only recently found out that Joseph had died. I tried to contact him a short while ago to let him know of my illness, but my letters to his address were returned. I then tried to write to your mother, Agnes, and the same thing happened, but I didn't know that she, too, had died. So I then contacted his employer, Mr Yates, who told me all about the terrible events of 1840. I had often wondered why Joseph had ceased to keep in touch, and now I know. Mr Yates said he was sure you were still living somewhere in Sheffield, so I decided to come and try to find you. I arrived here a couple of days ago and called on some neighbours near your mother's old house, but eventually it was the landlady at the Cutler's Arms, where you held your wedding breakfast, who told me where you and Eliza were now living and working.'

'Oh, that's Annie. She's been a very good friend to me since Joseph died. In fact it was her husband, Harry, who helped me to find the position with Mr and Mrs Brentnall. And I do feel bad not letting you know about Joseph. Mother and I wanted to, but we didn't know your surname and all we knew was that you lived somewhere in the West Riding, so it would have been very difficult to contact you. After Joseph was murdered I almost lost the will to live. Then not long after that mother died, and for a while it was only Eliza that gave me a reason to keep going. I'm sorry it's taken you so long to find out what happened to Joseph.'

'Oh, please don't blame yourself, Hannah. I do understand what you must have been going through at the time, and trying to contact me would have been the last thing on your mind.'

Emily's story was briefly interrupted when the waiter arrived with their first course, and in between eating, Emily continued.

'As I told Eliza yesterday, my surname is Bussey. I was born and brought up by my parents, now both deceased, at the family farmhouse a few miles south of Wakefield, where my father, Edwin, had a substantial acreage, sufficient for us to live a fairly comfortable lifestyle. I had just the one sister, Amelia, five years my junior, and it was she who was Joseph's mother. I myself have never married, but Amelia – oh, what a beauty she was! All the young men of the district were after her, but the one she finally chose lived some twenty miles away, at a small village called Westbrook, about twenty-five miles northwest of Sheffield, right up on the edge of the moors. His name was Henry Lambert. My father met him at the Corn Exchange in Wakefield and they soon became good friends. Henry used to visit us occasionally at the farmhouse and that's how he and Amelia met. Sometimes when Henry came to visit he would stay for the night, and I do recall that after he had first met Amelia his visits became much more frequent.

'And what I now have to tell you may come as a surprise, but a pleasant one, I hope. Henry Lambert was extremely wealthy, for he was the squire and lived at Westbrook Manor, where he owned an estate of several thousand acres. That's not particularly large compared with some Yorkshire estates, but the Lambert family was very well off. Their wealth came originally from a marriage between one of Henry's ancestors and the daughter and only heir of a much wealthier neighbour. Most of Henry's income came from agriculture, although I do recollect him saying that he had been investigating the potential of some coal deposits, which he had been told lay beneath estate lands on the lower parts of the moor. But he never did anything to exploit them.

'Henry hadn't known Amelia very long when they became engaged, and they were married in 1807. I remember that day as if it were yesterday – the 8th May, and what a splendid affair it was! They were married not at our local church, but at Westbrook, and afterwards there was a grand reception at the manor. Amelia looked stunning in her wedding dress with her flaming-red hair hanging down in ringlets. Everyone present that day was so happy for them and their future seemed so bright. But I'm afraid their hopes of years of happiness were soon to fade, and their time together was to be short.

'Their first son, Miles, was born a year after their marriage, then three daughters followed in quick succession but each died within a year of their birth. And then came the real tragedy. Amelia and Henry had only been married for eight years when Amelia died giving birth to their second son, Joseph – your Joseph, Hannah, the man you married. Amelia was only thirty, and Henry suddenly found himself a widower at the age of thirty-five with two young sons to bring up.

'Everyone naturally expected that after a time he would remarry, for he was still young and a man of some wealth, and there were plenty of young ladies in the neighbourhood who would have been delighted to become the squire's new wife. But it was never to be. Poor Henry soon slipped into long bouts of depression and found it difficult to spend any time with his two sons. And within a few weeks of Joseph's birth he asked me whether I would be willing to go and live at the manor and help him bring them up.

Well, as I said, I was unmarried and at that time mother and father were quite capable of looking after themselves, and so I agreed.

'At first, everything was fine and I enjoyed looking after Miles and Joseph. Miles was eight years older than Joseph, and he was the one who took after his mother, at least in looks – everyone could see that, what with the colour of his eyes and hair in particular. But that was as far as it went. Amelia was the kindest and gentlest person you could ever hope to meet, and Miles himself had always been a likeable lad when he was young, but shortly after Joseph was born he gradually began to change. I think he blamed Joseph for his mother's death, and the older he got the worse things became. He turned into a malicious and vindictive boy. He became obstinate, cruel and argumentative, and you wouldn't believe some of the things he did. Things got so bad that the tutor, whom Henry employed to teach Miles, simply walked out. And then Miles began to beat his younger brother, to the point of causing severe bruising. Then he turned his attentions to me. I had a lovely little kitten, which one of Henry's tenant farmers had given to me. I'd only had it for a week or two when it went missing, and when we went to look for it we found it hanging from a tree in the garden. Of course, we couldn't prove it, but we all knew who was responsible. I tell you, I was becoming very frightened at what he might do next, and eventually, I also left. By this time Joseph was nine and Miles seventeen, and Henry was so busy looking after the affairs of the estate that he had to rely more and more on his housekeeper, Jessie Hough, to keep the boys in order.'

At this point, there was another short interruption whilst the waiter returned with their next course, and Emily took this opportune moment to try and assess Hannah's reaction to the name she had just mentioned; but there was none.

'I take it, Hannah, the name Jessie Hough means nothing to you?'

'No, I've never heard it.'

'I thought not. Well, that confirms something I suspected and I'll explain that shortly. Anyway, Jessie suffered in exactly the same way that the tutor and I had, and eventually she told Henry that unless he did something she would have to leave, too. But she didn't really want to go, any more than Henry would have wanted to lose her, because she and her husband had been servants at the manor for many years and they were almost like a part of the family.

'So Henry decided that the best thing would be to send Joseph away to school, away from the unwanted attentions of his elder brother. Now, he had an old friend who was the proprietor of a boys' school near York, and he soon arranged for Joseph to become a border there. It took him a little while to settle down, but eventually he came to enjoy being at the school, and then, at Christmas, 1828, a terrible tragedy occurred. I'll never forget it, because Henry had invited me to go and stay at the manor for Christmas and the New Year. Joseph was back home from school, and it was nice to see them all again. Even Miles seemed a little more amenable than usual. I should explain, at this point, that Henry was having an appalling time with Miles. He was drinking and gambling heavily, and he hated the work he was having to do on the estate, in return for Henry having settled a particularly large gambling debt of his. Miles seemed to think that as he was the squire's eldest son he could do just as he wished.

'Then, on Boxing Day, the usual hunt took place, during which Henry had an accident. He was found lying in some woods apparently having hit his head on the branch of a tree. No one actually saw it happen, and most of the hunt members couldn't understand how such an experienced rider as Henry could have met such a fate. And it was Miles who found him. Nobody else was anywhere near. I do know that some people never believed it was an accident, but that Miles himself had had a hand in his father's death, although nothing could be proved. And then came the real blow. Henry had never made a will, but after the funeral, when we all returned to the manor, I overheard the family solicitor telling Miles that Henry had spoken to him on that very subject shortly before Christmas, and that they were due to meet in a few days time to draw up his will. But obviously, it was too late by then. The top and bottom of it was that Miles, as the eldest son, inherited the estate and all the money that went with it.

'As soon as he took over, things rapidly went from bad to worse for many of the estate workers, but the one to suffer most was young Joseph. Miles wrote to the school, saying that he was no longer prepared to pay his brother's fees. The poor lad was terrified to go home. He'd never had a mother to guide and comfort him, he'd recently lost his father and now he had to leave the school. So he set off early one morning and walked until he came to our farmhouse. He had no one else to turn to. He stayed with us for a while, but was adamant that he would never return to Westbrook, but would try and make his own way in the world.

'Joseph wasn't sure what he would do, and then one day he was admiring some cutlery we had, best Sheffield silver-plated steel it was, made by one of father's acquaintances from many years before, Solomon Yates. It was Solomon who had founded the cutlery business here in Sheffield which is now run by his son, Titus. I remember that, as a child, Joseph had always been good at drawing and painting and I can see him now, sitting quietly by himself, whittling away at a piece of old discarded wood, carving a human figure, an animal, or a toy of some sort. He seemed to have a natural, artistic talent and a love of beautiful, man-made objects. So father wrote to Titus, and he agreed to take Joseph on as an apprentice. I expect a lot of people would think it a strange thing for the son of a wealthy squire to do, but it suited Joseph. Even at his age, for he was only thirteen when he first arrived in Sheffield, he was determined to stand on his own two feet. And I think you know the rest, Hannah, because he came to lodge with your mother, and that, I guess, is how you met.'

Throughout this long account of Joseph's early life, Hannah and Eliza had sat, spellbound. They could never have imagined that Joseph could have had such a privileged background, for he had never spoken of any of it, and never given any hints or clues that he was anything other than a normal, working-class lad.

'You might be asking yourselves why I should come and tell you all this. You might think it a most interesting, or perhaps even, an unbelievable story. But if *I* don't tell you it, nobody else will. There is only one other person living who knows the truth about Joseph, and that's his brother, Miles; and *he'll* never volunteer any part of it. Because there is one final chapter to add to the story. You recall I mentioned Jessie Hough, the housekeeper at Westbrook Manor. Now, some years ago, 1840 to be precise, there was a quite sensational case which was reported in all the newspapers at the time, about a suspicious death that took place there. Well, it was Mrs Hough herself who was found dead one morning in unusual circumstances. So unusual, in fact, that the police suspected foul play and that Miles was responsible. He was arrested, and such was the evidence that he was sent for trial. Do you remember reading about it, Hannah?'

'No, I don't. I have to admit that I could barely read then, so I never looked at the newspapers, although Joseph always bought the weekly paper and seemed to spend hours reading it. I've learned to read and write since, but even if I could have read at that time, the names Jessie Hough and Westbrook Manor would have meant nothing to me.'

'Exactly. Well, the trial took place at York Assizes in July of that year, and ...' Suddenly, Emily's account was interrupted by Hannah.

'July, you say? 1840? York? That's where Joseph died. Saturday the 11th July. I'll never forget that date as long as I live. And you say his brother was on trial for murder there, and in the same month. What a coincidence!' Emily paused for a few moments before replying.

'You know, I do believe the trial was on that very same date. I know it was a Saturday, because our weekly paper is published on a Friday, and we had to wait a whole week before we could read the report. Now I come to think of it, it must have been that Saturday, because father's birthday was the nineteenth of July, and I distinctly remember going to Wakefield to collect a book I'd ordered as a present for him, and at the same time I purchased the paper, keen to read all the details. Of course, we'd already heard that Miles had been found not guilty, and we were eager to learn how the jury came to that verdict. From what we knew, it seemed there was a cast-iron case against him. But it turned out he had the very best attorney to defend him, and he obviously managed to persuade the jury that Miles was innocent.'

'But was there nothing in the paper about Joseph's death and the inquest?' asked Hannah. 'It was reported in the Sheffield newspapers.'

'Well, I don't remember reading anything about it. If it was mentioned, I must have missed it. But I was fully engrossed in reading all about Miles's trial.'

It was now Hannah's turn to sit, deep in thought. Eliza looked across at her mother who seemed to be in a trance, staring into space.

'What is it, mother? You've gone as white as a sheet. Are you all right?' Hannah stared at Eliza, then at Emily.

'Joseph always read the newspaper. He must have read about the case. He knew Jessie Hough and he knew that Miles would be on trial. He said he was going to York on business, but he must have known what else was happening there that day.'

'What are saying, mother?'

'I'm not sure what I'm saying, Eliza. So many coincidences and so many tragedies. My mind's in a complete whirl. But tell me, Emily, what happened to Miles after the trial. Is he still living at Westbrook? Did he ever marry?'

'As far as I know he still lives there. I occasionally meet people from that area and they give me all the gossip, and from what they say he's still the same dissolute and arrogant man he was all those years ago. And no, so far as I know, he never did marry. No decent woman would ever have him!'

Their meal was now over, but they carried on talking for another hour or so. There was so much Hannah wanted to know about Joseph, and Emily was able to answer most of her questions.

Eventually, Emily said that she wanted to retire to her room.

'I do get so very tired these days and usually take a nap in the afternoon. It's been so good meeting you again Hannah, and you too, Eliza. I've enjoyed our talk, even though it has been a little exhausting. And now that I've achieved what I came here for, I'd like to return home as soon as I can, so I think I'll go back tomorrow.'

'How will you get there?' asked Eliza.

'There's a train to Leeds at a quarter past eight, the only one on Sunday morning, so I'll have to be up quite early. I get off at Oakenshaw and there's an omnibus that meets the train there and goes to Wakefield. It passes right through the village where I now live. My goodness, how times have changed since I was a girl!'

'So you don't still live at the farmhouse?'

'No, not any more. After mother and father died I did carry on with it for a few years, but it was getting too much for me to manage, especially after I started to get ill. So I decided to sell up. I didn't get a great deal for it – it was a bad time for farming just then and land prices were depressed – but I got enough to rent a little cottage in the village and keep myself reasonably comfortable, so I can't complain.'

The three ladies got up from the table and went out into the hotel lobby. They said their goodbyes and that they'd try and keep in touch. But just before Hannah and Eliza left, Eliza turned to Emily.

'Emily, there's one more thing I'd like to ask you. When you came to the house yesterday looking for mother, and I said I was her daughter, you said that you knew that as soon as you saw me. But we'd never met before, so how could you know?'

'Oh, that's easy, my dear. As soon as you opened the door I knew who you must be. You're the very image of your father. Yes, I could tell at once that you are Joseph's daughter.'

Later on, when they were back home, having a cup of tea and a slice of cake, Hannah and Eliza talked about what they had found out that afternoon.

'What did you think about what Emily told us about Miles?' asked Hannah.

'Well, he was hardly the perfect elder brother! And that's putting it politely.'

'Yes, but didn't you detect the suggestion that he might have had something to do with his father's death, during the hunt?'

'Yes, I did,' replied Eliza, 'but she didn't really say much more, other than that some people found the affair rather suspicious.'

'But why should he want to kill his own father?'

'Well, from what Emily said, he was a complete and utter rogue. Or perhaps I should say, still is. But why do people commit murder? I suppose it's usually out of hate or greed. And you remember what Emily said about Henry not having made a will, but was about to do so? Just imagine that Miles knew that, and wanted to make sure he got his hands on the estate and all the money. He was the eldest son, so without a will he stood to inherit the lot, but a will might have disposed of the estate differently. So Henry's death was definitely to Miles's advantage. Of course, it would be impossible to prove anything now. If he did do it, then he's got away with it. And to think, he's my uncle!'

'And my brother-in-law,' added Hannah with a tone of disgust in her voice. 'But I can't stop thinking about poor Joseph. He died in York on the same day that his brother was standing trial for murder. And like I told Emily, Joseph always used to read the newspaper, so he must have known about Mrs Hough's death and that his own brother was to stand trial – and on the very day he went to York. It could just be a coincidence, but I'm not so sure. What is certain is that Joseph was murdered. I know I haven't told you many of the details, Eliza, but I'll never forget them. The police assumed that robbery was the motive, but they gave up trying to find the culprit. The one valuable item stolen was his gold watch and chain that used to belong to his father. His body was found in the yard of the Old Star Inn, and the police said he must have been killed late in the evening, as the innkeeper said he remembered him coming in for a drink, then leaving at about nine o'clock. But the trial would have been over long before then, and Miles, no doubt, walking the streets of York as a free man!'

'Oh, mother, it's all too awful to think about. But I don't suppose we'll ever be able to discover the truth, not after all these years.'

'I'm afraid you're probably right, Eliza. And there's nothing we can do to change what's happened. So I think it's best not to dwell on it. But I'll never forget Joseph. He was the most wonderful husband to me and the most loving father to you. And the saddest thing of all is that you probably don't even remember him.'

'No, mother, I don't.'

CHAPTER FIFTEEN

Decisions decisions decisions

It was a glorious summer's day; a red-hot, sultry Sunday morning in August. The sun beat down unmercifully from a cloudless sky and not a breath of wind blew. In Mortimer Street, as in every other part of the town, doors and windows had been thrown wide open to try and let in some air and alleviate the oppressive, stifling heat.

'Sarah, how do you fancy a stroll up to the Arboretum?' asked John. 'It's so hot and stuffy in here, and it's a while since we've been. There's nothing much else to do and I'm sure it'll be much cooler there. We could take some scraps of bread and feed the birds on the lake. What do you say?'

'I'd love to. And you're right, it would be nice to get out for a few hours. I'll go and ask ma and pa if they'd like to come along, too.' Sarah eased herself sluggishly from her chair and was about to go out into the street, where David and Margaret were chatting to some neighbours, when John put out a hand and gently grabbed her arm. 'No, Sarah, not today. Just the two of us.'

'Why, John? I'm sure they'd love to join us, and ...'

'Yes, I'm sure they would, but not today; just you and me. Please, Sarah.'

Sarah looked at her husband and could see the pleading in his eyes. She couldn't understand why he should not want to include her parents in their little jaunt. He was usually agreeable to anything she suggested, but she could tell that on this occasion he seemed to have a strong reason not to be. So she said nothing more, and as soon as they were ready they set off, having told David and Margaret of their plans.

'Don't be late back. I'll have the tea on the table at six o'clock,' said Margaret.

'Oh, we'll be back by then,' John assured her, 'and after tea we could all go out for a drink or two. My treat,' he added.

'My, my, you're splashing out, aren't you, John?' said Sarah as they walked round the corner into Finkhill Street. 'Have you come into some money? I thought things were a bit tight at the moment.'

'Well, yes, they are, Sarah, but your ma and pa have been so good to us since we moved in, it's nice to be able to treat them once in a while.'

They headed for the Market Place, then up Sheep Lane into Parliament Street, and along Goldsmith Street to Waverley Street. Ahead, on their right, the Arboretum stretched out almost to the top of the hill rising up before them. These grounds had been provided by the town council some five years before, affording a haven of relaxation for the town's residents. They were attractively laid out with grassy hills, tree-lined avenues, shrubs and beautiful floral displays, and a small lake stocked with a variety of native British aquatic birds. As John and Sarah entered the park, it was evident that countless others had the same idea.

'I don't think I've ever seen so many folk here before,' said Sarah.

'Well, I'm not surprised, on a day like today, and it is Sunday so it's free to come in. And I expect there'll be a band playing later on.'

They spent an hour or so slowly walking round the pathways, admiring the colourful flowerbeds and the exotic plants and shrubs, each neatly labelled with its botanical name and country of origin. The birds were duly fed, and then, as the band struck up, they found an empty bench in the shade of a willow tree and sat down. Sarah had brought some slices of cake that her mother had baked, and soon there was nothing left but a few crumbs, which were being noisily fought over by a family of ducks.

'Sarah, there's something I've been meaning to talk to you about for some time, but I don't seem to have had the opportunity recently. And I really wanted to wait till there was nobody else around.'

'Oh, and what's that?' asked Sarah with an inquisitive look on her face. 'Is that why you didn't want ma and pa to come along?'

John turned to her and took both her hands in his. 'Well, yes, it is. I thought today would be an ideal time and I really don't want to leave it any longer. Sarah, how would you like to go and live in Sheffield?' For a second or two Sarah remained silent, as if dumbstruck by this most unlikely of questions.

'Sheffield? Why Sheffield? I've heard it's a dirty, smoky town. And why move anyway? What's wrong with Nottingham?'

'There's nothing wrong with Nottingham, nothing at all. But you know that I've not been very busy recently. Things have been pretty bad for a while now, and I really can't see any future for stocking makers. At least, not for those like me, just one man and a hand frame. I can't compete with the large firms and their power frames. I'm sure things will only get worse and we have to look to the future. I think a complete change would be good for me – good for both of us. Somewhere new, new jobs, a new town.

'Do you remember the Christmas before last, when we were all together? I was talking to Thomas about how he was getting on in Sheffield. I told him I was worried about the future here, and he told me there were lots of opportunities in Sheffield; and not only in the iron and steel business. He says it's a really thriving town. Why don't we give it a try? It might be the best move we could make. And if things didn't work out we could always come back here.' John paused before continuing. 'And another thing, Sarah. I know I've never mentioned it, but it still saddens me when I walk down Isabella Street and past James's house. I hadn't known him long, but he was a very good friend, and every time I walk down there the memories come flooding back of that awful day. I know it was a long time ago but I can still remember it as if it was yesterday. Poor James got killed and I nearly did, too. I honestly think a change of scenery will be good for us. What do you think?'

'I don't know what to think, John. This is all so sudden. And what would I do? I don't think they make lace in Sheffield and that's what I've always been used to.'

'Yes, I know, but Thomas was telling me about a large tannery near where he lives. I'm sure we'd be able to find jobs there, or somewhere else, and Thomas could help us find a place to live. Why don't we go and visit him and stay for a day or two and have a look round? Then we could make up our minds. Treat it as a holiday.'

'A holiday! That would make a change. I'd have to ask permission to take time off work, but if we went on a Saturday I might only need to take one day off. I'd lose pay, of course, but it would be nice to see Thomas again; we've not seen him for ages.'

John and Sarah continued to discuss John's idea, and although Sarah wasn't too enamoured at the prospect of moving away from her home town and all her friends and relations, she agreed to go along with John's suggestion of an initial visit to Sheffield.

That evening, after tea, John and Sarah took David and Margaret along to the Hanging Gate, and whilst there they broke their news about what they intended to do. Margaret seemed quite upset at the thought of another of her children moving away, but David could understand the reasoning behind it.

'You must do what you think's best,' he told them. 'I always thought the stocking business would go into decline. That's why I insisted on our Matthew following me into the lace trade.'

'But couldn't you do that too, John?' asked Margaret, desperately trying to find a reason why Sarah and John should stay in Nottingham. 'Surely, lace making can't be all that different from using a stocking frame.'

'Now then, Margaret, give the lad a chance. I've no doubt he could adapt, but if they want to try their luck at doing something else, and in a different town, then we mustn't stand in their way. And if it doesn't work out, they can easily come back. They know there'll always be a home for them here.'

The next day, John went to the telegraph office and sent a short telegram to Thomas, saying that he and Sarah intended to come and visit him on Saturday, that they would arrive at the Wicker Station at 12.25, and would like to stay for a couple of days. The following evening a short reply was received – *Finish work at one. Will then come to station.*

On Saturday morning Sarah packed a bag with a few clothes for them both and some food and drink, and straight after breakfast they set off to catch the nine o'clock train to Derby, en route to Sheffield. The journey was uneventful, but they both enjoyed what was, for them, a rare treat. John had only made a handful of rail journeys, and for Sarah this was only the second time she had ever been on a train. As they pulled out of the station she told John how, when she was a young girl, her father had taken her, Matthew and her mother for a ride, a month after the line had opened in 1839. Many of the Nottingham folk were curious to try this new mode of travel, and she recalled how they had joined scores of others on the short ride to the first station down the line, Beeston, where the village wakes were being held. And afterwards they had had tea at a public house, the Boat and Horses, down near the river, then walked back home along the banks of the Trent to Nottingham.

After almost an hour they arrived at Derby, where they had thirty minutes to wait for the train to Sheffield. They then enjoyed a most agreeable trip of almost two hours through the Derbyshire countryside, until eventually they began to enter the outskirts of Sheffield, where houses, factories and smoking chimneys increasingly dominated the landscape and rapidly presented a stark contrast to the delightful rustic scenes they had been enjoying. Within minutes, the transformation from rural idyll to industrial squalor was complete, and presently the train came to a stop at the Sheffield terminus in The Wicker. They found an empty bench in the lofty entrance hall and sat and ate the lunch that Sarah had prepared. They were then temped to leave the station and explore the surrounding area but didn't want to risk missing Thomas when he arrived.

So they stayed where they were, and soon found themselves being amused by the lively and humorous banter of half a dozen men, armed with baskets and fishing rods, who were waiting for their train. It was clear that they had already partaken of a good quantity of ale, and from what was being said they were off for a weekend's fishing in Derbyshire, mention being made of a pub near to Ambergate, where they had booked rooms for the night. Sarah was fascinated by the men's accent and dialect, so different to her own, and by the time they staggered off to join their train, she and John had learned that they were work colleagues from a local foundry who were on their annual fishing trip, having been given permission by their wives to absent themselves for the weekend. How much actual fishing would be achieved, Sarah wondered, would have to remain a matter of conjecture, but she had no doubt that this jolly band of comrades was likely to spend almost as much time in the tap room as on the banks of the Derwent. As the men disappeared onto the platform, Sarah noticed John smiling to himself with a hint of longing on his face.

'Now don't you go getting any ideas, John. I don't want you starting that sort of tradition!'

'No, I won't. But I was thinking how long it's been since I did any fishing. I think the last time was with Matthew and James, and that was years ago. I wonder if Thomas ever goes fishing? If we do move here, perhaps me and Thomas could spend the odd afternoon down by the river. I think I've still got my rod at home somewhere.'

'Well you can ask him, 'cause here he is,' said Sarah, getting up from the bench and waving enthusiastically towards her brother, who had just come through the entrance to the station. He strode across the floor and Sarah ran towards him, throwing her arms around him and giving him a kiss. Then she stood back and looked him up and down.

'My, how you've grown!' she exclaimed.

'She's right,' added John, as he grasped Thomas by the hand and shook it firmly. 'You've really thickened out, and I reckon you've grown a few inches, too.'

'Well, maybe. It must be all that hard graft that's done it. It's no place for weaklings, working in an iron and steel mill, I can tell you. Anyway, it's good to see you both, but I've been wondering why you suddenly decided to come up. There's nothing the matter is there? No bad news, I hope.'

'No, nothing like that. But we do need to talk to you about something. Is there a pub nearby? We can have a drink while we tell you what it's all about.'

'I was going to suggest that myself. I'll take you to the Rutland Arms up at Neepsend, just round the corner from where I live. They do a delicious steak and kidney pie. Don't know about you, but I'm starving. I've not eaten since six this morning.'

Thomas led the way through the town, and Sarah's preconceived ideas of it appeared to be justified. Many tall chimneys towered above the rooftops, and although it was a Saturday afternoon a lot of them were belching thick black smoke. All the buildings, except for those that were newly constructed, were almost completely blackened by the soot that endlessly settled upon them, and the air was heavy with an acrid, almost sulphurous haze, which the bright sunlight seemed unable to penetrate. After a steady walk of about twenty minutes they turned a corner into a narrow street and saw the pub sign hanging over the door of a property a little way down. They went in and found themselves in a large and cheerful room, surprisingly busy, Sarah thought, for the early afternoon. Apart from two barmaids, the occupants were nearly all men, and by the look of their clothes and the dirt and sweat on their brows,

Sarah guessed they had all come straight from work. Thomas nodded to a number of them and exchanged greetings as he made his way to one of the last empty tables in the bar.

'Sit yourselves down, you two, and I'll go and get the drinks. Do you want anything to eat as well?'

'Not for me,' said Sarah, 'I brought some food with us and we ate it at the station while we were waiting for you.'

'Those pies smell good,' said John, glancing enviously at a nearby table where a group of men were eagerly tucking into their meal.

'Best pies in Sheffield. They do a roaring trade here. I'll get you one, shall I?' asked Thomas.

'Yes. Here, I'll pay,' insisted John, handing over a shilling piece. 'I'll have a pint of whatever you're having and Sarah will have a gin and lemonade.'

'Right you are. I'll not be a minute.'

Thomas was soon back, his large hands easily clasping two pint pots of brown ale and a smaller glass for Sarah. 'Dolly'll bring the pies over in a bit.'

'Thanks, Thomas. Well, here's to you,' said John, raising his tankard and taking a good long swig of the foaming brown liquid. 'Mmm; not bad, not bad at all, but I don't reckon it's quite as good as our Nottingham ale!' he added mischievously.

'You might be right, but I've got mixed feelings. I'm Nottingham born and bred, same as you, but I'm settled here now and I like the place. The people are really friendly and they made me welcome as soon as I arrived. It's a booming town right enough, but it can be noisy and dirty, what with all the iron and steelworks, and round here we get the smells from the tanneries as well, but after a while you hardly notice it. And I don't think it's any worse than some parts of Nottingham. Anyway, it's good to see you both again. Now then; how's ma and pa keeping? And how's our Matthew and Betsy getting on? I expect young Isabella must be shooting up now.'

'Yes, she is,' said Sarah, smiling pensively. 'She's five now, a real joy to both of them and a little bundle of energy. Matthew loves his daughter so much, and he's even happier now, after Betsy let it slip last week that she's expecting again.' And Thomas couldn't help noticing a wistful look on his sister's face. He knew she wanted children herself, but so far had had no luck.

'But tell me, what brings you both here? I must say, I was surprised when I got your telegram.' Just then, the barmaid arrived with two large plates, each almost full to overflowing with a huge, steaming-hot pie, smothered in thick gravy.

'Good gracious, John! You're not going to eat all that, are you?' asked Sarah.

'Well, I'm going to give it a good go. Everyone else in here seems to be managing.'

'Yes, but most of them have done a morning's hard graft. All we've done is sit back and enjoy a train ride through the countryside!'

'Ah well,' replied John, 'I wouldn't want to upset the locals by leaving anything on my plate,' and picking up his knife, he plunged it through the thick pastry crust, whereupon a plume of steam arose, carrying with it the most appetising aroma.

Ten minutes later, John placed his knife and fork on an empty plate, leant back in his chair, took another swig of ale, wiped his mouth on a handkerchief and turned to his wife. 'You know, Sarah, I'm beginning to get a liking for this town!'

'I take that to mean you enjoyed your pie. However, Thomas wants to know why we've come here.'

'Oh, yes, so you do, Thomas. Do you remember some time ago when I told you I was concerned about the future, and that I was worried about how long I could continue working for myself? Well, things haven't got any better; in fact, if anything, they've got worse. And then I thought about what you said; that there was always work to be had in Sheffield. So me and Sarah talked things over, and decided we wanted to come and have a look at the place; talk to you again, and possibly consider moving here. That is, provided we can find work. That's why we'd like to stay for a day or two – if you can put us up.'

'Of course I can, but it'll be a bit of a tight squeeze. I rent the ground floor of a house near here and I've only got a living room, a back parlour which I use as a bedroom, and a scullery, but I can sleep on the sofa in the living room and you two can use my bed. Mind you, it's only a single bed, but at least you'll be nice and cosy! And I'll be comfortable enough on the sofa. Once my head hits the pillow I'm usually out like a snuffed candle.'

The three of them stayed in the pub for a little while longer and had another drink, then Thomas suggested he show them around this part of the town. But first they went to his house. It was only a short walk, further down the street, then left and left again into a cul-de-sac. All the streets hereabouts were lined with rows of neat terraced houses, all pretty much identical and of recent construction. They were two storeys high and built of brick. After every fourth house was an alley leading to the rear of the properties, each of which had its own back door and small yard, provided with a water pump, a privy and a coal store. A vast improvement, Sarah and John both agreed, on the house they shared with her parents in Nottingham. Living in a house such as Thomas's, commented Sarah, would be almost luxurious in comparison.

Thomas stopped outside a house on the left-hand side near the end of the street, took a key from his pocket and unlocked the freshly painted dark-blue door. They stepped into a small hallway with a flight of stairs directly ahead and a door on the left. Thomas opened it and they walked straight into the living room.

'Here we are; follow me and I'll show you the rest of the house; it won't take long,' and he led the way through to the back parlour and beyond that to the scullery, where another door opened into the back yard.

'Who lives upstairs?' asked Sarah.

'No one. There are two bedrooms up there, but the landlord uses them. He's a dealer in all sorts of stuff, mainly furniture, and he uses those rooms as storage. It's a bit inconvenient, what with his men coming and going, but I managed to get the place at a lower rent. I could never have afforded it otherwise, so the arrangement suits me fine. I've not been here long, but it's much better than where I used to live. That was a really dirty, dingy place. Just one room in an old three-storey house facing north; so no sunlight, and cold and damp, especially in winter. And then this place came up. The landlord's the brother of a chap I work with, and he told me about it. It's a bit dearer than where I was before but I decided I could afford it, just about, so here I am. Look, why don't you leave your bag here, and we'll carry on. It's not four o'clock yet so we've got plenty of time to have a good look round. Then later on we'll go out for something to eat and a few drinks.'

'Perhaps we could go back to the Rutland Arms, I fancy another one of those pies,' suggested John.

'You'll get as fat as that fat lady we paid to see at the Goose Fair last year,' said Sarah, patting her husband on the stomach and laughing.

'Well, you'll not find a better night's entertainment round here and their food's second to none. And there's always a good crowd in there on a Saturday night,' Thomas added.

They were soon on their way and Thomas took them on a walk around the district, showing them first where he worked. It was within a large sprawling mass of buildings in an area known as Kelham Island; a man-made island, bounded on one side by the River Don and on the other by a millstream created many centuries before to turn the waterwheels used to power the machinery in the ancient mills.

'See that large building in the middle, the one with the tall chimney; that's where I work; *Potter, Simpson and Co.*'

'What exactly do you do?' asked John.

'When I first arrived I worked as an iron moulder, that's what I'd been doing in Nottingham. But now the firm's turning over most of its manufacturing to steel so we're doing less iron casting and more steel forging, and for the last few months I've been turning my hand to that. Just at the moment we've got a massive order to supply America with rails, so we're churning them out by the ton, every day. I'm told that new railways are being built all over the place but they can't roll out enough rails at their own works, so we benefit; it's good news for us. A man never needs to be out of work here.'

Some of the factories were still operating; others had closed for the weekend. Everyone, Thomas explained, worked till at least midday on Saturday, some all day. Most men worked twelve-hour shifts and the work was hard, physical graft, so they all looked forward to the weekend, with time to relax.

'And over there,' said Thomas, pointing to another large building nearby, 'is the tannery I mentioned to you. I was talking to a mate in the pub last week who works there, and he told me they're looking for more men to take on.'

They continued their tour for a couple of hours, taking in most of the immediate locality. It soon became apparent to both John and Sarah that this was an expanding industrial town, seemingly more so than Nottingham. The industries here seemed bigger, bolder and brasher; Nottingham had many hosiery and lace factories but these were almost genteel compared with the heavy industries to be found in Sheffield, a fact with which Thomas readily agreed.

'Mind you, there are lots of smaller workshops here, too, producing the finest cutlery in the world. Some of them only occupy one or two rooms, tucked in out-of-the-way places you could walk past and not even know existed. But for all their tumbledown appearance, that's where some of the most skilled artisans anywhere in the country are to be found. I know one or two of them and you'd never believe, just looking at them, that they could make such fine things, that only the wealthiest people can afford. I could never do what they do. I don't think I'd have the patience to spend seven years learning all their skills. Give me a rolling mill and a steam hammer any day!'

As they slowly made their way back to Thomas's house, Sarah thought hard over what she had seen. Most of the houses were similar to what she was used to in Nottingham, closely packed together and in terraces. But others, like Thomas's, seemed a step up. There had obviously been a lot of building in recent years, and some of these were clearly of a much higher quality than the older properties.

But what struck Sarah most was the ambience of the town. Compared with Nottingham it was, as she had suspected, much dirtier, smellier and noisier. When they walked past the River Don she couldn't help but notice the state of it. She was familiar with the River Leen back in Nottingham, now reduced to little more than a narrow, stinking drain, but even that seemed clean compared with the Don. This heavily polluted river appeared to be a conduit for every variety of filth imaginable, its surface a film of slime in which floated dead cats and dogs, and which was clearly used as a common sewer into which all the foul and unspeakable by-products from the adjacent industries were dumped, whilst the banks of the river seemed to be used as a depositary for offal, ash and dung. And the smell which arose from it, and from the nearby tanneries, combined to make it difficult to breathe freely without feeling a little nauseous. Thomas had said that after a while one got used to it. If she and John were to come and live here, she hoped, for their sakes, that he was right.

Later that evening they went back to the Rutland Arms, where Thomas introduced Sarah and John to some of his friends. Sarah might not have been impressed with the town itself, but one thing she had observed was how friendly the people were. After they had had a few drinks and a bite to eat, life suddenly seemed brighter. There was plenty of joking and laughter, and a great deal of singing, once one of the locals began to demonstrate his musical talents on the piano, and Thomas, who possessed a fine tenor voice, captivated everyone with a solo rendition of *Jeannie with the Light Brown Hair* which was greeted with much applause.

That night, tired out after a long day, John and Sarah both slept soundly, and it was only the noise of Thomas coming through to the scullery that woke them at gone ten o'clock the next morning. It being Sunday, things were much quieter as nearly all the factories were closed, the only signs of industrial life coming from those works where it was necessary to keep the blast furnaces working morning, noon and night.

They spent a lazy day, and after a late breakfast they strolled into the town centre where Sarah was keen to do some window-shopping, and compare the shops here with those she frequented in Nottingham.

The following morning Thomas had to be up early to go to work, so before they retired to bed that night John said that he and Sarah would call at the tannery and enquire about jobs before setting off for the station, and that once they had decided what they intended to do, they would let him know. And Thomas told them that if they did decide to move to Sheffield they could stay with him for a while, until they found somewhere to live.

After breakfast John and Sarah went along to the tannery, then called at Thomas's place of work and left his door key with the gatekeeper, as he had asked them to. On their way to the station they spotted some advertisements in the windows of business premises, or on boards outside with lists of 'hands required' and they made a note of any that sounded promising.

During the train journey back home they talked at length about their future. Sarah was still reluctant to move away from Nottingham, where she had so many friends and relatives, but John was quite clear in his own mind that he could see little future as a framework knitter. He knew that, sooner or later, he would have to find a different job, and he thought that a new start, in a new town, might just suit them both.

'I'm not so sure,' said Sarah, with a degree of hesitancy. 'We don't know anyone in Sheffield, other than Thomas, and it seems such a dirty and smelly town.'

'But you saw how friendly everyone was; all those friends of

Thomas, they all made us welcome at the pub. And as for being dirty, I suppose it was, but all towns are getting like that. Maybe we saw the worst parts of it. I expect it has some pleasant areas that we didn't see. But you heard what Thomas said; he soon got used to it and I'm sure we would, too.'

'Well, if we could find somewhere to live like Thomas's house, I would feel much happier about moving. Just think, our own privy and water supply, in our own back yard!'

'I doubt if we'd drop that lucky. But in any case, if we did move, and found after a while we didn't like it, we could always go back to Nottingham. There'll always be a place for us at your parents' house; they told us that. I'd have to find another job, but I'd have to do that anyway, and you'll never have any difficulty getting work at a lace factory, not with your years of experience.'

For almost a week they thought long and hard as to what they should do. They talked it over with David and Margaret. They deliberated, debated and discussed it at great length, until at last they decided to go. Margaret could tell that John was the keener of the two, but Sarah was content, once they had finally made up their minds. And once their minds were made up, they were determined not to delay things any longer. It was still summer, the best time to be traipsing round the streets looking for work and somewhere to live. Sarah gave her employer a week's notice, and John wrote a short note to Thomas, telling him of their decision, and that they would come up the following Saturday and would like to stop with him until they found a place of their own.

And so, on the Friday night, having packed all the belongings they needed to take with them, they joined their family and friends for a farewell drink at the Hanging Gate, and late the next morning, feeling a little hung over and light-headed, and accompanied by David and Margaret, they walked down to the station. As their train pulled out, Sarah leant out of the window, waving goodbye to her parents, and not until they were out of sight did she sit down again. John noticed a tear in her eye, so he put a comforting arm around her and told her not to fret.

'Now, Sarah, love; there's no need for tears. You've got me and your brother to look after you, and we can easily get back and visit everyone in Nottingham. I'm sure we've made the right decision.'

Thomas was waiting for them at the station, and they were soon back at his house. 'First thing Monday morning, we'll start looking for jobs,' said John, and that's just what they did.

It didn't take John long to find work. He had promised Sarah that he would take any job he could get, just to start earning some money, and then if he didn't like what he was doing he could always look round for something else. He glanced down his list of available jobs and concluded that the tannery seemed the best bet. It was close to where Thomas lived, and they seemed to have a number of positions for unskilled men, and as far as the tanning business went, the word 'unskilled' described John precisely, for he had no knowledge at all of this trade. He enquired within, as directed by the sign outside the factory entrance, and was instructed to speak to one of the foremen, who, once he had found out a little about John, looked him up and down, and having satisfied himself that he appeared to be of good character and a strong and healthy individual, offered him a job to start the next morning.

Funny, thought John, as he walked back home, for his own surname was Glover. The tannery cured leather hides, some of which were sold to glove makers in the town. Perhaps some of his ancestors had been men who made gloves and that's how his family had acquired the name. But whatever the truth of his ancestry, it made no difference to the nature of the job.

He was employed as a general porter, carrying the raw hides into a warehouse when they arrived at the tannery, then taking them to the various departments as required for processing, and finally helping to pack the finished hides ready for despatch. It was hard work and boring in the extreme. It was also smelly and dirty, and although he rapidly became immune to the stench he didn't think he'd like to remain employed there forever. He was not afraid of hard work, but the tediousness of it all got to him. At least, when he had worked for himself as a framework knitter there were skills involved, acquired during a seven-year apprenticeship, and he had always taken an immense pride in the quality of his work. But this job needed no skills and offered no opportunity for satisfaction. Each day was just like the last, and he was determined that he would eventually find something more to his liking, something which would, once again, restore in him a sense of pride in his work.

Sarah, meanwhile, had found work in one of the largest hotels in the town, the Commercial, a fifteen-minute walk away. The hotel had its own laundry and sewing room, where all its linen – sheets, tablecloths, napkins and so forth – were washed and ironed and, when necessary, repaired. The hotel had need of someone with good needlework skills, and Sarah's many years at the lace factory in Nottingham meant she was well qualified. She had done similar work there, as a finisher, checking the lace as it came off the machines, and repairing by hand any little defects that were found.

They stayed with Thomas for several weeks, but knew it was not fair to him to occupy his only bed whilst he had to sleep on the sofa, so having looked round, they found some rooms to rent in a large tenement building nearby. It was noisy, and the amenities were all situated in a rear courtyard, accessed by a narrow dark alley a little way down the street. They were, of course, both familiar with such arrangements, but here they had a considerable distance to go to fetch water or to use the privy, and one or two of the other tenants, with whom these amenities were shared, were not the most obliging or tolerant of neighbours.

At first, they both found living in Sheffield a bit strange and Sarah felt quite homesick for a while, but as they gradually got to know more people they soon found themselves feeling much more settled. John was still not enjoying his job at the tannery, and it was Sarah who seemed the happier of the two and more content in her work.

John continued to look for another job, and then one evening, over a drink at the Rutland Arms, Thomas told him that there was a vacancy for a clerk in the Despatch Department at the steel mill where he worked. One of the staff there, an elderly man whom Thomas knew quite well, had recently retired, having reached the age of seventy. John had never really thought about a clerk's job, having always worked with his hands, but he was quite capable of reading and writing, he had a quick and agile brain and was a fast learner.

When he was a young boy his mother had taught him to read and write and to memorise his times tables, and he had always been good with numbers, so he reckoned that a clerical job might suit him. No more smelly hides to hump around a draughty, dirty factory; a nice warm office, no doubt, in the winter; more regular and amenable hours and probably more pay into the bargain. So he went along to the company office to enquire about the position, and that evening he sat down and composed a letter of application then immediately went back and posted it through the large brass letterbox; and then he waited.

After two weeks, and no reply, he assumed he would hear nothing further. But having now convinced himself that his future lay in office work, and just as he had decided to start looking round for other similar positions, a letter arrived in a stiff, expensive-looking envelope, and tearing it open, he found himself invited to attend an interview the following Monday morning at ten o'clock.

He could barely sleep that night with excitement, relishing the prospect of a new job, and having managed to dream up a plausible reason for absenting himself from the tannery for a half-day, the next evening he went along to give Thomas the good news and to find out as much as he could about the firm in general and the clerk's position in particular.

'Well, I think the best thing you could do is talk to old Isaac, the man who did the job for over twenty years, I believe.

If we go down to the Rutland a bit later we might catch him; he often calls in there for a pint and a smoke about nine o'clock.' Thomas was correct in his assumption, and shortly after nine, the door opened and in walked a small, plumpish man with a bald head and a sallow complexion.

'There he is,' said Thomas. 'You wait here and I'll bring him over.'

'Here,' said John, taking a shilling from his pocket, 'get him a pint and two more for us.'

Thomas soon returned and introduced him to Isaac, who told John that he had worked for the firm for over twenty years. He explained what the job entailed and spoke about some of the staff who worked there.

'Mind you,' he added, then paused whilst he took another swig of ale and drew long and hard on his pipe, 'I don't want to put a damper on your hopes, but before I left I did hear a whisper that one of the senior clerks in the Goods Inwards Department is keen to get his nephew appointed, and if I know his uncle, which I do, he'll pull every string he can to try and get him selected. Having a relative already working there can often help, and it wouldn't be the first time nepotism ruled the day. Bristow's his name; full of his own importance, he is, and I'm told his nephew's just the same. You can rest assured his uncle will be dropping hints about who should get the job. Of course, it won't be up to him, but he's a crafty sod and I wouldn't trust him an inch. So if you do get the job, you'll need to watch your back.'

On the Monday morning at five minutes to ten, John presented himself, spick and span and in his Sunday best, at the offices of *Potter, Simpson and Co*. He was shown into a corridor, and asked to take a seat outside a door marked 'Despatch Office'. Three other men were already seated there – a pimply-faced youth who looked barely old enough to be let out alone, a man of about his own age who seemed excessively nervous, and a shabbily dressed middle-aged fellow who sat nonchalantly smoking a pipe and reading a newspaper. John nodded a greeting and wished them all a good morning then took a seat himself, but no sooner had he done so when they were joined by a young whippersnapper. He came swaggering down the corridor as if he were himself the factory owner, and taking the last remaining seat, dragged it noisily a little way from the others, sat down, leant back and stretched out his long, gangly legs. John took a quick glimpse at the latecomer, and quickly summed him up. He was about eighteen or nineteen, nattily dressed in the latest fashion, tall, slim and clean-shaven, and exhibiting all the arrogance that comes from an excess of self-confidence. He uttered not a word, so John wished him a good morning, a greeting that was met with total silence.

A couple of minutes later the door to the Despatch Office opened and a clerk emerged, a bewhiskered gentleman of uncertain years wearing a pair of spectacles, and instructed them all to enter. First out of his seat was the latest arrival, who swept past the others as if they were invisible and led the way into the office, with a haughty 'morning Jim' to the clerk. Once inside, they were told to take a seat at one of the five small desks spread out in the middle of the room. The clerk introduced himself and explained that they were firstly to be given a written test, to establish their abilities in reading, writing, arithmetic, logic and current affairs, after which they were each to undergo a short interview with the senior clerk, Mr Burdsall. Each desk was already provided with an inkstand and pen, and the clerk then handed to each of them a sheet of printed paper, along with some blank sheets on which to write.

'Now then, gentlemen,' said the clerk, 'you are to answer all the questions and write your answers on the blank sheets. Please write your name at the top, and number each sheet. You have thirty minutes and you may now start.'

John looked at the paper containing the various questions and read it through as quickly as he could. Tests like this were new to him, he having never been subjected to anything of the kind before, but he had a cool head and was determined to do his best. He worked diligently through all the questions, none of which was too tasking, but checked each one carefully as he went, taking care to write neatly. After about fifteen minutes, during which time one could have heard the proverbial pin drop, the silence was suddenly broken by the scraping of a chair, as the arrogant young whippersnapper rose noisily from the desk he was seated at, walked up to the clerk and handed him his papers.

'Finished, Jim. I'm going to go and have a word with my uncle, now. Let me know when you want me; you know where his office is,' he said condescendingly, and promptly strode out of the room. This announcement merely served to confirm to John what he had already guessed – that this was none other than Bristow junior, the candidate that Isaac had mentioned.

John tried to ignore this irritating interruption to his concentration, and carried on writing. He had almost finished when the clerk rose from his desk at the front and ordered them to stop immediately.

'You will now go outside and sit in the corridor again until you are called,' he announced, whereupon the four of them remaining did as requested.

They had no sooner taken their seats, when another gentleman came along the corridor and entered the room. This, it transpired, was Mr Burdsall, the senior clerk, and after about ten minutes the pimply-faced youth was called into the room, only to emerge a short while later looking somewhat flummoxed. The pipe-smoking man was next to be interviewed, followed by the nervous one, who very quickly reappeared, his ashen face having turned several shades lighter.

John, himself now feeling a little apprehensive, was the last to be summoned. His interview was short, no more than ten minutes, and was in no way intimidating. He was asked about his experience and what sort of work he had done in the past, then told what the required hours were and the wages, and advised that if he were successful he would hear within a week. If he heard nothing, it was explained, he could assume that he had not been successful. Of the arrogant young whippersnapper, he neither saw nor heard anything further.

After a week had passed, and no letter had arrived, John assumed that he had not been selected for the position. This was confirmed a couple of days later when he and Thomas went along to the Rutland one night and bumped into Isaac.

'Sorry to hear you didn't get the job, lad, but just as I thought, young Bristow's been appointed.' John was a little surprised that Isaac appeared to know for certain what he already suspected.

'Well, I haven't heard anything, so I guessed I hadn't got it. But how come you know who got the job?'

'Ah, I've got a lot of pals still working there, and they keep me up-to-date with everything that goes on.'

'Oh well, never mind. I'm sure there'll be other jobs, so I'll keep on looking. I'm determined to get out of that tannery.'

And that's exactly what John did – kept looking. But after a month, he still hadn't found anything he fancied, and was beginning to get a bit downhearted, when one evening, on returning home from work, he found he had received a rather official-looking letter.

'I wonder what this can be?' he said to Sarah, as they sat eating their tea. He took a knife from the table, carefully opened the envelope and took out the single sheet of paper. As he read it, a look of astonishment spread across his face.

'Who's it from, John? Read it to me.'

'You're never going to believe this, Sarah; it's from *Potter and Simpson*. They're asking if I would be interested in taking a position in the Despatch Office. It says a vacancy has arisen, and as they have already interviewed me they are aware of my capabilities and would like to offer me the job. Well, there's a turn up for the books!'

John didn't need asking twice, and straight after his tea he wrote a letter of acceptance. But being inquisitive, he made a special visit to the Rutland that night, hoping to see Isaac and find out if he knew any more about the firm's apparent change of mind. He wasn't disappointed, and didn't have long to wait until Isaac arrived. He had, indeed, heard the news, and it turned out that the two Bristows, uncle and nephew, were no longer in the employ of the firm. No official reason had been given for their sudden and unexpected departure, but Isaac had it on good authority that certain discrepancies had been found in the ledgers of both the Despatch and the Goods Inwards Departments, and rumours of 'fingers in the till' were rife. Whatever the truth, John was delighted at the opportunity that he had been afforded, and the following Monday morning, at seven o'clock sharp, he started his new job.

It was probably the best move John could have made. He soon settled down and made new friends. He enjoyed the work, and really believed that he'd at last found his true vocation. He was happy again and suddenly everything seemed to be looking up, especially when, a few weeks later, Thomas came round one evening with a proposition.

'The landlord came over the other day to tell me that he's found some new premises to use as a warehouse, so he won't be needing the upstairs rooms any more. I guessed his business had been growing, because his men have been coming and going a lot recently and storing more furniture up there.'

'Oh, that'll be good for you, Thomas, you'll have much more room now,' said Sarah.

'That's true enough, but the trouble is, he also told me that the rent's going up, and I can't afford it, so I thought I'd have to start looking for somewhere cheaper. But then I thought of you two. How do you fancy moving back in with me? At least, this time, we'd each have a proper bedroom upstairs. And with our three wages we could easily afford the rent. What do you say?'

'Oh yes!' exclaimed Sarah, excitedly. 'And just think, John, our own back yard and privy and even our own water supply! No more going out into a dark cold courtyard at night and sharing with everyone else. And your house is so much nicer than round here, Thomas. When can we move in?'

It was soon arranged, and the following Saturday afternoon, after they had all finished work, Thomas arrived with a cart he'd borrowed from a workmate, and in a couple of hours all of John and Sarah's possessions had been moved to their new home.

'Right, you two,' said Thomas, as the last remaining item was taken off the cart. 'Come on, let's have a night out to celebrate. I could do with a few pints, and one of those steak pies down at the Rutland, and I bet you could, too.'

'Agreed,' said John. 'And the first round's on me.'

CHAPTER SIXTEEN

Oh mother where art thou?

'Oh, bother and drat. Just when we were getting things sorted, she springs this on us!'

'Now then, mother, whatever's the matter?' asked Eliza as she came into the kitchen, her arms laden down with two large baskets of fresh food that the provision merchant's boy had just delivered. 'We're all organised for tonight and the food you ordered has arrived, so why all the fuss?'

'Has he left yet?'

'Who?'

'The grocer's lad, of course,' replied Hannah, tetchily. 'We need some more provisions. Quick, Eliza, go and see if you can stop him so we can ask him to fetch them for us, otherwise it means a special trip into town, and in this weather, too.'

'More provisions? We've ordered enough, haven't we? Anyway, it's too late. After he'd dropped these off, I stepped outside to have a quick word with the gardener, and I watched him trotting off down the lane. There's a mountain of stuff here. Why do we need any more?'

'Well, Mrs Brentnall's just sprung it on us that there'll be twelve for dinner, not the six she originally said. She's got another of her charity dos tonight, and one of the committee has only just told her about some wealthy donors she wanted to bring along. Mrs Brentnall was very apologetic, but we've got no choice. We can easily cater for twelve, we've done it often enough before, but it's very annoying to be told at such short notice. I'll have to go straight down into the town and sort it out.'

'It's all right, mother, I'll go. You know how cold it is; it's a bit frosty underfoot and there's a fog setting in.'

'No, Eliza, you stay here and carry on getting things ready. There's a couple of other errands I want to sort out too, and if I hurry up I can get those done as well. I'll be as quick as I can. Let's see, now, it's just gone one, so I should be back by about four, half past at the latest. I'm sure I can get a ride back with the delivery boy. They're not dining till eight, fortunately, so if I get a move on we should be ready by then.'

Before Eliza could protest further, Hannah had rushed out the kitchen and up the rear stairs, and a minute or two later Eliza heard steps coming down the main staircase followed by the front door being slammed. Oh dear, thought Eliza; her mother must really be in a bad mood to use the main staircase and front door. Mrs Brentnall didn't really approve of that. She and her mother were expected to use the rear stairs and back door at all times.

For the rest of the afternoon Eliza continued getting things ready for the dinner party. Mr and Mrs Brentnall regularly entertained and she knew exactly what had to be done, so she did as much as she could with what was available, and the rest would have to wait until her mother returned. It had been bitterly cold for several days and Eliza was glad of the warmth in the kitchen, where a fire was kept burning almost continuously and the heat from the ovens made this a cosy place to be on such a miserable, raw day.

She had barely stopped working since her mother set off for the town, but now, she decided, it was time for a well-earned break. Picking up a cloth, she lifted the hot iron kettle from its almost permanent perch on a hook over the fire, and poured some of its boiling contents into a small teapot. Whilst the tea brewed, she took a freshly baked scone from a tray on the kitchen table, cut it in half and smothered it with a generous portion of butter and raspberry jam, then pouring herself a large cup of tea, seated herself in the comfortable fireside chair.

Her mother had taught her well, she thought, and she now considered herself as good a cook as she was, and from what she had said, these culinary skills ran in the family. Her grandmother, Agnes, whom she could only vaguely remember, had ran quite a thriving little business from her home in Norfolk Street, supplying a number of pubs and small shops with her bread, cakes, pastries and pies, and those skills had now been passed down to her. Hannah had helped with this business but found it difficult to continue when Agnes died, what with having a young daughter to look after and also having recently been widowed. As she sat enjoying her afternoon tea and scone, Eliza continued to reminisce about the past.

It was now late January in 1861. She knew that her mother had come to work for Mr and Mrs Brentnall twenty years before, after her own mother had passed on. Eliza herself had only been three years old at the time, so this was really the only home she had ever known. It must have been a terrible time for her mother, she thought, because all this upheaval came only a year after her husband, Joseph, had died under tragic circumstances. Eliza was only two then, and, sadly, she had no memory of her father at all. Her mother had often said what a fine man he was, a skilled cutler who had some clever ideas and a determined ambition to make something of himself, and Eliza often wondered how different all their lives might have been had he lived. But she was happy enough here. She and her mother had a comfortable, if busy, life, and compared with many of the workers in Sheffield they really had no cause for complaint.

But, happy as she was, she had recently begun to think that she ought to seek pastures new. She was now twenty-three. Most young women of her age were married with children, and she didn't want to remain single forever. Working and living where she did, away from the town, and often having to work late into the evenings, her opportunities for getting out and meeting eligible young men were severely restricted.

Suddenly, her daydreams were interrupted as the large kitchen clock over the mantelpiece began to strike five. Her mother should have been back by now, but maybe the bad weather had delayed her; and she did say she had some other errands to see to. But as soon as she turned up they'd have to get on with preparing the rest of the food.

She got up out of the chair, and was taking her cup and plate over to the sink when she heard the front door bell ring. Mr Brentnall had not yet arrived home from work but she knew that Mrs Brentnall was in, and she usually answered callers at the front door, so Eliza ignored it. Perhaps Mrs Brentnall hadn't heard it, for after a very short pause it rang again, this time for much longer, and whoever the caller was they must have been pulling frantically at the bell handle. This time she heard steps in the hallway, followed by the door being opened, and immediately she heard a man's voice. She couldn't tell, from inside the kitchen, exactly what was being said, but she got the impression that whoever it was sounded in some distress, talking ten to the dozen and in an increasingly agitated tone.

She stopped what she was doing and moved nearer to the kitchen door, inquisitive to hear the animated conversation taking place between her mistress and the mystery visitor. Then she heard the voices getting louder and closer, and moved away from the door just before it opened and Mrs Brentnall entered. She was followed by a short, stout, middle-aged man, suitably dressed for such a wretched day in a heavy worsted coat, a thick woollen scarf wound several times around his neck, and a large brimmed hat, still sitting firmly on his head. Even beneath these voluminous layers of clothing she was able to recognise Mr Poynter, the owner of the shop where they purchased most of their food; the very place her mother had set out to visit some four hours earlier.

'Eliza, this is Mr Poynter, the provision merchant, but I'm sure you know him,' said Mrs Brentnall.

'Yes, of course. Good afternoon, Mr Poynter. Is mother with you? She set off a while ago to fetch some more food and she said she'd try and get a lift back with the delivery boy. Have you come, instead?'

There was no immediate answer from either Mr Poynter or Mrs Brentnall, and then Eliza noticed them glancing uneasily at each other, and that they each seemed to be waiting for the other to speak first. And Eliza knew that something was wrong. It was Mrs Brentnall who eventually spoke.

'Eliza, my dear, I'm sorry to have to tell you, but Mr Poynter has brought some bad news. There's been an accident and your mother's been taken to the infirmary. He came as quickly as he could, and he'll take you there at once so that you can see her.'

Eliza cried out in anguish, then buried her face in her hands and began to sob. Mrs Brentnall put a comforting arm around her shoulders. 'There, now, Eliza, don't fret. Run along and put your coat and hat on, it's very cold outside.'

'But what's happened? You say there's been an accident?'

'I'm afraid so, miss,' explained Mr Poynter. 'Your mother came to the shop, and the lad loaded everything she ordered into the van, and they set off to come back here. But from what I can make out they were going along Church Street past the cathedral, when a brewer's dray came hurtling round a corner without warning and collided with them. The drayman said the road was icy, and it was quite foggy, too. The van turned over and your mother was thrown out and got trapped underneath. My lad was a bit shaken, but some people stopped to help and they soon got the van upright and freed your mother. Fortunately, an empty cab was passing and the driver offered to take her to the hospital. The lad got back to the shop as quick as he could and told me what had happened, and I came straight here. I'm so sorry, miss, but if you'd like to get your coat, we can set off.'

'Yes, of course. I won't be a minute.' And Eliza hurried up the stairs to her room. She was soon back and ready to leave. 'But what about the dinner? I've got to finish preparing it, and mother's not here to help.'

'Now, don't you go worrying about that, Eliza; I'm sure we can sort something out,' said Mrs Brentnall. 'The important thing is for you to go and see how your mother is. Mr Poynter says he'll stay with you and then bring you back.'

The General Infirmary was a little way out of the town, on the northwest side, so it wasn't too far away, and before long they were turning off the road and into the grounds. Mr Poynter went into the hospital with Eliza, and they were soon able to find out where Hannah had been taken.

'I'll wait here for you and I'll take you back home whenever you're ready,' said Mr Poynter. He sat down on a bench in the entrance hall, and watched as Eliza hurried off down a long corridor. About half an hour later she returned. 'How is she?' he enquired.

'She's asleep now. I only managed to have a few words with her, but she seemed to be very confused. The nurse says she's suffering from mild concussion, and she's also got a broken arm and some fractured ribs. They've set the arm and done what they can for the time being. She says all they can do now is wait and hope things heal. But I can visit her as often as I like, so I'll come again tomorrow.'

Within twenty minutes they were back at *Aysgarth Villa*. Eliza thanked Mr Poynter for his help, then went in through the back door, where she found Mrs Brentnall busying herself in the kitchen.

'I can see to that, now,' Eliza said as she walked in.

'Not on your own, you can't. I might not do much cooking these days, but I haven't forgotten how. And I can't possibly expect you to do everything yourself. But how is your mother?'

Soon, Eliza had told Mrs Brentnall all about her visit, and although she seemed quite calm now, it was evident that Eliza was very worried about her. Over the coming weeks, she went to the infirmary every day. But as the days went by there was little improvement in Hannah's condition. Sometimes she was awake and able to talk a little, but more often than not she was asleep, and Eliza was not keen to wake her. The doctors now believed that the injury to her ribs may have been worse than at first thought, and that this might lead to other complications. And then, a month after the accident, Eliza arrived at the infirmary one morning and as usual went straight to the ward where her mother was being treated, only to find an empty bed. And suddenly, her worst fears seemed to have come true. As she stood there, staring at the bed where her mother had been sleeping the day before, the matron came in and saw her, looking utterly alone and distraught.

'Miss Lambert, if you could just come along with me, please,' she said, sympathetically. Eliza followed her into a small office at the far end of the ward and the matron closed the door behind them. 'I'm so very sorry to have to tell you that your mother passed away just an hour ago. We sent someone with a message, but you must already have left home.'

Poor Eliza was devastated. The matron said that the damage to her ribs was far worse than they thought, and that one of her lungs had probably been punctured. Pneumonia had set in, and the various injuries she had suffered in the accident had made her too weak to recover. Eliza made her way back home in a daze, but how she got there, she couldn't remember. Her mind was in a whirl. Only a month before, on the day her mother had set off for the town, she had sat in the kitchen, thinking about her father who had died so tragically, and now her mother was dead, too. If only she had gone to do the shopping that day, as she had wanted to, everything might have been different, and her mother would still be alive. But she had insisted on going herself. And now Eliza felt all alone in the world.

Mr and Mrs Brentnall were good to Eliza during those next few, difficult months. They helped with the funeral arrangements, and also found a girl to come in and assist her in the kitchen, but they could tell that she had lost her enthusiasm and that her heart was no longer in her work.

When her mother had been alive, Eliza had been happy here, but her mother was now gone. She decided that she needed a change. Her friends all lived in the town, and that's where she wanted to be. And so she resolved that she would look for another job and find somewhere else to live. But she knew she owed a lot to her employers, and so, one evening, she sat down with them and explained what she had decided to do, and why. They were both understanding and sympathetic, albeit sorry to lose her. Eliza promised to stay on until they had found suitable replacements for her and her mother, but they insisted that this would not be necessary, and she should not feel any disloyalty whatsoever by applying for other positions as soon as she wished.

For several weeks she perused the 'situations vacant' columns that appeared in the newspapers. Eventually, her eyes landed on a particular advertisement from the Commercial Hotel, the same establishment where she and her mother had met Emily over four years earlier, when she had travelled to Sheffield to tell them about her father's past. The hotel was looking for an assistant cook, but better still for her, one of the conditions was that the successful applicant must live in at the hotel, where accommodation and keep would be provided. And that would save her having to find somewhere to live. She was confident that, with her years of experience, she was capable of meeting all the requirements of the position, and without delay she penned her application then set off into the town to deliver it.

She was one of three invited to attend at the hotel a week later, where she was interviewed by the assistant manager, and within another week she had been offered, and had accepted, the job.

On the day of Eliza's departure, Mr Brentnall had his carriage waiting at the front door, and helped to put aboard the large trunk and a smaller suitcase, containing all her worldly belongings. He had offered to take her to the hotel on the way to his office, and as she climbed in, Mrs Brentnall was there to say goodbye. Although Eliza knew she was making the right move, it was still with much sadness that she left.

'Goodbye, Eliza. The very best of luck; and do please keep in touch with us,' said Mrs Brentnall. 'And don't forget, if ever you need any help, in any way, you know where we are. And do take care.'

'I will; and thank you for everything you've done for me. I'll never forget my time here.'

And so, with hope and anticipation, but a degree of trepidation, Eliza left *Aysgarth Villa* and set off for a new home and a new life, not knowing what the future might hold.

CHAPTER SEVENTEEN

A night at the halls

'I think, Thomas, it's high time you thought about settling down; you're twenty-six next, you know.'

Sarah, John and Thomas were seated round the table in the parlour one evening eating their tea, and Sarah was in one of her 'mother hen' moods as Thomas usually referred to them.

'I am settled down,' he replied with a grin, carefully directing a discreet wink at John. 'I'm settled down here with you and John.'

'You know exactly what I mean, Thomas. Don't try and be funny with me!'

'Now then Sarah, just because you're my older sister doesn't mean you can act like ma. Whenever I get to see her she asks the same questions – have you met a nice girl yet? Isn't it time you got married? And every time I give her the same answer, that I'll get married when I'm good and ready, and not before. Now you're beginning to sound just like her. Has she asked you to keep on nagging me on her behalf?'

'No, of course not. But she's right. You're not getting any younger; John was twenty-one when we got married and I was just seventeen. You've got a steady job, you're good-looking and fun to be with. You'd be a catch for any girl. You've had plenty of girlfriends to my knowledge. Why can't you stick with one of them and settle down?'

'Ah well, you know what they say, sis, variety's the spice of life!'

'Hmm; typical,' replied Sarah with a look of mild disapproval on her face.

'It's no use looking at me like that. I've told you before; I haven't found anyone who I really liked enough to marry. It's as simple as that. Anyway, what's brought this on, all of a sudden?'

'Nothing.'

'Come on, Sarah. I know you better than that. Something's made you raise the subject.'

'Well … since you've asked, I'll tell you. It's just that, there's a girl at the hotel, she's only been there a few months, and …'

'Oh, no!' interrupted Thomas, 'not another of your attempts at matchmaking. I remember the last time you introduced me to one of your work colleagues. What was she called? Dora, wasn't it? Dopy Dora, I called her. Dumpy little thing, had a laugh like a parrot with a sore throat. Started talking about weddings and babies within minutes of meeting her; and she stunk to high heaven.'

'Poor Dora. She wasn't that bad. Anyway, she's happily married now, so that proves that we don't all think alike.'

'So, who've you got lined up for me now? I assume you have, otherwise I don't think you'd have mentioned it.'

'Well, as I was saying, there's a girl who started work at the hotel some months ago. I hadn't actually met her until today. She's one of the cooks, and she lives in at the hotel, in the staff quarters. We don't normally get to meet the kitchen staff, but the curtains in her room got snagged and had a tear in them, so she came into the sewing room to ask if anyone could mend it for her, and I volunteered. It didn't take long, but while I was there we got talking. She's a really nice girl, very pretty, and was so interesting to listen to. I think she's a year or two younger than you, Thomas. They call her Eliza. She told me a bit about herself, not much, but when I asked her if her parents were still alive she went a bit quiet and said no, and she sounded quite sad then, so I changed the subject. But I did find out that there's no one special in her life at the moment. She's very friendly, and I know that she likes to go out and meet people, and I was thinking, you said you fancied going to that new music hall that's just opened on Saturday night, so maybe I could ask her to join us. What do you think, Thomas?'

'Well, if she's one of the cooks, I expect she'll be working on

Saturday night. It must be one of the hotel's busiest times.'

'It is, so I asked her about that, and she's off duty on Saturday. The kitchen staff work shifts but they each get one Saturday in six off, and this week it's Eliza's turn, so she's really looking forward to going out somewhere on Saturday night.'

'But she might not like the music hall. Not everybody does. Things can sometimes get out of hand, especially when people have had too much to drink.'

'Oh, she likes music halls; I've already asked her that. And I think she's quite broadminded.'

'I see. It looks like you've got it all sorted, then! All right, Sarah, invite her to come along. Anything for a quiet life, eh John. What do you say?'

'I'm saying nothing,' replied John. 'Sometimes it pays to keep quiet when the wife's got the bit between her teeth, as you'll no doubt find out one day.'

Saturday soon came round, and by early afternoon Thomas, Sarah and John were all back home, and work was over for another week. Sarah quickly prepared lunch for them, just some bread, cheese and fruit as they intended to eat later, before they went to the music hall. Sarah, in her usual efficient manner, had organised everything. She had arranged to meet Eliza at the Cutler's Arms, where they could get a meal; a pub not far from the Commercial Hotel, and quite close to the music hall.

'The Cutler's Arms? I've never been in there; in fact I don't know the pub. What's it like?' asked Thomas.

'I couldn't say. It was Eliza's suggestion that we meet there. She said she knows the landlady, and that they serve good food, and it seems convenient for where we're going. And she's a cook herself, so I expect her recommendation must count for something.'

Although he hadn't admitted it, Thomas was quite looking forward to meeting Eliza. From what Sarah had told him she seemed to be quite an amiable young lady, but he was still concerned that a night out at the music hall might not be to her liking.

Some of them could be extremely rough, especially the 'free

and easies', most of which were not the sort of venue to which one would want to take a lady of propriety. They were invariably thick with tobacco smoke and pungent with liquor fumes, where cheap ale and gin were available, and often attracted many people of a dubious character. Some were openly used by prostitutes to pick up clients, and many a time the police had to be called as drunken brawls broke out. He knew all that at first hand, for he had, on occasions, visited them with friends from work. But from what he had heard, this new hall appeared to be a far more respectable place. At least, he hoped so.

The three of them set off at half past four. Sarah had arranged to meet Eliza at about five o'clock, and it was five to when they opened the pub door and walked into a large and inviting room. A welcoming fire burned brightly in the hearth, for although it was May, the day had been cool. The room was pleasantly furnished and well equipped with tables and chairs; in one corner stood a piano, and along the far side was the bar. There were, perhaps, a dozen people already there, and as they entered, Sarah noticed her brother eagerly looking around, and she knew exactly who he was looking for. Most of the customers were seated in groups around tables, except for three young men propping up one end of the bar, behind which stood a barmaid with her back to the room, while she appeared to be talking to someone through a hatchway. Thomas continued to look round, but there was no sign of the one person he was expecting to see. Not only expecting, but keen, for Sarah had already described Eliza to him and he had decided that if her description was accurate, then this was one attempt at her matchmaking he was happy to go along with.

'You two go and sit down, and I'll get some drinks,' said Thomas. Sarah and John found a table near the fire while Thomas went up to the bar. The barmaid was still standing at the hatchway, but on hearing someone approach, she turned round.

'Sorry, love, I was talking to the landlady and her friend who's just called in. Now, what can I get you?' While the barmaid was busy pouring the drinks, Thomas was able to see through the hatchway into a room at the rear, which he could tell was the kitchen. Two women, of contrasting ages, were seated at a table, an elderly one, presumably the landlady, and a much younger woman, whom he took to be the friend. And it was the latter who instantly attracted his attention. For a brief moment, he had a feeling that he might have seen her somewhere before, but it was only when she turned round so that he could see her face clearly, that he knew he hadn't. And yet he seemed to recognise those features. He was immediately smitten, staring at the vision of loveliness before him, and then he realised that she fitted precisely the description Sarah had given him of Eliza. Could this really be her, he thought to himself.

'Here's your drinks, love,' said the barmaid, 'that'll be sixpence, please,' she added. Suddenly, Thomas became aware of the voice addressing him.

'Oh, sorry. I was miles away.'

'Yes, I noticed. Eyeing up our Eliza, if I'm not mistaken. She's very pretty, isn't she?' Thomas nodded his head in agreement. Eliza. So this *was* her. She had told Sarah that she knew the landlady, so it had to be her, he thought, as he carried the drinks over to the table and sat down.

'Don't worry, Thomas, I'm sure she'll be here soon,' said Sarah, teasingly, as she took a sip of her drink.

'I think she's here already. There's a girl in the kitchen talking to the landlady and she's called Eliza, and she looks just like you described her.' Sarah went over to the bar to have a look for herself.

'Eliza, it's me, Sarah,' she shouted through the hatchway.

In less than a minute Eliza had joined them in the bar, and Sarah introduced her to her brother and husband. Within half an hour, they were all tucking into the food they had ordered, and Thomas and Eliza were nattering away like they'd known each other for years. Sarah dreamed up an excuse and went outside for a minute with John.

'Now then, John, what do you think of that? They're getting on famously. Thomas obviously likes her, and I think the feeling might be mutual. I've never seen him like that with any other girl before.'

'Well, you could be right. But don't go getting your hopes up just yet. They've only known each other for five minutes! We'll have to wait and see how things go.'

They finished their meal and had another drink, and then it was time to set off for the music hall. It wasn't far, just a couple of streets away, and as they walked along, Thomas and Eliza dropped back a bit and walked a few yards behind Sarah and John, as if they wanted to be alone.

The music hall was one of a growing number in the town, for this form of entertainment was rapidly gaining popularity throughout the whole country. This one had only recently opened, and was situated in a large extension built at the rear of a public house, which had for some years been a venue for up-and-coming amateur entertainers of all kinds, providing impromptu performances for the pub's customers. Increasing numbers were being attracted to his pub, and the landlord had soon realised the financial benefits such entertainment brought.

But his existing premises were hardly big enough, and he had decided to invest a considerable sum in constructing a building specially designed for the purpose, where professional entertainers could perform and more customers could be accommodated. The hall had its own entrance in a passage along the side of the pub, and could also be accessed via a connecting door from within. And whilst the amateur entertainments had been free, a small charge was now made, and just inside the door was a booth where one purchased a ticket. Fourpence up in the balcony, threepence downstairs, the ticket price to include a free glass of beer or gin. The balcony was provided with more comfortable, upholstered seats, laid out in rows, as in a theatre, whilst downstairs, in the main body of the hall, were wooden tables and chairs where the audience sat. The hall also had its own separate bars, one upstairs and one downstairs, open continuously throughout the performance.

Once inside, they had a quick discussion and decided that more fun was likely to be had by remaining downstairs, where the atmosphere would no doubt be far livelier than in the more sedate setting of the balcony. So they handed over their money to the man in the ticket booth, and in return were given four tokens, to be exchanged at the bar for their drinks.

The performance was due to commence at seven o'clock, and it was now a quarter to. A sizeable number of people were already in the main hall as they entered, and others were still queuing at the ticket booth. Most of the tables were already occupied, but they were able to find an empty one, and took their seats. Thomas offered to go to the bar and fetch the drinks, and Sarah suggested that John go with him. He was happy to do so, but he and Thomas both knew that her motive was to get Eliza to herself, for it had been her suggestion that Eliza should join them that night and she was itching to find out just what she thought of her brother.

The hall, being newly built, had a clean and airy appearance, its size exaggerated by the many large mirrors fixed to the walls, which were finished in a stunning blend of crimson, green and gold, whilst the soft, yellow glow from the numerous gaslights was reflected in dazzling intensity by hundreds of lead crystal prisms hanging from eight large, chandeliers, themselves gas lit and suspended from the white ceiling. No expense had been spared in planning this majestic palace of varieties, designed to attract the townsfolk and entice them away from their usual drab surroundings.

The stage, which was shortly to become the focus of attention, was about twenty by thirty feet, with a dozen footlights, below which sat the 'orchestra', if one could give it such an exalted title. For it consisted merely of a pianist, a cellist and violinist and a fourth musician, who during the course of the evening, played a variety of wind instruments. Towards the front of the stage hung a pair of satin curtains in a deep shade of red. By the time these were drawn back, and the gaslights dimmed as the master of ceremonies introduced the first act, the hall was full, and looking around it was plain that some had already consumed more than their fair share of alcohol. There was a continuous scraping of chair legs as people got up to go to the bar, and in between the various acts, purveyors of sandwiches, hot pies, whelks, oysters and other tempting foodstuffs, came amongst the audience with their well-stocked baskets, whilst waiters were busily occupied in delivering drinks and collecting empty glasses.

The entertainment was many and varied; singers of comic, patriotic, tragic or sentimental songs, all intended to bring a smile to the face, a stirring of the heart, or a tear to the eye; a juggler; a comedian and ventriloquist; male and female impersonators; a troupe of dancers; a magician, and a small company of actors who performed a short, two-act rendering of that favourite melodramatic play, *Maria Marten and the murder in the Red Barn*. This brought forth both laughter and sighs, and then shouts of derision as the unfortunate murder victim was seen to get up and walk off stage before the curtain had quite closed. The crowd was a lively mix of both high and low life, and all degrees in between, and as the night wore on, and the general consumption of alcohol increased, Thomas became a little concerned lest Eliza might be offended. He had only met her that afternoon, but he already knew that he did want to see her again and wished to make a good impression, and he wondered whether she might want to disassociate herself from someone who clearly enjoyed such bawdy entertainment. But he need not have worried, for he observed how much she was enjoying herself and as she later confessed, she had been to far worse places than that.

The proprietor of the establishment, keen to see his investment bear fruit, was also anxious to avoid the excesses of bad behaviour which was frequently to be found in some of the lowest dives, where an evening out often culminated in a mass brawl. He had therefore hired a number of men – many of whom laboured by day in the steelworks – whose job was to evict anyone who threatened the good order and enjoyment of the majority. This was certainly not a place for those of a sensitive or retiring nature, but provided one was prepared to overlook the incidents of inebriation, and close one's ears to the more obscene and lewd comments directed at some of the performers, then it had to be said that a splendid night's entertainment could almost be guaranteed.

When the curtain eventually came down for the final time,

they returned to the Cutler's Arms for a last drink. This time the bar was full and there was not a seat to be had, but their evening's entertainment was not quite over yet, for the piano was now in use and soon they had joined the rest of the customers in a combined, if not always melodic, rendition of some of the popular songs of the day, many of which they had heard sung so much more professionally just a little while before. But Thomas, egged on by his sister, displayed his undoubted vocal talent with a fine solo performance of *The Rose of Tralee* which was received with a prolonged round of applause, and Sarah was delighted to observe how impressed Eliza appeared to be at her brother's musical ability.

It was shortly after eleven thirty when they finally emerged into the street. The night had turned cool, and all Sarah wanted to do now was get back home to a nice warm bed.

'You two go along,' said Thomas. 'I'll follow you but I want to see that Eliza gets back to the hotel safely. There can be some shifty characters around at this time of night.'

It was more than an hour later when Thomas arrived home. Sarah, tired as she was, but eager to find out just what he thought of Eliza, was still awake. As soon as she heard the door open she got out of bed and slipped on a dressing gown, and ignoring John, who was fast asleep and snoring loudly, she ran downstairs and walked into the living room even before her brother had taken off his coat.

'Well? How did you get on?' she asked excitedly.

'Oh, hello Sarah. I thought you'd be fast asleep by now. You said you were tired and wanted to get to bed.'

'Yes … well … never mind about that. What do you think of Eliza?'

'Well, what do you think?'

'What do you mean, what do I think? I want to know what you think.'

'You women can be quite nosey at times. And you know what they say – curiosity killed the cat.'

'And you men can be equally infuriating. Now, come along, Thomas. I only want to know whether you liked her. You seemed to be getting on like a house on fire.'

Thomas was enjoying having a bit of fun at his sister's expense. He knew full well that she'd be keen to find out everything she could. She was four years his senior, and some of his earliest childhood memories were of her fussing over him and forever getting involved in whatever was going on around the house. Nothing was allowed to happen without her being fully informed, and then having her say.

'We got on all right.'

'All right! Is that all you can say? I might be curious, but never mind the cat – it'll be you that gets killed if you don't tell me a bit more, and it'll be me doing the killing!'

'Right, sis, you win again. She's very nice. We got on well and I think she's one of the prettiest girls I've ever met. No, she is the prettiest girl I've ever met. She's kind and considerate, and she can take a joke. And before you ask, yes, I am seeing her again. We thought we might go for a walk if it's fine tomorrow, maybe up to the cricket ground at Hyde Park. There's often a game there on a Sunday, and she told me she enjoys watching cricket. She's working all day but she's got a few hours off in the afternoon. Anyway, Sarah, that's all there is to tell, for now, so I'm off to bed.'

'Oh, Thomas, that's wonderful. I'm so pleased for you. But make sure you get her back to the hotel in time. You wouldn't want her to be late for work.'

It was usual for them to sleep in on a Sunday, the only day they didn't have to get up early and go to work, and the next day was no exception, especially after their night out. But when Sarah came downstairs just after eleven o'clock, she was surprised to find Thomas already up, washed, shaved and dressed in his Sunday best, which he rarely wore, even on a Sunday. Now it was her turn to tease him.

'My, my, we are looking dapper this morning. Going somewhere special, Thomas?' she asked with a cheeky smile on her face.

'You know I am. I told you last night.'

'Oh, do tell me again.'

While Sarah made a pot of tea, there was a deal of good-natured banter between them, but Sarah was, of course, delighted for her brother, almost as much as he was himself.

He left the house at one o'clock, and twenty minutes later arrived at the Cutler's Arms, where he had promised to meet her. She was not in the bar when he arrived, so he ordered a pint while he waited.

'You're becoming quite a regular,' said the barmaid, the same one who had served him the previous day, both before and after their visit to the music hall. 'A little bird tells me you're seeing Eliza again today. Seems she's quite taken with you.'

'And how do you know that?'

'Well, she's a friend of Annie, the landlady here, but I think you know that. Been the landlady ever since her husband, Harry, died. That must be all of ten years ago. Nice chap he was. Anyway, as I say, Eliza's a friend of her's, and they're upstairs having a chat right now. I'll go and tell her you're here.'

The barmaid disappeared, but shortly returned, followed by Eliza. She had to be back at work by five o'clock, so Thomas quickly finished his drink, and they set off for Hyde Park to see if there was a cricket match being played.

'How come you know the landlady at the Cutler's Arms?' Thomas asked her, as they went.

'She was a friend of my mother and my grandmother. Grandmother had a little business that she ran from her home in Norfolk Street, supplying bread and pies and so on to a number of pubs, and the Cutler's Arms was one of them. When my mother was old enough, she used to help out, but after grandmother died, she found it difficult to carry the business on by herself, especially as she had me to look after. So she had to find something else instead, and it was Annie's husband, Harry, who told her about a job at a big house on Glossop Road. They were looking for someone to live in and be the cook and housekeeper, and of course that suited mother down to the ground, as it provided a home for the two of us. I was only about three at the time, so I don't remember very much, but my mother told me all about it when I was a bit older. And we continued to keep in touch with Annie and Harry, although he died about ten years ago and Annie took over as landlady. She's still going strong, but she's only two or three years younger than my grandmother would have been, had she lived. Sad really, when you think about it. All the women in our family seem to die young. Anyway, Thomas,' she said all of a sudden, as if wanting to change the subject, 'here we are. Oh good, they're playing. Let's find somewhere to sit. I've brought us some cakes and a bottle of lemonade. It's one of the perks of the job; but don't let on!'

They spent a pleasant couple of hours watching the cricket and enjoying the refreshments Eliza had brought, and continuing their conversation. But Thomas could tell that Eliza was reluctant to say much more about her family. He already knew that neither her mother nor her father was still alive – Sarah had told him that much. But Eliza had said very little about her mother and had never even mentioned her father, and Thomas got the impression that it might all be a bit too painful for her to relate. He would have liked to have asked her about them, but thought it best to leave that for her to tell him, if and when she was ready. And so he said nothing more on the subject.

But there were to be plenty more opportunities when she could have told him, because that afternoon was to be only the first of many more times they spent together. Within a short while, it became clear to everyone who knew them that this was more than just a passing friendship, and six months later, on Christmas Day, they became engaged to be married. Together, and with Annie's help, Eliza and Thomas arranged a celebration at the Cutler's Arms the following Saturday, and as soon into the new year as possible, when they could both arrange a day off work together, Thomas took Eliza to Nottingham to meet his family. David and Margaret were delighted that their youngest son had at last found a wife-to-be, and immediately took to their prospective daughter-in-law. It was only a flying visit, but they promised to come again later, and possibly stay for a day or two. Margaret, of course, was keen to know when they planned to get married.

'Don't worry, ma, you'll be the first to know,' Thomas told her, as he gave her a hug and a kiss, just before he and Eliza set off to walk back to the station.

They had decided that there was no point in a long engagement, but one slight problem emerged to prevent them making any immediate plans, something they had overlooked in their recently found happiness. Eliza's job at the hotel required her to live in. That had been one of the strict conditions of taking the job, but a condition that suited her admirably when she had applied for it; in fact, it was one of the reasons she had applied for it. She had been single then, but circumstances were about to change. There was no way that the hotel management would allow her to continue to work there, but live somewhere else. And equally, they would not allow her husband to come and live at the hotel. The choice was simple. Give up her job, or give up her wedding plans. But there was no choice. She knew she would have to give up her job. But she wanted to keep on working, so she and Thomas decided to postpone their wedding for a bit longer, until she could find a suitable job elsewhere.

Disappointing as this was, not least for Margaret who was looking forward to a wedding, Thomas and Eliza saw each other as often as work permitted. When Eliza's shift suited, they would meet up at the Cutler's Arms. One particular evening, after he had had a rather long and tiring day, with no break for lunch, Thomas arrived at the pub, desperate for a drink and a bite to eat. Eliza was already there, having finished her shift an hour before, and come straight over to have a natter with Annie.

'Bad news, I'm afraid, Thomas,' Eliza said to him as he joined her at the bar. Annie was behind the bar, serving drinks, Eliza sitting at a stool, keeping her company.

'That's right, Thomas,' added Annie. 'There'll be no hot food tonight. The lady who helps me out in the kitchen and does most of the cooking has sent a message saying that her mother, who lives over at Chesterfield, has fallen over and injured herself quite badly, and she's had to go there to look after her, and doesn't know when she'll be back. Turns out her mother's a widow who lives by herself, so I don't expect to see her again for ages, if at all. And to cap that, the new barmaid's not turned up again, you know the one I mean, that slip of a girl who's only been here two minutes, which is why I'm having to serve tonight. Mind you, she's no great shakes, not a patch on the others, and this is the third time she's let me down, so I might have to look for some new staff. I can easily find another barmaid, but replacing the cook's a different matter. Anyway, enough of my problems. What can I get you to drink, Thomas? This one's on the house, and I'm sure we can rustle up a sandwich.'

Annie poured Thomas a pint of ale, and after downing half of it in one go, he put it back down on the bar. 'I needed that! Now then, Annie, I think the solution's staring you straight in the face, so to speak.'

'What do you mean?'

'Well, you want a cook. Eliza's a cook, and she's looking for a new job so she can leave the hotel and marry me. Simple, really. Provided she wants the job and you'll have her. And assuming she still wants me!'

'Thomas, you're a genius,' said Eliza, throwing her arms round him and giving him a kiss.

'Yes, I suppose I am. Still, it usually takes a man to come up with the solution to a problem!' he replied with a grin on his face, then ducked out of the way to avoid an imaginary clip round the ear.

'What a good idea,' said Annie. 'Are you interested, Eliza?'

She was, indeed, and after pouring Thomas another pint, Annie went into the kitchen and soon returned with a plate of sandwiches and a large slice of cold pork pie.

'Here you are, Thomas; get this down you.'

'Thanks, Annie. It looks delicious. But you're right, the pub can't do without a cook. So why don't you and Eliza put your heads together and sort something out?'

Whilst Thomas enjoyed the food Annie had prepared, she and

Eliza talked it over and were soon able to come to an arrangement. Eliza was to work at the pub most lunchtimes and evenings, except on Sundays, when food wasn't served. She knew that she would not been earning as much as she did at the hotel, but she would be working less hours. And more importantly, she and Thomas would be able to get married. The very next day Eliza handed in her notice, and a week after that she left the Commercial Hotel for the last time.

She moved into the pub, where Annie said she could stay until they were married, and she and Thomas started making plans for the wedding, which was duly arranged for the last Sunday in June. They chose a Sunday, as Thomas, John and Sarah all worked on Saturdays, and there were also Thomas's relatives from Nottingham to consider. They all travelled up on the Saturday afternoon after they had finished work for the week, and Annie kindly offered to put them up for two nights at the Cutler's Arms. The pub had, many years before, provided accommodation for travellers, but that facility had long since been discontinued. But she had some spare rooms, and so David and Margaret used one, while Matthew and Betsy and their two children used another.

They were married at St. Peter's, the ancient cathedral church of Sheffield. Eliza loved this old church, the one that she and her mother had sometimes attended together on their day off. After the ceremony, there was, of course, only one place where the wedding breakfast could be held – the Cutler's Arms – where the celebrations went on long into the evening, and Thomas was delighted at having all his family together again, the first time in years.

During the afternoon, Annie took Eliza on one side and handed her a little package wrapped in green paper and tied with a ribbon. 'This is for you, Eliza. It's rightfully yours, so I want you to have it.'

Eliza was curious to know what it was, and quickly untied the ribbon and removed the paper, revealing a small polished wooden box. She lifted the lid, and inside, resting on a tiny cushion of black velvet there lay an exquisite heart-shaped silver locket and chain.

'Oh, it's beautiful,' she said as she examined it, and turning it over she noticed an engraving on the back. Intertwined were the letters *JL* and *HW,* and underneath these was the date *25th June 1836.* 'Look, it's got some initials, and a date. Where did it come from?'

'It belonged to your mother. It was a present to her from your father on their wedding day. That's their initials engraved on it – Joseph Lambert and Hannah Whitworth. And look at the date – it's almost twenty-seven years to the day since they were wed. And they had their wedding breakfast here, too. I didn't know the locket existed until a couple of years ago, when, one day, your mother was telling me all about it. She told me that your father made it himself, just as he was finishing his apprenticeship, shortly before they got married. I said I'd like to see it, so she brought it over and left it with me to have a look at. I put it away in a drawer for safekeeping until she next called by, but she never did. It was only a few days later that she had the accident. To be honest, I'd forgotten that I still had it; I think I must be getting forgetful in my old age! But I came across it yesterday when I was doing some clearing out, and I know your mother would have wanted you to have it. And look inside it.' Eliza did as Annie told her, and there she found a tiny lock of blond hair. 'That's your father's. See, it's almost as blond as yours. You have his eyes, too. Anyone who knew your father could tell you're his daughter.'

'It's strange, but mother never showed me this. But then she never spoke much about my father, and it was only some years ago when we had a visit from an old aunt of his, that we both learned anything about his past.'

Eliza rushed to show it to Thomas, and he placed it around her neck. Henceforth, she wore it often, the only memento she had of the father she never knew.

The next day, the Brown family travelled back to Nottingham, while Thomas and Eliza set off in the opposite direction. Thomas had been able to arrange for a full week off work, and Annie, of course, was more than happy to manage without her new cook. They caught a train to York, en route for Scarborough, for a short honeymoon. Neither of them had ever been to the seaside before, and for five days they were enthralled by the novel sights and experiences that this genteel resort had to offer. They strolled along the promenade and wandered lazily through the spa gardens, amused by the antics of the seagulls swooping down and fighting over scraps of food; they climbed to the top of the cliffs above the town and marvelled at the vastness of the ocean, stretching to the distant horizon; they walked, barefoot along the beach and paddled in the sea, breathing in the air, so pure and sweet compared to the sour and polluted atmosphere they had become used to.

But all too soon they were heading home to Sheffield and back to work. They had just enjoyed the best week of their lives, and they promised each other that one day they would make a return visit to Scarborough.

While they had been away, Sarah and John had been to the Cutler's Arms to collect all Eliza's possessions and take them back to the house at Neepsend. And so, Thomas and Eliza began married life together.

CHAPTER EIGHTEEN

Water water everywhere

William Horsfield was glad that it was Friday once more, and that he could now go home and put his feet up for a couple of days. William was a quarryman, hard physical work for a man now in his forty-eighth year. And this particular Friday, 11th March 1864, he was especially pleased. For it had been a dreadful week, one of almost incessant rain, culminating that day with a torrential downpour accompanied by a biting, cold and progressively strengthening westerly wind. Bad enough for anyone who had to leave the comfort of their home for even a short time; but his work kept him outdoors where there was no respite or shelter from the elements, and as he left the quarry he looked forward to reaching the warmth of the fireside at his home in the hamlet of Thompson Houses, some three miles northwest of the village of Low Bradfield on the opposite side of the valley.

He knew this valley well. He had been born and brought up here and he loved its wild seclusion. He had worked in the quarry for more years than he cared to remember, but his route to and from work had recently been made longer, now that the construction of a huge embankment had been completed, damming the valley and creating a vast reservoir. The Dale Dyke Reservoir as it was called, was to be the first of several in the area being built by the Sheffield Waterworks Company to meet the needs of the growing population, and to feed the hungry demands of both the older water mills along the valley and the increasing number of modern steelworks in the town, eight miles to the southeast. Once the reservoir had started to fill, what had formerly been a short walk to and from the quarry via a footbridge over the Dale Dyke Beck, now required a detour down the valley, across the embankment, and back up the other side.

Further up the valley, several miles above Bradfield, in the desolate mountainous countryside that borders Derbyshire, lay the source of the River Loxley. For the first few miles of its course it was known as the Dale Dyke and was little more than a brook, or dyke, as its name suggested. But as it flowed gently down, between rising hills, this insignificant stream gradually gained width and depth as other springs and watercourses fed into it. William had often walked along the valley of the Dale Dyke, from its source in the hills and down past his home to the first village of any size, Low Bradfield. Further down the valley lay other small settlements; Damflask and then Loxley, which gave its name to the substantial river it had now become. As it continued on its journey towards Sheffield, further centres of population were to be found; Little Matlock, named after its equally romantic namesake in Derbyshire's Derwent Valley; Malin Bridge; Hillsborough and then Owlerton, where the Loxley twisted and turned before falling into the river Don. From here onwards the countryside became flatter and wider as the outskirts of Sheffield were reached, and the Don soon became a river of some size as it passed through Neepsend and Kelham Island, where the hum of modern industry shattered the peace. And yet, north of the Loxley's meeting with the Don, the countryside was exceedingly picturesque. Here, the river flowed through a narrow gorge, scooped out through the rocks, in places rising in precipitous crags; and by its rippling waters, woods and groves added a charm to delight any poet or artist.

But whilst the valley of the Loxley displayed a rural and bucolic charm, where agriculture was the principal occupation, it had, for centuries, also been a place of industry. For its fast-flowing waters had been harnessed by man to drive water wheels, and along its banks, amid this quiet and pastoral scene, in and around the villages and hamlets clustered by its side, were little pockets of industry; corn mills; a paper mill; a knife-grinding mill; rolling mills and forges, all providing employment for its inhabitants and adding to the prosperity of the area.

It was five o'clock when William left the quarry. He was already sopping wet and chilled to the marrow, but he still fastened his coat tightly about him and pulled down his cap in a vain attempt to protect himself. He walked along the lane by the reservoir, watching the surface of the icy water being whipped into a frenzy of white horses by the increasingly violent wind. This man-made lake covered an area about a mile in length by a quarter of a mile wide. At its centre, its depth was over ninety feet, and he had been told it contained nearly seven hundred million gallons. The embankment, which held back this enormous volume of water, had been five years in the making. It was a hundred feet high, five hundred feet wide at its base, tapering to twelve feet wide at the top. He had never seen the reservoir so full, and if it were to rise just another six inches it would breach the overflow weir, provided to direct excess water down to the river below. It was along the top that he would normally walk, just above the water level. But he knew that if he were foolish enough to try that on such a wild night, he would certainly lose his cap, and possibly his life, for the wind was becoming stronger and could easily have blown him down the steep side of the embankment. So he took a detour and crossed it a little further down, where it afforded him some shelter from the full fury of the blast.

But as he walked along he suddenly noticed, just above him, about twelve feet from the top, a long horizontal crack extending for perhaps fifty yards. He stopped, scrambled up and examined it. It was not a wide crack, no wider than would admit the blade of a knife. He knew all about knives, did William. One of his cousins was a cutler, and on days like this he wished he had also chosen that profession. At first, he thought it might be a frost crack, such as he had often seen in the earth in winter, and although he did not remember seeing it the day before it did not unduly concern him. But on reaching the other side of the dam he met an employee of the waterworks company and mentioned it to him, and before long word had got round and a group of about two dozen men went to inspect it more closely. By now, the crack had widened and could take a man's finger. One of those present was a Mr Fountain, one of the contractor's men, and despite declaring that he believed the crack constituted no danger, he thought it best to advise the chief engineer of the waterworks company, Mr John Gunson, who resided in Sheffield. He therefore instructed his son, Stephenson, a lad of seventeen, to set off on horseback to inform him.

The young man rode as fast as the appalling weather, the creeping darkness, and the mountainous nature of the road would allow. But he had only gone about two miles when his horse's saddle girth broke, so he called at the Barrel Inn at Damflask to get it repaired, and whilst there he told the landlord of the reason for his journey. Once the repair had been made he quickly set off again, and as soon as the message was delivered, Mr Gunson, along with the principal contractor, Mr Craven, were on their way by gig to inspect the dam.

They pressed on as fast as they could, but the fierce wind, coming howling down the valley straight into their faces, hampered their progress. Struggling on, they eventually reached Damflask, and as their gig descended the road into the village they noticed flickering lights in the distance, and, unusually for such a night, a large number of villagers out and about, some herding cattle and sheep up into the surrounding hills, others loading carts with bundles and bags, like absconding tenants performing a night-time flit. But their actions had been prompted solely by a desire for self-preservation. The landlord of the inn had spread the news he had been given by young master Fountain, and fearing a possible breach of the dam, some of those inhabiting the lower parts of the valley had decided to quit their homes and seek the safety of higher ground. Others, confident that this was merely scaremongering, and that the embankment was sufficiently robust and resilient, preferred to remain in the warmth and apparent security of their solidly built stone houses and cottages.

By the time Gunson and Craven reached the dam it was past ten o'clock, and more workmen were already there, inspecting it. By now, the crack was wide enough to take a man's arm, but both men still considered it was safe and that there was no danger of a collapse. Nevertheless, the water was dangerously high, and Mr Fountain convinced them that unless swift action was taken to relieve the pressure, the result could be catastrophic. Already, he explained, he and George Swinden, another of the waterworks' overseers had, after much difficulty, managed to open some of the sluices in the valve house at the foot of the dam in order to allow some water to flow out, but that had had little effect. A more radical solution was needed, and so the decision was taken to get some gunpowder and use it to blow up the overflow weir. A desperate measure, but one that they decided was worthwhile. So Gunson ordered some of the workmen to go and fetch the powder. And whilst they waited for their return, they watched; and hoped; and prayed.

'Good God. What a night!' said Thomas, as he opened the door to the living room and walked in. It was seven o'clock. John and Sarah were sitting by the fire, drinking tea.

'You're late tonight, Thomas. Go and get out of those wet clothes while I make you a cup,' said Sarah.

'Yes, I know I'm late. We had a rush job on, and the foreman insisted we got it finished before we left. And can I have a slice of that parkin you made, as well? I'm famished.'

'Of course you can. We've just finished our supper. We weren't sure what time you'd be back so we didn't wait. Shall I get you some? It won't take long; it's only stew and dumplings and I can soon warm some up in the oven.'

'No. It's all right, Sarah. I'm going to walk down to the Cutler's to meet Eliza. She finishes at nine, so I'll get off shortly and have something there.'

Ten minutes later Thomas was back downstairs, having dried himself and changed out of his work clothes. He joined the other two by the fire as he hungrily devoured the thick slice of cake Sarah had brought him.

'It's raw out there,' Thomas said, as he sipped his tea. 'And the wind's getting worse. I'll bet there'll be some damage tonight if this keeps up.'

'There has been already,' added Sarah, 'I noticed quite a lot of slates that had been blown off some roofs as I walked home. And I got a soaking, too. You can't put an umbrella up, not in this wind.'

'And have you seen how the river's rising?' said John. 'It must be a good foot higher than it was last week. Still, it's not surprising, not with all the rain we've had. But you know what they say about March – *in like a lion, out like a lamb*. By the end of the month we'll probably be basking in sunshine!'

'Well, you'll not hear me complaining if we are,' replied Thomas as he got up out of his chair and went to put his coat on. 'Right, I'd better get going. I don't think we'll be late back. Once we've had a drink and a bite to eat we'll set off. I don't want to be in bed late tonight, I've got to be in early tomorrow. There's another big job on and the boss wants it finished as soon as possible. So we'll see you later.'

Thomas left, but the moment he opened the front door an icy blast rushed in, blowing open the living room door, rattling the window in its frame and rustling the curtains. John got up to close the door, then put another shovelful of coal on the fire. He picked up the now empty coal scuttle from the hearth and went through the back parlour into the scullery. 'Just going outside to get some more coal. Put the kettle on, love; I could do with another cuppa.'

He opened the door into the yard, and was nearly blown off his feet as the gale hit him full in the face. Outside, evidence of the storm could be heard all around, both near and far; outhouse doors rattled and banged; tin baths, suspended by hooks on privy doors, clattered and clanged; loose chimneypots rocked and vibrated and the wind hummed mournful tunes as it whistled under the eaves and between loose-fitting slates. A loud crash, then another, as slates and tiles were dashed to the ground. John pitied those living in older, poorly maintained houses and slums, but more so those who had no home at all. And God help anyone out on the moors on a night like this, he thought to himself, as he returned to the warmth of the house, and locked and bolted the back door behind him.

At the Dale Dyke Dam the workmen had returned with the gunpowder, and John Gunson and George Swinden now prepared to use it to blow up the overflow weir. This was about sixty feet long and was situated on the south side of the dam. It was made of concrete, and below it was a channel down which excess water flowed to the river below. Holes had already been drilled into the concrete and these were now filled with powder, and a trail laid a short distance away. This was lit, and the men quickly retreated to a safe distance, waiting for the expected explosion. But it did not come. Perhaps, they thought, the combination of wind and rain had blown it out. But before attempting to relight it, Gunson went to re-examine the crack in the dam wall, and glancing up, he now saw water, foaming and bubbling and beginning to pour over the top of the embankment. It reached his feet and vanished into the now widening crack. So he and Swinden then went down to the valve house, to see if the sluices could be opened further to relieve the water pressure above, but Swinden, realising the danger of remaining there, persuaded

Gunson to leave. And not a moment too soon. For, looking up to the top of the dam wall, they were horrified to see that a breach had now appeared, about thirty feet wide, the water gushing out at an immense speed and cascading down the embankment.

'My God, Swinden, look at that!' cried Gunson. 'Come away man, quick. It's all up; the embankment's going.'

As fast as they could, the two men ran to the side, away from the advancing avalanche of water, and just at that moment they heard an explosion as the powder, at last, went off. Gunson was aghast at what he saw. The overflow weir had gone, but that had become an irrelevancy, for nothing could now be done to prevent the destructive power of nature taking its course. A gigantic mountain of water was now plunging headlong down towards the valley below. Gunson, in an almost trance-like state, stood transfixed, watching at the disaster unfolding before his eyes. But just in time, Swinden grabbed his arm and pulled him away before they both became engulfed. Instinctively, Gunson took his pocket watch from his waistcoat and with difficulty managed to read the time. Midnight; almost exactly to the minute. He raised his eyes once more towards the top of the embankment. The breach was now wider and deeper and the crack in the wall had now vanished forever, replaced by a void, as earth, rocks and masonry were tossed aside by the millions of gallons of water pouring relentlessly and with increasing ferocity from the lake above.

There was no gradual escape of water, but a sudden and overwhelming torrent. After the initial surge there quickly followed a second terrific burst. By now the gap was over three hundred feet wide at the top, and seventy feet deep – almost the depth of the reservoir. And with such an enormous opening, Gunson knew that it would not take long for the whole of the reservoir to be emptied. He looked on with mounting dread as seven hundred million gallons of freezing cold water hurtled down the valley towards Sheffield. And he knew that it would not be long before this destructive mountain of death would reach the sleeping residents of the town. And there was nothing, absolutely nothing, he could do to warn them.

It was just past midnight when Thomas and Eliza arrived back home. To their surprise, John and Sarah were still up, sitting by the fireside as they had been when Thomas had left for the pub, and enjoying a mug of hot cocoa. 'Ah, you're here at last,' said Sarah, 'we expected you back long before now.'

'Yes, and we would have been but I was late finishing tonight,' explained Eliza. 'We were unusually busy, considering the weather. We didn't expect so many folk to turn out on a night like this. Just goes to show. We had quite a big crowd come in, celebrating something or other and all wanting to eat, so that really set us back, and then Thomas turned up wanting something as well. Then we got chatting with some of the regulars and Jim got going on the piano – you know Jim, he often plays the piano there – and before we knew it, it was eleven o'clock and Annie wanted to shut up shop. So I helped her clear up, then we left. But you're both still up. We thought you'd have turned in by now.'

'We've been keeping an eye on the weather,' said John, 'and we were getting a bit worried about you two; thought something might have happened. That wind's not dropped much, and we've been a bit concerned that it might cause some damage to the house; but I think we're all right. Mind you, not everyone's been lucky. I went out for some coal earlier and you could hear things being blown about and smashed all over the place.'

'We saw quite a lot of damage as we walked home, didn't we, Thomas? A couple of slates came flying down off one roof and nearly hit us, and then we had to climb over a tree that had been blown down across the road. Anyway, I've had a long day so I'm off to bed. Don't be long, Thomas, you've got to be up at five tomorrow. Or should I say today – look, it's almost quarter past midnight already.'

'All right, Eliza. You go on up; I shan't be long. I'm just going to clean my boots first to save time in the morning, then I'll be up. What about you two?' asked Thomas.

'Yes, we'll be going up in a minute,' replied Sarah. 'We'll just finish our cocoa first.'

Thomas went through to the scullery and took a shoe brush from a drawer in the tall cabinet that stood against the wall next to the back door. He picked up his boots from the floor, where he had left them earlier when he came in from work, went over to the sink, and taking a damp rag wiped away the mud and grime, then started to brush them vigorously. As he worked he began to whistle a tune, a haunting, lilting melody. He had a good ear for music, did Thomas, and a fine singing voice, and whenever he heard a song, even for the first time, he had the knack of picking up the melody immediately and remembering the words.

'I've not heard that one before,' shouted Sarah, 'where did you hear it?'

'In the Cutler's, tonight. Jim was playing it on the piano. I'd never heard it before, either, and now I can't get the tune out of my head. He only bought the sheet music today. It's a new song by Stephen Foster, only just been published. You know, the American chap who died a couple of months ago; he's written no end of songs, but I think this is one of his best – a real tear-jerker. Half the women had tears in their eyes, especially after a few gins,' and Thomas started to sing:

Beautiful dreamer, beam on my heart,
E'en as the morn on the streamlet and sea;
Then will all clouds of sorrow depart,
Beautiful dreamer, awake unto me
Beautiful dreamer...

Suddenly, and without warning, he stopped singing.

'Whatever is that?' he cried, 'did you hear it?' The noise clearly came from afar, but it was unmistakeable and getting louder. He went over to the one tiny window, next to the back door, and put his ear against the thin lace curtain draped over it, listening carefully. It was a roaring, rolling sound, like thunder, only continuous and getting louder and nearer.

In the front living room, Sarah and John had just got up from the sofa to go to bed when they, too, heard it. They also made straight for the window, which overlooked the street, and drew back the curtains. An intermittent, flickering light came from the almost new moon, shining faintly through the fleeting clouds scurrying across the night sky, but there was nothing they could see to account for this inexplicable and alarming sound. Sarah started to tremble. John, seeing her distress, put a reassuring arm around her, but he too was afraid. More so because they had no idea what it was, and there is no fear as bad as the fear of the unknown. The noise continued to grow louder and louder, and whatever was causing it was getting closer, as if all the hounds of hell had been unleashed and were bearing down on them.

All of a sudden, there came a mighty blast of wind, and then, for a few brief seconds as the clouds parted and the moon cast a brighter light on the scene outside, Sarah and John looked on in horror as a colossal wall of water, half as high as their house, came thundering down the street. In an instant it was upon them. With an almighty, reverberating thump it hit the front of the house, smashing the window into a thousand splinters of glass and wood. Sarah screamed and John cried out for help. All went black. The two oil lamps in the room, and the candles they had lit to light their way upstairs, were instantly extinguished, as was the fire in the hearth. The force of the water slammed shut the doors into the parlour and the scullery and knocked Sarah and John off their feet, submerging them beneath the rising tide.

John had long had a fear of drowning. And a recurring

nightmare of his – of being locked in a room as water rushed in and rose up all around him – had suddenly become a terrifying reality, a fight for survival. Battling strongly against a growing sense of panic he managed to find his feet again, and feeling around in the darkness he found Sarah and helped her up above the water. They both surfaced, gasping for breath as they tried to recover from the shock of the icy cold deluge that had hit them, coughing and spluttering and spitting out mouthfuls of the foul, dirty liquid.

By now, the room was waist deep, and anything that could float was bobbing about. Gripping Sarah by the arm, John dragged her towards the door leading to the hall, hoping to get up the stairs and above the deepening flood. But the door was stuck fast. He pulled hard on it, trying frantically to open it but the pressure of water against it was too great and he was unable to shift it. In a last desperate bid to save themselves, they now attempted to reach the window, and make their escape there.

But fate transpired against them. Outside, the wall of water rolled on past the house, but the street was a cul-de-sac with a terrace of houses at the far end, forming a barrier. This end terrace took the full force, the water rebounding and rolling back to meet the still advancing tide, and a second, even more destructive wave surged in through the cavity where the window had been, hurling them both underwater again, as the level rose ever upwards towards the ceiling.

In the scullery, Thomas was fighting his own battle for survival. The water had entered this small room somewhat more slowly, getting under the back door and the door from the parlour. There was no sudden inrush, but the level was rising rapidly. His first thought, on hearing John and Sarah's cries for help, was to try and reach them, but the rising level inside the parlour made it impossible to open the door. And his thoughts then turned to Eliza. She had gone up to bed before the flood arrived, and hopefully would be safer up there. He knew he must try and help all of them, but the water was already up to his chest, so he waded across to the back door, his only possible means of escape, grabbed the handle and turned it, but to no avail. The door was fitted with a lock and two bolts, so taking a deep breath, he dived under the freezing cold water, feeling for the bolt at the bottom, and was easily able to release it. Then the bolt at the top, but still the door would not open. Damn! It was locked. Just one barrier remained between him and safety – the solid mortise lock – but for that he needed the key. This was kept in the left-hand drawer of the scullery cabinet, so he moved towards it, felt for the drawer, opened it and started to feel inside. His hand rummaged haphazardly through its now waterlogged contents, searching blindly for the one item that could mean the difference between life and death. It was full of odds and ends; bits of old metal, nails and screws, a few tools, some odd items of cutlery, a box of candles and wicks for the oil lamps. He cursed himself that he hadn't sorted out that drawer as he had meant to. He had also intended to fix some hooks on the side of the cabinet on which to hang all the spare keys. If only he had done that. He continued to feel his way through the drawer's contents, then felt a sudden pain as he cut his hand on a sharp edge.

By now, the water was almost at shoulder level and still rising, and he was beginning to feel numb. He started to panic. Still he could not find the key, and he knew that before long his head would be underwater. He looked up. The cabinet reached almost to the ceiling, but there was a gap of about a foot at the top. If he could climb up, he could just about squeeze onto the top, and pray that the water didn't get any higher. The cabinet was an old, solid oak dresser, with a cupboard at the bottom, two drawers above, and above that four shelves where plates, cups and saucers were kept. Fortunately, the cupboard was stuffed full of all sorts of paraphernalia, and this gave it weight and stability. He reached up and grasped the top shelf, then using the open drawer and shelves like rungs on a ladder, he scrambled up. He was fit and agile, and was soon able to position himself on top of the cabinet. He lay there, face up, soaked to the skin and shivering uncontrollably, the ceiling just a few inches away. And then, after a little while, he noticed how much quieter it had become. The rumbling and roaring of the water had ceased. Whatever had caused it and wherever it had come from, it had now passed. The gale, which had persisted for almost twenty-four hours, appeared to be easing, and an eerie silence was now descending, punctuated only by an occasional gust of wind and distant cries and screams.

His eyes had gradually adjusted to the darkness, and a hint of moonlight shining through a gap in the lace curtain was just enough to give a dim view of his surroundings. He looked down, and got the impression that the level had stopped rising, so he put his hand over the side of the cabinet until it reached the surface of the water. He left it there for a minute or two but could detect no change. Thank goodness, he thought. If anything, it seemed to have dropped slightly, unless this was wishful thinking. And then he realised that in his efforts to save himself, he had not heard another word from John or Sarah. He shouted out to them, but got no reply. Of Eliza, he had heard not a sound, and he prayed that she was safe, upstairs. If only they had all gone to bed at the same time! Several times he shouted out Eliza's name, but there was no response. Their bedroom was at the front of the house, and he was now marooned at the back. Two rooms and three doors separated him from the foot of the stairs, so possibly that was why she couldn't hear him. But he tried again, and then, faintly at first, he thought he heard her voice. Once more he shouted her name, and this time he was sure he recognised her voice, very softly, in the distance. Overjoyed, he cried out, trying to let her know he was still alive.

It seemed like hours that he had lain there, on top of that cabinet. In truth, it was probably no more than half an hour, but he now knew for certain that the water level was slowly dropping, and provided it continued to do so he would soon be able to free himself. But his joy at the thought was tempered by the realisation of what he might find in the front room. Before long, he was able to climb down. The water was now only waist high, and he quickly opened the drawer and located the key. He unlocked the back door, and with much effort began to force it open, pulling it hard against the pressure of the water. The moment a gap appeared, the water began to pour out into the yard, until eventually it had receded to little more than a few inches deep, and he found himself standing in thick, evil-smelling mud.

Water continued to seep under the door from the back parlour, so he went to it, and after more effort was able to open that door too, whereupon he was temporarily hit by a wave of water escaping from within. He repeated the exercise with the door to the front room, opening it with some trepidation. As the water flowed out, through the house and into the yard, the scale of devastation that greeted him was dramatic.

Facing him across the room was a gaping hole where the window had been, but strangely, the curtains were still hanging from the rail above, wafting gently, seemingly unscathed by the combined force of wind, water and debris. A pale moonlight cast ghostly shafts of light upon this scene of chaos and mayhem. Every piece of furniture they owned lay scattered about, ruined and of no further use; thick mud covered the floor to a depth of over two feet, and the chimney was completely blocked with the same slimy sludge.

And then Thomas saw what he feared he would. He had hoped, against hope, that somehow they might have survived, but as he gazed down from the curtains to the floor below, he knew they hadn't. Almost invisible under the layer of mud, he could just make out two human forms lying together, face down, entwined in each other's arms. He hadn't the heart to disturb them. Not just yet. Instead, he went to the door leading to the hall, and had no difficulty in opening it. The front door stood wide open, forced inwards by the pressure of the water, and hanging at a crazy angle on its one remaining twisted hinge, its mud-splattered blue panels splintered and cracked beyond repair.

Stepping over yet more debris, he turned to climb the stairs, and there, on the top step, dressed only in her nightdress, sat Eliza, head in hands, and shivering with the cold. She looked up, but seemed unable to move. Thomas ran up the stairs and picked her up, holding her tightly as she sobbed gently. It was the best sound he had ever heard. She was alive. She had survived this horrific catastrophe.

CHAPTER NINETEEN

Aftermath

Thomas was meant to be starting work early that Saturday morning, but any such thoughts were far from his mind. He didn't sleep a wink the rest of that night. After he'd found Eliza sitting at the top of the stairs, shivering, and clearly in shock, he'd carried her to the bedroom and put her to bed, whispering words of comfort until she drifted off into sleep.

He then set about removing his sodden, mud-stained clothes. Outside, the yard now resembled a deep trough of filthy, syrupy, sludge and much of it had seeped into the water pump and the well beneath, and there was no clean water to be had. But he cleaned himself as best as he could then dressed in dry clothes, just as the birds began their dawn chorus to herald another day, as if nothing untoward had happened.

Leaving Eliza asleep, he ventured back downstairs. The mud lay thick on the floor, so he rolled up his trouser legs. With a degree of foreboding, he opened the door to the living room, and as dawn continued to break, the strengthening light confirmed the full extent of the flooding. He could hardly bear to look down to where John and Sarah lay. He knew he would have to make arrangements to have their bodies removed, but he hadn't the heart to face that particular task just yet. He went through into the back parlour and scullery, astounded at the level of damage. The only item of furniture left relatively unscathed was the scullery cabinet. Thank God he had bought that, he thought. It was old and second-hand and had cost him five shillings from the market. The best five shillings he had ever spent though, for it had saved his life. And as he looked around him at what remained of their home, one thing became abundantly clear. It would take weeks, maybe months, for the house to be made fit for habitation again, and in the meantime they would have to find somewhere else to live.

He walked out into the street and found others, just like himself, surveying the aftermath of the disaster. It immediately became apparent that they were the lucky ones. The tidal wave, as it had come down their street, had only reached about halfway up each house. In other nearby streets, lying somewhat lower and closer to the river, the houses had been completely engulfed, and it was in these that many more fatalities had occurred. Thomas talked to some of his neighbours and soon learned the cause of the flood – the bursting of the Dale Dyke Dam.

He went back inside and gently roused Eliza from her sleep. He now had the unenviable job of telling her what had happened to Sarah and John. He held her tenderly as he related the tragic news. For a moment she said nothing, then looking up, spoke softly in between her sobs, 'I thought as much. When I heard them scream, then didn't hear anything more, I guessed something dreadful had happened. I tried to get down the stairs, but the water was up to the top of the door. I thought you must have drowned, too, until I heard you shout my name, but that was much later. Oh, Thomas, it's all so awful. What are we going to do?'

Thomas knew precisely what they were going to do. He needed to get her away from there to somewhere safe, and had a hunch that the Cutler's Arms might be the answer. The town centre was on higher ground than where they were, and if he was correct the pub should have remained unaffected. He was sure that Annie would be able to offer them temporary accommodation, so, while Eliza got dressed, he packed all their clothes into two cases, the sum total of their worldly possessions, and led her down the stairs and straight through the open front door into the street. He did not want her going into the living room.

The sights that met their eyes as they made their way into

the town were ones neither of them would ever forget. By now, the water had receded, but the legacy of its destructive force was plain to see. Everywhere, there was debris and an oozing, stinking, treacly, mud, strewn with the remains of anything that had lain in the path of the flood as it made its deadly journey down the valley of the Loxley. Uprooted trees and branches; rocks and boulders, some weighing several tons; stones and bricks from what had once been houses; baulks of timber and pieces of machinery from now vanished workshops; items of household goods, and furniture – here an iron bedstead, there an armchair; dead animals – cats, dogs, horses, sheep and cattle; but saddest of all, the bodies of those unfortunate victims unable to save themselves.

They picked their way carefully amongst this nightmare scene of death and destruction, and at every turn in the road, round every corner, a new horror faced them. At one point, where the road dipped, the flood had simply smashed its way through a building that dared to block its path, tearing off the roof and the front and side walls, so all that remained was the rear wall, and, astonishingly, the timber floor of one of the bedrooms, hanging precariously at a precipitous angle. Here and there they noticed people sitting on the ground, dazed and confused, or wandering around aimlessly, dressed only in their nightclothes, some staring piteously at the remains of what had once been their homes; others crying out pitifully and searching frantically for loved ones.

As they approached the town centre these scenes of destruction eased, until only minor evidence of damage was apparent. They turned a corner, and were relieved to see that the Cutler's Arms was intact. Eliza had a key to the back door, but this had been lost along with many of her possessions, so they knocked at the front door, forgetting that it was still only eight o'clock. But Annie was already up, and had been for some time. Like most others in the town, she had hardly slept for the past eight hours and had already been out and about to see the damage for herself.

'Eliza, Thomas, you're both safe!' she exclaimed as she opened the door. 'Thank goodness. But come on in. I was just thinking about you. I've already had a few people call by, and they've been telling me all about what's happened further up the valley. I've heard things are very bad at Neepsend and I'm just as worried about Malin Bridge. I have a nephew who lives there with his wife and six children, and they reckon things are even worse there, so I must go along and see if they are safe, as well.'

'I'll come with you if you want,' said Thomas without hesitation.

'Oh, that's kind of you, Thomas. But I don't suppose you've had anything to eat or drink yet, so come through to the kitchen and I'll get you both something.'

Annie soon brought them a pot of tea and a large plate of piping hot toast, along with pots of jam, marmalade and dripping, and they all sat round the kitchen table while Thomas related the events of the previous night, and the terrible news about Sarah and John.

'We didn't know where else to go,' explained Thomas. 'We can't possibly stay in the house; it'll take months to put right. We wondered whether you could put us up for a little while, just until we can find somewhere else to live. I doubt we'll be able to return there, even when the landlord's sorted it out. There's only the two of us now, God rest their souls, and we couldn't afford the rent by ourselves.'

'Oh, I'm so terribly sorry to hear about Sarah and John. But please don't worry; of course you can stay here. I've some spare rooms upstairs as you know, so you can use one of those. But now, Thomas, I think we'd better get going. It's a good four miles, and with all this flooding it might take a lot longer than usual to get there.'

'Take as long as you need,' said Eliza, 'I'll look after the pub.'

Thomas and Annie were about to set out, when they heard voices coming from the bar. Annie went through from the kitchen to see who it was.

'Wilfred and Laura, and the children, too! Oh, thank the Lord you're all here, safe and sound. Come in, do come in. I was just about to walk over and see how you are – I've been hearing such dreadful things about Malin Bridge.' The bedraggled group followed Annie into the kitchen, mother, father and six children, the youngest asleep in his father's arms. 'Here, come and warm yourselves by the fire. This is Thomas and Eliza, two good friends of mine. They'll be staying here for a while. They've been made homeless, but that's not the worst of it. Thomas's sister and her husband weren't so lucky; they haven't survived.'

Before long, Annie had made another pot of tea and more toast and everyone had been properly introduced. For the next hour or so, they sat and swapped horror stories of what they had experienced and witnessed during the past tumultuous twelve hours. Wilfred and Laura lived in a small house close to the file cutter's shop where Wilfred worked. They had six children, aged between two and fourteen. Wilfred explained that they had, fortunately, all been upstairs when the water reached their house, but they were marooned there for most of the night until the flood receded and they were able to get down the stairs again.

'We've lost nearly everything. All we've got left are the clothes we're wearing and some bits and bobs we could salvage,' he said, pointing to a couple of dirty, sodden bags lying on the floor. 'As soon as we could get out of the house we set off here, but it's taken us over four hours to come as many miles. Both the bridges at Malin are washed away, and you couldn't begin to imagine the destruction. It's like a battlefield up there. There's whole rows of cottages completely ruined, and some houses have just vanished. And it's not only the water that's caused the damage; it's what it's brought down the valley with it – trees, rocks, and even bits of machinery – and all this debris acted like cannon fire. The Stag Inn's gone and they reckon the whole family were drowned, along with a servant girl and a couple of lodgers. And the Cleakum pub has almost disappeared as well; only a bit of one wall's still standing, and there's no sign of anyone alive there, either. I hate to think how many have perished. We're lucky that our house is a bit higher up and protected by a row of cottages that took the full force. And if we hadn't been upstairs, well, we might have perished, too.

'As we were coming here, we saw crowds in the streets, and there's already rescue parties out searching for survivors. They had some harrowing tales to tell about what they'd seen and heard, all too heartbreaking to listen to, really. There was one bit of good news, though, if you can call anything good after what's happened. When we came through Hillsborough we saw a house with its front wall completely missing, and on the upper storey, in a corner of a room there was an iron bedstead, still there, where they'd just found a sleeping child, alive and well. But they haven't found the other occupants yet.'

'Well,' said Annie, after Wilfred had finished, 'it looks like I've got some more lodgers, and of course, you're all welcome to stay! Laura, why don't you take the children upstairs and get them cleaned up. You can use the two spare rooms at the back; Eliza'll show you where they are. I'm afraid they're all I've got and you'll be a bit cramped, but I'm sure you'll manage. Now I must go and open up. My regulars will be along soon and they'll not be happy if the pub's shut!'

And so, just like the old days, the Cutler's Arms once more echoed to the sound of overnight guests, and for a while it was pandemonium as they all tried to get their lives back to some sort of normality. And it had to be business as usual, so everyone mucked in and helped as best they could. But for thousands of people, life would never be the same again. Thomas and Eliza were just two of many left to grieve, to identify the bodies of their loved ones, to arrange funerals and to try and find somewhere new to live.

The first task for Thomas, later that Saturday morning, was to go to the steelworks to let them know he was still alive, and to ask for a couple of days off work so he could deal with the aftermath of the death of his sister and brother-in-law. Having done that, his second task was one he was dreading, for he had to arrange for the removal of John and Sarah's bodies. On his way to Neepsend he had called at an undertaker and asked them to meet him at the house that same afternoon. Thomas was reluctant to enter the house again, but had to go in to show the undertaker's men where John and Sarah were lying. He couldn't bear to watch, so he went back outside, and was relieved when the men had finally done their job and taken the bodies away to the funeral parlour.

Although the final death count was so far unknown, the funeral director told Thomas that there were bound to be many burials to be arranged in the coming days, and he was advised to agree a date very quickly. And so, after a brief discussion, the funeral was set for the following Tuesday. This left very little time to inform all those who might wish to attend, so the next day he and Eliza had to be up early to catch the morning train to Nottingham, and break the tragic news to his mother and father.

David and Margaret had already heard something about the flood and were desperate to learn whether Thomas, Sarah and John were safe, for as early as Saturday morning snippets of information had begun to spread throughout the land, and within days every newspaper in the country, and many abroad, were carrying lengthy and dramatic reports of the terrible event.

That Tuesday, a party of nine came up to Sheffield, the most distressing journey any of them had ever had to make. There was David and Margaret, Matthew and Betsy, Zachariah and Joan, and two of John's siblings. Nancy had also insisted on coming, despite the fact that she was now almost eighty years old and not in the best of health. George had passed away three years earlier, but she was determined to be at the funeral, as Sarah had always been her and George's favourite grandchild – not that they would ever have let that be known. And during the seven years that John had lived with them as an apprentice, she and George had become very fond of him, looking upon him as almost another grandchild, and were naturally delighted when he married Sarah and really did become their grandson-in-law.

A simple ceremony was held at St. John's Church in the Park district, where John and Sarah were laid to rest in the same grave.

Before they returned home, the mourners went back to the Cutler's for the wake and Joan reminded them how John had always had a fear of water, and how he was wary of using the ferry across the Trent at Wilford whenever he travelled to or from Nottingham.

But for other grieving families, things were not so straightforward. Many of the bodies that were recovered were taken to the workhouse, which became a temporary mortuary where relatives or friends had to go to undertake the traumatic and grisly task of trying to identify missing loved ones. But some of those who had gone missing, and presumed drowned, were never found. Others were, eventually, discovered as far away as Doncaster, having been carried for many miles down the Rivers Loxley and Don. And many of those who were recovered were unrecognisable, and were buried in the General Cemetery at the cost of the Board of Guardians, without formal identification but with all the decency and solemnity of a private burial.

The eventual death toll was estimated at about 240, but thousands more, who had survived, were rendered homeless, some with barely a possession left to their name. Immediately following the disaster the mayor called a meeting of the town council, and a relief fund was quickly established. Donations soon began to pour in, and most of the town's manufacturers donated large sums. Many of Sheffield's workers agreed to donate a day's pay, recognising that some families no longer had a breadwinner to provide for them. And not only from the immediate area did help come. From far and wide donations were received, as more details of the tragedy became known. Not just money, but clothing and other essentials, too. The Queen sent a letter of sympathy, along with a cheque for £200, and other wealthy individuals followed suit; and in towns and villages across the country subscription funds were set up to raise money for those in the most desperate need.

It took many months for things to begin to get back to normal. The priority was to try and rebuild those areas that had been so badly affected, and to help those who had been rendered homeless. And the very first job had to be the removal of the debris.

This was a monumental task, as countless numbers of houses were knee-deep in thick mud, their cellars full of the foul-smelling stuff. It all had to be removed by hand, and every wall, floor and surface, from top to bottom, thoroughly cleaned. And until this was done, there remained the danger of some epidemic breaking out or disease spreading, adding to the misery already caused by the flood. But the biggest, and most immediate problem, was finding shelter for all those who had been left homeless. Some, like Thomas and Eliza, and Annie's nephew and his family, were fortunate in having friends or relatives able to take all of them in together.

But not everyone was so lucky. Heart-rending stories abounded of families who had lost everything and were struggling, often without success, to find anywhere to live. Or of being split up, with parents separated from their children, one here, another there, staying with neighbours, friends or family in already overcrowded accommodation. Pubs, hotels, inns and lodging houses with rooms to spare did a roaring trade, to those who could afford it.

But what had caused hardship and ruin for so many turned out to be a goldmine for a few, for there is always money to be made from the suffering of others. Photographers were soon doing brisk business, selling pictures of the most damaged areas. One character was even seen hawking copies of hymns, especially composed for the occasion, at 'remunerative prices'. Other enterprising freeloaders arranged donkey carts or horse-drawn omnibuses to take tourists to view the most sensational scenes of devastation, as hundreds poured into the town by train, carriage, on horseback or on foot, eager to view for themselves the horrors they had read about in their newspapers. For it was the journalists, from near and far, who had been the first to arrive, some as early as the day after the flood, and the resources of the Post Office were soon stretched to the very limit as the telegraph staff struggled to wire the pages of copy the reporters heaped upon them, to be sent to their respective editors, all hungry to feed the morbid appetites of their readers.

The Cutler's Arms itself was not immune from all this heightened attention the town was experiencing, and was busier than usual, with Eliza working more hours and Laura also helping out. Many times, in the weeks immediately following the flood, Annie was approached by strangers looking for accommodation, and asking whether she was able to offer them a room. Kind-hearted as she was, she would gladly have helped every one of them, had she been able to; but she had no more spare rooms.

'I'm sure Thomas and me could find somewhere else to live,' Eliza told Annie one night, 'then you could use our room for one of those other poor families. There's only the two of us, and the room is big enough for a small family,' she suggested.

'That's very good of you,' said Annie, 'but I'd still want you to carry on helping me run the pub.'

'Yes, of course I would, you know that. But I'll keep my eyes and ears open, and so will Thomas, and if we hear of anywhere we'll let you know. You've done us a favour, Annie, and it would be nice if we could help some others. And I can easily walk to work, that would be the least of my problems. In any case, I've been doing that for almost a year now.'

As each day went by, and people were able to see for themselves the trail of destruction, more details of the devastating effects became known. A coroner's inquest had already begun to establish the events leading to the disaster, and the government had instituted a full enquiry to determine the exact reason for the dam's collapse, but that would take nearly two months to complete.

In the meantime, what everyone did know for certain was that whatever had caused the dam wall to give way, the consequences had been catastrophic and clear for everyone to see. Once the dam had been breached the force of the water quickly enlarged the gap, and within minutes, millions of gallons were hurtling down the Loxley Valley towards Sheffield at a speed approaching twenty miles per hour. Buildings were severely damaged or washed away entirely, adding to the debris being borne along on the fast-flowing and rapidly advancing wall of water, and intensifying its destructive power. Objects, which would have been regarded as virtually immovable, were picked up and tossed around like flotsam and jetsam. A huge piece of rock, about forty feet long and weighing almost sixty tons, had been torn from the mountainside and deposited in the river half a mile below the reservoir. Large items of heavy iron machinery from some of the mills were unceremoniously plucked from their mountings, adding further to the destruction as they were carried down the valley on the surging tide, destroying everything in their path.

But it was the loss of life that caused the greatest sadness, and all along the eight miles from the reservoir down to Sheffield, men, women and children had been swept to their deaths. Many a family lost one or two members, but the most harrowing accounts were those of whole families being wiped out, generations gone in the blink of an eye. A family of five at Little Matlock; at Malin Bridge a family of seven, and at the same place another of five, and worst of all, one of nine, six of them children. And so it went on down the valley. Seven in one house at Hillsborough and another five nearby; and at Neepsend a family of eight, most of whom were known to Thomas. Every day, for the first week following the flood, the news seemed to get worse, until eventually the seemingly endless list of fatalities petered out, and it was time for the rebuilding, both of lives and property, to begin. But that would take months. And for many, the scars would remain with them for the rest of their lives.

A couple of weeks later, Eliza was passing the Town Hall one afternoon when a group of important-looking men and women emerged from the main entrance. Eliza glanced in their direction and suddenly recognised someone she had not seen for almost two years – Mrs Frances Brentnall, her former employer. Mrs Brentnall recognised Eliza, too, and immediately came over to have a word with her.

'Eliza, my dear, what a lovely surprise. I think this is the first time we've met since you left. How have you been keeping and how is your new job? You must tell me all your news. I've just come out of a meeting at the Town Hall, and I did promise to meet Robert when he finishes work, so I've got about an hour to kill. Why don't you join me for afternoon tea?'

They were soon seated in a cosy little restaurant, enjoying a pot of tea and a selection of fancy cakes. Time quickly passed as Eliza told Mrs Brentnall everything that had happened to her since she had left her employ; her new job at the Commercial Hotel and how she had met Sarah there, and then Sarah's brother Thomas, now her husband; her change of job, and moving to Neepsend to share a house with Sarah and her husband, John. And then she related the terrifying and tragic events of 12th March. When she had finished, Mrs Brentnall laid a comforting hand on hers.

'Oh, Eliza, how awful for you. I'm so very sorry to hear your sad news. I've heard a lot of similar stories recently and I'm still finding it hard to comprehend the damage that water can cause, not to mention the horrendous loss of life. You know I'm involved with a number of charities. Well, I'm now helping with organising the flood-relief fund, too. That's where I'd been today, to a meeting with the council. It's very heartening to receive so many generous donations, some from the most unexpected quarters, but the most upsetting thing is firstly having to read about the circumstances some families have been reduced to, and then not being able to meet every request for help to the extent that we would like. But how long do you think it will be before you can move back into your home?'

'Oh, I doubt if we ever will. Even after the landlord's sorted it out, I think the rent will be too much for Thomas and me. There were four of us sharing it before; but there's only the two of us now, so we'll have to find somewhere new, sooner or later. We're lodging at the Cutler's Arms for the time being, and Annie, the landlady, also has her nephew and his family living there, and there's eight of them. And there are lots of other needy families who would also like to stay there, but Annie just hasn't got any more spare rooms. I've said I'll try and find somewhere else for me and Thomas, then one of them could have our room, but I've had no luck so far.'

Mrs Brentnall took another sip from the bone china cup, then placing it back on the saucer, she daintily wiped her mouth with her napkin.

'Now then, Eliza. Do you recall what I said to you the day you left? If I remember rightly, I said that if ever you need any help, in any way, you know where we are. I think, Eliza, it's time for me to keep that promise. I know it's not you that is in need of help, but maybe I could help one of those other poor families you were just telling me about. Why don't you and Thomas come and stay at *Aysgarth Villa*, so one of them can move to the Cutler's Arms? You can stay as long as you want, until you find somewhere else. We have plenty of room, as you know. If you like, you could have the same room you and your mother had. It's large enough, and it's got all the furniture you'll need. I've only the one housekeeper living in now, Elsie, and she uses one of the smaller rooms, and there's a local girl who comes in daily to help out. Now, my dear, what do you say?'

Eliza thanked Mrs Brentnall for her kind offer, and promised to discuss it with Thomas. It would mean a twenty-minute walk to work each day, and back at night, but she didn't mind that, and for Thomas it would be no further than from the Cutler's. That evening, they talked it over, and agreed that they would accept the offer, so the next morning Eliza went along first thing after breakfast to see Mrs Brentnall. Fortunately she was in, and everything was soon arranged. Two days later, Eliza and Thomas packed up their few possessions and headed up the Glossop Road. A bit like coming home for me, thought Eliza, as they approached *Aysgarth Villa*. As they turned off the road into the driveway, Thomas, who had never been here before, stopped for a moment and stared in admiration at the impressive house standing before him. And he mentally compared it with his childhood home, back in Mortimer Street in Nottingham, and could scarcely believe that he was going to live in such a grand place, even if it was only to be for a short time.

They walked on down the drive to the front door, and as Eliza rang the bell memories suddenly came flooding back of the many long, and mainly happy, years she had spent here. And with everything that had happened recently, she fervently hoped that things would once more return to normal.

CHAPTER TWENTY

Truth will out

'Oh, there you are, Eliza. I was hoping I'd catch you before you left.' Mrs Brentnall had come into the hallway just as Eliza was about to set off for the Cutler's Arms. It was shortly after three on a warm Friday afternoon in May, a little earlier than her usual time to go to work, but a large party of newly qualified cutlers from one of the local factories, along with many of their work colleagues and families, was booked in that evening to celebrate the successful culmination of their long apprenticeships, and there was much work to be done in preparation.

'Robert and I were talking last night, and we wondered if you and Thomas would like to have lunch with us on Sunday. We usually eat out on Sundays, as you know, but we'll be eating at home this week, and I know you both have Sundays off work, so if you've nothing else arranged it would be nice if you could join us. We all seem to have been so busy over the last few weeks, what with one thing and another, that we've barely had a moment to talk. We could have a chat and you can let us know how you're settling in.'

Eliza and Thomas had now been living at *Aysgarth Villa* for just over a fortnight, and things had been hectic for them, following the flood, with every spare hour seemingly taken up with trying to find a new place to live. 'Yes, that would be lovely; thank you for asking us. I don't need to check with Thomas; I know he won't be working, and we've nothing else planned.'

'Excellent. We'll be eating about one. Now, I must go and find Elsie and let her know; it's her day off, too, but she did say she'd cook lunch for us.'

To sit down to a proper Sunday lunch in such splendid surroundings as that of the Brentnall's dining room, was a rare treat for Thomas and Eliza. Eliza had, on numerous occasions, helped her mother serve meals at this very same table, but not once, during all the years they had lived and worked there, had they actually dined there.

At first, they were both a little overwhelmed by the occasion, Thomas, in particular. His background and upbringing were a world apart from that of the Brentnalls. Robert Brentnall was a successful and fairly prosperous solicitor, a partner in a long-established Sheffield practice, and it was evident from their demeanour that they were both well bred, refined and had received good educations. The trappings of wealth were everywhere to be seen in the house, and the shelves of books in the study indicated an interest in many subjects beyond the narrow confines of the law, which profession had provided the means for such a high standard of living.

Thomas had been somewhat reticent when Eliza had first told him of Mrs Brentnall's offer to let them stay at *Aysgarth Villa*. He had grown up amongst rough, working-class folk in Nottingham. His father was a lace maker and his father had been a framework knitter, and the family, for generations had lived in one of the poorest areas of the town. Now here he was in Sheffield, sweating his way through twelve-hour shifts in the searing heat and deafening clamour of a steelworks. His world was a million miles away from the surroundings he now found himself in.

Thomas had rarely come into contact with anyone from the upper echelons of society, but his natural inclination was to believe that they all considered themselves superior and looked down on people like him, and this had left him with a simmering distrust and dislike of the whole lot of them.

But possibly he had been wrong to judge so quickly. As Elsie served the soup, the conversation began, and it quickly became apparent that both Mr and Mrs Brentnall were not of that same ilk, and immediately put Thomas at ease. Eliza had, of course, already told him much about them both, and how kind and considerate they had been in the past. Mrs Brentnall, he knew, spent most of her time in charity work, so, he thought, that must be something in her favour.

'Now, before we go any further,' announced Mrs Brentnall, 'I think we should dispose of any unnecessary formalities, particularly as you're now guests in our house. So from now on, please call us Frances and Robert.' And immediately, Thomas's sense of ease was strengthened even more.

In the course of their meal, they spoke of many things and it soon became obvious to Thomas that Mr Brentnall was very well read, but he made no attempt to use such knowledge in an intimidating way. On the contrary, he seemed to go out of his way to seek his opinions on a number of topics, and took a genuine interest in learning of Thomas's former life in Nottingham, and the processes of the steel industry which now provided his living.

At the conclusion of lunch, Frances suggested that they retire to the comfort of the drawing room, where Elsie proceeded to serve coffee.

'Well, Thomas,' said Robert, after Elsie had taken away the empty coffee pot and cups, 'I think you and I deserve a brandy to finish off with. And what about the ladies?' he asked, glancing in the direction of his wife and Eliza who were seated at a long settee. 'Would you both like one, too?'

'Oh, not for me dear,' Frances replied, 'but I'd love a sherry, and I'm sure Eliza would as well,' to which suggestion Eliza nodded her agreement. Robert went to a tall mahogany cabinet and took out two cut-glass decanters and four equally fine glasses, and poured generous portions into each.

'Now, Eliza,' said Frances, 'I don't want you take this the wrong way, because Robert and I are happy to have you both stay here for as long as you need to, but tell me, have you had any luck yet in finding somewhere new to live? I know you've been looking. And what about your old house – have you had second thoughts about moving back there?'

'I'm afraid the answer's no on both counts,' replied Eliza. 'It seems there are so many others doing the same thing as us, and anything that becomes available soon gets snapped up, at least where the rent's not too high, although some landlords are cashing in on the shortage and upping rents. Thomas saw our old landlord last week and he reckons it'll be months before the damage is sorted out. And even if he doesn't up the rent, I know we won't be able to afford it, not just the two of us. And it was such a nice little house,' then as an afterthought she added, 'but it now holds some awful memories, and I don't think I'd ever want to go back there, anyway.'

'And you don't have any family in the area, any relatives who could help out?' Eliza sat in quiet contemplation for a few seconds before replying, a look of sadness on her face.

'No, I'm afraid not. Not that I know of.'

'No aunts or uncles or cousins close by?'

'No, I haven't. My mother was an only child, like me.'

'But what about your father?' chipped in Robert. 'Do you have no relatives on his side?' Again, there was a slight pause before Eliza replied. Thomas took a drink of his brandy and looked across at his wife. He knew only a little about her father. She had only ever told him the briefest of details, and seemed reluctant to discuss it, so he had never pressed the issue, believing that she would tell him, if and when she was ready to. Maybe, now, that time had come. But he could sense the pain showing on her face as she resumed.

'It's something that I've never spoken about much, not even to Thomas. But after everything that's happened recently, I think the time has come to break my silence. And you've both been so good to us of late, so I'd like to tell you. Even Thomas doesn't know the full story either. So here goes.

'My mother never talked much about my father's early life, mainly because it was always a complete mystery to her. She always used to say that he never liked to talk about his past, and it wasn't until we received a visit one day from an elderly lady that we got to know anything. You might remember it, Frances. I think we told you about her at the time. It must have been, let me think now, about eight years ago. Yes, that's right, and it was about this same time of the year. She arrived here one morning, unannounced, asking after mother. She was down in the town, doing some shopping, and you were also both out, as well. Her name was Emily and she told me that she was an aunt of my father, his mother's sister, and that she'd come to Sheffield from her home near Wakefield to see mother, as she had something very important to tell her; something that couldn't wait. It was all very mysterious. So I suggested that mother could go and see her the next day, which was a Saturday, at the Commercial Hotel where she was staying, and she kindly invited us both to have lunch with her. I'd never been in there before, but as you know, that's where I eventually ended up working. Anyway, we had lunch, and she told us the most extraordinary story about my father. I could hardly believe it. If I'd read it in a book I'd have probably thought it was a little far-fetched.' Eliza stopped and took a sip of her sherry.

'Oh, I do hope you're not going to leave us all in suspense,' exclaimed Robert, before Eliza had the chance to continue. 'I do love a good mystery, and this sounds as if it has all the hallmarks of a rattling good one. Just hang on a minute, though, and I'll top up our glasses.'

Glasses duly replenished, Eliza resumed her tale. As her audience sat riveted to their seats, she proceeded to relate everything she and Hannah had learned from Emily. All about Joseph's childhood as the younger son of a wealthy landowner in the West Riding, living at Westbrook Manor, some twenty miles to the northwest of Sheffield, but growing up without a mother and being mercilessly bullied by his elder brother; of being sent to a boarding school near York to escape these unwanted and undeserved attacks, and then of his father's sudden and unexpected death, days before he intended to make a will; of being forced out of his school after his brother inherited the estate and cut Joseph off without a penny, and how he had managed to find his way to Emily's home, where she lived with her parents, Joseph's grandparents. And how his grandfather secured for him an apprenticeship with a cutler in Sheffield, where he took lodgings with a widow, Agnes Whitworth, Eliza's grandmother. She had a daughter, Hannah, and she and Joseph eventually fell in love and were married in 1836, and Eliza herself was born in early 1838. And then came the most painful part of her story; of how, in July 1840, Joseph had gone to York, supposedly in connection with a business venture, but had never returned. And how, it quickly transpired, he had been found murdered in the back yard of an inn.

'How terrible,' said Robert. 'Was the culprit ever apprehended and brought to court?'

'No. His assailant was never found, but the plot thickens. Emily told us that in 1840, the same year that father died, the housekeeper at Westbrook Manor, Jessie Hough, had been found dead there under suspicious circumstances, and father's brother, who of course was now the owner of the estate, had been charged with her murder and sent for trial at York Assizes. And despite all the evidence, he was found not guilty. It turns out he had a very good advocate to defend him. I know nothing more about what happened to him, although Emily thought he was still alive, but that was eight years ago. But the most amazing coincidence, if indeed that is what it was, is that the trial took place on the very same day that father had gone to York. So you see, Robert, in answer to your question, I might, possibly, have a living relative, an uncle. But from what Emily told us, not the sort of uncle one would want to have anything to do with.'

Robert, as a solicitor himself, was now even more intrigued than ever. 'This case is beginning to ring a bell with me. Whilst I don't practice in criminal law myself, I do, vaguely remember reading about some such trial in the Sheffield newspapers, although it was a long time ago. Tell me, Eliza, what was this man's name, your uncle? I don't think you mentioned it, did you?'

'No, I didn't; how silly of me. It was Miles, Miles Lambert.'

'Miles Lambert, you say. That's not a particularly common name, and yet it does seem familiar. I'm sure I've heard it before.'

'Perhaps it was when you read about the murder trial,' suggested Frances.

Robert took a drink of his brandy, leant back in his chair and closed his eyes, concentrating hard.

'No, I don't think so. That would have been almost twenty-five years ago. This was much more recent than that, a month or two back, and I'm pretty sure it was at the office, but the name meant nothing to me at the time, so I didn't think any more about it. But I'll ask tomorrow morning and see if anyone else can recall the name.'

The following evening Eliza arrived back from work at about nine o'clock. Mondays were never very busy at the Cutler's, and she had just settled down in their room to do a bit of sewing when there came a knock at the door.

'Ah, there you are, Eliza. I thought I heard you come in,' said Frances. 'Robert has some news that I think you'll be interested to hear. Why don't you come down to the drawing room and he can tell you all about it. And bring Thomas, too. I'll go and put the kettle on and make us all a cup of tea.'

Ten minutes later, Frances was pouring out the tea as Robert began.

'I made some enquiries, as I said I would, about Miles Lambert. I've no precise details yet, but I have established that the name *was* mentioned and in what connection. We have a recent recruit to the practice, an articled clerk by the name of Arthur Newton. He's a keen lad, and his family has been involved with the law for several generations, on the right side, I hasten to add,' he explained, in response to a mischievous grin that had spread across Thomas's face. 'His father's retired now, but Arthur has an uncle, Samuel Newton, a partner in a firm of solicitors in Penistone. About a month ago, Arthur was assisting us with the administration of a rather complicated estate, and the subject of intestacy cropped up – you know, when someone dies without making a will – and he started to relate a recent example he had heard about from his uncle. Of course, many people don't make wills because they have very little to leave, but when the opposite is the case, all sorts of problems can arise.

'His uncle's practice had recently been requested by the Court of Exchequer – that's the body that oversees such matters – to act as local agents in one such case that had recently arisen up in the West Riding, although Arthur didn't know precisely where. It concerns the death of a wealthy landowner who, it appears, died without ever making a will – a most unusual and extremely foolhardy thing to do where such large amounts of property and other assets are involved. And the name of the deceased was Miles Lambert. Arthur said he particularly remembered the name, because his uncle had told him that there was a deal of speculation in the local press regarding not only the nature of his death, but also certain scandalous events in which he was believed to be implicated. That's about all that Arthur could remember, but he said that he will be visiting his uncle at the weekend and will try and find out as much as he can. I'm afraid that's all I can tell you for now, but hopefully, by this time next week, I should be able to enlighten you both a little more.'

Eliza and Thomas were both fascinated by what they had been told; not only that, but also quite excited. They were both reluctant to speculate, lest such hopes might tempt fate, but they both realised that, if this was Eliza's uncle, and if he had died intestate, then she, as a descendent, might be entitled to inherit some of the estate. The next week went by so painfully slowly, so eager were they to learn the truth. Eventually Monday came round, and straight after work Thomas went to the Cutler's for something to eat, but by nine o'clock he and Eliza were hurrying up the Glossop Road, and another half-hour later found them seated once more in the drawing room at *Aysgarth Villa*. This time, there were to be no cups of tea. Instead, Robert had already laid out glasses and decanters of brandy and sherry on the sideboard.

'I thought we might all like to have something a little stronger than tea,' he said, with a satisfied smile on his face, as he poured out the drinks. Having seated himself comfortably in an armchair, he picked up a briefcase from the carpet, and taking out a handful of papers placed them beside him on a low table.

'Now then, Eliza, this time I really do have something of interest to tell you. Young Arthur has come up trumps,' he added, as he began to sift through the papers. 'I'd like you to have a look at this, first. It's an advertisement that appeared recently in both the *Leeds Intelligencier* and the *Sheffield Independent*, both of which circulate quite widely in the West Riding. I expect the same notice has also appeared in the *London Gazette*,' and he handed her a single sheet of paper. It consisted merely of a small newspaper cutting, pasted in the middle, underneath which was written, in a neat and flowing hand, *Leeds Intelligencier, Fri. 11th March '64*.

Eliza quietly read the item to herself as Thomas looked on, expectantly. 'What does it say?' he asked. 'Come on, Eliza, don't keep me in the dark.'

'I'll read it to you.'

All persons claiming to be related to MILES LAMBERT, late of the parish of Westbrook, near Penistone in the County of West Yorkshire, and who recently died intestate, are desired to send a statement of the grounds of their respective Claims, with sufficient evidence in support thereof, to Messrs. Newton and Harcourt, Solicitors, at their office in Penistone.

'Westbrook!' exclaimed Eliza, 'that's where Emily said my father and his brother Miles lived. It must be the same Miles. Surely, there can't be two men with the same name in the same place, not both owning large estates.'

'It certainly seems unlikely,' agreed Robert. 'But the Court of Exchequer never takes anything for granted, and it will be up to claimants to verify their entitlement.'

'So how do we go about that?' asked Eliza.

'Well, from what you've already told me, it does seem that this Miles is your uncle. If you like, I'll get Arthur to put all the evidence together, and he can send it on to his uncle. But first, I'll need more details – names, dates of birth and marriage, that sort of thing. Are you happy for me to do that?'

'Oh, yes please. I'll obviously pay you whatever it costs.'

'Well, let's not worry about that just at the moment. And this will be a good practical case for young Arthur to get his teeth into. We can start right away, if you're not too tired.'

'No, let's get on with it. I'm so excited I couldn't sleep anyway.'

'Excellent,' said Robert, picking up a notepad and pencil. 'Firstly, do you know whether Miles ever married?'

'I don't know for certain. We did ask Emily that when we saw her, and she said he never had. But that was eight years ago.'

'Well, that will be something else for Arthur to check. Now, Eliza, tell me about yourself. Where were you born and what was your date of birth?'

'Sheffield. 16th January, 1838.'

'Ah, that means there should be a birth certificate for you. Registration of births and so on started in 1837, and although it isn't compulsory, most births are registered. I'll get Arthur to check it. Now, I need the same information for your parents.'

'Well, I know my mother's birthday, just a week before mine, 9th January. And she was born, I think, in 1818, in Sheffield.'

'There'll be no birth certificate for her, then; do you know if she was christened, and at what church?'

'I really don't know, but she used to attend St. Peters, the Cathedral, and take me along with her, so she might have been christened there; and I know that's where she was married, because she told me so. That's why Thomas and I also got married there.'

'And do you know exactly when she got married? This is most important. As you'll be claiming to be related to the Lambert family, we have to prove she did marry into that family.'

'Oh, I can tell you that; it was the 25th June 1836,' and as she spoke she removed the silver chain and locket from round her neck and laid it on the table. 'If you look on the back, you'll find the date and my mother's and father's initials. This was a present from my father on their wedding day. Evidently he made it himself, just as he finished his apprenticeship, shortly before they got married.'

'And your father, Joseph Lambert. Would you know when and where he was born?'

'I'm afraid I don't know his birthday. The truth is, I don't know much about him at all. But I do know he was a few years older than mother, and I can only assume he was born at Westbrook. When his Aunt Emily came to see us she told us that her sister, Amelia, had married Henry Lambert at Westbrook in 1807. Yes, I'm fairly certain that's the year, but I can't remember the actual date. I think she said that Miles was born first, then there were some daughters who all died young, and finally, my father. He was the youngest, and Amelia died giving birth to him.'

'I can see Arthur will have to take a trip over to Westbrook. I'm sure the local churchwarden will let him examine the parish register and that should provide all the information and dates we need about the Lambert family and prove that your father was a brother to Miles. But what about Emily; would she be able to corroborate any of this, if necessary?'

'I very much doubt it. When she came to see us, she explained that she didn't have very long to live. We did say we'd try and keep in touch with each other, but we've never heard from her since, so I can only assume she has passed away. I don't think she had any other relatives, either, so there was nobody to let us know.'

'I see. But if we should need any more evidence, I expect your father's old employer could provide that. Yates, I think you said, is where he used to work.'

'That's right, in Eyre Street. I know they're still trading, because I walked down there the other day.'

'Well, Eliza,' said Robert, as he put his notepad and pencil back on the table, 'I think what you've told me should be enough to build a cast-iron case to substantiate your claim. I'll pass all this on to Arthur tomorrow morning and he can get to work on it right away. As soon as I have anything more to tell you, I'll let you know.'

'How long do think it will all take?' asked Eliza.

'Difficult to say. I would expect Arthur to have everything checked out and written up within three or four weeks, even though he'll have to go over to Westbrook. Then we'll send everything to the solicitor in Penistone who's dealing with it. After that, it's down to the Court of Exchequer. And it will also depend on whether there are any other claimants. I know you said you thought Miles never married, but that doesn't mean he didn't father any children, and from what you've said about him, that could be a real possibility.'

Robert was as good as his word, and in just under a month he was able to confirm that Arthur's research had been completed, all the relevant information had been found, and everything had been written up and sent to *Newton and Harcourt* at Penistone. Another month went by before Arthur was able to wheedle out of his uncle, entirely unofficially of course, that they had received no other claims of kinship to Miles, and that they had consequently forwarded Eliza's claim to the Court of Exchequer. But the wheels of the law grind slowly, and there was to be another agonising wait of over six months, before Robert returned home from the office one evening in mid-February with a broad grin on his face, as wide as the cold, damp, clinging fog that had descended on the town that afternoon.

'You seem remarkably jolly tonight, Robert,' said Frances as he entered the drawing room, humming a merry tune to himself, 'especially on such a foul night as this. Something must have tickled your fancy.'

'Well, I think there's someone else who's fancy is going to be far more tickled than mine,' he said, brandishing above his head a sheaf of papers, tied in pink ribbon. 'I take it Eliza and Thomas are still out.'

'Yes. I think Thomas must have gone straight from work to meet Eliza. He usually does when the weather's so bad. I expect they'll be back soon after nine.'

'Very good. That'll give us time for supper and for me to put you in the picture. And I think tonight might be the time to open that exceedingly fine bottle of champagne that's been laid up waiting for such an occasion since last Christmas.'

CHAPTER TWENTY-ONE

Treasures untold

It was approaching nine thirty when Frances heard the front door open. Hurrying into the hallway, she stopped Eliza and Thomas just as they were about to go up the stairs to their room.

'I'm glad I've caught you. Would you like to come and join us? Robert has something important he wants to tell you,' she explained, trying hard not to smile too much and give the game away.

'Yes, of course we will,' replied Eliza, and, having removed their coats, they followed Frances into the warm and cosy drawing room, and sat on the settee by the fire.

'Now then,' said Robert, as he picked up the file of papers resting on his lap. 'I have something here that I know will interest you,' and he began to untie the pink ribbon. 'So I won't prolong things any further, as I've no doubt you may already have guessed what this is. We've waited long enough, but we now have the ruling from the Court of Exchequer. It arrived in the office today from *Newton and Harcourt*.' He dropped the ribbon on the floor and began to sift through the papers. 'I won't bore you with all the legal jargon, but you're welcome to read it at your leisure. With your permission, I'll just explain what it says. Is that acceptable?'

'Oh yes, Robert, please do,' urged Eliza, with a mounting sense of anticipation.

'Very well. It says that your claim to be an heir to Miles's estate has been checked and accepted as true. It does go on to say that two other late claims were also received, and that caused a further delay, but they have now been declared spurious. Arthur found no evidence of a wife, or any legitimate children, but it seems that once word got out that Miles had died intestate, two single women, both now residing in the area, put in claims alleging that Miles was the father of their children, and that they believed they were therefore entitled to a share of his estate. But when the court discovered that one of them had already made a successful claim for financial support against the cellar man at an inn near Holmfirth, naming him as the father, whilst the other turned out to have spent the year prior to the birth of her son residing in Durham, much of it at Her Majesty's pleasure in Durham Gaol following a conviction for fraud, these two claims were dismissed out of hand. Which means, Eliza, that you are the sole heir to the Westbrook estate.'

'Does that mean I'll have to refer to you as the Lady of the Manor, now?' asked Thomas, tongue firmly in cheek.

'A good point, Thomas. Technically, that is precisely what Eliza is, but I'll leave it to you to decide that little matter between yourselves,' added Robert, smiling, but trying to appear serious. 'But the estate is now officially yours, and that means you are entitled to all income from the rents on the various properties and farms.'

'But what exactly does the estate consist of?' asked Eliza. 'I've never been there, never seen it. Just what have I inherited?'

'You'll find a full inventory here,' said Robert, pointing to the file of papers, 'but briefly, the Westbrook estate includes most of the village of Westbrook, which is about half a mile from Westbrook Manor. This is an early seventeenth-century stone building, although I understand it's in need of some repair and maintenance. It seems your uncle has neglected it somewhat. Then there are almost six thousand acres of land and quite a number of farms. The lower parts of the estate are good for arable farming, but the higher, moorland, is really only good for sheep, although it is understood that some of the lower parts of the moor are sitting on reserves of coal. It seems your grandfather was looking into exploiting these shortly before his death, but Miles has, evidently, not pursued the matter further. That is surprising, because a number of mining companies have shown an interest.

'From what the Penistone solicitor has been told by some of the tenants, Miles cared little for the wellbeing of the estate, and devoted most of his energy in the pursuit of pleasure. Fortunately, the tenants have been more conscientious, so the farms are in reasonable fettle, and the coal reserves could prove to be very valuable. In terms of the overall assets, there is little in the way of actual money – Miles saw to that! But there is some exceptionally fine furniture at the manor. There was, however, one small item that I want to give you now; it came with the paperwork,' and Robert reached into his jacket pocket and handed to Eliza a small cardboard box. She opened it, and took out a beautiful gold pocket watch on a rose gold chain and carefully examined it.

'I've never seen this before. Where did it come from?'

'It was the only item of any value found on Miles's body. The only other things in his pockets were an empty hip flask, a few copper coins and some old IOUs – gambling debts, it's believed. But if you open the case, you'll find something that will interest you.'

Eliza did as Robert suggested, and there, on the inside of the watchcase, were engraved the words – *For HL with fondest love from AB 8th May 1807*. For a moment or two, Eliza stared at the inscription, and then a look of both surprise and delight spread across her face.

'I think I know what this is. I remember my mother telling me that the one thing my father had to remind him of his father was a gold watch. And look at these initials – *HL* and *AB*. They must be for Henry Lambert and Amelia Bussey, father's parents – and see, that must be the date of their wedding. I said I thought that was the year they got married. And when mother told me about father's murder, she explained that when the policeman came from York to break the news she asked him whether they had found his watch, but they said they had found nothing of value on him. That's why they suspected that robbery had been the motive. And when we eventually found out that Miles had been on trial in York the very same day, we did begin to wonder whether he might have had something to do with father's death. And now that his watch has been found on Miles's body, well, it makes you think.'

'You might be right, Eliza, but I doubt we'll ever know the truth for certain. But I can confirm that that was the date of Henry and Amelia's wedding, so it must have been a gift from Amelia to Henry.'

'But how did Miles die; and where was he found?' asked Thomas, who had been listening intently to everything being said.

'One of Miles's tenant farmworkers found him lying face down in a ditch. He'd gone out early one morning to do a spot of hedging and found him there. He was only fifty yards from the gates of the manor, and his horse was nearby. It appears that he'd spent the previous night at the Black Boar in Westbrook, gambling and drinking heavily; a regular pastime of his, by all accounts. There was an inquest, of course, and the coroner's verdict was "accidental death", and that he'd drowned in a mixture of ditch water and his own vomit.'

'A fitting end, some might say,' observed Eliza, 'and I know we shouldn't speak ill of the dead, but from what I've found out about my uncle I don't think there would have been many to mourn his passing.'

'There weren't, so I'm led to believe. His burial was a very quiet affair, alongside his ancestors in the local churchyard. According to Arthur's uncle, there were only a handful of village folk present, who were probably there more out of curiosity. But no real mourners.'

'But what happens next? I've never owned much more than a few sticks of furniture and the clothes I wear. Now, it seems, I'm rich!'

'Indeed you are. The estate farms and other property bring in a considerable annual rent. Miles spent all that as fast as it came in, but I expect you'll be much more sensible. You'll also have to decide whether to keep the estate, sell it – or maybe parts of it – or lease it. And I've already mentioned the interest from coal mining companies.'

'Yes, Robert, you're right. There's going to be a lot for me to think about and decide on. Would you be able to help me? I mean, this is all so new to me, and I really wouldn't know how to deal with it myself.'

'I'd be more than happy to administer it for you. And there's an excellent land agent here in Sheffield with whom we regularly do business, who could handle that side of things for you, while I sort out all the legal bits. But I suggest, Eliza, that before you come to any decision, you and Thomas take a trip over there and view your inheritance. However, right now, I propose that we celebrate your good fortune. I take it you won't refuse a glass or two of champagne?'

Two weeks later, the appropriate arrangements having been made, Eliza and Thomas caught a Saturday morning train to Penistone, where they were met by Samuel Newton, a middle-aged gentleman, neatly dressed and precise in his manner; reserved, yet friendly, and displaying a sense of reliability and honesty. Having introduced themselves, they climbed into his trap and set off at a brisk pace, quickly leaving the town behind them. It was a cool day, and Mr Newton kindly offered Eliza a thick woollen rug to wrap around her.

Before long they had reached open countryside, heading in a northwesterly direction, the watery sun on their backs offering only scant warmth, and after a journey of some three or four miles the landscape gradually became bleaker, with moorlands rising up on all sides. A few miles further on the road narrowed and descended into a broad valley through which a shallow river meandered, and they entered a quaint village of weather-beaten stone cottages and houses. Mr Newton slowed down as they passed through, and Eliza noticed the faded wooden sign hanging outside one ancient building, bearing a name she had heard just a couple of weeks before – the Black Boar. So this was Westbrook. Eliza looked around, finding it hard to believe that she was now the owner of most of these properties.

But in no time at all they had left the village and were travelling once more along a narrow country lane. Turning a sharp bend, a stone wall, some six feet in height, came into view on their right, running for a considerable distance downhill from the high moorlands above and then alongside the lane, clearly marking the boundary of a large landed estate. Turning yet another corner, Mr Newton began to pull gently on the reins and brought the trap to a halt next to a pair of wrought-iron gates.

'There it is,' said Mr Newton, nodding towards the house that stood broodingly at the end of a long driveway. 'It's all yours now; the house, the grounds, and the land right up onto those moors. Not to mention nearly all the cottages in the village and most of the surrounding farms.'

The house itself was of limestone, three storeys high and with three gables; small, mullioned windows and a huge front door in the middle.

'The gates are locked,' added Mr Newton pointing to a padlock and heavy iron chain fastening them tightly together and hanging almost to the ground, 'but I've got the key here, if you'd like to look round.'

Eliza turned to Thomas. 'What do you think, Thomas? I suppose we should, now we've come all this way.'

Mr Newton unlocked the gates and swung them back on their rusty hinges. He climbed back into the trap and they trotted on down the driveway towards the house, the horse's hooves and iron-shod wheels of the carriage crunching over the rough stone chippings. To each side lay a wide strip of grass, bordering trees and shrubs, all showing signs of neglect, whilst beyond the immediate grounds, behind the house, the land rose up towards the moors stretching as far as the eye could see.

Pulling up outside the porch, Mr Newton dug deep into his pocket and took out another bunch of heavy keys, the largest of which he used to unlock the massive oak front door. With some effort, assisted by Thomas, he pushed this open and they made their way into a wood-panelled hallway, into which little natural light penetrated. Doors led off in all directions, whilst a handsome carved staircase ascended towards a landing running the full length of the house. For an hour or so they explored every nook and cranny, from below stairs up into the attic rooms. An impression of severe gloominess permeated throughout, for the windows were small and the panes of glass thickly coated with grime, both inside and out, as dirty as the heavy curtains draped forlornly over some of them.

Every room told the same story. It was a solid enough house, obviously built with every indication of having had no expense spared in its construction and having employed only the finest craftsmen. But at the same time it showed signs of many years of neglect. Little or no housekeeping seemed to have been done, and everywhere was in a state of decline. And yet, exactly as they had been told, there were some magnificent pieces of furniture to be seen, and it was clear that whilst the most recent generation of the Lambert family had neglected his property, earlier ones clearly hadn't. It saddened Eliza, looking around, to think that such wanton negligence and lack of care had been bestowed on such a fine old house. And she wondered how much better it would have fared had it been her father instead of Miles who had inherited the estate. But of course, had that been the case, he would never have moved to Sheffield and met her mother, and she would not be standing there now.

Seeking to escape the overwhelming sense of decay they had found inside, they wandered out into the grounds that surrounded the house, and strolled through the walled kitchen-garden that would once have provided much of the food required at the manor. But here, too, everything had also been abandoned and left to the ravages of time and the effects of nature.

Having seen all they wanted to, they set off back to Penistone, but as they were passing the Black Boar in Westbrook, Eliza suddenly asked Mr Newton to pull up. 'Come with me Thomas, there's something I'd like to have a look at.' Once inside the inn, Eliza exchanged a few quiet words with the landlord then asked Thomas to follow her. She led the way up the stairs to a small room overlooking the stable yard, and stood there for a moment or two in silent contemplation. In the centre of the room was a large circular table covered with a green baize cloth, as if patiently waiting for a school of card players to arrive. 'This is it, Thomas. This is where Miles spent most of his time and much of my inheritance,' she explained. 'I just needed to see it for myself before we left.'

Two hours later Eliza and Thomas settled themselves into the deeply upholstered and comfortable seats of an empty first-class compartment in the train taking them back to Sheffield. It was a journey of less than forty minutes, but they were happy to pay the extra for a luxury they had never before been able to afford.

After sitting quietly for a little while, Eliza turned to Thomas. 'I've made my mind up, Thomas. I've decided I'm going to sell the estate, lock, stock and barrel. It's certainly a lovely old house, Westbrook Manor, but it does need some money spending on it and it's far too big for us. And I don't think I could ever get used to living in such a remote place. It's a very pretty area, but imagine it in the depths of winter, with rain and wind and snow coming down off those moors. I was brought up in the town, same as you, and that's what I'm used to. I don't really think I could live without the attractions that a town can offer. I suppose we could keep one of the small cottages in the village, and go and stop there in the summer if we wanted to get away for a week or two.'

'I'm glad you've said that, Eliza. I'd have gone along with whatever you decided, but I think I'd much rather remain where we are.'

'Well, not *exactly* where we are. We still have to find somewhere else to live, but money won't be a problem now. When we get back I'll let Robert know of our decision and ask him to set the wheels in motion to dispose of the estate. And we'll have to make sure he and Frances are well rewarded for putting us up for so long and for everything that they've done for us. And talking about finding somewhere else to live, have you noticed that lovely little villa that's for sale, down towards the bottom of Glossop Road? It's on the left, set back from the road, with a neat front garden. It looks just right for us. It's far enough out of the town to be quiet and away from all the noise and smells, but near enough to get to all the shops easily, and … Thomas, Thomas! Are you listening to me?'

'Oh, sorry, Eliza. I was just looking at those pictures,' and he pointed to some small, framed prints above the seats opposite, scenes of various locations served by the railway company. 'Look, there's one of the seafront at Cleethorpes and that reminded me of when we went to Scarborough for our honeymoon. We did promise ourselves we'd go back there again, one day. Well, why don't we go now? I think it's about time we had a holiday, especially after everything that's happened over the last year. And this time we can afford the best hotel in town!'

'What a good idea! But it's only March and it's a bit too cold to be walking along those cliffs right now. Why don't we wait until the summer? That will give Robert time to start sorting out the sale of the estate and I expect he'll have lots of documents for me to sign. And I know you want to go and visit your folks in Nottingham. We could stop there for a few days. And I'd like to give your parents some money to make their lives a bit easier now they're approaching old age, and I bet your Matthew and Betsy wouldn't say no to a little windfall, either. We could go to Scarborough at the end of June. That'll be our second wedding anniversary; cotton isn't it, the second anniversary? You could buy me something made of cotton, some nice Nottingham lace perhaps. You could get it for me when we go down there.

'But don't forget, Thomas, we must go and have a look at that house down Glossop Road I was telling you about, before someone else buys it. It's sounds very nice. When I went past it the other day, a gardener was pruning some rose bushes, so I stopped and had a word with him and he told me a bit about it. It's got a sitting room and a dining room, a large kitchen and scullery and five bedrooms; and it's even got a bathroom and I thought we could keep some of that beautiful old furniture we saw at Westbrook Manor today, and I was also thinking …'

'Five bedrooms! Whatever would we do with five bedrooms?

There's only the two of us.'

'Yes; but one day there might be more than just us two.'

'Of course, Eliza, and I hope there will be. But *five* bedrooms. When I was a kid, three of us had to share one tiny room, and Matthew and me shared the same bed.'

'Yes, but we can afford better now. Your folks might like to come and stay with us sometimes. And we'll need a bigger house soon anyway. I was about to suggest that if you do buy me something made of Nottingham lace, I think a christening shawl would be just the thing. I bet your father could make us one specially at the lace factory.'

'A christening shawl? You mean ...'

'Oh, yes. I've suspected it for some weeks now, but I didn't want to say anything until I'd seen the doctor, which I did yesterday, and he confirmed it. By the beginning of October, all being well, you're going to be a father.'

'Oh, Eliza, that's wonderful news. Come here,' and Thomas gave his wife a hug and a kiss.

'And I did think that if it's a girl we'll call her Sarah, and if it's a boy, we'll call him John.'

'Yes, I think that's a nice idea, naming the baby after one of them.'

The train had been slowing down and came to a stop. 'Look, we're at Wadsley Bridge already. We'll be back at Sheffield in ten minutes. I think we'd better get a cab. Don't want you walking up that hill, not in your condition.'

'Oh, stop fussing, Thomas. I'll be fine. But I'd like to call and see Annie at the Cutler's on the way and give her all the news and let her know that I'll have to stop work soon. And I think we ought to give her something towards her retirement, because I know she's been talking about giving up the pub before too long, and she was so good to us after the flood. And that reminds me; I'm going to let Frances have a donation for the flood relief fund – I know they'll make good use of it. And you'll need to hand in your notice, too. No need for you to go on working any longer.'

'First thing Monday morning. But you know what I'd like to do tonight?'

'What's that, Thomas?'

'I'd like to go to the music hall. The one we went to the first time we met. I see that George Leybourne's topping the bill there tonight. He's one of the big stars on the London halls right now, so he should be worth seeing. Then, afterwards, we could go along to the Cutler's. It'll be just like the old days. What do you say, Eliza?'

'Yes, I'd like that; I'd like that very much.'

Two years later, shortly before Christmas, in the comfort of the sitting room at *Westbroook Villa*, the house they had purchased on Glossop Road, Eliza and Thomas sat on a settee, Eliza cradling their baby daughter, Sarah, in her arms, Thomas reading the newspaper, whilst their two-year-old son, John, played noisily on the carpet.

'Oh, by the way, Thomas, I meant to ask you to have a look at the bureau; the inside top drawer on the left won't shut properly and it's a bit stiff when you try and open it.'

'I'll do it now while I think about,' he said, putting his newspaper to one side.

In one corner of the room stood a handsome eighteenth-century French escritoire in walnut, one of a number of pieces of furniture they had kept from Westbrook Manor prior to the sale of the estate. Thomas lowered the hinged top, to reveal inside a number of small drawers, and examined the offending one, trying to open and close it.

'I see what you mean; I think there must be something stuck at the back.' Removing the drawer beneath it, he put his hand in and felt around. 'Ah, here we are, I've found it,' and he removed some sheets of paper, folded and tied with a ribbon. 'I wonder what these can be?' he said as he sat down on the settee again. The paper looked old and somewhat faded, and on the front sheet was writing in an immaculate copperplate hand.

'What does it say?' asked Eliza.

'Here, pass Sarah over to me and you can read it.'

Eliza untied the ribbon, revealing three sheets of yellowing and rather musty-smelling paper and began to read it to herself, turning the pages quickly.

'Well, Thomas just listen to this. It's dated December 1828, and addressed to Nathaniel Cartwright, Cartwright & Dickens, solicitors, with a note underneath which reads – *here's the draft for my will, please write it up as soon as you can* – and it's signed by Henry Lambert; that's my grandfather. You remember I told you that Emily said he was going to make a will, but then died before he got round to doing it. This must be what he'd drafted out, ready to give to the solicitor.'

'So what exactly does it say?' enquired Thomas, anxious to learn its secrets.

'Well, firstly he appoints his sister-in-law, Emily, and the solicitors as joint executors and trustees. Then there are several small legacies to various charities, and quite a few to people I've never heard of, although I do recognise two names – Alfred and Jessie Hough – they were the old retainers at the manor, and Jessie of course was the one Miles was accused of murdering. But this is the really interesting bit; I'll read it to you:

> *I leave the whole of the Westbrook Estate, the house and all its contents, buildings, farms and other properties, and all the land and any mineral deposits found there, in its entirety to my younger son, Joseph, in the sure and certain knowledge that he will administer it wisely for the benefit of himself and future generations of the Lambert family.*
> *To my eldest son, Miles, I leave the old gamekeeper's cottage for his use for as long as he lives, along with an annuity of £50, but in the event that he agrees to leave the country and seek his fortune abroad, and never to return, the above annuity is to be increased to £100, payable until his death.*

'So, there we have it, Thomas. Henry didn't trust his eldest son – he wanted Joseph, my father, to inherit. It's taken many years and a great deal of good fortune for the truth about this Westbrook affair to come out, and all the wrongs caused by Miles to be put right, but Henry's wishes have been fulfilled at long last. And one thing's for certain, you and I will make sure these two are well provided for,' she said as she leant over and kissed her daughter.

NARROW MARSH
A R DANCE

An exciting historical saga set in
Nottingham in the early years of
the 19th century

Nottingham, 1811 – a time of fear and hardship for the town's framework knitters. With low wages and long working hours, desperate men turn to direct action. And when a man is killed, someone has to pay the ultimate price. Young William Daniels witnesses the public execution, and from that day onwards he develops a burning desire for justice and freedom. But his chance encounter with the headstrong daughter of a wealthy factory owner sets in motion a tumultuous chain of events that will change his life forever. Set in early 19th century Nottingham, in an era of bitter social unrest, *Narrow Marsh* is a dramatic story of life, love and hope.

'One of the best novels I have read. The story just flew through my fingers and I couldn't turn the pages fast enough.'
East Midlands Arts

'A highly evocative story of early 19th century high and low life. At its heart, one of England's most notorious slums. Unputdownable.'
John Brunton, journalist and author

'The sense of overriding hope against unrest and misfortune will stay with you long after you finish this rewarding novel.'
Nottinghamshire Today

Narrow Marsh is published by Arundel Books
ISBN 978-0-9558133-0-6

Available from all good book shops, price £6.99
Also available post-free direct from the publisher.
Please send cheques payable to Arundel Books.

LEEN TIMES
A R DANCE

The dramatic sequel to *Narrow Marsh*

Having returned to Nottingham from exile in France, William Daniels has now settled in his home town and is developing a successful business as a canal carrier. But ever resourceful, and always looking to the future, he also becomes involved in plans to bring the railway to Nottingham.

Meanwhile, on the other side of the world, one man has not forgotten the past. Residing at his Majesty's pleasure in a penal colony in Van Diemen's Land, an old adversary of William waits patiently for the day when he will become a free man again. And as he waits, he carefully plans his revenge against the one whom he regards as responsible for his downfall.

Nottingham in the 1820s and 1830s, an era of brutal and uncompromising change, and of fierce political upheaval, is the setting for the dramatic sequel to *Narrow Marsh*. A fast-moving story of retribution, radical politics and criminal conspiracies.

'Excellent story-telling. A fascinating marriage of fact and fiction.'
Andy Smart, Nottingham Post

'A thrilling sequel to *Narrow Marsh*, with as many twists and turns as the courts and alleys of 19th century Nottingham. I never knew my ancestors' town had experienced so much turmoil, political chicanery and mob violence.'
Jean Boht, actress

Leen Times is published by Arundel Books
ISBN 978-0-9558133-1-3

Available from all good book shops, price £7.99
Also available post-free direct from the publisher.
Please send cheques payable to Arundel Books.

Coming soon from Arundel Books

CANARY CHILD *by* David Field and Alan Dance

In 1968, in a small Nottinghamshire country churchyard, an embittered divorcée has a strange encounter with the apparition of a girl who claims to have died in an explosion at a nearby First World War shell-filling factory fifty years before. Unable to dismiss from her mind the girl's desperate plea for help, Dorothy Younger begins her search for further details surrounding the events leading to the girl's death, in the hope of finding the child left orphaned by the blast.

Enlisting the help of veteran army officer Tim Mildmay, together they learn of one of the greatest wartime civilian tragedies, which claimed the lives of almost 140 workers. Dorothy and Tim grapple with the mystery of a young woman who apparently died in the explosion, but who was never officially there, and the survival of another who should have been blown to pieces, but was later discovered safely at home.

Of those who died in the tragedy, there were no doubt many tales which could have been told of their lives and the events which led to their last, fatal, few moments on earth. Perhaps this is one of them.

Canary Child is a supernatural mystery drama, at times tragic, yet immensely humorous.

IN LUD'S NAME *by* David Field

It is the second decade of the nineteenth century in the rapidly expanding industrial town of Nottingham. The emerging hosiery industry is the only means of livelihood for hundreds of refugees from the surrounding agricultural villages who have fled to the town in search of a less hazardous way of life. They are herded into hastily built slums, and grudgingly paid subsistence wages for a skilled product which is funding several private fortunes among the more wealthy entrepreneurs.

But the terms of international trade, blighted by the Napoleonic Wars, render the hosiery product hard to sell in Europe, whilst at the same time forcing domestic food prices ever upward. Starvation and disease are rife in the festering courtyards of the resentful workers, who are desperate for a champion to their cause.

Then into this tinderbox someone throws a lighted fuse called Ned Lud...

For further details of all these books, see www.arundelbooks.co.uk